The Story So Far

◆

Fleur Forsyte grows up the spoiled darling of her wealthy father Soames and her mother Annette. In the first 20 years of her life, she does not know her cousin Jon, son of Jolyon Forsyte and his wife Irene, who used to be married to Soames. Hatred between Soames and Jolyon, because of Irene, has kept the two families apart. Jon's sister Holly has married Val Dartie and they are raising race horses deep in the country. Jon goes to visit his sister and brother-in-law, with some idea of trying farming, and there he encounters for the first time the visiting Fleur. The two young people fall deeply in love; they have no real idea of the reasons why their respective branches of the family have been feuding. Later, Fleur learns the entire story, but is still determined to marry Jon, although she is being courted by Michael Mont, the suitor her father approves. Jolyon reluctantly reveals to Jon all the unhappy details of Soames' past ill-treatment of Irene, Jon's mother. Jon decides with a wrench that he cannot marry Soames' daughter. Jolyon dies soon after, and Jon goes to America with his mother. In her bitter disappointment, Fleur marries Michael Mont.

The nine volumes of
THE FORSYTE SAGA

The Man of Property
In Chancery
To Let
The White Monkey
The Silver Spoon
Swan Song
Maid in Waiting
Flowering Wilderness
One More River

Available from
Ballantine Books

THE WHITE MONKEY

A SILENT WOOING

JOHN GALSWORTHY

BALLANTINE BOOKS • NEW YORK
An Intext Publisher

SBN 345-02611-X-150

This edition published by arrangement with Charles
Scribner's Sons

First Printing: May, 1972

Printed in the United States of America

Cover photo courtesy BBC/MGM TV.

BALLANTINE BOOKS, INC.
101 Fifth Avenue, New York, N.Y. 10003

To
MAX BEERBOHM

CONTENTS

PART ONE

1 Promenade	1
2 Home	7
3 Musical	19
4 Dining	27
5 Eve	33
6 "Old Forsyte" and "Old Mont"	37
7 "Old Mont" and "Old Forsyte"	45
8 Bicket	55
9 Confusion	65
10 Passing of a Sportsman	77
11 Venture	87
12 Figures and Facts	93
13 Tenterhooks	103

PART TWO

1 The Mark Falls	109
2 Victorine	123
3 Michael Walks and Talks	133

4 Fleur's Body   143

5 Fleur's Soul   153

6 Michael Gets "What-for"   159

7 The Altogether   169

8 Soames Takes the Matter Up   177

9 Sleuth   185

10 Face   193

11 Cocked Hat   197

12 Going East   203

PART THREE

1 Bank Holiday   207

2 Office Work   215

3 "Afternoon of a Dryad"   223

4 Afternoon of a Bicket   229

5 Michael Gives Advice   235

6 Quittance   243

7 Looking into Elderson   247

8 Levanted   253

9 Soames Doesn't Give a Damn   263

10 But Takes No Chances   269

11 With a Small "n"   277

12 Ordeal by Shareholder   283

13 Soames at Bay   295

14 On the Rack   305

15 Calm   311

INTERLUDE

A Silent Wooing   315

·THE FORSYTE FAMILY

FORSYTE FAMILY TREE

b. 1741, JOLYON FORSYTE (Farmer, of Hays, Dencombe, Dorset), *d.* 1812. *m.* Julia Hayter, 1768.

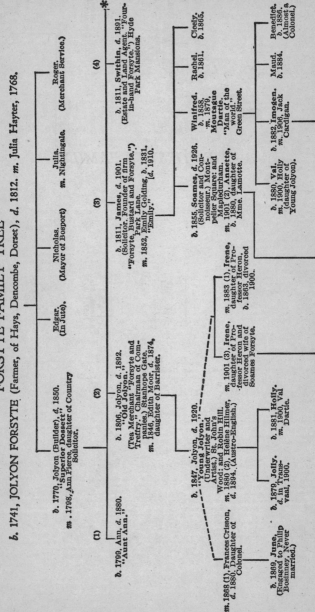

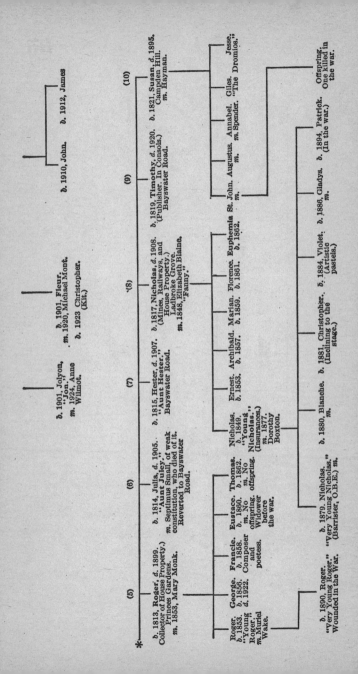

b. 1910, John.   b. 1912, James

b. 1901, Fleur.
m. 1920, Michael Mont.
b. 1923 Christopher.
(Kit.)

b. 1901, Jolyon,
"Jon,"
m. 1924, Anne
Wilmot.

*

(5)
b. 1813, Roger, d. 1899.
Collector of House Property.)
Princes Gardens.
m. 1853, Mary Monk.

Roger.
b. 1853.
"Young
Roger."
m. Muriel
Wake.

George.
b. 1856.
d. 1922.

Francie.
b. 1858.
Composer
and
poetess.

Eustace.
b. 1860.
m. No
offspring.
Widower
before
the war.

Thomas.
b. 1862.
m. No
offspring.

b. 1890, Roger,
"Very Young Roger."
Wounded in the War.

b. 1879, Nicholas.
"Very Young Nicholas."
(Barrister, O.B.E.) m.

(6)
b. 1814, Julia, d. 1905.
"Aunt Juley,"
m. Septimus Small, of weak
constitution, who died of it.
Reverted to Bayswater
Road.

(7)
b. 1815, Hester, d. 1907.
"Aunt Hester,"
Bayswater Road.

Nicholas,
b. 1849,
"Young,
Nicholas,"
(Insurance.)
m. 1877,
Dorothy
Boxton.

Ernest,
b. 1853.

Archibald.
b. 1857.

Marian.
b. 1859.

Florence.
b. 1861.

Euphemia
b. 1862.

b. 1880, Blanche.
m.

b. 1881, Christopher.
(Inclining to the
stage.)

(8)
b. 1817, Nicholas, d. 1908.
(Mines. Railways, and
House Property.)
Ladbroke Grove.
m. 1848, Elizabeth Blaine,
"Fanny."

(9)
b. 1819, Timothy, d. 1920.
(Publisher. In Consols.)
Bayswater Road.

St. John.
m.

Augustus.
m.

Annabel.
m. Spender.

Giles,
"The Dromios,"

Jesse,

b. 1884, Violet.
(Artistic
pastels.)

b. 1886, Gladys.
m.

b. 1894, Patrick.
(In the war.)

(10)
b. 1821, Susan, d. 1895.
Campden Hill.
m. Hayman.

Offspring.
One killed in
the war.

THE WHITE MONKEY

"No retreat, no retreat;
They must conquer or die
Who have no retreat!"
—*Mr. Gay*

PART ONE

Chapter One

PROMENADE

COMING down the steps of 'Snooks' Club, so nick-named by George Forsyte in the 'eighties,' on that momentous mid-October afternoon of 1922, Sir Lawrence Mont, ninth baronet, set his fine nose towards the east wind, and moved his thin legs with speed. Political by birth rather than by nature, he reviewed the revolution which had restored his Party to power with a detachment not devoid of humour. Passing the Remove Club, he thought: 'Some sweating into shoes, there! No more confectioned dishes. A woodcock—without trimmings, for a change!'

The captains and the kings had departed from 'Snooks' before he entered it, for he was not of "that catchpenny crew, now paid off, no, sir; fellows who turned their tails on the Land the moment the war was over. Pah!" but for an hour he had listened to echoes, and his lively twisting mind, embedded in deposits of the past, sceptical of the present, and of all political protestations and pronouncements, had recorded with amusement the confusion of patriotism and personalities left behind by the fateful gathering. Like most landowners, he distrusted doctrine. If he had a political belief, it was a tax on wheat; and so

1

far as he could see, he was now alone in it—but then he was not seeking election; in other words, his principle was not in danger of extinction from the votes of those who had to pay for bread. Principles—he mused—*au fond* were pocket; and he wished the deuce people wouldn't pretend they weren't! Pocket, in the deep sense of that word, of course, self-interest as a member of a definite community. And how the devil was this definite community, the English nation, to exist, when all its land was going out of cultivation, and all its ships and docks in danger of destruction by aeroplanes? He had listened that hour past for a single mention of the Land. Not one! It was not practical politics! Confound the fellows! They had to wear their breeches out—keeping seats or getting them. No connection between posteriors and posterity! No, by George! Thus reminded of posterity, it occurred to him rather suddenly that his son's wife showed no signs as yet. Two years! Time they were thinking about children. It was dangerous to get into the habit of not having them, when a title and estate depended. A smile twisted his lips and eyebrows which resembled spinneys of dark pothooks. A pretty young creature, most taking; and knew it too! Whom was she not getting to know? Lions and tigers, monkeys and cats—her house was becoming quite a menagerie of more or less celebrities. There was a certain unreality about that sort of thing! And opposite a British lion in Trafalgar Square Sir Lawrence thought: 'She'll be getting these to her house next! She's got the collecting habit. Michael must look out—in a collector's house there's always a lumber-room for old junk, and husbands are liable to get into it. That reminds me: I promised her a Chinese Minister. Well, she must wait now till after the General Election.'

Down Whitehall, under the grey easterly sky, the towers of Westminster came for a second into view. 'A certain unreality in that, too,' he thought. 'Michael and his fads! Well, it's the fashion—Socialistic principles and a rich wife. Sacrifice with safety! Peace with plenty! Nostrums—ten a penny!'

Passing the newspaper hubbub of Charing Cross, frenzied by the political crisis, he turned up to the left towards Danby and Winter, publishers, where his son was junior partner. A new theme for a book had just begun to bend a mind which had already produced a "Life of Montrose," "Far Cathay," that work of Eastern travel, and a fanciful conversation between the shades of Gladstone and Disraeli—entitled "Duet." With every step taken, from 'Snooks' eastward, his erect thin figure in Astrakhan-collared coat, his thin grey-moustached face, and tortoise-shell-rimmed monocle under the lively dark eyebrow, had seemed more rare. It became almost a phenomenon in this dingy back street, where carts stuck like winter flies, and persons went by with books under their arms, as if educated.

He had nearly reached the door of Danby's when he encountered two young men. One of them was clearly his son, better dressed since his marriage, and smoking a cigar—thank goodness—instead of those eternal cigarettes; the other—ah! yes—Michael's sucking poet and best man, head in air, rather a sleek head under a velour hat! He said:

"Ha, Michael!"

"Hallo, Bart! You know my governor, Wilfrid? Wilfrid Desert. 'Copper Coin'—some poet, Bart, I tell you. You must read it. We're going home. Come along!"

Sir Lawrence went along.

'What happened at 'Snooks'?"

"Le roi est mort. Labour can start lying, Michael—election next month."

"Bart was brought up, Wilfrid, in days that knew not Demos."

"Well, Mr. Desert, do *you* find reality in politics now?"

"Do you find reality in anything, sir?"

"In income tax, perhaps."

Michael grinned.

"Above knighthood," he said, "there's no such thing as simple faith."

"Suppose your friends came into power, Michael—in

some ways not a bad thing, help 'em to grow up—what could they do, eh? Could they raise national taste? Abolish the cinema? Teach English people to cook? Prevent other countries from threatening war? Make us grow our own food? Stop the increase of town life? Would they hang dabblers in poison gas? Could they prevent flying in war-time? Could they weaken the possessive instinct—anywhere? Or do anything, in fact, but alter the incidence of possession a little? All party politics are top dressing. We're ruled by the inventors, and human nature; and we live in Queer Street, Mr. Desert."

"Much my sentiments, sir."

Michael flourished his cigar.

"Bad old men, you two!"

And, removing their hats, they passed the Cenotaph.

"Curiously symptomatic—that thing," said Sir Lawrence; "monument to the dread of swank—most characteristic. And the dread of swank——"

"Go on, Bart," said Michael.

"The fine, the large, the florid—all off! No far-sighted views, no big schemes, no great principles, no great religion, or great art—æstheticism in cliques and backwaters, small men in small hats."

"As panteth the heart after Byron, Wilberforce, and the Nelson Monument. My poor old Bart! What about it, Wilfrid?"

"Yes, Mr. Desert—what about it?"

Desert's dark face contracted.

"It's an age of paradox," he said. "We all kick up for freedom, and the only institutions gaining strength are Socialism, and the Roman Catholic Church. We're frightfully self-conscious about art—and the only art development is the cinema. We're nuts on peace—and all we're doing about it is to perfect poison gas."

Sir Lawrence glanced sideways at a young man so bitter.

"And how's publishing, Michael?" he said.

"Well, 'Copper Coin' is selling like hot cakes; and there's quite a movement in 'Duet.' What about this for a new ad.: 'A Duet, by Sir Lawrence Mont, Bart. The most distinguished Conversation ever held between the Dead.' That ought to get the psychic. Wilfred suggested 'G. O. M. and Dizzy—broadcasted from Hell.' Which do you like best?"

They had come, however, to a policeman holding up his hand against the nose of a van horse, so that everything marked time. The engines of the cars whirred idly, their drivers' faces set towards the space withheld from them; a girl on a bicycle looked vacantly about her, grasping the back of the van, where a youth sat sideways with his legs stretched out towards her. Sir Lawrence glanced again at young Desert. A thin, pale-dark face, good-looking, but a hitch in it, as if not properly timed; nothing *outré* in dress or manner, and yet socially at large; less vivacious than that lively rascal, his own son, but as anchorless, and more sceptical—might feel things pretty deeply though! The policeman lowered his arm.

"You were in the war, Mr. Desert?"

"Oh, yes."

"Air service?"

"And line. Bit of both."

"Hard on a poet."

"Not at all. Poetry's only possible when you may be blown up at any moment, or when you live in Putney."

Sir Lawrence's eyebrow rose. "Yes?"

"Tennyson, Browning, Wordsworth, Swinburne—they could turn it out; *ils vivaient, mais si peu.*"

"Is there not a third condition, favourable?"

"And that, sir?"

"How shall I express it—a certain cerebral agitation in connection with women?"

Desert's face twitched, and seemed to darken.

Michael put his latch-key into the lock of his front door.

Chapter Two

HOME

━━━◆◆━━━◆◆◆━━━◆◆━━━

THE house in South Square, Westminster, to which
the young Monts had come after their Spanish
honeymoon two years before, might have been called
"emancipated." It was the work of an architect whose
dream was a new house perfectly old, and an old house
perfectly new. It followed, therefore, no recognised style
or tradition, and was devoid of structural prejudice; but it
soaked up the smuts of the metropolis with such special
rapidity that its stone already respectably resembled that
of Wren. Its windows and doors had gently rounded tops.
The high-sloping roof, of a fine sooty pink, was almost
Danish, and two "ducky little windows" looked out of it,
giving an impression that very tall servants lived up there.
There were rooms on each side of the front door, which
was wide and set off by bay-trees in black-and-gold bind-
ings. The house was thick through, and the staircase, of a
broad chastity, began at the far end of a hall which had
room for quite a number of hats and coats and cards.
There were four bathrooms; and not even a cellar underneath. The Forsyte instinct for a house had co-operated
in its acquisition. Soames had picked it up for his daughter, undecorated, at that psychological moment when the

bubble of inflation was pricked, and the air escaping from
the balloon of the world's trade. Fleur, however, had
established immediate contact with the architect—an ele-
ment which Soames himself had never quite got over—
and decided not to have more than three styles in her
house: Chinese, Spanish, and her own. The room to the
left of the front door, running the breadth of the house,
was Chinese, with ivory panels, a copper floor, central
heating, and cut-glass lustres. It contained four pictures—
all Chinese—the only school in which her father had not
yet dabbled. The fireplace, wide and open, had Chinese
dogs with Chinese tiles for them to stand on. The silk was
chiefly of jade-green. There were two wonderful old black
tea-chests, picked up with Soames' money at Jobson's—
not a bargain. There was no piano, partly because pianos
were too uncompromisingly occidental, and partly because it would have taken up much room. Fleur aimed at
space—collecting people rather than furniture or bibe-
lots. The light, admitted by windows at both ends, was
unfortunately not Chinese. She would stand sometimes in
the centre of this room, thinking—how to "bunch" her
guests, how to make her room more Chinese without
making it uncomfortable; how to seem to know all about
literature and politics; how to accept everything her
father gave her, without making him aware that his taste
had no sense of the future; how to keep hold of Sibley
Swan, the new literary star, and to get hold of Gurdon
Minho, the old; of how Wilfrid Desert was getting too
fond of her; of what was really her style in dress; of why
Michael had such funny ears; and sometimes she stood
not thinking at all—just aching a little.

When those three came in she was sitting before a red-
lacquer tea-table, finishing a very good tea. She always
had tea brought in rather early, so that she could have a
good quiet preliminary "tuck in" all by herself, because
she was not quite twenty-one, and this was her hour for
remembering her youth. By her side Ting-a-ling was
standing on his hind feet, his tawny fore paws on a Chi-

nese footstool, his snubbed black-and-tawny muzzle turned up towards the fruits of his philosophy.

"That'll do, Ting. No more, ducky! No *more!*"

The expression of Ting-a-ling answered:

"Well, then, stop, too! Don't subject me to torture!"

A year and three months old, he had been bought by Michael out of a Bond Street shop-window on Fleur's twentieth birthday, eleven months ago.

Two years of married life had not lengthened her short dark chestnut hair; had added a little more decision to her quick lips, a little more allurement to her white-lidded, dark-lashed hazel eyes, a little more poise and swing to her carriage, a little more chest and hip measurement; had taken a little from waist and calf measurement, a little colour from cheeks a little less round, and a little sweetness from a voice a little more caressing.

She stood up behind the tray, holding out her white round arm without a word. She avoided unnecessary greetings or farewells. She would have had to say them so often, and their purpose was better served by look, pressure, and slight inclination of head to one side.

With a circular movement of her squeezed hand, she said:

"Draw up. Cream, sir? Sugar, Wilfrid? Ting has had too much—don't feed him! Hand things, Michael. I've heard all about the meeting at 'Snooks.' You're not going to canvass for Labour, Michael—canvassing's so silly. If any one canvassed me, I should vote the other way at once."

"Yes, darling; but you're not the average elector."

Fleur looked at him. Very sweetly put! Conscious of Wilfrid biting his lips, of Sir Lawrence taking that in, of the amount of silk leg she was showing, of her black-and-cream teacups, she adjusted these matters. A flutter of her white lids—Desert ceased to bite his lips; a movement of her silk legs—Sir Lawrence ceased to look at him. Holding out her cups, she said:

"I suppose I'm not modern enough?"

Desert, moving a bright little spoon round in his magpie cup, said without looking up:

"As much more modern than the moderns, as you are more ancient."

" 'Ware poetry!" said Michael.

But when he had taken his father to see the new cartoons by Aubrey Greene, she said:

"Kindly tell me what you meant, Wilfrid."

Desert's voice seemed to leap from restraint.

"What does it matter? I don't want to waste time with that."

"But I want to know. It sounded like a sneer."

"A sneer? From me? Fleur!"

"Then tell me."

"I meant that you have all their restlessness and practical getthereness; but you have what they haven't, Fleur—power to turn one's head. And mine is turned. You know it."

"How would Michael like that—from *you*, his best man?"

Desert moved quickly to the window.

Fleur took Ting-a-ling on her lap. Such things had been said to her before; but from Wilfrid it was serious. Nice to think she had his heart, of course! Only, where on earth could she put it, where it wouldn't be seen except by her? He was incalculable—did strange things! She was a little afraid—not of him, but of that quality in him. He came back to the hearth, and said:

"Ugly, isn't it? Put that dam' dog down, Fleur; I can't see your face. If you were really fond of Michael—I swear I wouldn't; but you're not, you know."

Fleur said coldly:

"You know very little; I *am* fond of Michael."

Desert gave his little jerky laugh.

"Oh, yes; not the sort that counts."

Fleur looked up.

"It counts quite enough to make one safe."

"A flower that I can't pick?"

Fleur nodded.

"Quite sure, Fleur? Quite, quite sure?"

Fleur stared; her eyes softened a little, her eyelids, so excessively white, drooped over them; she nodded again. Desert said slowly:

"The moment I believe that, I shall go East."

"East?"

"Not so stale as going West, but much the same—you don't come back."

Fleur thought: 'The East? I should love to know the East! Pity one can't manage that, too. Pity!'

"You won't keep me in your Zoo, my dear. I shan't hang around and feed on crumbs. You know what I feel —it means a smash of some sort."

"It hasn't been my fault, has it?"

"Yes; you've collected me, as you collect everybody that comes near you."

"I don't know what you mean."

Desert bent down, and dragged her hand to his lips.

"Don't be riled with me; I'm too unhappy."

Fleur let her hand stay against his hot lips.

"Sorry, Wilfrid."

"All right, dear. I'll go."

"But you're coming to dinner to-morrow?"

Desert said violently:

"*To-morrow?* Good God—no! What d'you think I'm made of?"

He flung her hand away.

"I don't like violence, Wilfrid."

"Well, good-bye; I'd better go."

The words "And you'd better not come again" trembled up to her lips, but were not spoken. Part from Wilfrid— life would lose a little warmth! She waved her hand. He was gone. She heard the door closing. Poor Wilfrid!— nice to think of a flame at which to warm her hands! Nice—but rather dreadful! And suddenly, dropping Ting-a-ling, she got up and began to walk about the room. To-morrow! Second anniversary of her wedding-day! Still an ache when she thought of what it had not been. But there was little time to think—and she made less. What

good in thinking? Only one life, full of people, of things
to do and have, of things wanted—a life only void of—
one thing, and that—well, if people had it, they never had
it long! On her lids two tears, which had gathered, dried
without falling. Sentimentalism! No! The last thing in the
world—the unforgivable offence! Whom should she put
next whom tomorrow? And whom should she get in place
of Wilfrid, if Wilfrid wouldn't come—silly boy! One day
—one night—what difference? Who should sit on her
right, and who on her left? Was Aubrey Greene more
distinguished, or Sibley Swan? Were they either as distinguished as Walter Nazing or Charles Upshire? Dinner
of twelve, exclusively literary and artistic, except for Michael and Alison Charwell. Ah! Could Alison get her
Gurdon Minho—just one writer of the old school, one
glass of old wine to mellow effervescence? He didn't
publish with Danby and Winter; but he fed out of Alison's hand. She went quickly to one of the old tea-
chests, and opened it. Inside was a telephone.

"Can I speak to Lady Alison—Mrs. Michael Mont. . . .
Yes. . . . That you, Alison? . . . Fleur speaking. Wilfrid has
fallen through to-morrow night. . . . Is there any chance
of your bringing Gurdon Minho? I don't know him, of
course; but he might be interested. You'll try? . . . That'll
be ever so delightful. Isn't the 'Snooks' Club meeting rather exciting? Bart says they'll eat each other now they've
split. . . . About Mr. Minho. Could you let me know to-
night? Thanks—thanks awfully! . . . Good-bye!"

Failing Minho, whom? Her mind hovered over the
names in her address book. At so late a minute it must be
some one who didn't stand on ceremony; but except Alison, none of Michael's relations would be safe from Sibley
Swan or Nesta Gorse, and their subversive shafts; as to
the Forsytes—out of the question; they had their own
subacid humour (some of them), but they were not modern, not really modern. Besides, she saw as little of them
as she could—they dated, belonged to the dramatic period,
had no sense of life without beginning or end. No! If
Gurdon Minho was a frost, it would have to be a musician,

whose works were hieroglyphical with a dash of surgery; or, better perhaps, a psychoanalyst. Her fingers turned the pages till she came to those two categories. Hugo Solstis? A possibility; but suppose he wanted to play them something recent? There was only Michael's upright grand, and that would mean going to his study. Better Gerald Hanks—he and Nesta Gorse would get off together on dreams; still, if they did, there would be no actual loss of life. Yes, failing Gurdon Minho, Gerald Hanks; he would be free—and put him between Alison and Nesta. She closed the book, and, going back to her jade-green settee, sat gazing at Ting-a-ling. The little dog's prominent round eyes gazed back; bright, black, very old. Fleur thought: 'I *don't* want Wilfrid to drop off.' Among all the crowd who came and went, here, there, and everywhere, she cared for nobody. Keep up with them, keep up with everything, of course! It was all frightfully amusing, frightfully necessary! Only—only—what?

Voices! Michael and Bart coming back. Bart had noticed Wilfrid. He *was* a noticing old Bart. She was never very comfortable when he was about—lively and twisting, but with something settled and ancestral in him; a little like Ting-a-ling—something judgmatic, ever telling her that she was fluttering and new. He was anchored, could only move to the length of his old-fashioned cord, but he could drop on to things disconcertingly. Still, he admired her, she felt—oh! yes.

Well! What had he thought of the cartoons? Ought Michael to publish them, and with letter-press or without? Didn't he think that the cubic called "Still Life"—of the Government, too frightfully funny—especially the "old bean" representing the Prime? For answer she was conscious of a twisting, rapid noise; Sir Lawrence was telling her of his father's collection of electioneering cartoons. She did wish Bart would not tell her about his father; he had been so distinguished, and he must have been so dull, paying all his calls on horseback, with trousers strapped under his boots. He and Lord Charles Cariboo and the Marquis of Forfar had been the last three "callers" of that sort. If only they hadn't, they'd have been clean forgot. She had that dress to try, and fourteen things to see to, and Hugo's concert began at eight-fifteen! Why did people of the last generation always have so much time? And, suddenly, she looked down. Ting-a-ling was licking the copper floor. She took him up: "Not that, darling; nasty!" Ah! the spell was broken! Bart was going, reminiscent to the last. She waited at the foot of the stairs till Michael shut the door on him, then flew. Reaching her room, she turned on all the lights. Here was her own style—a bed which did not look like one, and many mirrors. The couch of Ting-a-ling occupied a corner, whence he could see himself in three. She put him down, and said: "Keep quiet, now!" His attitude to the other dogs in the room had long become indifferent; though of his own breed and precisely his colouring, they had no smell and no licking power in their tongues—nothing to be done with them, imitative creatures, incredibly unresponsive.

Stripping off her dress, Fleur held the new frock under her chin.

"May I kiss you?" said a voice, and there was Michael's image behind her own reflection in the glass.

"My dear boy, there isn't time! Help me with this." She slipped the frock over her head. "Do those three top hooks. How do you like it? Oh! and, Michael! Gurdon Minho may be coming to dinner to-morrow—Wilfrid can't. Have you read his things? Sit down and tell me something about them. All novels, aren't they? What sort?"

"Well, he's always had something to say. And his cats are good. He's a bit romantic, of course."

"Oh! Have I made a gaff?"

"Not a bit; jolly good shot. The vice of our lot is, they say it pretty well, but they've nothing to say. They won't last."

"But that's just why they will last. They won't date."

"Won't they? My gum!"

"Wilfrid will last."

"Ah! Wilfrid has emotions, hates, pities, wants; at least,

sometimes; when he does, his stuff is jolly good. Otherwise, he just makes a song about nothing—like the rest."

Fleur tucked in the top of her undergarment.

"But, Michael, if that's so, we—I've got the wrong lot."

Michael grinned.

"My dear child! The lot of the hour is always right; only you've got to watch it, and change it quick enough."

"But d'you mean to say that Sibley isn't going to live?"

"Sib? Lord, no!"

"But he's so perfectly sure that almost everybody else is dead or dying. Surely he has critical genius?"

"If I hadn't more judgment than Sib, I'd go out of publishing tomorrow."

"You—more than Sibley Swan?"

"Of course, I've more judgment than Sib. Why! Sib's judgment is just his opinion of Sib—common or garden impatience of any one else. He doesn't even read them. He'll read one specimen of every author and say: 'Oh! that fellow! He's dull, or he's moral, or he's sentimental, or he dates, or he drivels'—I've heard him dozens of times. That's if they're alive. Of course, if they're dead, it's different. He's always digging up and canonising the dead; that's how he's got his name. There's always a Sib in literature. He's a standing example of how people can get taken at their own valuation. But as to lasting—of course he won't; he's never creative, even by mistake."

Fleur had lost the thread. Yes! It suited her—quite a nice line! Off with it! Must write those three notes before she dressed!

Michael had begun again.

"Take my tip, Fleur. The really big people don't talk—and don't bunch—they paddle their own canoes in what seem backwaters. But it's the backwaters that make the main stream. By Jove, that's a *mot,* or is it a bull; and are bulls *mots* or *mots* bulls?"

"Michael, if you were me, would you tell Frederic Wilmer that he'll be meeting Hubert Marsland at lunch next week? Would it bring him or would it put him off?"

"Marsland's rather an old duck, Wilmer's rather an old goose—I don't know."

"Oh! do be serious, Michael—you never give me any help in arranging—No! Don't maul my shoulders, please."

"Well, darling, I *don't* know. I've no genius for such things, like you. Marsland paints windmills, cliffs, and things—I doubt if he's heard of the future. He's almost a Mathew Maris for keeping out of the swim. If you think he'd like to meet a Vertiginist——"

"I didn't ask you if he'd like to meet Wilmer; I asked you if Wilmer would like to meet him."

"Wilmer will just say: 'I like little Mrs. Mont, she gives deuced good grub'—and so you do, ducky. A Vertiginist wants nourishing, you know, or it wouldn't go to his head."

Fleur's pen resumed its swift strokes, already becoming slightly illegible. She murmured:

"I think Wilfrid would help—you won't be there; one —two—three. What women?"

"For painters—pretty and plump; no intellect."

Fleur said crossly:

"I can't get them plump; they don't go about now." And her pen flowed on:

"DEAR WILFRID, Wednesday—lunch; Wilmer, Hubert Marsland, two other women. Do help me live it down.

                                        "Yours ever,
                                                    "FLEUR."

"Michael, your chin is like a boot-brush."

"Sorry, old thing; your shoulders shouldn't be so smooth. Bart gave Wilfrid a tip as we were coming along."

Fleur stopped writing. "Oh!"

"Reminded him that the state of love was a good stunt for poets."

"*À propos* of what?"

"Wilfrid was complaining that he couldn't turn it out now."

"Nonsense! his last things are his best."

"Well, that's what I think. Perhaps he's forestalled the tip. Has he?"

Fleur turned her eyes towards the face behind her shoulder. No, it had its native look—frank, irresponsible, slightly faun-like, with its pointed ears, quick lips, and nostrils.

She said slowly:

"If *you* don't know, nobody does."

A snuffle interrupted Michael's answer. Ting-a-ling, long, low, slightly higher at both ends, was standing between them, with black muzzle upturned. "My pedigree is long," he seemed to say: "but my legs are short—what about it?"

Chapter Three

MUSICAL

———◄►◄—————◄►——

ACCORDING to a great and guiding principle, Fleur and Michael Mont attended the Hugo Solstis concert, not because they anticipated pleasure, but because they knew Hugo. They felt, besides, that Solstis, an Englishman of Russo-Dutch extraction, was one of those who were restoring English music, giving to it a wide and spacious freedom from melody and rhythm, while investing it with literary and mathematical charms. And one never could go to a concert given by any of this school without using the word "interesting" as one was coming away. To sleep to this restored English music, too, was impossible. Fleur, a sound sleeper, had never even tried. Michael had, and complained afterwards that it had been like a nap in Liège railway station before the war. On this occasion they occupied those gangway seats in the front row of the dress circle of which Fleur had a sort of natural monopoly. There Hugo and the rest could see her taking her place in the English restoration movement. It was easy, too, to escape into the corridor and exchange the word "interesting" with side-whiskered cognoscenti; or, slipping out a cigarette from the little gold case, wedding-present of Cousin Imogen Cardigan, get a whiff or two's repose.

19

To speak quite honestly, Fleur had a natural sense of rhythm which caused her discomfort during those long and "interesting" passages which evidenced, as it were, the composer's rise and fall from his bed of thorns. She secretly loved a tune, and the impossibility of ever confessing this without losing hold of Solstis, Baff, Birdigal, Mac-Lewis, Clorane, and other English restoration composers, sometimes taxed to its limit a nature which had its Spartan side. Even to Michael she would not "confess"; and it was additionally trying when, with his native disrespect of persons, accentuated by life in the trenches, and a publisher's office, he would mutter: "Gad! Get on with it!" or: "Cripes! Ain't he took bad!" especially as she knew that Michael was really putting up with it better than herself, having a more literary disposition, and a less dancing itch in his toes.

The first movement of the new Solstis composition—"Phantasmagoria Piemontesque"—to which they had especially come to listen, began with some drawn-out chords.

"What oh!" said Michael's voice in her ear: "Three pieces of furniture moved simultaneously on a parquet floor!"

In Fleur's involuntary smile was the whole secret of why her marriage had not been intolerable. After all, Michael was a dear! Devotion and mercury—jesting and loyalty—combined, they piqued and touched even a heart given away before it was bestowed on him. "Touch" without "pique" would have bored; "pique" without "touch" would have irritated. At this moment he was at peculiar advantage! Holding on to his knees, with his ears standing up, eyes glassy from loyalty to Hugo, and tongue in cheek, he was listening to that opening in a way which evoked Fleur's admiration. The piece would be "interesting"—she fell into the state of outer observation and inner calculation very usual with her nowadays. Over there was L.S.D., the greater dramatist; she didn't know him—yet. He looked rather frightening, his hair stood up so straight. And her eye began picturing him on her copper floor against a Chinese picture. And there—yes! Gurdon Minho!

Imagine *his* coming to anything so modern! His profile *was* rather Roman—of the Aurelian period! Passing on from that antique, with the pleased thought that by this time to-morrow she might have collected it, she quartered the assembly face by face—she did not want to miss any one important.

"The furniture" had come to a sudden standstill.

"Interesting!" said a voice over her shoulder. Aubrey Greene! Illusive, rather moonlit, with his silky fair hair brushed straight back, and his greenish eyes—his smile always made her feel that he was "getting" at her. But, after all, he was a cartoonist!

"Yes, isn't it?"

He curled away. He might have stayed a little longer—there wouldn't be time for any one else before those songs of Birdigal's! Here came the singer Charles Powls! How stout and efficient he looked, dragging little Birdigal to the piano.

Charming accompaniment—rippling, melodious!

The stout, efficient man began to sing. How different from the accompaniment! The song hit every note just off the solar plexus, it mathematically prevented her from feeling pleasure. Birdigal must have written it in horror of some one calling it "vocal." Vocal! Fleur knew how catching the word was; it would run like a measle round the ring, and Birdigal would be no more! Poor Birdigal! But this was "interesting." Only, as Michael was saying: 'O, my Gawd!"

Three songs! Powls was wonderful—so loyal! Never one note hit so that it rang out like music! Her mind fluttered off to Wilfrid. To him, of all the younger poets, people accorded the right to say something; it gave him such a position—made him seem to come out of life, instead of literature. Besides, he had done things in the war, was a son of Lord Mullyon, would get the Mercer Prize probably, for "Copper Coin." If Wilfrid abandoned her, a star would fall from the firmament above her copper floor. He had no right to leave her in the lurch. He must learn not to be violent—not to think physically. No! she couldn't let Wilfrid slip away; nor could she have any more sob-stuff in her life, searing passions, *cul de sacs*, aftermaths. She had tasted of that; a dulled ache still warned her.

Birdigal was bowing, Michael saying: "Come out for a whiff! The next thing's a dud!" Oh! ah! Beethoven. Poor old Beethoven! So out of date—one did *rather* enjoy him!

The corridor, and refectory beyond, were swarming with the restoration movement. Young men and women with faces and heads of lively and distorted character, were exchanging the word "interesting." Men of more massive type, resembling sedentary matadors, blocked all circulation. Fleur and Michael passed a little way along, stood against the wall, and lighted cigarettes. Fleur smoked hers delicately—a very little one in a tiny amber holder. She had the air of admiring blue smoke rather than of making it; there were spheres to consider beyond this sort of crowd—one never knew who might be about!—the sphere, for instance, in which Alison Charwell moved, politico-literary, catholic in taste, but, as Michael always put it, "Convinced, like a sanitary system, that it's the only sphere in the world; look at the way they all write books of reminiscence about each other!" They might, she always felt, disapprove of women smoking in public halls. Consorting delicately with iconoclasm, Fleur never forgot that her feet were in two worlds at least. Standing there, observant of all to left and right, she noted against the wall one whose face was screened by his program. 'Wilfred,' she thought, 'and doesn't mean to see me!' Mortified, as a child from whom a sixpence is filched, she said:

"There's Wilfrid! Fetch him, Michael!"

Michael crossed, and touched his best man's sleeve; Desert's face emerged, frowning. She saw him shrug his shoulders, turn and walk into the throng. Michael came back.

"Wilfrid's got the hump to-night; says he's not fit for human society—queer old son!"

How obtuse men were! Because Wilfrid was his pal,

Michael did not see; and that was lucky! So Wilfrid really meant to avoid her! Well, she would see! And she said:

"I'm tired, Michael; let's go home."

His hand slid round her arm.

"Sorry, old thing; come along!"

They stood a moment in a neglected doorway, watching Woomans, the conductor, launched towards his orchestra.

"Look at him," said Michael; "guy hung out of an Italian window, legs and arms all stuffed and flying! And look at the Frapka and her piano—that's a turbulent union!"

There was a strange sound.

"Melody, by George!" said Michael.

An attendant muttered in their ears: "Now, sir, I'm going to shut the door." Fleur had a fleeting view of L.S.D. sitting upright as his hair, with closed eyes. The door was shut—they were outside in the hall.

"Wait here, darling; I'll nick a rickshaw."

Fleur huddled her chin in her fur. It was easterly and cold.

A voice behind her said:

"Well, Fleur, am I going East?"

Wilfrid! His collar up to his ears, a cigarette between his lips, hands in pockets, eyes devouring.

"You're very silly, Wilfrid!"

"Anything you like; am I going East?"

"No; Sunday morning—eleven o'clock at the Tate. We'll talk it out."

"Convenu!" And he was gone.

Alone suddenly, like that, Fleur felt the first shock of reality. Was Wilfrid truly going to be unmanageable? A taxicab ground up; Michael beckoned; Fleur stepped in.

Passing a passionately lighted oasis of young ladies displaying to the interested Londoner the acme of Parisian undress, she felt Michael incline towards her. If she were going to keep Wilfrid, she must be nice to Michael. Only:

"You needn't kiss me in Piccadilly Circus, Michael!"

"Sorry, ducky! It's a little previous—I mean to get you opposite the Partheneum."

Fleur remembered how he had slept on a Spanish sofa for the first fortnight of their honeymoon; how he always insisted that she must not spend anything on him, but must always let him give her what he liked, though she had two thousand five hundred a year and he twelve hundred; how jumpy he was when she had a cold—and how he always came home to tea. Yes, he was a dear! But would she break her heart if he went East or West to-morrow?

Snuggled against him, she was surprised at her own cynicism.

A telephone message written out, in the hall, ran: "Please tell Mrs. Mont I've got Mr. Gurding Minner. Lady Alison."

It was restful. A real antique! She turned on the lights in her room, and stood for a moment admiring it. Truly pretty! A slight snuffle from the corner—Ting-a-ling, tan on a black cushion, lay like a Chinese lion in miniature; pure, remote, fresh from evening communion with the Square railings.

"I see you," said Fleur.

Ting-a-ling did not stir; his round black eyes watched his mistress undress. When she returned from the bathroom he was curled into a ball. Fleur thought: 'Queer! How does he know Michael won't be coming?' And slipping into her well-warmed bed, she too curled herself up and slept.

But in the night, contrary to her custom, she awoke. A cry—long, weird, trailing, from somewhere—the river —the slums at the back—rousing memory—poignant, aching—of her honeymoon—Granada, its roofs below, jet, ivory, gold; the watchman's cry, the lines in Jon's letter:

"Voice in the night crying, down in the old sleeping
   Spanish city darkened under her white stars.
   What says the voice—its clear, lingering anguish?
   Just the watchman, telling his dateless tale of safety?
   Just a road-man, flinging to the moon his song?

No! 'Tis one deprived, whose lover's heart is weeping,
　　Just his cry: 'How long?' "

A cry, or had she dreamed it? Jon, Wilfrid, Michael!
No use to have a heart!

Chapter Four

DINING

———◆◆◆◆◆———

LADY ALISON CHARWELL, born Heathfield, daughter of the first Earl of Campden, and wife to Lionel Charwell, K.C., Michael's somewhat young uncle, was a delightful Englishwoman brought up in a set accepted as the soul of society. Full of brains, energy, taste, money, and tinctured in its politico-legal ancestry by blue blood, this set was linked to, but apart from 'Snooks,' and the duller haunts of birth and privilege. It was gay, charming, free-and-easy, and, according to Michael, "Snobbish, old thing, æsthetically and intellectually, but they'll never see it. They think they're the top notch—quick, healthy, up-to-date, well-bred, intelligent; they simply can't imagine their equals. But you see their imagination is deficient. Their really creative energy would go into a pint pot. Look at their books'—they're always *on* something—philosophy, spiritualism, poetry, fishing, themselves; why, even their sonnets dry up before they're twenty-five. They know everything—except mankind outside their own set. Oh! they work—they run the show—they have to; there's no one else with their brains, and energy, and taste. But they run it round and round in their own blooming circle. It's the world

27

to them—and it might be worse. They've patented their
own golden age; but it's a trifle flyblown since the war."

Alison Charwell—in and of this world, so spryly soulful, debonnaire, free, and cosy—lived within a stone's
throw of Fleur, in a house pleasant, architecturally, as any
in London. Forty years old, she had three children and
considerable beauty, wearing a little fine from mental and
bodily activity. Something of an enthusiast, she was fond
of Michael, in spite of his strange criticisms, so that his
matrimonial venture had piqued her from the start. Fleur
was dainty, had quick natural intelligence—this new niece
was worth cultivation. But though adaptable and assimila-
tive, Fleur had remained curiously unassimilated; she continued to whet the curiosity of Lady Alison, accustomed to
the close borough of choice spirit, and finding a certain
poignancy in contact with the New Age, on Fleur's copper
floor. She met with an irreverence there, which, not taken
too seriously, flipped her mind. On that floor she almost
felt a back number. It was stimulating.

Receiving Fleur's telephonic enquiry about Gurdon
Minho, she had rung up the novelist. She knew him, if
not well. Nobody seemed to know him well; amiable,
polite, silent, rather dull and austere; but with a discon-
certing smile, sometimes ironical, sometimes friendly. His
books were now caustic, now sentimental. On both counts
it was rather the fashion to run him down, though he still
seemed to exist.

She rang him up. Would he come to a dinner to-morrow at her young nephew, Michael Mont's, and meet the
younger generation? His answer came, rather high-pitched:

"Rather! Full fig, or dinner jacket?"

"How awfully nice of you! they'll be ever so pleased.
Full fig, I believe. It's the second anniversary of their
wedding." She hung up the receiver with the thought: 'He
must be writing a book about them!'

Conscious of responsibility, she arrived early.

It was a grand night at her husband's Inn, so that she
brought nothing with her but the feeling of adventure,
pleasant after a day spent in fluttering over the decision at

'Snooks.' She was received only by Ting-a-ling, who had his back to the fire, and took no notice beyond a stare. Sitting down on the jade-green settee, she said:

"Well, you funny little creature, don't you know me after all this time?"

Ting-a-ling's black shiny gaze seemed saying: "You recur here, I know; most things recur. There is nothing new about the future."

Lady Alison fell into a train of thought: The new generation! Did she want her own girls to be of it? She would like to talk to Mr. Minho about that—they had had a very nice talk down at Beechgroves before the war. Nine years ago—Sybil only six, Joan only four then! Time went, things changed! A new generation! And what was the difference? "I think we had more tradition!" she said to herself softly.

A slight sound drew her eyes up from contemplation of her feet. Ting-a-ling was moving his tail from side to side on the hearthrug, as if applauding. Fleur's voice, behind her, said:

"Well, darling, I'm awfully late. It *was* good of you to get me Mr. Minho. I do hope they'll all behave. He'll be between you and me, anyway; I'm sticking him at the top, and Michael at the bottom, between Pauline Upshire and Amabel Nazing. You'll have Sibley on your left, and I'll have Aubrey on my right, then Nesta Gorse and Walter Nazing; opposite them Linda Frewe and Charles Upshire. Twelve. You know them all. Oh! and you mustn't mind if the Nazings and Nesta smoke between the courses. Amabel will do it. She comes from Virginia—it's the reaction. I do hope she'll have some clothes on; Michael always says it's a mistake when she has; but having Mr. Minho makes one a little nervous. Did you see Nesta's skit in 'The Bouquet'? Oh, too frightfully amusing—clearly meant for L.S.D.! Ting, my Ting, are you going to stay and see all these people? Well, then, get up here or you'll be trodden on. Isn't he Chinese? He does so round off the room."

Ting-a-ling laid his nose on his paws, in the centre of a jade-green cushion.

"Mr. Gurding Minner!"

The well-known novelist looked pale and composed. Shaking the two extended hands, he gazed at Ting-a-ling, and said:

"How nice! How are *you*, my little man?"

Ting-a-ling did not stir. "You take me for a common English dog, sir!" his silence seemed to say.

"Mr. and Mrs. Walter Nazon, Miss Linda Frow."

Amabel Nazing came first, clear alabaster from her fair hair down to where her gleaming back ended at her waist, shrouded alabaster from two inches below the knee to the gleaming toes of her shoes; the eminent novelist mechanically ceased to commune with Ting-a-ling.

Walter Nazing, who followed a long way up above his wife, had a tiny line of collar emergent from swathes of black, and a face, cut a hundred years ago, that slightly resembled Shelley's. His literary productions were sometimes felt to be like the poetry of that bard, and sometimes like the prose of Marcel Proust. "What oh!" as Michael said.

Linda Frewe, whom Fleur at once introduced to Gurdon Minho, was one about whose work no two people in her drawing-room ever agreed. Her books "Trifles" and "The Furious Don" had quite divided all opinion. Genius according to some, drivel according to others, those tomes always roused an interesting debate whether a slight madness enhanced or diminished the value of art. She herself paid little attention to criticism—she produced.

"*The* Mr. Minho? How interesting! I've never read anything of yours."

Fleur gave a little gasp.

"What—don't you know Mr. Monho's cats? But they're wonderful. Mr. Minho, I do want Mrs. Walter Nazing to know you. Amabel—Mr. Gurdon Minho."

"Oh! Mr. Minho—how perfectly lovely! I've wanted to know you ever since my cradle."

Fleur heard the novelist say quietly:

"I could wish it had been longer;" and passed on in doubt to greet Nesta Gorse and Sibley Swan, who came in, as if they lived together, quarrelling over L.S.D., Nesta upholding him because of his "panache," Sibley maintaining that wit had died with the Restoration; this fellow was alive!

Michael followed with the Upshires and Aubrey Greene, whom he had encountered in the hall. The party was complete.

Fleur loved perfection, and that evening was something of a nightmare. Was it a success? Minho was so clearly the least brilliant person there; even Alison talked better. And yet he had such a fine skull. She did hope he would not go away early. Some one would be almost sure to say: "Dug up!" or "Thick and bald!" before the door closed behind him. He was pathetically agreeable, as if trying to be liked, or, at least, not despised too much. And there must, of course, be more in him than met the sense of hearing. After the crab soufflé he did seem to be talking to Alison, and all about youth. Fleur listened with one ear.

"Youth feels . . . main stream of life . . . not giving it what it wants. Past and future getting haloes. . . . Quite! Contemporary life no earthly just now. . . . No. . . . Only comfort for us—we'll be antiquated, some day, like Congreve, Sterne, Defoe . . . have our chance again. . . . *Why?* What *is* driving them out of the main current? Oh! Probably surfeit . . . newspapers . . . photographs. Don't see life itself, only reports . . . reproductions of it; all seems shoddy, lurid, commercial. . . . Youth says 'Away with it, let's have the past or the future!' "

He took some salted almonds, and Fleur saw his eyes stray to the upper part of Amabel Nazing. Down there the conversation was like Association football—no one kept the ball for more than one kick. It shot from head to head. And after every set of passes some one would reach out and take a cigarette, and blow a blue cloud across the unclothed refectory table. Fleur enjoyed the glow of her Spanish room—its tiled floor, richly coloured fruits in porcelain, its tooled leather, copper articles, and

Soames' Goya above a Moorish divan. She headed the ball promptly when it came her way, but initiated nothing. Her gift was to be aware of everything at once. "Mrs. Michael Mont presented" the brilliant irrelevancies of Linda Frewe, the pricks and stimulations of Nesta Gorse, the moonlit sliding innuendoes of Aubrey Greene, the up-turning strokes of Sibley Swan, Amabel Nazing's little cool American audacities, Charles Upshire's curious bits of lore, Walter Nazing's subversive contradictions, the critical intricacies of Pauline Upshire; Michael's happy-go-lucky slings and arrows, even Alison's knowledgeable quickness, and Gurdon Minho's silences—she presented them all, showed them off, keeping her eyes and ears on the ball of talk lest it should touch earth and rest. Brilliant evening; but—a success?

On the jade-green settee, when the last of them had gone and Michael was seeing Alison home, she thought of Minho's "Youth—not getting what it wants." No! Things didn't fit. "They don't fit, do they, Ting?" But Ting-a-ling was tired, only the tip of one ear quivered. Fleur leaned back and sighed. Ting-a-ling uncurled himself, and putting his forepaws on her thigh, looked up in her face. "Look at me," he seemed to say, "I'm all right. I get what I want, and I want what I get. At present I want to go to bed."

"But I don't," said Fleur, without moving.

"Just take me up!" said Ting-a-ling.

"Well," said Fleur, "I suppose— It's a nice person, but not the right person, Ting."

Ting-a-ling settled himself on her bare arms.

"It's all right," he seemed to say. "There's a great deal too much sentiment and all that, out of China. Come on!"

Chapter Five

EVE

———— ❖ ————

THE Honourable Wilfrid Desert's rooms were opposite a picture-gallery off Cork Street. The only male member of the aristocracy writing verse that any one would print, he had chosen them for seclusion rather than for comfort. His "junk," however, was not devoid of the taste and luxury which overflows from the greater houses of England. Furniture from the Hampshire seat of the Cornish nobleman, Lord Mullyon, had oozed into two vans, when Wilfrid settled in. He was seldom to be found, however, in his nest, and was felt to be a rare bird, owing his rather unique position among the younger writers partly to his migratory reputation. He himself hardly, perhaps, knew where he spent his time, or did his work, having a sort of mental claustrophobia, a dread of being hemmed-in by people. When the war broke out he had just left Eton; when the war was over he was twenty-three, as old a young man as ever turned a stave. His friendship with Michael, begun in hospital, had languished and renewed itself suddenly, when in 1920 Michael joined Danby and Winter, publishers, of Blake Street, Covent Garden. The scattery enthusiasm of the sucking publisher had been roused by Wilfrid's verse. Hobnobbing lunches over the

poems of one in need of literary anchorage, had been
capped by the firm's surrender to Michael's insistence. The
mutual intoxication of the first book Wilfrid had written
and the first book Michael had sponsored was crowned at
Michael's wedding. Best man! Since then, so far as Desert
could be tied to anything, he had been tied to those two;
nor, to do him justice, had he realised till a month ago
that the attraction was not Michael, but Fleur. Desert never
spoke of the war, it was not possible to learn from his
own mouth an effect which he might have summed up
thus: "I lived so long with horror and death; I saw men so
in the raw; I put hope of anything out of my mind so
utterly, that I can never more have the faintest respect
for theories, promises, conventions, moralities, and principles. I have hated too much the men who wallowed in
them while I was wallowing in mud and blood. Illusion is
off. No religion and no philosophy will satisfy me—words,
all words. I have still my senses—no thanks to them; am
still capable—I find—of passion; can still grit my teeth
and grin; have still some feeling of trench loyalty, but
whether real or just a complex, I don't yet know. I am
dangerous, but not so dangerous as those who trade in
words, principles, theories, and all manner of fanatical
idiocy to be worked out in the blood and sweat of other
men. The war's done one thing for me—converted life to
comedy. Laugh at it—there's nothing else to do!"

Leaving the concert hall on the Friday night, he had
walked straight home to his rooms. And lying down full
length on a monk's seat of the fifteenth century, restored
with down cushions and silk of the twentieth, he crossed
his hands behind his head and delivered himself to these
thoughts: 'I am not going on like this. She has bewitched
me. It doesn't mean anything to her. But it means hell to
me. I'll finish with it on Sunday—Persia's a good place.
Arabia's a good place—plenty of blood and sand! She's
incapable of giving anything up. How has she hooked herself into me? By trick of eyes, and hair, by her walk, by
the sound of her voice—by trick of warmth, scent, colour.
Fling her cap over the windmill—not she! What then?

Am I to hang about her Chinese fireside and her little Chinese dog; and have this ache and this fever because I can't be kissing her? I'd rather be flying again in the middle of Boche whiz-bangs! Sunday! How women like to drag out agonies! It'll be just this afternoon all over again. "How unkind of you to go, when your friendship is so precious to me! Stay, and be my tame cat, Wilfrid!" No, my dear, for once you're up against it! And—so am I, by the Lord! . . .'

When in that gallery which extends asylum to British art, those two young people met so accidentally on Sunday morning in front of Eve smelling at the flowers of the Garden of Eden, there were present also six mechanics in various stages of decomposition, a custodian and a couple from the provinces, none of whom seemed capable of observing anything whatever. And, indeed, that meeting was inexpressive. Two young people, of the disillusioned class, exchanging condemnations of the past. Desert with his offhand speech, his smile, his well-tailored informality, suggested no aching heart. Of the two Fleur was the paler and more interesting. Desert kept saying to himself: "No melodrama—that's all it would be!" And Fleur was thinking: 'If I can keep him ordinary like this, I shan't lose him, because he'll never go away without a proper outburst.'

It was not until they found themselves a second time before the Eve, that he said:

"I don't know why you asked me to come, Fleur. It's playing the goat for no earthly reason. I quite understand your feeling. I'm a bit of 'Ming' that you don't want to lose. But it's not good enough, my dear; and that's all about it."

"How horrible of you, Wilfrid!"

"Well! Here we part! Give us your flipper."

His eyes—rather beautiful—looked dark and tragic above the smile on his lips, and she said stammering:

"Wilfrid—I—I don't know. I want time. I can't bear you to be unhappy. Don't go away! Perhaps I—I shall be unhappy, too; I—I don't know."

Through Desert passed the bitter thought: 'She *can't* let go—she doesn't know how.' But he said quite softly: "Cheer up, my child; you'll be over all that in a fortnight. I'll send you something to make up. Why shouldn't I make it China—one place is as good as another? I'll send you a bit of real 'Ming,' of a better period than this."

Fleur said passionately:

"You're insulting! Don't!"

"I beg your pardon. I don't want to leave you angry."

"What is it you want of me?"

"Oh! no—come! This is going over it twice. Besides, since Friday I've been thinking. I want nothing, Fleur, except a blessing and your hand. Give it me! Come on!"

Fleur put her hand behind her back. It was too mortifying! He took her for a cold-blooded, collecting little cat—clutching and playing with mice that she didn't want to eat!

"You think I'm made of ice," she said, and her teeth caught her upper lip: "Well, I'm not!"

Desert looked at her; his eyes were very wretched. "I didn't mean to play up your pride," he said. "Let's drop it, Fleur. It isn't any good."

Fleur turned and fixed her eyes on the Eve—rumbustious-looking female, care-free, avid, taking her fill of flower perfume! Why not be care-free, take anything that came along? Not so much love in the world that one could afford to pass, leaving it unsmelled, unplucked. Run away! Go to the East! Of course, she couldn't do anything extravagant like that! But, perhaps—— What did it matter? —one man or another, when neither did you really love!

From under her drooped, white, dark-lashed eyelids she saw the expression on his face, and that he was standing stiller than the statues. And suddenly she said: "You will be a fool to go. Wait!" And without another word or look, she walked away, leaving Desert breathless before the avid Eve.

Chapter Six

"OLD FORSYTE" AND "OLD MONT"

———◆——◆——◆———

MOVING away, in the confusion of her mood, Fleur almost trod on the toes of a too-familiar figure standing before an Alma Tadema with a sort of grey anxiety, as if lost in the mutability of market values. "Father! *You* up in town? Come along to lunch, I have to get home quick."

Hooking his arm and keeping between him and Eve, she guided him away, thinking: 'Did he see us? Could he have seen us?'

"Have you got enough on?" muttered Soames.

"Heaps!"

"That's what you women always say. East wind, and your neck like that! Well, I don't know."

"No, dear, but I do."

The grey eyes appraised her from head to foot.

"What are you doing here?" he said. And Fleur thought: 'Thank God he didn't see. He'd never have asked if he had.' And she answered:

"I take an interest in art, darling, as well as you."

"Well, I'm staying with your aunt in Green Street. This east wind has touched my liver. How's your—how's Michael?"

37

"Oh, he's all right—a little cheap. We had a dinner last night."

Anniversary! The realism of a Forsyte stirred in him, and he looked under her eyes. Thrusting his hand into his overcoat pocket, he said:

"I was bringing you this."

Fleur saw a flat substance wrapped in pink tissue-paper.

"Darling, what is it?"

Soames put it back into his pocket.

"We'll see later. Anybody to lunch?"

"Only Bart."

"Old Mont! Oh, Lord!"

"Don't you like Bart, dear?"

"Like him? He and I have nothing in common."

"I thought you fraternised rather over the state of things."

"He's a reactionary," said Soames.

"And what are you, ducky?"

"I? What should *I* be?" With these words he affirmed that policy of non-commitment which, the older he grew, the more he perceived to be the only attitude for a sensible man.

"How is Mother?"

"Looks well. I see nothing of her—she's got her own mother down—they go gadding about."

He never alluded to Madame Lamotte as Fleur's grandmother—the less his daughter had to do with her French side, the better.

"Oh!" said Fleur. "There's Ting and a cat!" Ting-a-ling, out for a breath of air, and tethered by a lead in the hands of a maid, was snuffling horribly and trying to climb a railing whereon was perched a black cat, all hunch and eyes.

"Give him to me, Ellen. Come with Mother, darling!"

Ting-a-ling came, indeed, but only because he couldn't go, bristling and snuffling and turning his head back.

"I like to see him natural," said Fleur.

"Waste of money, a dog like that," Soames commented.

"You should have had a bull-dog and let him sleep in the hall. No end of burglaries. Your aunt had her knocker stolen."

"I wouldn't part with Ting for a hundred knockers."

"One of these days you'll be having *him* stolen—fashionable breed."

Fleur opened her front door. "Oh!" she said, "Bart's here, already!"

A shiny hat was reposing on a marble coffer, present from Soames, intended to hold coats and discourage moth. Placing his hat alongside the other, Soames looked at them. They were too similar for words, tall, high, shiny, and with the same name inside. He had resumed the "tall hat" habit after the failure of the general and coal strikes in 1921, his instinct having told him that revolution would be at a discount for some considerable period.

"About this thing," he said, taking out the pink parcel, "I don't know what you'll do with it, but here it is."

It was a curiously carved and coloured bit of opal in a ring of tiny brilliants.

"Oh!" Fleur cried: "What a delicious thing!"

"Venus floating on the waves, or something," murmured Soames. "Uncommon. You want a strong light on it."

"But it's lovely. I shall put it on at once."

Venus! If Dad had known! She put her arms round his neck to disguise her sense of *à propos*. Soames received the rub of her cheek against his own well-shaved face with his usual stillness. Why demonstrate when they were both aware that his affection was double hers?

"Put it on then," he said, "and let's see."

Fleur pinned it at her neck before an old lacquered mirror. "It's a jewel. Thank you, darling! Yes, your tie is straight. I like that white piping. You ought always to wear it with black. Now, come along!" And she drew him into her Chinese room. It was empty.

"Bart must be up with Michael, talking about his new book."

"Writing at his age?" said Soames.

"Well, ducky, he's a year younger than you."

"I don't write. Not such a fool. Got any more new-fangled friends?"

"Just one—Gurdon Minho, the novelist."

"Another of the new school?"

"Oh, no, dear! Surely you've heard of Gurdon Minho; he's older than the hills."

"They're all alike to me," muttered Soames. "Is he well thought of?"

"I should think his income is larger than yours. He's almost a classic—only waiting to die."

"I'll get one of his books and read it. What name did you say?"

"Get 'Big and Little Fishes,' by Gurdon Minho. You can remember that, can't you? Oh! here they are! Michael, look at what Father's given me."

Taking his hand, she put it up to the opal at her neck. 'Let them both see,' she thought, 'what good terms we're on.' Though her father had not seen her with Wilfrid in the gallery, her conscience still said: 'Strengthen your respectability, you don't quite know how much support you'll need for it in future.'

And out of the corner of her eye she watched those two. The meetings between "Old Mont" and "Old Forsyte" —as she knew Bart called her father when speaking of him to Michael—always made her want to laugh, but she never quite knew why. Bart knew everything, but his knowledge was beautifully bound, strictly edited by a mind tethered to the eighteenth century. Her father only knew what was of advantage to him, but the knowledge was unbound, and subject to no editorship. If he *was* late Victorian, he was not above profiting if necessary by even later periods. "Old Mont" had faith in tradition; "Old Forsyte" none. Fleur's acuteness had long perceived a difference which favoured her father. Yet "Old Mont's" talk was so much more up to date, rapid, glancing, garrulous, redolent of precise information; and "Old Forsyte's" was constricted, matter-of-fact. Really impossible to tell which of the two was the better museum specimen; and both so well-preserved!

They did not precisely shake hands; but Soames mentioned the weather. And almost at once they all four sought that Sunday food which by a sustained effort of will Fleur had at last deprived of reference to the British character. They partook, in fact, of lobster cocktails, and a mere risotto of chickens' livers, an omelette *au rhum,* and dessert trying to look as Spanish as it could.

"I've been in the Tate," Fleur said; "I do think it's touching."

"Touching?" queried Soames with a sniff.

"Fleur means, sir, that to see so much old English art together is like looking at a baby show."

"I don't follow," said Soames stiffly. "There's some very good work there."

"But not grown-up, sir."

"Ah! You young people mistake all this crazy cleverness for maturity."

"That's not what Michael means, Father. It's quite true that English painting has no wisdom teeth. You can see the difference in a moment, between it and any Continental painting."

"And thank God for it!" broke in Sir Lawrence. "The beauty of this country's art is its innocence. We're the oldest country in the world politically, and the youngest æsthetically. What do you say, Forsyte?"

"Turner is old and wise enough for me," said Soames curtly. "Are you coming to the P.P.R.S. Board on Tuesday?"

"Tuesday? We were going to shoot the spinneys, weren't we, Michael?"

Soames grunted. "I should let them wait," he said. "We settle the report."

It was through "Old Mont's" influence that he had received a seat on the Board of that flourishing concern, the Providential Premium Reassurance Society, and, truth to tell, he was not sitting very easily in it. Though the law of averages was, perhaps, the most reliable thing in the world, there were circumstances which had begun to cause him disquietude. He looked round his nose. Light weight, this narrow-headed, twisting-eyebrowed baronet of a chap—like his son before him! And he added suddenly: "I'm not easy. If I'd realised how that chap Elderson ruled the roost, I doubt if I should have come on to that Board."

One side of "Old Mont's" face seemed to try to leave the other.

"Elderson!" he said. "His grandfather was my grandfather's parliamentary agent at the time of the Reform Bill; he put him through the most corrupt election ever fought —bought every vote—used to kiss all the farmers' wives. Great days, Forsyte, great days!"

"And over," said Soames. "I don't believe in trusting a man's judgment as far as we trust Elderson's; I don't like this foreign insurance."

"My dear Forsyte—first-rate head, Elderson; I've known him all my life, we were at Winchester together."

Soames uttered a deep sound. In that answer of "Old Mont's" lay much of the reason for his disquietude. On the Board they had all, as it were, been at Winchester together! It was the very deuce! They were all so honourable that they dared not scrutinise each other, or even their own collective policy. Worse than their dread of mistake or fraud was their dread of seeming to distrust each other. And this was natural, for to distrust each other was an immediate evil. And, as Soames knew, immediate evils are those which one avoids. Indeed, only that tendency, inherited from his father, James, to lie awake between the hours of two and four, when the chrysalis of faint misgiving becomes so readily the butterfly of panic, had developed his uneasiness. The P.P.R.S. was so imposing a concern, and he had been connected with it so short a time, that it seemed presumptuous to smell a rat; especially as he would have to leave the Board and the thousand a year he earned on it if he raised smell of rat without rat or reason. But what if there were a rat? That was the trouble! And here sat "Old Mont" talking of his spinneys and his grandfather. The fellow's head was too small! And visited by the cheerless thought: 'There's nobody here, not even my own daughter, capable of taking a thing seriously,' he kept silence. A sound at his elbow roused him. That marmoset of a dog, on a chair between him and his daughter, was sitting up! Did it expect him to give it something? Its eyes would drop out one of these days. And he said: "Well what do *you* want?" The way the little beast stared with those boot-buttons! "Here," he said, offering it a salted almond. "You don't eat these."

Ting-a-ling did.

"He has a passion for them, Dad. Haven't you, darling?"

Ting-a-ling turned his eyes up at Soames, through whom a queer sensation passed. 'Believe the little brute likes me,' he thought, 'he's always looking at me.' He touched the dog's nose with the tip of his finger. Ting-a-ling gave it a slight lick with his curly blackish tongue.

"Poor fellow!" muttered Soames involuntarily, and turned to "Old Mont."

"Don't mention what I said."

"My dear Forsyte, what was that?"

Good Heavens! And he was on a Board with a man like this! What had made him come on, when he didn't want the money, or any more worries—goodness knew. As soon as he had become a director, Winifred and others of his family had begun to acquire shares to neutralise their income tax—seven per cent preference—nine per cent ordinary—instead of the steady five they ought to be content with. There it was, he couldn't move without people following him. He had always been so safe, so perfect a guide in the money maze! To be worried at his time of life! His eyes sought comfort from the opal at his daughter's neck —pretty thing, pretty neck! Well! She seemed happy enough—had forgotten her infatuation of two years ago! That was something to be thankful for. What she wanted now was a child to steady her in all this modern scrimmage of twopenny-ha'penny writers and painters and musicians. A loose lot, but she had a good little head on her.

If she had a child, he would put another twenty thousand into her settlement. That was one thing about her mother —steady in money matters, good French method. And Fleur—so far as he knew—cut her coat according to her cloth. What was that? The word "Goya" had caught his ear. New life of him coming out? H'm! That confirmed his slowly growing conviction that Goya had reached top point again.

"Think I shall part with that," he said, pointing to the picture. "There's an Argentine over here."

"Sell your Goya, sir?" It was Michael speaking. "Think of the envy with which you're now regarded!"

"One can't have everything," said Soames.

"That reproduction we've got for 'The New Life' has turned out first-rate. 'Property of Soames Forsyte, Esquire.' Let's get the book out first, sir, anyway."

"Shadow or substance, eh, Forsyte?"

Narrow-headed baronet chap—was he mocking?

"*I've* no family place," he said.

"No, but we have, sir," murmured Michael; "you could leave it to Fleur, you know."

"Well," said Soames, "we shall see if that's worth while." And he looked at his daughter.

Fleur seldom blushed, but she picked up Ting-a-ling and rose from the Spanish table. Michael followed suit. "Coffee in the other room," he said. "Old Forsyte" and "Old Mont" stood up, wiping their moustaches.

Chapter Seven

"OLD MONT" AND "OLD FORSYTE"

———— ❦ ————

THE offices of the P.P.R.S. were not far from the
College of Arms. Soames, who knew that "three
dexter buckles on a sable ground gules" and a "pheasant
proper" had been obtained there at some expense by his
Uncle Swithin in the 'sixties of the last century, had always
pooh-poohed the building, until, about a year ago, he had
been struck by the name Golding in a book which he had
absently taken up at the Connoisseurs' Club. The affair
purported to prove that William Shakespeare was really
Edward de Vere, Earl of Oxford. The mother of the earl
was a Golding—so was the mother of Soames! The coincidence struck him; and he went on reading. The tome
left him with judgment suspended over the main issue, but
a distinct curiosity as to whether he was not of the same
blood as Shakespeare. Even if the earl were not the bard,
he felt that the connection could only be creditable,
though, so far as he could make out, Oxford was a shady
fellow. Recently appointed on the Board of the P.P.R.S.,
so that he passed the college every other Tuesday, he
had thought: 'Shan't go spending a lot of money on it,
but might look in one day.' Having looked in, it was
astonishing how taken he had been by the whole thing.

45

Tracing his mother had been quite like a criminal investigation, nearly as ramified and fully as expensive. Having begun, the tenacity of a Forsyte could hardly bear to stop short of the mother of Shakespeare de Vere, even though she would be collateral; unfortunately, he could not get past a certain William Gouldyng, Ingerer—whatever that might be, and he was almost afraid to enquire—of the time of Oliver Cromwell. There were still four generations to be unravelled, and he was losing money and the hope of getting anything for it. This it was which caused him to gaze askance at the retired building while passing it on his way to the Board on the Tuesday after the lunch at Fleur's. Two more wakeful early mornings had screwed him to the pitch of bringing his doubts to a head and knowing where he stood in the matter of the P.P.R.S.; and this sudden reminder that he was spending money here, there and everywhere, when there was a possibility, however remote, of financial liability somewhere else, sharpened the edge of a nerve already stropped by misgivings. Neglecting the lift and walking slowly up the two flights of stairs, he "went over" his fellow-directors for the fifteenth time. Old Lord Fontenoy was there for his name, of course; seldom attended, and was what they called "a dud"—h'm!—nowadays; the Chairman, Sir Luke Sharman, seemed always to be occupied in not being taken for a Jew. His nose was straight, but his eyelids gave cause for doubt. His surname was impeccable, but his Christian dubious; his voice was reassuringly roughened, but his clothes had a suspicious tendency towards gloss. Altogether a man who, though shrewd, could not be trusted—Soames felt—to be giving his whole mind to other business. As for "Old Mont"— what was the good of a ninth baronet on a Board? Guy Meyricke, King's Counsel, last of the three who had been "together," was a good man in court, no doubt, but with no time for business and no real sense of it! Remained that converted Quaker, old Cuthbert Mothergill—whose family name had been a by-word for successful integrity throughout the last century, so that people still put Mothergills on to Boards almost mechanically—rather deaf, nice clean old chap, and quite bland, but nothing more. A perfectly honest lot, no doubt, but perfunctory. None of them really giving their minds to the thing! In Elderson's pocket, too, except perhaps Sharman, and he on the wobble. And Elderson himself—clever chap, bit of an artist, perhaps; managing director from the start, with everything at his finger-tips! Yes! That was the mischief! Prestige of superior knowledge, and years of success—they all kowtowed to him, and no wonder! Trouble with a man like that was that if he once admitted to having made a mistake he destroyed the legend of his infallibility. Soames had enough infallibility of his own to realise how powerful was its impetus towards admitting nothing. Ten months ago, when he had come on to the Board, everything had seemed in full sail; exchanges had reached bottom, so they all thought—the "reassurance of foreign contracts" policy, which Elderson had initiated about a year before, had seemed, with rising exchanges, perhaps the brightest feather in the cap of possibility. And now, a twelve-month later, Soames suspected darkly that they did not know where they were—and the general meeting only six weeks off! Probably not even Elderson knew; or, if he did, he was keeping knowledge which ought to belong to the whole directorate severely to himself.

He entered the Board room without a smile. All there—even Lord Fontenoy and "Old Mont"—given up his spinneys, had he! Soames took his seat at the end on the fire side. Staring at Elderson, he saw, with sudden clearness, the strength of the fellow's position; and, with equal clearness, the weakness of the P.P.R.S. With this rising and falling currency, they could never know exactly their liability—they were just gambling. Listening to the minutes and other routine business, with his chin clasped in his hand, he let his eyes move from face to face—old Mothergill, Elderson, Mont opposite; Sharman at the head; Fontenoy, Meyricke, back to himself—decisive Board of the year. He could not, must not, be placed in any dubious position! At his first general meeting on this concern, he must not face the shareholders without knowing exactly where he stood. He looked again at Elderson—sweetish face, bald head rather like Julius Cæsar's, nothing to suggest irregularity or excessive optimism—in fact, somewhat resembling that of old Uncle Nicholas Forsyte, whose affairs had been such an example to the last generation but one. The managing director having completed his exposition, Soames directed his gaze at the pink face of dosey old Mothergill, and said:

"I'm not satisfied that these accounts disclose our true position. I want the Board adjourned to this day week, Mr. Chairman, and during the week I want every member of the Board furnished with exact details of the foreign contract commitments which do *not* mature during the present financial year. I notice that those are lumped under a general estimate of liability. I am not satisfied with that. They ought to be separately treated." Shifting his gaze past Elderson to the face of "Old Mont," he went on: "Unless there's a material change for the better on the Continent, which I don't anticipate (quite the contrary), I fully expect those commitments will put us in Queer Street next year."

The scraping of feet, shifting of legs, clearing of throats which accompany a slight sense of outrage greeted the words "Queer Street"; and a sort of satisfaction swelled in Soames; he had rattled their complacency, made them feel a touch of the misgiving from which he himself was suffering.

"We have always treated our commitments under one general estimate, Mr. Forsyte."

Plausible chap!

"And to my mind wrongly. This foreign contract business is a new policy. For all I can tell, instead of paying a dividend, we ought to be setting this year's profits against a certain loss next year."

Again that scrape and rustle.

"My dear sir, absurd!"

The bulldog in Soames snuffled.

"So you say!" he said. "Am I to have those details?"

"The Board can have what details it likes, of course. But permit me to remark on the general question that it *can* only be a matter of estimate. A conservative basis has always been adopted."

"That is a matter of opinion," said Soames; "and in my view it should be the Board's opinion after very careful discussion of the actual figures."

"Old Mont" was speaking.

"My dear Forsyte, to go into every contract would take us a week, and then get us no further; we can but average it out."

"What we have not got in these accounts," said Soames, "is the relative proportion of foreign risk to home risk—in the present state of things a vital matter."

The Chairman spoke.

"There will be no difficulty about that, I imagine, Elderson. But in any case, Mr. Forsyte, we should hardly be justified in penalising the present year for the sake of eventualities which we hope will not arise."

"I don't know," said Soames. "We are here to decide policy according to our common sense, and we must have the fullest opportunity of exercising it. That is my point. We have not enough information."

That "plausible chap" was speaking again:

"Mr. Forsyte seems to be indicating a lack of confidence in the management." Taking the bull by the horns —was he?

"Am I to have that information?"

The voice of old Mothergill rose cosy in the silence.

"The Board could be adjourned, perhaps, Mr. Chairman; I could come up myself at a pinch. Possibly we could all attend. The times are very peculiar—we mustn't take any unnecessary risks. The policy of foreign contracts is undoubtedly somewhat new to us. We have no reason so far to complain of the results. And I am sure we have the utmost confidence in the judgment of our managing director. Still, as Mr. Forsyte has asked for this information, I think perhaps we ought to have it. What do you say, my lord?"

"I can't come up next week. I agree with the Chairman that on these accounts we couldn't burke this year's dividend. No good getting the wind up before we must. When do the accounts go out, Elderson?"

"Normally at the end of this week."

"These are not normal times," said Soames. "To be quite plain, unless I have that information I must tender my resignation." He saw very well what was passing in their minds. A newcomer making himself a nuisance— they would take his resignation readily—only it would look awkward just before a general meeting unless they could announce "wife's ill-health" or something satisfactory, which he would take very good care they didn't.

The Chairman said coldly:

"Well, we will adjourn the Board to this day week; you will be able to get us those figures, Elderson?"

"Certainly."

Into Soames' mind flashed the thought: 'Ought to ask for an independent scrutiny.' But he looked round. 'Going too far—perhaps—if he intended to remain on the Board —and he had no wish to resign—after all, it was a big thing, and a thousand a year! No! Mustn't overdo it!'

Walking away, he savoured his triumph doubtfully, by no means sure that he had done any good. His attitude had only closed the "all together" attitude round Elderson. The weakness of his position was that he had nothing to go on, save an uneasiness, which when examined was found to be simply a feeling that he hadn't enough control himself. And yet, there couldn't be two managers —you must trust your manager!

A voice behind him tittupped: "Well, Forsyte, you gave us quite a shock with your alternative. First time I remember anything of the sort on that Board."

"Sleepy hollow," said Soames.

"Yes, I generally have a nap. It gets very hot in there. Wish I'd stuck to my spinneys. They come high, even as early as this."

Incurably frivolous, this tittupping baronet!

"By the way, Forsyte, I wanted to say: With all this

modern birth control and the rest of it, one gets uneasy. We're not the royal family; but don't you feel with me it's time there was a movement in heirs?"

Soames did, but he was not going to confess to anything so indelicate about his own daughter.

"Plenty of time," he muttered.

"I don't like that dog, Forsyte."

Soames stared.

"Dog!" he said. "What's that to do with it?"

"I like a baby to come before a dog. Dogs and poets distract young women. My grandmother had five babies before she was twenty-seven. She was a Montjoy; wonderful breeders, you remember them—the seven Montjoy sisters—all pretty. Old Montjoy had forty-seven grandchildren. You don't get it nowadays, Forsyte."

"Country's over-populated," said Soames grimly.

"By the wrong sort—less of them, more of ourselves. It's almost a matter for legislation."

"Talk to your son," said Soames.

"Ah! but they think us fogeys, you know. If we could only point to a reason for existence. But it's difficult. Forsyte, it's difficult."

"They've got everything they want," said Soames.

"Not enough, my dear Forsyte, not enough; the condition of the world is on the nerves of the young. England's dished, they say, Europe's dished. Heaven's dished, and so is Hell! No future in anything but the air. You can't breed in the air; at least, I doubt it—the difficulties are considerable."

Soames sniffed.

"If only the journalists would hold their confounded pens," he said; for, more and more of late, with the decrescendo of scare in the daily Press, he was regaining the old sound Forsyte feeling of security. "We've only to keep clear of Europe," he added.

"Keep clear and keep the ring! Forsyte, I believe you've hit it. Good friendly terms with Scandinavia, Holland, Spain, Italy, Turkey—all the outlying countries that we can get at by sea. And let the others dree their weirds. It's an idea!" How the chap rattled on!

"I'm no politician," said Soames.

"Keep the ring! The new formula. It's what we've been coming to unconsciously! And as to trade—to say we can't do without trading with this country or with that— bunkum, my dear Forsyte. The world's large—we can."

"I don't know anything about that," said Soames. "I only know we must drop this foreign contract assurance."

"Why not confine it to the ring countries? Instead of 'balance of power,' 'keep the ring'! Really, it's an inspiration!"

Thus charged with inspiration, Soames said hastily:

"I leave you here, I'm going to my daughter's."

"Ah! I'm going to my son's. Look at these poor devils!"

Down by the Embankment at Blackfriars a band of unemployed were trailing dismally with money-boxes.

"Revolution in the bud! There's one thing that's always forgotten, Forsyte, it's a great pity."

"What's that?" said Soames, with gloom. The fellow would tittup all the way to Fleur's!

"Wash the working-class, put them in clean, pleasant-coloured jeans, teach 'em to speak like you and me, and there'd be an end of class feeling. It's all a matter of the senses. Wouldn't you rather share a bedroom with a clean, neat-clothed plumber's assistant who spoke and smelled like you than with a profiteer who dropped his aitches and reeked of opoponax? Of course you would."

"Never tried," said Soames, "so don't know."

"Pragmatist! But believe me, Forsyte—if the working class would concentrate on baths and accent instead of on their political and economic tosh, equality would be here in no time."

"I don't want equality," said Soames, taking his ticket to Westminster.

The "tittupping" voice pursued him entering the tube lift.

"Æsthetic equality, Forsyte, if we had it, would remove the wish for any other. Did you ever catch an impecunious professor wishing he was the King?"

"No," said Soames, opening his paper.

Chapter Eight

BICKET

━━━━◀━━━▶━━━◀━

ℬENEATH its veneer of cheerful irresponsibility, the character of Michael Mont had deepened during two years of anchorage and continuity. He had been obliged to think of others; and his time was occupied. Conscious, from the fall of the flag, that he was on sufferance with Fleur, admitting as whole the half-truth, *"Il y a toujours un qui baise, et l'autre qui tend la joue,"* he had developed real powers of domestic consideration; and yet he did not seem to redress the balance in his public or publishing existence. He found the human side of his business too strong for the monetary. Danby and Winter, however, were bearing up against him, and showed, so far, no signs of the bankruptcy prophesied for them by Soames on being told of the principles which his son-in-law intended to introduce. No more in publishing than in any other walk of life was Michael finding it possible to work too much on principle. The field of action was so strewn with facts—human, vegetable, and mineral.

On this same Tuesday afternoon, having long tussled with the price of those vegetable facts, paper and linen, he was listening with his pointed ears to the plaint of a packer discovered with five copies of "Copper Coin" in his overcoat pocket, and the too obvious intention of converting them to his own use.

Mr. Danby had "given him the sack"—he didn't deny that he was going to sell them, but what would Mr. Mont have done? He owed rent—and his wife wanted nourishing after penumonia—wanted it bad. 'Dash it!' thought Michael, 'I'd snoop an edition to nourish Fleur after pneumonia!'

"And I can't live on my wyges with prices what they are. I can't, Mr. Mont, so help me!"

Michael swivelled. "But look here, Bicket, if we let you snoop copies, all the packers will snoop copies; and if they do, where are Danby and Winter? In the cart. And, if they're in the cart, where are all of you? In the street. It's better that one of you should be in the street than that all of you should, isn't it?"

"Yes, sir, I quite see your point—it's reason; but I can't live on reason, the least thing knocks you out, when you're on the bread line. Ask Mr. Danby to give me another chance."

"Mr. Danby always says that a packer's work is particularly confidential, because it's almost impossible to keep a check on it."

"Yes, sir, I should feel that in future; but with all this unemployment and no reference, I'll never get another job. What about my wife?"

To Michael it was as if he had said "What about Fleur?" He began to pace the room; and the young man Bicket looked at him with large dolorous eyes. Presently he came to a standstill, with his hands deep plunged into his pockets and his shoulders hunched.

"I'll ask him," he said; "but I don't believe he will; he'll say it isn't fair on the others. You had five copies; it's pretty stiff, you know—means you've had 'em before, doesn't it? What?"

"Well, Mr. Mont, anything that'll give me a chance, I don't mind confessin'. I have 'ad a few previous, and it's just about kept my wife alive. You've no idea what that pneumonia's like for poor people."

Michael pushed his fingers through his hair.

"How old's your wife?"

"Only a girl—twenty."

Twenty! Just Fleur's age!

"I'll tell you what I'll do, Bicket; I'll put it up to Mr. Desert; if he speaks for you, perhaps it may move Mr. Danby."

"Well, Mr. Mont, thank you—you're a gentleman, we all sy that."

"Oh! hang it! But look here, Bicket, you were reckoning on those five copies. Take this to make up, and get your wife what's necessary. Only for goodness' sake don't tell Mr. Danby."

"Mr. Mont, I wouldn't deceive you for the world—I won't sy a word, sir. And my wife—well!"

A sniff, a shuffle—Michael was alone, with his hands plunged deeper, his shoulders hunched higher. And suddenly he laughed. Pity! Pity was pop! It was all dam' funny. Here he was rewarding Bicket for snooping "Copper Coin"! A sudden longing possessed him to follow the little packer and see what he did with the two pounds—see whether "the penumonia" was real or a figment of the brain behind those dolorous eyes. Impossible, though! Instead he must ring up Wilfrid and ask him to put in a word with old Danby. His own word was no earthly. He had put it in too often! Bicket! Little one knew of anybody, life was deep and dark, and upside down! What was honesty? Pressure of life *versus* power of resistance—the result of that fight, when the latter won, was honesty! But why resist? Love thy neighbour as thyself—but not more! And wasn't it a darned sight harder for Bicket on two pounds a week to love him, than for him on twenty-four pounds a week to love Bicket? . . .

"Hallo! . . . That you, Wilfrid? . . . Michael speaking. . . . One of our packers has been snooping copies of 'Copper Coin.' He's 'got the sack'—poor devil! I wondered if you'd mind putting in a word for him—old Dan won't listen to me . . . yes, got a wife—Fleur's age; pneumonia, so he says. Won't do it again with yours anyway, insurance by common gratitude—what! . . . Thanks, old man, awfully good of you—will you bob in, then? We can go round home together. . . . Oh! Well! You'll bob in anyway. Aurev!"

Good chap, old Wilfrid! Real good chap—underneath! Underneath—what?

Replacing the receiver, Michael saw a sudden great cloud of sights and scents and sounds, so foreign to the principles of his firm that he was in the habit of rejecting instantaneously every manuscript which dealt with them. The war might be "off"; but it was still "on" within Wilfrid, and himself. Taking up a tube, he spoke:

"Mr. Danby in his room? Right! If he shows any signs of flitting, let me know at once." . . .

Between Michael and his senior partner a gulf was fixed, not less deep than that between two epochs, though partially filled in by Winter's middle-age and accommodating temperament. Michael had almost nothing against Mr. Danby except that he was always right—Philip Norman Danby, of Sky House, Campden Hill, a man of sixty and some family, with a tall forehead, a preponderance of body to leg, and an expression both steady and reflective. His eyes were perhaps rather close together, and his nose rather thin, but he looked a handsome piece in his well-proportioned room. He glanced up from the formation of a correct judgment on a matter of advertisement when Wilfrid Desert came in.

"Well, Mr. Desert, what can I do for you? Sit down!"

Desert did not sit down, but looked at the engravings, his fingers, at Mr. Danby, and said:

"Fact is, I want you to let that packer chap off, Mr. Danby."

"Packer chap. Oh! Ah! Bicket. Mont told you, I suppose?"

"Yes; he's got a young wife down with penumonia."

"They all go to our friend Mont with some tale or other, Mr. Desert—he has a very soft heart. But I'm afraid I can't keep this man. It's a most insidious thing. We've been trying to trace a leak for some time."

Desert leaned against the mantelpiece and stared into the fire.

"Well, Mr. Danby," he said, "your generation may like the soft in literature, but you're precious hard in life. Ours won't look at softness in literature, but we're a deuced sight less hard in life."

"I don't think it's hard," said Mr. Danby, "only just."

"Are you a judge of justice?"

"I hope so."

"Try four years' hell, and have another go."

"I really don't see the connection. The experience you've been through, Mr. Desert, was bound to be warping."

Wilfrid turned and stared at him.

"Forgive my saying so, but sitting here and being just is much more warping. Life is pretty good purgatory, to all except about thirty per cent of grown-up people."

Mr. Danby smiled.

"We simply couldn't conduct our business, my dear young man, without scrupulous honesty in everybody. To make no distinction between honesty and dishonesty would be quite unfair. You know that perfectly well."

"I don't know anything perfectly well, Mr. Danby; and I mistrust those who say they do."

"Well, let us put it that there are rules of the game which must be observed, if society is to function at all."

Desert smiled, too: "Oh! hang rules! Do it as a favour to me. I wrote the rotten book."

No trace of struggle showed in Mr. Danby's face; but his deep-set, close-together eyes shone a little.

"I should be only too glad, but it's a matter—well, of conscience, if you like. I'm not prosecuting the man. He must leave—that's all."

Desert shrugged his shoulders.

"Well, good-bye!" and he went out.

On the mat was Michael in two minds.

"Well?"

"No go. The old blighter's too just."

Michael stivered his hair.

"Wait in my room five minutes while I let the poor beggar know, then I'll come along."

"No," said Desert, "I'm going the other way."

Not the fact that Wilfrid was going the other way—he almost always was—but something in the tone of his voice and the look on his face obsessed Michael's imagination while he went downstairs to seek Bicket. Wilfrid was a rum chap—he went "dark" so suddenly!

In the nether regions he asked:

"Bicket gone?"

"No, sir, there he is."

There he was, in his shabby overcoat, with his pale narrow face, and his disproportionately large eyes, and his sloping shoulders.

"Sorry, Bicket, Mr. Desert has been in, but it's no go."

"No, sir?"

"Keep your pecker up, you'll get something."

"I'm afryde not, sir. Well, I thank you very 'eartily; and I thank Mr. Desert. Good-night, sir; and good-bye!"

Michael watched him down the corridor, saw him waver into the dusky street.

"Jolly!" he said, and laughed. . . .

The natural suspicions of Michael and his senior partner that a tale was being pitched were not in fact justified. Neither the wife nor the pneumonia had been exaggerated; and wavering away in the direction of Blackfriars Bridge, Bicket thought not of his turpitude nor of how just Mr. Danby had been, but of what he should say to her. He should not, of course, tell her that he had been detected in stealing; he must say he had "got the sack for cheeking the foreman"; but what would she think of him for doing that, when everything as it were depended on his not cheeking the foreman? This was one of those melancholy cases of such affection that he had been coming to his work day after day feeling as if he had "left half his guts" behind him in the room where she lay, and when at last the doctor said to him:

"She'll get on now, but it's left her very run down—you must feed her up," his anxiety had hardened into a resolution to have no more. In the next three weeks he had "snooped" eighteen "Copper Coins," including the five found in his overcoat. He had only pitched on Mr. Desert's book because it was "easy sold," and he was sorry now that he hadn't pitched on some one else's. Mr. Desert had been very decent. He stopped at the corner of the Strand, and went over his money. With the two pounds given him by Michael and his wages he had seventy-five shillings in the world, and going into the Stores he bought a meat jelly and a tin of Benger's food that could be made with water. With pockets bulging he took a 'bus, which dropped him at the corner of his little street on the Surrey side. His wife and he occupied the two ground floor rooms, at eight shillings a week, and he owed for three. 'Better py that!' he thought, 'and have a roof until she's well.' It would help him over the news, too, to show her a receipt for the rent and some good food. How lucky they had been careful to have no baby! He sought the basement. His landlady was doing the week's washing. She paused, in sheer surprise at such full and voluntary payment, and inquired after his wife.

"Doing nicely, thank you."

"Well, I'm glad of that, it must be a relief to your mind."

"It is," said Bicket.

The landlady thought: 'He's a thread-paper—reminds me of a shrimp before you bile it, with those eyes.'

"Here's your receipt, and thank you. Sorry to 'ave seemed nervous about it, but times are 'ard."

"They are," said Bicket. "So long!"

With the receipt and the meat jelly in his left hand, he opened the door of his front room.

His wife was sitting before a very little fire. Her bobbed black hair, crinkly towards the ends, had grown during her illness; it shook when she turned her head and smiled. To Bicket—not for the first time—that smile seemed queer, "pathetic-like," mysterious—as if she saw things that one didn't see oneself. Her name was Victorine, and he said: "Well, Vic.? This jelly's a bit of all right, and

I've pyde the rent." He sat on the arm of the chair and
she put her hand on his knee—her thin arm emerged
blue-white from the dark dressing-gown.

"Well, Tony?"

Her face—thin and pale with those large dark eyes and
beautifully formed eyebrows—was one that "looked at
you from somewhere; and when it looked at you—well!
it got you right inside!"

It got him now and he said: "How've you been
breathin'?"

"All right—much better. I'll soon be out now."

Bicket twisted himself round and joined his lips to
hers. The kiss lasted some time, because all the feelings
which he had not been able to express during the past
three weeks to her or to anybody, got into it. He sat up
again, "sort of exhausted," staring at the fire, and said:
"News isn't bright—lost my job, Vic."

"Oh! Tony! Why?"

Bicket swallowed.

"Fact is, things are slack and they're reducin'."

There had surged into his mind the certainty that
sooner than tell her the truth he would put his head under
the gas!

"Oh! dear! What shall we do, then?"

Bicket's voice hardened.

"Don't you worry—I'll get something"; and he
whistled.

"But you liked that job."

"Did I? I liked some o' the fellers; but as for the job—
why, what was it? Wrappin' books up in a bysement all
dy long. Let's have something to eat and get to bed early
—I feel as if I could sleep for a week, now I'm shut of
it."

Getting their supper ready with her help, he carefully
did not look at her face for fear it might "get him agyne
inside"! They had only been married a year, having made
acquaintance on a tram, and Bicket often wondered what
had made her take to him, eight years her senior and C_3

during the war! And yet she must be fond of him, or she'd never look at him as she did.

"Sit down and try this jelly."

He himself ate bread and margarine and drank cocoa, he seldom had any particular appetite.

"Shall I tell you what I'd like?" he said: "I'd like Central Austrylia. We had a book in there about it; they sy there's quite a movement. I'd like some sun. I believe if we 'ad sun we'd both be twice the size we are. I'd like to see colour in your cheeks, Vic."

"How much does it cost to get out there?"

"A lot more than we can ly hands on, that's the trouble. But I've been thinkin'. England's about done. There's too many like me."

"No," said Victorine; "there aren't enough."

Bicket looked at her face, then quickly at his plate.

"What myde you tyke a fancy to me?"

"Because you don't think first of yourself, that's why."

"Used to before I knew you. But I'd do anything for you, Vic."

"Have some of this jelly, then, it's awful good."

Bicket shook his head.

"If we could wyke up in Central Austrylia," he said. "But there's only one thing certain, we'll wyke up in that blighted little room. Never mind, I'll get a job and earn the money yet."

"Could we win it on a race?"

"Well, I've only got forty-seven bob all told, and if we lose it, where'll you be? You've got to feed up, you know. No, I must get a job."

"They'll give you a good recommend, won't they?"

Bicket rose and heaped his plate and cup.

"They would, but that job's off—overstocked."

Tell her the truth? Never! So help him!

In their bed, one of those just too wide for one and just not wide enough for two, he lay, with her hair almost in his mouth, thinking what to say to his Union, and how to go to work to get a job. And in his thoughts as the hours drew on he burned his boats. To draw his unemployment money he would have to tell his Union what the trouble was. Blow the Union! He wasn't going to be accountable to them! *He* knew why he'd sneaked the books; but it was nobody else's business, nobody else could understand his feelings, watching her so breathless, pale and thin. Strike out for himself! And a million and a half out o' work! Well, he had a fortnight's keep, and something would turn up—and he might risk a bob or two and win some money, you never knew. She turned in her sleep. 'Yes,' he thought, 'I'd do it agyne. . . .'

Next day, after some hours on foot, he stood under the grey easterly sky in the grey street, before a plate-glass window protecting an assortment of fruits, and sheaves of corn, lumps of metal, and brilliant blue butterflies, in the carefully golden light of advertised Australia. To Bicket, who had never been out of England, not often out of London, it was like standing outside Paradise. The atmosphere within the office itself was not so golden, and the money required considerable; but it brought Paradise nearer to take away pamphlets which almost burned his hands, they were so warm.

Later, he and she, sitting in the one armchair—advantage of being thin—pored over these alchemised pages and inhaled their glamour.

"D'you think it's true, Tony?"

"If it's thirty per cent true it's good enough for me. We just must get there somehow. Kiss me."

From around the corner in the main road the rumbling of the trams and carts, and the rattling of their windowpane in the draughty dry easterly wind increased their feeling of escape into a gas-lit Paradise.

Chapter Nine

CONFUSION

———◆◆◆◆◆◆———

TWO hours behind Bicket, Michael wavered towards home. Old Danby was right as usual—if you couldn't trust your packers, you might shut up shop! Away from Bicket's eyes, he doubted. Perhaps the chap hadn't a wife at all! Then Wilfrid's manner usurped the place of Bicket's morals. Old Wilfrid had been abrupt and queer the last three times of meeting. Was he boiling-up for verse?

He found Ting-a-ling at the foot of the stairs in a conservative attitude. "I am not going up," he seemed saying, "until some one carries me—at the same time it is later than usual!"

"Where's your mistress, you heraldic little beast?"

Ting-a-ling snuffled. "I could put up with it," he implied, "if you carried me—these stairs are laborious!"

Michael took him up. "Let's go and find her."

Squeezed under an arm harder than his mistress', Ting-a-ling stared as if with black-glass eyes; and the plume of his emergent tail quivered.

In the bedroom Michael dropped him so absent-mindedly that he went to his corner plume pendent, and couched there in dudgeon.

65

Nearly dinner time and Fleur not in! Michael went over his sketchy recollection of her plans. To-day she had been having Hubert Marsland and that Vertiginist—what was his name?—to lunch. There would have been fumes to clear off. Vertiginists—like milk—made carbonic acid gas in the lungs! Still! Half-past seven! What was happening to-night? Weren't they going to that play of L.S.D.'s? No—that was to-morrow! Was there conceivably nothing? If so, of course she would shorten her unoccupied time as much as possible. He made that reflection humbly. Michael had no illusions, he knew himself to be commonplace, with only a certain redeeming liveliness, and, of course, his affection for her. He even recognised that his affection was a weakness, tempting him to fussy anxieties, which on principle he restrained. To enquire, for instance, of Coaker or Philps—their man and their maid—when she had gone out, would be thoroughly against that principle. The condition of the world was such that Michael constantly wondered if his own affairs were worth paying attention to; but then the condition of the world was also such that sometimes one's own affairs seemed all that were worth paying attention to. And yet his affairs were, practically speaking, Fleur; and if he paid too much attention to them, he was afraid of annoying her.

He went to his dressing-room and undid his waistcoat.

'But no!' he thought; 'If she finds me "dressed" already, it'll put too much point on it.' So he did up his waistcoat and went downstairs again. Coaker was in the hall.

"Mr. Forsyte and Sir Lawrence looked in about six, sir. Mrs. Mont was out. What time shall I serve dinner?"

"Oh! about a quarter past eight. I don't think we're going out."

He went into the drawing-room and passing down in Chinese emptiness, drew aside the curtain. The square looked cold and dark and draughty; and he thought: 'Bicket—pneumonia—I hope she's got her fur coat.' He took out a cigarette and put it back. If she saw him at the

window she would think him fussy; and he went up again
to see if she had put on her fur!

Ting-a-ling, still couchant, greeted him plume dansetti
arrested as at disappointment. Michael opened a wardrobe. She had! Good! He was taking a sniff round, when
Ting-a-ling passed him trottant, and her voice said: "Well,
my darling!" Wishing that he was, Michael emerged from
behind the wardrobe door. Heaven! She looked pretty,
coloured by the wind! He stood rather wistfully silent.

"Hallo, Michael! I'm rather late. Been to the Club and
walked home."

Michael had a quite unaccountable feeling that there
was suppression in that statement. He also suppressed,
and said: "I was just looking to see that you'd got your
fur, it's beastly cold. Your dad and Bart have been here
and went away fasting."

Fleur shed her coat and dropped into a chair. "I'm
tired. Your ears are sticking up so nicely to-night,
Michael."

Michael went on his knees and joined his hands behind
her waist. Her eyes had a strange look, a scrutiny which
held him in suspense, a little startled.

"If *you* got pneumonia," he said, "I should go clean
out of curl."

"Why on earth should I?"

"You don't know the connection—never mind, it
wouldn't interest you. We're not going out, are we?"

"Of course we are. It's Alison's monthly."

"Oh! Lord! If you're tired we could cut that."

"My dear! Impos.! She's got all sorts of people
coming."

Stifling a disparagement, he sighed out: "Right-o! War-
paint?"

"Yes, white waistcoat. I like you in white waistcoats."

Cunning little wretch! He squeezed her waist and rose.
Fleur laid a light stroke on his hand, and he went into his
dressing-room comforted. . . .

But Fleur sat still for at least five minutes—not precisely "a prey to conflicting emotions," but the victim of

very considerable confusion. *Two* men within the last
hour had done this thing—knelt at her knees and joined
their fingers behind her waist. Undoubtedly she had been
rash to go to Wilfrid's rooms. The moment she got there
she had perceived how entirely unprepared she really was
to commit herself to what was physical. True he had done
no more than Michael. But—Goodness!—she had seen
the fire she was playing with, realised what torment he
was in. She had strictly forbidden him to say a word to
Michael, but intuitively she knew that in his struggle
between loyalties she could rely on nothing. Confused,
startled, touched, she could not help a pleasant warmth
in being so much loved by two men at once, nor an itch
of curiosity about the upshot. And she sighed. She had
added to her collection of experiences—but how to add
further without breaking up the collection, and even perhaps the collector, she could not see.

After her words to Wilfrid before the Eve: "You will
be a fool to go—wait!" she had known he would expect
something before long. Often he had asked her to come
and pass judgment on his "junk." A month, even a
week, ago she would have gone without thinking more
than twice about it, and discussed his "junk" with
Michael afterwards! But now she thought it over many
times, and but for the fumes of lunch, and the feeling, en-
gendered by the society of the "Vertiginist," of Amabel
Nazing, of Linda Frewe, that scruples of any kind were
"stuffy," sensations of all sorts "the thing," she would
probably still have been thinking it over now. When they
departed, she had taken a deep breath and her telephone
receiver from the Chinese tea chest.

If Wilfrid were going to be in at half-past five, she
would come and see his "junk."

His answer: "My God! Will you?" almost gave her
pause. But dismissing hesitation with the thought: 'I *will*
be Parisian—Proust!' she had started for her Club.
Three-quarters of an hour, with no more stimulant than
three cups of Chinese tea, three back numbers of the
Glass of Fashion, three back views of country members

"dead in chairs," had sent her forth a careful quarter of an hour behind her time.

On the top floor Wilfrid was standing in his open doorway, pale as a soul in purgatory. He took her hand gently, and drew her in. Fleur thought with a little thrill: 'Is this what it's like? *Du côté de chez Swann!*' Freeing her hand, she began at once to flutter round the "junk," clinging to it piece by piece.

Old English "junk" rather manorial, with here and there an eastern or First Empire bit, collected by some bygone Desert, nomadic, or attached to the French court. She was afraid to sit down, for fear that he might begin to follow the authorities; nor did she want to resume the intense talk of the Tate Gallery. "Junk" was safe, and she only looked at him in those brief intervals when he was not looking at her. She knew she was not playing the game according to "La Garçonne" and Amabel Nazing; that, indeed, she was in danger of going away without having added to her sensations. And she couldn't help being sorry for Wilfrid; his eyes yearned after her, his lips were bitter to look at. When at last from sheer exhaustion of "junk" she sat down, he had flung himself at her feet. Half hypnotised, with her knees against his chest, as safe as she could hope for, she really felt the tragedy of it—his horror of himself, his passion for herself. It was painful, deep; it did not fit in with what she had been led to expect; it was not in the period, and how—how was she to get away without more pain to him and to herself? When she *had* got away, with one kiss received but not answered, she realised that she had passed through a quarter of an hour of real life, and was not at all sure that she liked it. . . . But now, safe in her own room, undressing for Alison's monthly, she felt curious as to what she would have been feeling if things had gone as far as was proper according to the authorities. Surely she had not experienced one-tenth of the thoughts or sensations that would have been assigned to her in any advanced piece of literature! It had been disillusioning, or else she was deficient, and Fleur could not bear to feel

deficient. And, lightly powdering her shoulders, she bent
her thoughts towards Alison's monthly.

Though Lady Alison enjoyed an occasional encounter
with the younger generation, the Aubrey Greenes and
Linda Frewes of this life were not conspicuous by their
presence at her gatherings. Nesta Gorse, indeed, had
once attended, but one legal and two literary politicos
who had been in contact with her, had complained of it
afterwards. She had, it seemed, rent little spiked holes in
the garments of their self-esteem. Sibley Swan would have
been welcome, for his championship of the past, but he
seemed, so far, to have turned up his nose and looked
down it. So it was not the intelligentsia, but just intellec-
tual society, which was gathered there when Fleur and
Michael entered, and the conversation had all the sparkle
and all the *"savoir faire"* incidental to talk about art and
letters by those who—as Michael put it—"fortunately had
not to *faire.*"

"All the same, these are the guys," he muttered in
Fleur's ear, "who make the names of artists and writers.
What's the stunt, tonight?"

It appeared to be the London *début* of a lady who
sang Balkan folk songs. But in a refuge to the right were
four tables set out for bridge. They were already filled.
Among those who still stood listening, were, here and
there, a Gurdon Minho, a society painter and his wife, a
sculptor looking for a job. Fleur, wedged between Lady
Feynte, the painter's wife, and Gurdon Minho himself,
began planning an evasion. There—yes, there was Mr.
Chalfont! At Lady Alison's, Fleur, an excellent judge of
"milieu," never wasted her time on artists and writers—
she could meet *them* anywhere. Here she intuitively
picked out the biggest "bug," politico-literary, and waited
to pin him. Absorbed in the idea of pinning Mr. Chalfont, she overlooked a piece of drama passing without.

Michael had clung to the top of the stairway, in no
mood for talk and skirmish; and, leaning against the
balustrade, wasp-thin in his long white waistcoat, with

hands deep thrust into his trousers' pocket, he watched the
turns and twists of Fleur's white neck, and listened to the
Balkan songs, with a sort of blankness in his brain. The
word: "Mont!" startled him. Wilfrid was standing just
below. Mont! He had not been that to Wilfrid for two
years!

"Come down here."

On that half-landing was a bust of Lionel Charwell,
K.C., by Boris Strumolowski, in the genre he had cynically adopted when June Forsyte gave up supporting his
authentic but unrewarded genius. It had been almost in-
distinguishable from any of the other busts in that year's
Academy, and was used by the young Charwells to chalk
moustaches on.

Beside this object Desert leaned against the wall with
his eyes closed. His face was a study to Michael.

"What's wrong, Wilfrid?"

Desert did not move. "You've got to know—I'm
in love with Fleur."

"What!"

"I'm not going to play the snake. You're up against
me. Sorry, but there it is! You can let fly!" His face was
death-pale, and its muscles twitched. In Michael, it was
the mind, the heart that twitched. What a very horrible,
strange, "too beastly" moment! His best friend—his best
man! Instinctively he dived for his cigarette case—instinctively handed it to Desert. Instinctively they both
took cigarettes, and lighted each other's. Then Michael
said:

"Fleur—knows?"

Desert nodded: "She doesn't know I'm telling you—
wouldn't have let me. You've nothing against her—yet."
And, still with closed eyes, he added: "I couldn't help it."

It was Michael's own subconscious thought! Natural!
Natural! Fool not to see how natural! Then something
shut-to within him, and he said: "Decent of you to tell
me; but—aren't you going to clear out?"

Desert's shoulders writhed against the wall.

"I thought so; but it seems not."

"Seems? I don't understand."

"If I knew for certain I'd no chance—but I don't," and he suddenly looked at Michael: "Look here, it's no good keeping gloves on. I'm desperate, and I'll take her from you if I can."

"Good God!" said Michael. "It's the limit!"

"Yes! Rub it in! But, I tell you, when I think of you going home with her, and of myself," he gave a dreadful little laugh, "I advise you *not* to rub it in."

"Well," said Michael, "as this isn't a Dostoievsky novel, I suppose there's no more to be said."

Desert moved from the wall and laid his hand on the bust of Lionel Charwell.

"You realise, at least, that I've gone out of my way— perhaps dished myself—by telling you. I've not bombed without declaring war."

"No," said Michael dully.

"You can chuck my books over to some other publisher." Michael shrugged.

"Good-night, then," said Desert. "Sorry for being so primitive."

Michael looked straight into his "best man's" face. There was no mistaking its expression of bitter despair. He made a half-movement with his hand, uttered half the word "Wilfrid," and, as Desert went down, he went upstairs.

Back in his place against the balustrade, he tried to realise that life was a laughing matter, and couldn't. His position required a serpent's cunning, a lion's courage, a dove's gentleness; he was not conscious of possessing such proverbial qualities. If Fleur had loved him as he loved her, he would have had for Wilfrid a real compassion. It was so natural to fall in love with Fleur! But she didn't— oh! no, she didn't! Michael had one virtue—if virtue it be—a moderate opinion of himself, a disposition to think highly of his friends. He had thought highly of Desert; and—odd!—he still did not think lowly of him. Here was his friend trying to do him mortal injury, to alienate the affection—more honestly, the toleration—of his wife; and yet he did not think him a cad. Such leniency, he knew, was hopeless; but the doctrines of free-will, and free contract, were not to him mere literary conceptions, they were part of his nature. To apply duress, however desirable, would not be on his cards. And something like despair ravaged the heart of him, watching Fleur's ingratiating little tricks with the great Gerald Chalfont. If she left him for Wilfrid! But surely—no—her father, her house, her dog, her friends, her—her collection of—of—she would not—could not give *them* up? But suppose she kept everything—Wilfrid included! No, no! She wouldn't! Only for a second did that possibility blur the natural loyalty of his mind.

Well, what to do? Tell her—talk the thing out? Or wait and watch? For what? Without deliberate spying, he could not watch. Desert would come to their house no more. No! Either complete frankness; or complete ignoring—and that meant living with the sword of Damocles above his head! No! Complete frankness! And not do anything that seemed like laying a trap! He passed his hand across a forehead that was wet. If only they were at home, away from that squalling and these cultivated jackanapes! Could he go in and hook her out? Impossible without some reason! Only his brain-storm for a reason! He must just bite on it. The singing ceased. Fleur was looking round. Now she would beckon! On the contrary, she came towards him. He could not help the cynical thought: 'She's hooked old Chalfont!' He loved her, but he knew her little weaknesses. She came up and took hold of his sleeve.

"I've had enough, Michael, let's slip off; d'you mind?"

"Quick!" he said, "before they spot us!"

In the cold air outside he thought: 'Now? Or in her room?'

"I think," said Fleur, "that Mr. Chalfont is overrated —he's nothing but a mental yawn. He's coming to lunch to-morrow week."

Not now—in her room!

"Whom do you think to meet him, besides Alison?"

"Nothing jazzy."

"Of course not; but it must be somebody intriguing, Michael. Bother! sometimes I think it isn't worth it."

Michael's heart stood still. Was that a portent—sign of "the primitive" rising within his adored practitioner of social arts? An hour ago he would have said:

"You're right, old dear; it jolly well isn't!" But now—any sign of change was ominous! He slipped his arm in hers.

"Don't worry, we'll dig up the just-right cuckoos, somehow."

"A Chinese Minister would be perfect," mused Fleur, "with Minho and Bart—four men—two women—cosy. I'll talk to Bart."

Michael had opened their front door. She passed him; he lingered to see the stars, the plane trees, a man's figure motionless, collared to the eyes, hatted down to them. 'Wilfrid!' he thought: 'Spain! Why Spain? And all poor devils who are in distress—the heart—oh! darn the heart!' He closed the door.

But soon he had another to open, and never with less enthusiasm. Fleur was sitting on the arm of a chair, in the dim lavender pyjamas she sometimes wore just to keep in with things, staring at the fire. Michael stood, looking at her and at his own reflection beyond in one of the five mirrors—white and black, the pierrot pyjamas she had bought him. 'Figures in a play,' he thought, 'figures in a play! Is it real?' He moved forward and sat on the chair's other arm.

"Hang it!" he muttered. "Wish I were Antinous!" And he slipped from the arm into the chair, to be behind her face, if she wanted to hide it from him.

"Wilfrid's been telling me," he said, quietly.

Off his chest! What now? He saw the blood come flushing into her neck and cheek.

"Oh! what business—how do you mean 'telling you'?"

"Just that he's in love with you—nothing more—there's nothing more to tell, is there?" And drawing his feet up on to the chair, he clasped his hands hard round his knees. Already—already he had asked a question! Bite on it! Bite on it! And he shut his eyes.

"Of course," said Fleur, very slowly, "there's nothing more. If Wilfrid chooses to be so silly."

Chooses! The word seemed unjust to one whose own "silliness" was so recent—so enduring! And—curious!—his heart wouldn't bound. Surely it ought to have bounded at her words!

"Is that the end of Wilfrid, then?"

"The end? I don't know."

Ah! Who knew anything—when passion was about?

"Well," he said, holding himself hard together, "don't forget I love you awfully!"

He saw her eyelids flicker, her shoulders shrugging.

"Am I likely to?"

Bitter, cordial, simple—which? Suddenly her hand came round and took him by the ears. Holding them fast she looked down at him, and laughed. And again his heart *would* not bound. If she did not lead him by the nose, she—! But he clutched her to him in the chair. Lavender and white and black confused—she returned his kiss. But from the heart? Who knew? Not Michael.

Chapter Ten

PASSING OF A SPORTSMAN

———◆——◆——◆———

SOAMES, disappointed of his daughter, said: "I'll
wait," and took his seat in the centre of the jade-
green settee, oblivious of Ting-a-ling before the fire, sleeping off the attentions of Amabel Nazing, who had found
him "just too cunning." Grey and composed, with one
knee over the other, and a line between his eyes, he
thought of Elderson and the condition of the world, and
of how there was always something. And the more he
thought, the more he wondered why he had ever been
such a flat as to go on to a Board which had anything
to do with foreign contracts. All the old wisdom that in
the nineteenth century had consolidated British wealth,
all the Forsyte philosophy of attending to one's own business, and taking no risks, the close-fibred national in-
dividualism which refused to commit the country to
chasing this wild goose or that, held within him silent
demonstration. Britain was on the wrong tack politically
to try and influence the Continent, and the P.P.R.S. on
the wrong tack monetarily to insure business outside
Britain. The special instinct of his breed yearned for re-
sumption of the straight and private path. Never meddle
with what you couldn't control! "Old Mont" had said:

77

"Keep the ring!" Nothing of the sort; mind one's own business! That was the real "formula." He became conscious of his calf—Ting-a-ling was sniffing at his trousers.

"Oh!" said Soames. "It's you!"

Placing his forepaws against the settee, Ting-a-ling licked the air.

"Pick you up?" said Soames. "You're too long." And again he felt that faint warmth of being liked.

'There's something about me that appeals to him,' he thought, taking him by the scruff and lifting him on to a cushion. "You and I," the little dog seemed saying with his stare—Chinese little object! The Chinese knew what they were about, they had minded their own business for five thousand years!

'I shall resign,' thought Soames. But what about Winifred, and Imogen, and some of the Rogers and Nicholases who had been putting money into this thing because he was a director? He wished they wouldn't follow him like a lot of sheep! He rose from the settee. It was no good waiting, he would walk on to Green Street and talk to Winifred at once. She would have to sell again, though the shares had dropped a bit. And without taking leave of Ting-a-ling, he went out.

All this last year he had almost enjoyed life. Having somewhere to come and sit and receive a certain sympathy once at least a week, as in old days at Timothy's, was of incalculable advantage to his spirit. In going from home Fleur had taken most of his heart with her; but Soames had found it almost an advantage to visit his heart once a week rather than to have it always about. There were other reasons conducing to light-heartedness. That diabolical foreign chap, Prosper Profond, had long been gone he didn't know where, and his wife had been decidedly less restive and sarcastic ever since. She had taken up a thing they called Coué, and grown stouter. She used the car a great deal. Altogether she was more domestic. Then, too, he had become reconciled to Gauguin—a little slump in that painter had convinced him that he was still worth attention, and he had bought three more.

Gauguin would rise again! Soames almost regretted his intuition of that second coming, for he had quite taken to the chap. His colour, once you got used to it, was very attractive. One picture, especially, of a South Sea girl with nothing on, had a way of making you keep your eyes on it. He even felt uneasy when he thought of having to part with the thing at an enhanced price. But, most of all, he had been feeling so well, enjoying a recrudescence of youth in regard to Annette, taking more pleasure in what he ate, while his mind dwelt almost complacently on the state of money. The pound going up in value; Labour quiet! And now they had got rid of that Jack-o'-lantern, they might look for some years of solid Conservative administration. And to think, as he did, stepping across St. James' Park towards Green Street, that he had gone and put his foot into a concern which he could not control, made him feel—well, as if the devil had been in it!

In Piccadilly he moused along on the Park side, taking his customary look up at the 'Iseeum' Club. The curtains were drawn, and chinks of light glowed, long and cosy. And that reminded him—some one had said George Forsyte was ill. Certainly he had not seen George in the bay window of the club he had so appropriately nicknamed, for months past. Well, George had always eaten and drunk too much. He crossed over and passed beneath the Club; and a sudden feeling—he didn't know what—a longing for his own past, a sort of nostalgia—made him stop and mount the steps.

"Mr. George Forsyte in the Club?"

The janitor stared, a grey-haired, long-faced chap, whom he had known from away back in the 'eighties.

"Mr. Forsyte, sir," he said, "is very ill indeed. They say he won't recover, sir."

"What?" said Soames. "Nobody told me that."

"He's very bad—*very* bad indeed. It's the heart."

"The heart! Where is he?"

"At his rooms, sir; just round the corner. They say the doctors have given him up. He *will* be missed here. Forty years I've known him. One of the old school, and a wonderful judge of wine and horses. We none of us last for ever, they say, but I never thought to see *him* out. Bit too full-blooded, sir, and that's a fact."

With a slight shock Soames realised that he had never known where George lived, so utterly anchored had he seemed to that bay window above.

"Just give me the number of his rooms," he said.

"Belville Row—No. 11, sir; I'm sure I hope you'll find him better. I shall miss his jokes—I shall, indeed."

Turning the corner into Belville Row, Soames made a rapid calculation. George was sixty-six, only one year younger than himself! If George was really *in extremis* it would be quite unnatural! 'Comes of not leading a careful life,' he thought; 'always rackety—George! When was it I made his will?' So far as he remembered, George had left his money to his brothers and sisters—no one else to leave it to. The feeling of kinship stirred in Soames, the instinct of family adjustment. George and he had never got on—opposite poles of temperament—still he would have to be buried, and who would see to it if not Soames, who had seen to so many Forsyte burials in his time? He recalled the nickname George had once given him, "the undertaker!" H'm! Here was poetical justice! Belville Row! Ah! No. 11—regular bachelor-looking place! And putting his hand up to the bell, he thought: 'Women!' What had George done about women all his life?

His ring was answered by a man in a black cut-away coat, with a certain speechless reticence.

"My cousin, Mr. George Forsyte? How is he?"

The man compressed his lips.

"Not expected to last the night, sir."

Soames felt a little clutch beneath his Jaeger vest.

"Conscious?"

"Yes, sir."

"Could you show him my card? He might possibly like to see me."

"Will you wait in here, sir?" Soames passed into a low room panelled up to the level of a man's chest, and above that line decorated with prints. George—a collector!

Soames had never supposed he had it in him! On those
walls, wherever the eye roved, were prints coloured and
uncoloured, old and new, depicting the sports of racing
and prize-fighting! Hardly an inch of the red wall space
visible! About to examine them for marks of value,
Soames saw that he was not alone. A woman—age uncertain in the shaded light—was sitting in a very high-
backed chair before the fire with her elbow on the arm of
it, and a handkerchief held to her face. Soames looked
at her, and his nostrils moved in a stealthy sniff. 'Not a
lady,' he thought. 'Ten to one but there'll be complica-
tions.' The muffled voice of the cut-away man said:

"I'm to take you in, sir." Soames passed his hand
over his face and followed.

The bedroom he now entered was in curious contrast.
The whole of one wall was occupied by an immense
piece of furniture, all cupboards and drawers. Otherwise
there was nothing in the room but a dressing-table with
silver accoutrements, an electric radiator alight in the fireplace, and a bed opposite. Over the fireplace was a single
picture, at which Soames glanced mechanically. What!
Chinese! A large whitish sidelong monkey, holding the
rind of a squeezed fruit in its outstretched paw. Its
whiskered face looked back at him with brown, almost
human eyes. What on earth had made his inartistic cousin
buy a thing like that and put it up to face his bed? He
turned and looked at the bed's occupant. "The only
sportsman of the lot," as Montague Dartie in his prime
had called him, lay with his swollen form outlined beneath a thin quilt. It gave Soames quite a turn to see that
familiar beef-coloured face pale and puffy as a moon,
with dark corrugated circles round eyes which still had
their japing stare. A voice, hoarse and subdued, but with
the old Forsyte timbre, said:

"Hallo, Soames! Come to measure me for my coffin?"

Soames put the suggestion away with a movement of
his hand; he felt queer looking at that travesty of George.
They had never got on, but——!

And in his flat, unemotional voice he said:

"Well, George! You'll pick up yet. You're no age. Is there anything I can do for you?"

A grin twitched George's pallid lips.

"Make me a codicil. You'll find paper in the dressing table drawer."

Soames took out a sheet of 'Iseeum' Club notepaper. Standing at the table, he inscribed the opening words of a codicil with his stylographic pen, and looked round at George. The words came with a hoarse relish.

"My three screws to young Val Dartie, because he's the only Forsyte that knows a horse from a donkey." A throaty chuckle sounded ghastly in the ears of Soames. "What have you said?"

Soames read: "I hereby leave my three race-horses to my kinsman, Valerius Dartie, of Wansdon, Sussex, because he has special knowledge of horses."

Again the throaty chuckle. "You're a dry file, Soames. Go on. To Milly Moyle, of 12, Claremont Grove, twelve thousand pounds, free of legacy duty."

Soames paused on the verge of a whistle.

The woman in the next room!

The japing in George's eyes had turned to brooding gloom.

"It's a lot of money," Soames could not help saying.

George made a faint choleric sound.

"Write it down, or I'll leave her the lot."

Soames wrote. "Is that all?"

"Yes. Read it!"

Soames read. Again he heard that throaty chuckle.

"That's a pill. You won't let *that* into the papers. Get that chap in, and you and he can witness."

Before Soames reached the door, it was opened and the man himself came in.

"The—er—vicar, sir," he said in a deprecating voice, "has called. He wants to know if you would like to see him."

George turned his face, his fleshy grey eyes rolled.

"Give him my compliments," he said, "and say I'll see him at the funeral."

With a bow the man went out, and there was silence.

"Now," said George, "get him in again. I don't know when the flag'll fall."

Soames beckoned the man in. When the codicil was signed and the man gone, George spoke:

"Take it, and see she gets it. I can trust you, that's one thing about you, Soames."

Soames pocketed the codicil with a very queer sensation.

"Would you like to see her again?" he said.

George stared up at him a long time before he answered.

"No. What's the good? Give me a cigar from that drawer."

Soames opened the drawer.

"Ought you?" he said.

George grinned. "Never in my life done what I ought; not going to begin now. Cut it for me."

Soames nipped the end of the cigar. 'Shan't give him a match,' he thought. 'Can't take the responsibility.' But George did not ask for a match. He lay quite still, the unlighted cigar between his pale lips, the curved lids down over his eyes.

"Good-bye," he said, "I'm going to have a snooze."

"Good-bye," said Soames. "I—I hope—you—you'll soon——"

George reopened his eyes—fixed, sad, jesting, they seemed to quench the shams of hope and consolation. Soames turned hastily and went out. He felt bad, and almost unconsciously turned again into the sitting-room. The woman was still in the same attitude; the same florid scent was in the air. Soames took up the umbrella he had left there, and went out.

"This is my telephone number," he said to the servant waiting in the corridor; "let me know."

The man bowed.

Soames turned out of Belville Row. Never had he left George's presence without the sense of being laughed at. Had he been laughed at now? Was that codicil George's last joke? If he had not gone in this afternoon, would George ever have made it, leaving a third of his property away from his family to that florid woman in the high-backed chair? Soames was beset by a sense of mystery. How could a man joke at death's door? It was, in a way, heroic. Where would he be buried? Somebody would know—Francie or Eustace. And what would they think when they came to know about that woman in the chair —twelve thousand pounds! 'If I can get hold of that white monkey, I will,' he thought, suddenly. 'It's a good thing.' The monkey's eyes, the squeezed-out fruit—was life all a bitter jest and George deeper than himself? He rang the Green Street bell.

Mrs. Dartie was very sorry, but Mrs. Cardigan had called for her to dine and make a fourth at the play.

Soames went in to dinner alone. At the polished board below which Montague Dartie had now and again slipped, if not quite slept, he dined and brooded. "I can trust you, that's one thing about you, Soames." The words flattered and yet stung him. The depths of that sardonic joke! To give him a family shock and trust him to carry the shock out! George had never cared twelve thousand pounds for a woman who smelled of patchouli. No! It was a final gibe at his family, the Forsytes, at Soames himself! Well! one by one those who had injured or gibed at him—Irene, Bosinney, old and young Jolyon, and now George, had met their fates. Dead, dying, or in British Columbia! He saw again his cousin's eyes above that unlighted cigar, fixed, sad, jesting—poor devil! He got up from the table, and nervously drew aside the curtains. The night was fine and cold. What happened to one—after? George used to say that he had been Charles the Second's cook in a former existence! But reincarnation was all nonsense, weak-minded theorising! Still, one would be glad to hold on if one could, after one was gone. Hold on, and be near Fleur! What noise was that? Gramophone going in the kitchen! When the cat was away, the mice—! People were all alike—take what they could get, and give as little as they could for it. Well! he would smoke a cigarette. Lighting it at a candle—Winifred dined by candle-light, it was the "mode" again—he thought: 'Has he still got that cigar between his teeth?' A funny fellow, George—all his days a funny fellow! He watched a ring of smoke he had made without intending to—very blue, he never inhaled! Yes! George had lived too fast, or he would not have been dying twenty years before his time—too fast! Well, there it was, and he wished he had a cat to talk to! He took a little monster off the mantelboard. Picked up by his nephew Benedict in an Eastern bazaar the year after the War, it had green eyes—'Not emeralds,' thought Soames, 'some cheap stone!'

"The telephone for you, sir."

He went into the hall and took up the receiver.

"Yes?"

"Mr. Forsyte has passed away, sir—in his sleep, the doctor says."

"Oh!" said Soames: "Had he a cig—? Many thanks." He hung up the receiver.

Passed away! And, with a nervous movement, he felt for the codicil in his breast pocket.

Chapter Eleven

VENTURE

———◄►————◄►————◄►———

FOR a week Bicket had seen "the job," slippery as an eel, evasive as a swallow, for ever passing out of reach. A pound for keep, and three shillings invested on a horse, and he was down to twenty-four bob. The weather had turned sou'-westerly and Victorine had gone out for the first time. That was something off his mind, but the cramp of the unemployed sensation, that fearful craving for the means of mere existence, a protesting, agonising anxiety, was biting into the very flesh of his spirit. If he didn't get a job within a week or two, there would be nothing for it but the workhouse, or the gas. 'The gas,' thought Bicket, 'if she will, I will. I'm fed up. After all, what is it? In her arms I wouldn't mind.' Instinct, however, that it was not so easy as all that to put one's head under the gas, gave him a brain-wave that Monday night. Balloons—that chap in Oxford Street to-day! Why not? He still had the capital for a flutter in them, and no hawker's licence needed. His brain, working like a squirrel in the small hours, grasped the great, the incalculable advantage of coloured balloons over all other forms of commerce. You couldn't miss the man who sold them—there he was for every eye to see, with his many

87

radiant circumferences dangling in front of him! Not
much profit in them, he had gathered—a penny on a sixpenny globe of coloured air, a penny on every three small
two-penny globes; still their salesman was alive, and
probably had pitched him a poor tale for fear of making
his profession seem too attractive. Over the bridge, just
where the traffic—no, up by St. Paul's! He knew a passage where he could stand back a yard or two, like that
chap in Oxford Street! But to the girl sleeping beside him
he said nothing. No word to her till he had thrown the
die. It meant gambling with his last penny. For a bare
living he would have to sell—why, three dozen big and
four dozen small balloons a day would only be twenty-six
shillings a week profit, unless that chap was kidding. Not
much towards "Austrylia" out of that! And not a career—
Victorine would have a shock! But it was neck or nothing now—he must try it, and in off hours go on looking
for a job.

Our thin capitalist, then, with four dozen big and
seven dozen small on a tray, two shillings in his pocket,
and little in his stomach, took his stand off St. Paul's at
two o'clock next day. Slowly he blew up and tied the
necks of two large and three small, magenta, green and
blue, till they dangled before him. Then with the smell of
rubber in his nostrils, and protruding eyes, he stood back
on the kerb and watched the stream go by. It gratified
him to see that most people turned to look at him. But the
first person to address him was a policeman, with:

"I'm not sure you can stand there."

Bicket did not answer, his throat felt too dry. He had
heard of the police. Had he gone the wrong way to work?
Suddenly he gulped, and said: "Give us a chance, constable; I'm right on my bones. If I'm in the way, I'll
stand anywhere you like. This is new to me, and two
bob's all I've got left in the world besides a wife."

The constable, a big man, looked him up and down.
"Well, we'll see. I shan't make trouble for you if no one
objects."

Bicket's gaze deepened thankfully.

"I'm much obliged," he said; "tyke one for your little girl—to please me."

"I'll buy one," said the policeman, "and give you a start. I go off duty in an hour, you 'ave it ready—a big one, magenta."

He moved away. Bicket could see him watching. Edging into the gutter, he stood quite still; his large eyes clung to every face that passed; and, now and then, his thin fingers nervously touched his wares. If Victorine could see him! All the spirit within him mounted. By golly! he would get out of this somehow into the sun, into a life that was a life!

He had been standing there nearly two hours, shifting from foot to unaccustomed foot, and had sold four big and five small—sixpenny worth of profit—when Soames, who had changed his route to spite those fellows who couldn't get past William Gouldyng Ingerer, came by on his way to the P.P.R.S. board. Startled by a timid murmur: "Balloon, sir,—best quality," he looked round from that contemplation of St. Paul's which had been his life-long habit, and stopped in sheer surprise.

"Balloon!" he said, "What should I want with a balloon?"

Bicket smiled. Between those green and blue and orange globes and Soames' grey self-containment there was incongruity which even he could appreciate.

"Children like 'em—no weight, sir, waistcoat pocket."

"I daresay," said Soames, "but I've no children."

"Grandchildren, sir."

"Nor any grandchildren."

"Thank you, sir."

Soames gave him one of those rapid glances with which he was accustomed to gauge the character of the impecunious. 'A poor, harmless little rat!' he thought. "Here, give me two—how much?"

"A shilling, sir, and much obliged."

"You can keep the change," said Soames hurriedly, and passed on, astonished. Why on earth he had bought the things, and for more than double their price, he could not conceive. He did not recollect such a thing having happened to him before. Extremely peculiar! And suddenly he realised why. The fellow had been humble, mild —to be encouraged, in these days of Communistic bravura. After all, the little chap was—was on the side of Capital, had invested in those balloons! Trade! And, raising his eyes towards St. Paul's again, he stuffed the nasty-feeling things down into his overcoat pocket. Somebody would be taking them out, and wondering what was the matter with him! Well, he had other things to think of! . . . .

Bicket, however, stared after him, elated. Two hundred and fifty odd per cent profit on those two—that was something like. The feeling, that not enough women were passing him here, became less poignant—after all, women knew the value of money, no extra shillings out of them! If only some more of these shiny-hatted old millionaires would come along!

At six o'clock, with a profit of three and eightpence, to which Soames had contributed just half, he began to add the sighs of deflating balloons to his own; untying them with passionate care he watched his coloured hopes one by one collapse, and stored them in the drawer of his tray. Taking it under his arm, he moved his tired legs in the direction of the Bridge. In a full day he might make four to five shillings— Well, it would just keep them alive, and something might turn up! He was his own master, anyway, accountable neither to employer nor to Union. That knowledge gave him a curious lightness inside, together with the fact that he had eaten nothing since breakfast.

'Wonder if he was an alderman,' he thought; 'they say those aldermen live on turtle soup.' Nearing home, he considered nervously what to do with the tray? How prevent Victorine from knowing that he had joined the ranks of Capital, and spent his day in the gutter? Ill luck! She was at the window! He must put a good face on it. And he went in whistling.

"What's that, Tony?" she said, pointing to the tray.

"Ah! ha! Great stunt—this! Look 'ere!"

Taking a balloon out from the tray, he blew. He blew with a desperation he had not yet put into the process. They said the things would swell to five feet in circumference. He felt somehow that if he could get it to attain those proportions, it would soften everything. Under his breath the thing blotted out Victorine, and the room, till there was just the globe of coloured air. Nipping its neck between thumb and finger, he held it up, and said:

"There you are; not bad value for sixpence, old girl!" and he peered round it. Lord, she was crying! He let the "blymed" thing go; it floated down, the air slowly evaporating till a little crinkled wreck rested on the dingy carper. Clasping her heaving shoulders, he said desperately:

"Cheerio, my dear, don't quarrel with bread and butter. I shall get a job, this is just to tide us over. I'd do a lot worse than that for you. Come on, and get my tea, I'm hungry, blowin' up those things."

She stopped crying, looked up, said nothing—mysterious with those big eyes! You'd say she had thoughts! But what they were Bicket could not tell. Under the stimulus of tea, he achieved a certain bravado about his new profession. To be your own master! Go out when you liked, come home when you liked—lie in bed with Vic if he jolly well pleased. A lot in that! And there rose in Bicket something truly national, something free and happy-go-lucky, resenting regular work, enjoying a spurt, and a laze-off, craving independence—something that accounted for the national life, the crowds of little shops, of middlemen, casual workers, tramps, owning their own souls in their own good time, and damning the consequences—something inherent in the land, the race, before the Saxons and their conscience and their industry came in—something that believed in swelling and collapsing coloured air, demanded pickles and high flavours without nourishment—yes, all that something exulted above Bicket's kipper and his tea, good and strong. He would

rather sell balloons than be a packer any day, and don't
let Vic forget it! And when she was able to take a job,
they would get on fine, and not be long before they'd
saved enough to get out of it to where those blue butterflies came from. And he spoke of Soames. A few more
aldermen without children—say two a day, fifteen bob a
week outside legitimate trade. Why, in under a year
they'd have the money! And once away, Vic would blow
out like one of those balloons; she'd be twice the size, and
a colour in her cheeks to lay over that orange and
magenta. Bicket became full of air. And the girl, his
wife, watched with her large eyes and spoke little; but
she did not cry again, or, indeed, throw any water, warm
or cold, on him who sold balloons.

Chapter Twelve

FIGURES AND FACTS

———◆◆◆———

WITH the exception of old Fontenoy—in absence as in presence ornamental—the Board was again full, Soames, conscious of special ingratiation in the manner of "that chap" Elderson, prepared himself for the worst. The figures were before them; a somewhat colourless show, appearing to disclose a state of things which would pass muster, if within the next six months there were no further violent disturbances of currency exchange. The proportion of foreign business to home business was duly expressed in terms of two to seven; German business, which constituted the bulk of the foreign, had been lumped—Soames noted—in the middle section, of countries only half bankrupt, and taken at what might be called a conservative estimate.

During the silence which reigned, while each member of the Board digested the figures, Soames perceived more clearly than ever the quandary he was in. Certainly, these figures would hardly justify the foregoing of the dividend earned on the past year's business. But suppose there were another Continental crash and they became liable on the great bulk of their foreign business, it might swamp all profits on home business next year, and more besides.

And then his uneasiness about Elderson himself—founded
he could not tell on what, intuitive, perhaps silly.

"Well, Mr. Forsyte," the Chairman was speaking;
"there are the figures. Are you satisfied?"

Soames looked up; he had taken a resolution.

"I will agree to this year's dividend on condition that
we drop this foreign business in future, lock, stock and
barrel." The manager's eyes, hard and bright, met his,
then turned towards the Chairman.

"That appears to savour of the panicky," he said; "the
foreign business is responsible for a good third of our
profit this year."

The Chairman seemed to garner the expressions of his
fellow-directors, before he said:

"There is nothing in the foreign situation at the moment, Mr. Forsyte, which gives particular cause for alarm.
I admit that we should watch it closely——"

"You can't," interjected Soames. "Here we are four
years from the Armistice, and we know no more where we
stand than we did then. If I'd realised our commitment to
this policy, I should never have come on the Board. We
must drop it."

"Rather an extreme view. And hardly a matter we can
decide in a moment."

The murmur of assent, the expression, faintly ironical,
of "that chap's" lips, jolted the tenacity in Soames.

"Very well! Unless you're prepared to tell the shareholders in the report that we are dropping foreign business, you drop me. I must be free to raise the question myself at the general meeting." He did not miss the shift and
blink in the manager's eyes. That shot had gone home!

The Chairman said:

"You put a pistol to our heads."

"I am responsible to the shareholders," said Soames,
"and I shall do my duty by them."

"So we all are, Mr. Forsyte; and I hope we shall all
do our duty."

"Why not confine the foreign business to the small
countries—their currency is safe enough?"

"Old Mont," and his precious "ring"!

"No," said Soames, "we must go back to safety."

"Splendid isolation, Forsyte?"

"Meddling was all very well in the war, but in peace— politics or business—this half-and-half interference is no good. We can't control the foreign situation."

He looked around him, and was instantly conscious that with those words he had struck a chord. 'I'm going through with this!' he thought.

"I should be glad, Mr. Chairman"—the manager was speaking—"if I might say a word. The policy was of my initiation, and I think I may claim that it has been of substantial benefit to the Society so far. When, however, a member of the Board takes so strong a view against its continuance, I certainly don't press the Board to continue it. The times *are* uncertain, and a risk, of course, is involved, however conservative our estimates."

'Now why?' thought Soames: 'What's he ratting for?'

"That's very handsome of you, Elderson; Mr. Chairman, I think we may say this is very handsome of our manager."

Old Dosey Cosey! Handsome! The old woman!

The Chairman's rather harsh voice broke a silence.

"This is a very serious point of policy. I should have been glad to have Lord Fontenoy present."

"If I am to endorse the report," said Soames shortly, "it must be decided to-day. I have made up my mind. But please yourselves."

He threw in those last three words from a sort of fellow feeling—it was unpleasant to be dragooned! A moment's silence, and then discussion assumed that random volubility which softens a decision already forced on one. A quarter of an hour thus passed before the Chairman said:

"We are agreed then, gentlemen, that the report shall contain the announcement that, in view of Continental uncertainty, we are abandoning foreign risks for the present."

Soames had won. Relieved and puzzled, he walked away alone.

He had shown character; their respect for him had gone up, he could see; their liking for him down, if they'd ever had any—he didn't know! But why had Elderson veered round? He recalled the shift and blink of the fellow's steely eyes at the idea of the question being raised at the general meeting.

That had done it! But why? Were the figures faked? Surely not! That would be too difficult, in the face of the accountants. If Soames had faith, it was in chartered accountants. Sandis and Jevon were tip-top people. It couldn't be that! He glanced up from the pavement. The dome of St. Paul's was dim already in evening sky— nothing to be had out of it! He felt badly in need of some one to talk to; but there was nobody; and he quickened his pace among the hurrying crowd. His hand, driven deep into his overcoat pocket, came into sudden contact with some foreign sticky substance. 'Gracious!' he thought: 'those things!' Should he drop them in the gutter? If only there were a child he could take them home to! He must get Annette to speak to Fleur. He knew what came of bad habits from his own experience of long ago. Why shouldn't he speak to her himself? He was staying the night there! But there came on him a helpless sense of ignorance. These young people! What did they really think and feel? Was old Mont right? Had they given up interest in everything except the moment, abandoned all belief in continuity, and progress? True enough that Europe was in Queer Street. But look at the state of things after the Napoleonic Wars. He couldn't remember his grandfather "Superior Dosset," the old chap had died five years before he was born, but he perfectly remembered how Aunt Ann, born in 1799, used to talk about "that dreadful Bonaparte—we used to call him Boney, my dear"; of how her father could get eight or ten per cent for his money; and of what an impression "those Chartists" had made on Aunts Juley and Hester, and that was long afterwards. Yet, in spite of all that, look at the Victorian era—a golden age, things worth collecting, children worth having! Why not again? Consols had risen almost continuously since Timothy died. Even if Heaven and Hell had gone, that couldn't be the reason; none of his uncles had believed in either, and yet had all made fortunes, and all had families, except Timothy and Swithin. No! It couldn't be the want of Heaven and Hell! What, then, was the reason of the change—if change there really were? And suddenly it was revealed to Soames. They talked too much —too much and too fast! They got to the end of interest in this and that and the other. They ate life and threw away the rind, and—and— By the way, he must buy that picture of George's! . . . Had these young folk more mind than his own generation? And if so—why? Was it diet? That lobster cocktail Fleur had given him the Sunday before last. He had eaten the thing—very nasty! But it hadn't made him want to talk. No! He didn't think it could be diet. Besides—Mind! Where were the minds now that equalled the Victorians—Darwin, Huxley, Dickens, Disraeli, even old Gladstone? Why, he remembered judges and advocates who seemed giants compared with those of the present day, just as he remembered that the judges of James his father's youth had seemed giants to James compared with those of Soames' prime. According to that, mind was steadily declining. It must be something else. There was a thing they called psycho-analysis, which so far as he could understand attributed people's action not to what they ate at breakfast, or the leg they got out of bed with, as in the good old days, but to some shock they had received in the remote past and entirely forgotten. The subconscious mind! Fads! Fads and microbes! The fact was this generation had no digestion. His father and his uncles had all complained of liver, but they had never had anything the matter with them—no need of any of these vitamins, false teeth, mental healing, newspapers, psycho-analysis, spiritualism, birth control, osteopathy, broadcasting, and what not. 'Machines!' thought Soames. 'That's it—I shouldn't wonder!' How could you believe in anything when everything was going round so fast? When you couldn't count your chickens—they ran about so? But Fleur had got a good little head on her! 'Yes,' he mused, 'and French teeth, she can digest anything. Two years! I'll speak to her before she gets the habit confirmed. Her mother was quick enough about it!' And perceiving the Connoisseurs' Club in front of him, he went in.

The hall porter came out of his box. A gentleman was waiting.

"What gentleman?" said Soames, sidelong.

"I think he's your nephew, sir, Mr. Dartie."

"Val Dartie! H'm! Where?"

"In the little room, sir."

The little room—all the accommodation considered worthy of such as were not Connoisseurs—was at the end of a passage, and in no taste at all, as if the Club were saying: "See what it is not to be one of us!" Soames entered it, and saw Val Dartie smoking a cigarette and gazing with absorption at the only object of interest, his own reflection in the glass above the fire.

He never saw his nephew without wondering when he would say: "Look here, Uncle Soames, I'm up a stump." Breeding racehorses! There could only be one end to that!

"Well?" he said, "how are *you?*"

The face in the glass turned round, and became the back of a clipped sandyish head.

"Oh! bobbish, thanks! *You* look all right, Uncle Soames. I just wanted to ask you: Must I take these screws of old George Forsyte's? They're dashed bad."

"Gift horse in the mouth?" said Soames.

"Well," said Val, "but they're *so* dashed bad; by the time I've paid legacy duty, boxed them to a sale, and sold them, there won't be a sixpence. One of them falls down when you look at it. And the other two are broken-winded. The poor old boy kept them, because he couldn't get rid of them. They're about five hundred years old."

"Thought you were fond of horses," said Soames. "Can't you turn them out?"

"Yes," said Val, drily; "but I've got my living to make. I haven't told my wife, for fear she should suggest that. I'm afraid I might see them in my dreams if I sold them.

They're only fit for the kennels. Can I write to the executors and say I'm not rich enough to take them?"

"You can," said Soames, and the words: "How's your wife?" died unspoken on his lips. She was the daughter of his enemy, young Jolyon. That fellow was dead, but the fact remained.

"I will, then," said Val. "How did his funeral go off?"

"Very simple affair—I had nothing to do with it." The days of funerals were over. No flowers, no horses, no plumes—a motor hearse, a couple of cars or so, was all the attention paid nowadays to the dead. Another sign of the times!

"I'm staying the night at Green Street," said Val. "I suppose you're not there, are you?"

"No," said Soames, and did not miss the relief in his nephew's countenance.

"Oh! by the way, Uncle Soames—do you advise me to buy P.P.R.S. shares?"

"On the contrary. I'm going to advise your mother to sell. Tell her I'm coming in to-morrow."

"Why? I thought——"

"Never mind my reasons!" said Soames shortly.

"So long, then!"

Exchanging a chilly hand-shake, he watched his nephew withdraw.

So long! An expression, old as the Boer war, that he had never got used to—meant nothing so far as he could see! He entered the reading-room. A number of Connoisseurs were sitting and standing about, and Soames, least clubbable of men, sought the solitude of an embrasured window. He sat there polishing the nail of one forefinger against the back of the other, and chewing the cud of life. After all, what was the point of anything? There was George! He had had an easy life—never done any work! And here was himself, who had done a lot of work! And sooner or later they would bury him too, with a motor hearse probably! And there was his son-in-law, young Mont, full of talk about goodness knew what— and that thin-cheeked chap who had sold him the balloons

this afternoon. And old Fontenoy, and that waiter over
there; and the out-of-works and the in-works; and those
chaps in Parliament, and the parsons in their pulpits—
what were they all for? There was the old gardener down
at Mapledurham pushing his roller over and over the
lawn, week after week, and if he didn't, what would the
lawn be like? That was life—gardener rolling lawn! Put it
that there was another life—he didn't believe it, but for
the sake of argument—that life must be just the same.
Rolling lawn—to keep it lawn! What point in lawn? Conscious of pessimism, he rose. He had better be getting
back to Fleur's—they dressed for dinner! He supposed
there was something in dressing for dinner, but it was
like lawn—you came unrolled—undressed again, and
so it went on! Over and over and over to keep up to a
pitch, that was—ah! what *was* the pitch for?

Turning into South Square, he cannoned into a young
man, whose head was craned back as if looking after
some one he had parted from. Uncertain whether to
apologise or to wait for an apology, Soames stood still.

The young man said abruptly: "Sorry, sir," and moved
on; dark, neat-looking chap with a hungry look obviously
unconnected with his stomach. Murmuring: "Not at all!"
Soames moved forward and rang his daughter's bell. She
opened to him herself. She was in hat and furs—just in.
The young man recurred to Soames. Had he left her
there? What a pretty face it was! He should certainly speak
to her. If she once took to gadding about!

He put it off, however, till he was about to say "Good-
night"—Michael having gone to the political meeting of a
Labour candidate, as if he couldn't find something better
to do!

"Now you've been married two years, my child, I suppose you'll be looking towards the future. There's a great
deal of nonsense talked about children. The whole thing's
much simpler. I hope you feel that."

Fleur was leaning back among the cushions of the
settee, swinging her foot. Her eyes became a little restless,
but her colour did not change.

"Of course!" she said; "only there's no hurry, Dad."

"Well, I don't know," Soames murmured. "The French and the royal family have a very sound habit of getting it over early. There's many a slip, and it keeps them out of mischief. You're very attractive, my child—I don't want to see you take too much to gad-about ways. You've got all sorts of friends."

"Yes," said Fleur.

"You get on well with Michael, don't you?"

"Oh! yes."

"Well, then, why not? You must remember that your son will be a what-you-call-it."

In those words he compromised with his instinctive dislike of titles and flummery of that nature.

"It mightn't be a son," said Fleur.

"At your age that's easily remedied."

"Oh, I don't want a lot, Dad. One, perhaps, or two."

"Well," said Soames, "I should almost prefer a daughter, something like—well, something like you."

Her softened eyes flew, restive, from his face to her foot, to the dog, all over the room.

"I don't know, it's a tie—like digging your own grave in a way."

"I shouldn't put it as high as that," murmured Soames, persuasively.

"No man would, Dad."

"Your mother wouldn't have got on at all without you," and recollection of how near her mother had been to not getting on at all with her—of how, but for him, she would have made a mess of it, reduced him to silent contemplation of the restive foot.

"Well," he said, at last, "I thought I'd mention it. I—I've got your happiness at heart."

Fleur rose and kissed his forehead.

"I know, Dad," she said: "I'm a selfish pig. I'll think about it. In fact, I—I have thought about it."

"That's right," said Soames; "that's right! You've got a good head on you—it's a great consolation to me. Good-night, my dear!"

And he went up to his bed. If there was point in anything, it was in perpetuation of oneself, though, of course,
that begged the question. 'Wonder,' he thought, 'if I
ought to have asked her whether that young man—!' But
young people were best left alone. The fact was, he didn't
understand them. His eye lighted on the paper bag con-
taining those—those things he had bought. He had
bought them up from his overcoat to get rid of them—but
how? Put into the fire, they would make a smell. He
stood at his dressing-table, took one up and looked at it.
Good Lord! And, suddenly, rubbing the mouthpiece with
his handkerchief, he began to blow the thing up. He blew
until his cheeks were tired, and then, nipping the aperture,
took a bit of the dental cotton he used on his teeth every
night and tied it up. There the thing was! With a pettish
gesture he batted the balloon. Off it flew—purple and
extravagant, alighting on his bed. H'm! He took up the
other, and did the same to it. Purple and green! The
deuce! If any one came in and saw! He threw up the
window, batted them, balloon after balloon, into the night,
and shut the window down. There they'd be in the
dark, floating about. His lips contracted in a nervous grin.
People would see them in the morning. Well! What else
could you do with things like that?

Chapter Thirteen

TENTERHOOKS

~~~~~~~~~~~~~~~~

MICHAEL had gone to the Labour candidate's meeting partly because he wanted to, and partly out of fellow feeling for "old Forsyte," whom he was always conscious of having robbed. His father-in-law had been very decent about Fleur, and he liked the "old man" to have her to himself when he could.

In a constituency which had much casual and no trades-union labour to speak of, the meeting would be one of those which enabled the intellectuals of the Party to get it "off their chests." Sentiment being "slop," and championship mere condescension, one might look for sound economic speeches which left out discredited factors, such as human nature. Michael was accustomed to hearing people disparaged for deprecating change because human nature was constant; he was accustomed to hearing people despised for feeling compassion; he knew that one ought to be purely economic. And anyway that kind of speech was preferable to the tub-thumpings of the North or of the Park, which provoked a nasty underlying class spirit in himself.

The meeting was in full swing when he arrived, the candidate pitilessly exposing the fallacies of a capitalism which, in his view, had brought on the war. For fear that it should bring on another, it must be changed for a system which would ensure that nations should not want anything too much. The individual—said the candidate— was in every respect superior to the nation of which he formed a part; and the problem before them was to secure an economic condition which would enable the individual to function freely in his native superiority. In that way alone, he said, would they lose those mass movements and emotions which imperilled the sanity of the world. He spoke well; Michael listened, purring almost audibly, till he found that he was thinking of himself, Wilfrid and Fleur. Would he ever function so freely in a native superiority that he did not want Fleur too much? And did he wish to? He did not. That seemed to introduce human nature into the speaker's argument. Didn't everybody want something too much? Wasn't it natural? And if so, wouldn't there always be a collective wanting too much—poolings of primary desire, such as the desire of keeping your own head above water? The candidate's argument seemed to him suddenly to leave out heat, to omit friction, to be that of a man in an armchair after a poor lunch. He looked attentively at the speaker's shrewd, dry, doubting face. 'No juice!' he thought. And when "the chap" sat down, he got up and left the hall.

This Wilfrid business had upset him horribly. Try as he had to put it out of his mind, try as he would to laugh it off, it continued to eat into his sense of security and happiness. Wife and best friend! A hundred times a day he assured himself that he trusted Fleur. Only, Wilfrid was so much more attractive than himself, and Fleur deserved the best of everything. Besides, Wilfrid was going through torture, and it was not a pleasant thought! How end the thing, restore peace of mind to himself, to him, to her? He had heard no more; and it simply was impossible to ask. No way even of showing his anxiety! The whole thing was just "dark," and, so far as he could see, would have to stay so; nothing to be done but screw the lid on tighter, be as nice as he could to her, try not to feel bitter about Wilfrid. Hades!

He turned down Chelsea Embankment. Here the sky was dark and wide and streaming with stars. The river wide, dark and gleaming with oily rays from the Embankment lamps. The width of it all gave him relief. Dash the dumps! A jolly, queer, muddled, sweet and bitter world; an immensely intriguing game of chance, no matter how the cards were falling at the moment! In the trenches he had thought: 'Get out of this, and I'll never mind anything again!' How seldom now he remembered thinking that! The human body renewed itself—they said—in seven years. In three years' time his body would not be the body of the trenches, but a whole-time peace body with a fading complex. If only Fleur would tell him quite openly what she felt, what she was doing about Wilfrid, for she must be doing something! And Wilfrid's verse? Would his confounded passion—as Bart suggested—flow in poetry? And, if so, who would publish it? A miserable business! Well, the night was beautiful, and the great thing not to be a pig. Beauty and not being a pig! Nothing much else to it—except laughter—the comic side! Keep one's sense of humour, anyway! And Michael searched, while he strode beneath plane trees half-stripped of leaves and plume-like in the dark, for the fun in his position. He failed to find it. There seemed absolutely nothing funny about love. Possibly he might fall out of love again some day, but not so long as she kept him on her tenterhooks. Did she do it on purpose? Never! Fleur simply could not be like those women who kept their husbands hungry and fed them when they wanted dresses, furs, jewels. Revolting!

He came in sight of Westminster. Only half-past ten! Suppose he took a cab to Wilfrid's rooms, and tried to have it out with him. It would be like trying to make the hands of a clock move backwards to its ticking. What use in saying: "You love Fleur—well, don't!" or in Wilfrid saying it to him? 'After all, I was first with Fleur,' he thought. Pure chance, perhaps, but fact! Ah! And wasn't that just the danger? He was no longer a novelty to her—nothing unexpected about him now! And he and she had agreed times without number that novelty was the salt of life, the essence of interest and drama. Novelty now lay with Wilfrid! Lord! Lord! Possession appeared far from being nine points of the law! He rounded-in from the Embankment towards home—jolly part of London, jolly Square; everything jolly except just this infernal complication. Something, soft as a large leaf, tapped twice against his ear. He turned, astonished; he was in empty space, no tree near. Floating in the darkness, a round thing—he grabbed, it bobbed. What? A child's balloon! He secured it between his hands, took it beneath a lamppost—green, he judged. Queer! He looked up. Two windows lighted, one of them Fleur's! Was this the bubble of his own happiness expelled? Morbid! Silly ass! Some gust of wind—a child's plaything lodged and loosened! He held the balloon gingerly. He would take it in and show it to her. He put his latch-key in the door. Dark in the hall—gone up! He mounted, swinging the balloon on his finger. Fleur was standing before a mirror.

"What on earth's that?" she said.

The blood returned to Michael's heart. Curious how he had dreaded its having anything to do with her!

"Don't know, darling; fell on my hat—must belong to heaven." And he batted it.

The balloon floated, dropped, bounded twice, wobbled and came to rest.

"You *are* a baby, Michael. I believe you bought it."

Michael came closer, and stood quite still.

"My hat! What a misfortune to be in love!"

"You think so!"

"*Il y a toujours un qui baise, et l'autre qui ne tend pas la joue.*"

"But I do."

"Fleur!"

Fleur smiled.

"*Baise* away."

Embracing her, Michael thought: 'She holds me—does with me what she likes; I know nothing of her!'

And there arose a small sound—from Ting-a-ling sniffing at the balloon.

{ PART TWO }

Chapter One

THE MARK FALLS

THE state of the world had been getting more and more on Soames' nerves ever since the general meeting of the P.P.R.S. It had gone off with that fatuity long associated by him with such gatherings—a water-tight rigmarole from the chairman; butter from two reliable shareholders; vinegar from shareholders not so reliable; and the usual "gup" over the dividend. He had gone there glum, come away glummer. From a notion once taken into his head Soames parted more slowly than a cheese parts from its mites. Two-sevenths of foreign business, nearly all German! And the mark falling! It had begun to fall from the moment that he decided to support the dividend. And why? What was in the wind? Contrary to his custom, he had taken to sniffing closely the political columns of his paper. The French—he had always mistrusted them, especially since his second marriage—the French were going to play old Harry, if he were not greatly mistaken! Their papers, he noticed, never lost a chance of having a dab at English policy; seemed to think they could always call the tune for England to pipe to! And the mark and the franc, and every other sort of money, falling. And though in Soames was that which rejoiced in the thought that one of his country's bits of paper could buy a great quantity of other countries' bits of paper, there was also that which felt the whole thing silly and unreal, with an ever-growing consciousness that the P.P.R.S. would pay no dividend next year. The P.P.R.S. was a big concern; no dividend would be a sign, and no small one, of bad management. Assurance was one of the few things on God's earth which could and should be conducted without real risk. But for that he would never have gone on the Board. And to find assurance had not been so conducted and that by himself, was—well! He had caused Winifred to sell, anyway, though the shares had already fallen slightly. "I thought it was such a good thing, Soames," she had said plaintively: "it's rather a bore, losing money on the shares." He had answered without mercy: "If you don't sell, you'll lose more." And she had done it. If the Rogers and Nicholases who had followed him into it hadn't sold to—well, it was their look out! He had made Winifred warn them. As for himself, he had nothing but his qualifying shares, and the missing of a dividend or two would not hurt one whose director's fees more than compensated. It was not, therefore, private uneasiness so much as resentment at a state of things connected with foreigners and the slur on his infallibility.

Christmas had gone off quietly at Mapledurham. He abominated Christmas, and only observed it because his wife was French, and her national festival New Year's Day. One could not go so far as to observe that, encouraging a foreign notion. But Christmas with no child about—he still remembered the holly and snapdragons of Park Lane in his own childhood—the family parties; and how disgusted he had been if he got anything symbolic—the thimble or the ring—instead of the shilling. They had never gone in for Santa Claus at Park Lane, partly because they could see through the old gentleman, and partly because he was not at all a novelty. Emily, his mother, had seen to that. Yes; and, by the way, that William Gouldyng, Ingerer, had so stumped those fellows at the Heralds' College, that Soames had dropped the enquiry—it was just encouraging them to spend his money for sentimental satisfaction which did not materialise. That narrow-headed chap, "Old Mont," peacocked about his ancestry; all the more reason for having no ancestry to peacock about. The Forsytes and the Goldings were good English country stock—that was what mattered. And if Fleur and her child, if one came, had French blood in them—well, he couldn't help it now.

In regard to the coming of a grandchild, Soames knew no more than in October. Fleur had spent Christmas with the Monts; she was promised to him, however, before long, and her mother must ask her a question or two!

The weather was extremely mild; Soames had even been out in a punt fishing. In a heavy coat he trailed a line for perch and dace, and caught now and then a roach —precious little good, the servants wouldn't eat them, nowadays. His grey eyes would brood over the grey water under the grey sky; and in his mind the mark would fall. It fell with a bump on that eleventh of January when the French went and occupied the Ruhr. He said to Annette at breakfast: "Your country's cracked! Look at the mark now!"

"What do I care about the mark?" she had answered over her coffee. "I care that they shall not come again into my country. I hope they will suffer a little what we have suffered."

"You," said Soames; "you never suffered anything."

Annette put her hand where Soames sometimes doubted the existence of a heart.

"I suffered here," she said.

"I didn't notice it. You never went without butter. What do you suppose Europe's going to be like now for the next thirty years? How about British trade?"

"We French see before our noses," said Annette with warmth. "We see that the beaten must be kept the beaten, or they will take revenge. You English are so sloppy."

"Sloppy, are we?" said Soames. "You're talking like a child. Could a sloppy people ever have reached our position in the world?"

"That is your selfishness. You are cold and selfish."

"Cold, selfish and sloppy—they don't go together. Try again."

"Your slop is in your thought and your talk; it is your instinct that gives you your success, and your English instinct is cold and selfish, Soames. You are a mixture, all of you, of hypocrisy, stupidity, and egoism."

Soames took some marmalade.

"Well," he said, "and what are the French?—cynical, avaricious, and revengeful. And the Germans are sentimental, heady and brutal. We can all abuse each other. There's nothing for it but to keep clear. And that's what you French won't do."

Annette's handsome person stiffened.

"When you are tied to a person, as I am tied to you, Soames, or as we French are tied to the Germans, it is necessary to be top dog, or to be bottom dog."

Soames stayed his toast.

"Do you suppose yourself top dog in this house?"

"Yes, Soames."

"Oh! Then you can go back to France to-morrow."

Annette's eyebrows rose quizzically.

"I would wait a little longer, my friend; you are still too young."

But Soames had already regretted his remark; he did not wish any such disturbance at his time of life, and he said more calmly:

"Compromise is the essence of any reasonable existence between individuals or nations. We can't have the fat thrown into the fire every few years."

"That is so English," murmured Annette. "We others never know what you English will do. You always wait to see which way the cat jumps."

However deeply sympathetic with such a reasonable characteristic, Soames would have denied it at any ordinary moment—to confess to temporising was not, as it were, done. But, with the mark falling like a cartload of bricks, he was heated to the point of standing by his nature.

"And why shouldn't we? Rushing into things that

you'll have to rush out of! I don't want to argue. French and English never did get on, and never will."

Annette rose. "You speak the truth, my friend. *Entente, mais pas cordiale.* What are you doing to-day?"

"Going up to town," said Soames glumly. "Your precious Government has put business into Queer Street with a vengeance."

"Do you stay the night?"

"I don't know."

"Adieu, then, *jusqu'au revoir!"* And she got up.

Soames remained brooding above his marmalade—with the mark falling in his mind—glad to see the last of her handsome figure, having no patience at the moment for French tantrums.

An irritable longing to say to somebody "I told you so" possessed him. He would have to wait, however, till he found somebody to say it to.

A beautiful day, quite warm; and, taking his umbrella as an assurance against change, he set out for the station.

In the carriage going up they were talking about the Ruhr. Averse from discussion in public, Soames listened from behind his paper. The general sentiment was surprisingly like his own. In so far as it was unpleasant for the Huns—all right; in so far as it was unpleasant for British trade—all wrong; in so far as love of British trade was active and hate of Huns now passive—more wrong than right. A Francophil remark that the French were justified in making themselves safe at all costs, was coldly received. At Maidenhead a man got in whom Soames connected automatically with disturbance. He had much grey hair, a sanguine face, lively eyes, twisting eyebrows, and within five minutes had asked in a breezy voice whether any one had heard of the League of Nations. Confirmed in his estimate, Soames looked round the corner of his paper. Yes, that chap would get off on some hobby-horse or other! And there he went! The question—said the newcomer—was not whether the Germans should get one in the eye, the British one in the pocket, or the French one in the heart, but whether the world should get peace and goodwill. Soames lowered his paper. If—this fellow said—they wanted peace, they must sink their individual interests, and think in terms of collective interest. The good of all was the good of one! Soames saw the flaw at once: That might be, but the good of one was not the good of all. He felt that if he did not take care he would be pointing this out. The man was a perfect stranger to him, and no good ever came of argument. Unfortunately his silence amid the general opinion that the League of Nations was "no earthly," seemed to cause the newcomer to regard him as a sympathiser; the fellow kept on throwing his eyebrows at him! To put up his paper again seemed too pointed, and his position was getting more and more false when the train ran in at Paddington. He hastened to a cab. A voice behind him said:

"Hopeless lot, sir, eh! Glad to see *you* saw my point."

"Quite!" said Soames. "Taxi!"

"Unless the League of Nations functions, we're all for Gehenna."

Soames turned the handle of the cab door.

"Quite!" he said again. "Poultry!" and got in. He was not going to be drawn. The fellow was clearly a firebrand!

In the cab the measure of his disturbance was revealed. He had said "Poultry," an address that "Forsyte, Bustard and Forsyte" had abandoned two-and-twenty years ago when, merged with "Cuthcott, Holliday and Kingson," they became "Cuthcott, Kingson and Forsyte." Rectifying the error, he sat forward, brooding. Fall of the mark! The country was sound about it, yes—but when they failed to pay the next dividend, could they rely on resentment against the French instead of against the directors? Doubtful! The directors ought to have seen it coming! That might be said of the other directors, but not of himself—here was a policy that he personally never would have touched. If only he could discuss the whole thing with some one—but old Gradman would be out of his depth in a matter of this sort. And, on arrival at his office, he gazed with a certain impatience at that changeless old fellow, sitting in his swivel chair.

"Ah! Mr. Soames, I was hopin' you might come in this morning. There's a young man been round to see you from the P.P.R.S. Wouldn't give his business, said he wanted to see you privately. Left his number on the 'phone."

"Oh!" said Soames.

"Quite a young fellow—in the office."

"What did he look like?"

"Nice, clean young man. I was rather favourably impressed—name of Butterfield."

"Well, ring him up, and let him know I'm here." And going over to the window, he stood looking out on to a perfectly blank wall.

Suited to a sleeping partner, his room was at the back, free from disturbance. Young man! The call was somewhat singular! And he said over his shoulder: "Don't go when he comes, Gradman, I know nothing of him."

The world changed, people died off, the mark fell, but Gradman was there—embodiment, faithful and grey, of service and integrity—an anchor.

Gradman's voice, grating, ingratiating, rose.

"This French news—it's not nice, Mr. Soames. They're a hasty lot. I remember your father, Mr. James, coming into the office the morning the Franco-Prussian war was declared—quite in his prime then, not more than sixty, I should say. Why, I recall his very words: 'There,' he said, 'I told them so.' And here they are—at it still. The fact is, they're cat and dog."

Soames, who had half turned, resumed his contemplation of a void. Poor old Gradman dated! What would he say when he heard that they had been insuring foreign business? Stimulated by the old-time quality of Gradman's presence, his mind ranged with sudden freedom. He himself had another twenty years, perhaps. What would he see in that time? Where would old England be at the end of it? 'In spite of the papers, we're not such fools as we look,' he thought. 'If only we can steer clear of flibberty-gibberting, and pay our way!'

"Mr. Butterfield, sir." H'm! The young man had been very spry. Covered by Gradman's bluff and greasy greet-

ing, he "took a lunar," as his Uncle Roger used to call it.
The young fellow, in a neat suit, a turndown collar, with
his hat in his hand, was a medium modest-looking chap.
Soames nodded.

"You want to see me?"

"Alone, if I might, sir."

"Mr. Gradman here is my right-hand man."

Gradman's voice purred gratingly: "You can state your
business. Nothing goes outside these walls, young man."

"I'm in the office of the P.P.R.S., sir. The fact is,
accident has just put some information in my hands, and
I'm not easy in my mind. Knowing you to be a solicitor,
sir, I preferred to come to you, rather than go to the
chairman. As a lawyer, would you tell me: Is my first
duty to the Society, being in their employ?"

"Certainly," said Soames.

"I don't like this job, sir, and I hope you'll understand
that I'm not here for any personal motive—it's just because I feel I ought to."

Soames regarded him steadily. Though large and rather
swimming, the young man's eyes impressed him by
their resemblance to a dog's. "What's it all about?" he
said.

The young man moistened his lips.

"The insurance of our German business, sir."

Soames pricked his ears, already slightly pointed by
Nature.

"It's a very serious matter," the young man went on,
"and I don't know how it'll affect me, but the fact is, this
morning I overheard a private conversation."

"Oh!" said Soames.

"Yes, sir. I quite understand your tone, but the very
first words did it. I simply couldn't make myself known
after hearing them. I think you'll agree, sir."

"Who were the speakers?"

"The manager, and a man called Smith—I fancy by
his accent his name's a bit more foreign—who's done
most of the agenting for the German business."

"What were the words?" said Soames.

"Well, sir, the manager was speaking, and then this

Smith said: 'Quite so, Mr. Elderson, but we haven't paid you a commission on all this business for nothing; if the mark goes absolutely phut, you will have to see that your Society makes it good for us!' "

The intense longing, which at that moment came on Soames to emit a whistle, was checked by sight of Gradman's face. The old fellow's mouth had opened in the nest of his grizzly short beard; his eyes stared puglike, he uttered a prolonged: "A-ow!"

"Yes," said the young man, "it was a knockout!"

"Where were you?" asked Soames, sharply.

"In the lobby between the manager's room and the board room. I'd just come from sorting some papers in the board room, and the manager's door was open an inch or so. Of course I know the voices well."

"What after?"

"I heard Mr. Elderson say, 'H'ssh! Don't talk like that!' and I slipped back into the board room. I'd had more than enough, sir, I assure you."

Suspicion and surmise clogged Soames' thinking apparatus. Was this young fellow speaking the truth? A man like Elderson—the risk was monstrous! And, if true, what was the directors' responsibility? But proof—proof? He stared at the young man, who looked upset and pale enough, but whose eyes did not waver. Shake him if he could! And he said sharply:

"Now mind what you're saying! This is most serious!"

"I know that, sir. If I'd consulted my own interest, I'd never have come here. I'm not a sneak."

The words rang true, but Soames did not drop his caution.

"Ever had any trouble in the office?"

"No, sir, you can make enquiry. I've nothing against Mr. Elderson, and he's nothing against me."

Soames thought suddenly: 'Good heavens! He's shifted it on to me, and in the presence of a witness! And I supplied the witness!'

"Have you any reason to suppose," he said, "that they became aware of your being there?"

"They couldn't have, I think."

The implications of this news seemed every second more alarming. It was as if Fate, kept at bay all his life by clever wrist-work, had suddenly slipped a thrust under his guard. No good to get rattled, however—must think it out at leisure!

"Are you prepared, if necessary, to repeat this to the Board?"

The young man pressed his hands together.

"Well, sir, I'd much rather have held my tongue; but if you decide it's got to be taken up, I suppose I must go through with it now. I'm sure I hope you'll decide to leave it alone; perhaps it isn't true—only why didn't Mr. Elderson say: 'Commission! You ruddy liar!'?"

Exactly! Why hadn't he? Soames gave a grunt of intense discomfort.

"Anything more?" he said.

"No, sir."

"Very well. You've not told any one?"

"No, sir."

"Then don't, and leave it to me."

"I'll be only too happy to, sir. Good-morning."

"Good-morning!"

No—very bad morning! No satisfaction whatever in this sudden fulfilment of his prophetic feeling about Elderson. None!

"What d'you think of that young fellow, Gradman? Is he lying?"

Thus summoned, as it were, from stupor, Gradman thoughtfully rubbed a nose both thick and shining.

"It's one word against another, Mr. Soames, unless you get more evidence. But I can't see what the young man has to gain by it."

"Nor I; but you never know. The trouble will be to get more evidence. Can I act without it?"

"It's delicate," said Gradman. And Soames knew that he was thrown back on himself. When Gradman said a thing was delicate, it meant that it was the sort of matter on which he was accustomed to wait for orders—presumptuous even to hold opinion! But had he got one?

Well, one would never know! The old chap would sit and rub his nose over it till Kingdom Come.

"I shan't act in a hurry," he said, almost angrily: "I can't see to the end of this."

Every hour confirmed that statement. At lunch the tape of his city club showed the mark still falling—to unheard-of depths! How they could talk of golf, with this business on his mind, he could not imagine!

"I must go and see that fellow," he said to himself. "I shall be guarded. He may throw some light." He waited until three o'clock and repaired to the P.P.R.S.

Reaching the office, he sought the board room. The chairman was there in conference with the manager. Soames sat down quietly to listen; and while he listened he watched that fellow's face. It told him nothing. What nonsense people talked when they said you could tell character from faces! Only a perfect idiot's face could be read like that. And here was a man of experience and culture, one who knew every rope of business life and polite society. The hairless, neat features exhibited no more concern than the natural mortification of one whose policy had met with such a nasty knock. The drop of the mark had already wiped out any possible profit on the next half-year. Unless the wretched thing recovered, they would be carrying a practically dead load of German insurance. Really it was criminal that no limit of liability had been fixed! How on earth could he ever have overlooked that when he came on the Board? But he had only known of it afterwards. And who could have foreseen anything so mad as this Ruhr business, or realised the slack confidence of his colleagues in this confounded fellow? The words "gross negligence" appeared 'close up' before his eyes. What if an action lay against the Board! Gross negligence! At his age and with his reputation! Why! The thing was plain as a pikestaff; for omitting a limit of liability this chap had got his commission! Ten per cent, probably, on all that business—he must have netted thousands! A man must be in Queer Street indeed to take a risk like that! But conscious that his fancy was running on, Soames rose, and turned his back. The action suggested another. Simulate anger, draw some sign from that fellow's self-control! He turned again, and said pettishly: "What on earth were you about, Mr. Manager, when you allowed these contracts to go through without limit of liability? A man of your experience! What was your motive?"

A slight narrowing of the eyes, a slight compression of the lips. He had relied on the word "motive," but the fellow passed it by.

"For such high premiums as we have been getting, Mr. Forsyte, a limited liability was not possible. This is a most outrageous development, and I'm afraid it must be considered just bad luck."

"Unfortunately," said Soames, "there's no such thing as luck in properly regulated assurance, as we shall find, or I'm much mistaken. I shouldn't be surprised if an action lay against the Board for gross negligence!"

That had got the chairman's goat!—Got his goat? What expressions they used nowadays! Or did it mean the opposite? One never knew! But as for Elderson—he seemed to Soames to be merely counterfeiting a certain flusteration. Futile to attempt to spring anything out of a chap like that. If the thing were true, the fellow must be entirely desperate, prepared for anything and everything. And since from Soames the desperate side of life—the real holes, the impossible positions which demand a gambler's throw—had always been carefully barred by the habits of a prudent nature, he found it now impossible to imagine Elderson's state of mind, or his line of conduct if he were guilty. For all he could tell, the chap might be carrying poison about with him; might be sitting on a revolver like a fellow on the film. The whole thing was too unpleasant, too worrying for words. And without saying any more he went away, taking nothing with him but the knowledge that their total liability on this German business, with the mark valueless, was over two hundred thousand pounds. He hastily reviewed the fortunes of his co-directors. Old Fontenoy was always in low water; the chairman a dark horse; Mont was in land, land right down in value, and mortgaged at that; old Cosey Mothergill had nothing but his name and his director's fees; Meyricke must have a large income, but light come, light go, like most of those big counsel with irons in many fires and the certainty of a judgeship. Not a really substantial man among the lot, except himself! He ploughed his way along, head down. Public companies! Preposterous system! You had to trust somebody, and there you were! It was appalling!

"Ballons, sir—beautiful colours, five feet circumference. Take one, gentlemen!"

"Good gad!" said Soames. As if the pricked bubble of German business were not enough!

Chapter Two

VICTORINE

━━━◆━━━◆━━━

ALL through December balloons had been slack—
hardly any movement about them, even in Christmas week, and from the Bickets Central Australia was as
far as ever. The girl Victorine, restored to comparative
health, had not regained her position in the blouse de-
partment of Messrs. Boney Blayds & Co. They had given
her some odd sewing, but not of late, and she had spent
much time trying to get work less uncertain. Her trouble
was—had always been—her face. It was unusual. People
did not know what to make of a girl who looked like
that. Why employ one who without qualification of wealth,
rank, fashion, or ability (so far as they knew) made them
feel ordinary? For—however essential to such as Fleur
and Michael—dramatic interest was not primary in the
manufacture or sale of blouses, in the fitting-on of shoes,
the addressing of envelopes, making-up of funeral wreaths,
or the other ambitions of Victorine. Behind those large
dark eyes and silent lips, what went on? It worried Boney
Blayds & Co., and the more wholesale forms of commerce. The lurid professions—film-super, or mannequin
—did not occur to one, like Victorine of self-deprecating
nature, and born in Putney.

When Bicket had gone out of a morning with his tray

and his balloons not yet blown up, she would stand biting her finger, as though to gnaw her way to some escape from this hand-to-mouth existence which kept her husband thin as a rail, tired as a rook, shabby as a tailless sparrow, and, at the expense of all caste feeling, brought them in no more than just enough to keep them living under a roof. It had long been clear to them both that there was no future in balloons, just a cadging present. And there smouldered in the silent, passive Victorine a fierce resentment. She wanted better things for herself, for him, chiefly for him.

On the morning when the mark was bumping down, she was putting on her velveteen jacket and toque (best remaining items of her wardrobe), having taken a resolve. Bicket never mentioned his old job, and his wife had subtly divined some cause beyond the ordinary for his loss of it. Why not see if she could get him taken back? He had often said: "Mr. Mont's a gent and a sort o' socialist; been through the war, too; no high-and-mighty about *him*." If she could "get at" this phenomenon! With the flush of hope and daring in her sallow cheeks, she took stock of her appearance from the window-glasses of the Strand. Her velveteen of jade-green always pleased one who had an eye for colour, but her black skirt—well, perhaps the wear and tear of it wouldn't show if she kept behind the counter. Had she brass enough to say that she came about a manuscript? And she rehearsed with silent lips, pinching her accent: "Would you ask Mr. Mont, please, if I could see him; it's about a manuscript." Yes! and then would come the question: "What name, please?" "Mrs. Bicket?" Never! "Miss Victorine Collins?" All authoresses had maiden names. Victorine—yes! But Collins! It didn't sound like. And no one would know what her maiden name had been. Why not choose one? They often chose. And she searched. Something Italian, like—like—— Hadn't their landlady said to them when they came in: "Is your wife Eyetalian?" Ah! Manuelli! That was certainly Italian—the ice-cream man in Little Ditch Street had it! She walked on practising beneath her breath. If only she could get to see this Mr. Mont!

She entered, trembling. All went exactly as foreseen, even to the pinching of her accent, till she stood waiting for them to bring an answer from the speaking tube, concealing her hands in their very old gloves. Had Miss Manuelli an appointment? There was no manuscript.

"No," said Victorine, "I haven't sent it yet. I wanted to see him first." The young man at the counter was looking at her hard. He went again to the tube, then spoke.

"Will you wait a minute, please—Mr. Mont's lady secretary is coming down."

Victorine inclined her head towards her sinking heart. A lady secretary! She would never get there now! And there came on her the sudden dread of false pretences. But the thought of Tony standing at his corner, ballooned up to the eyes, as she had spied out more than once, fortified her desperation.

A girl's voice said: "Miss Manuelli? I'm Mr. Mont's secretary, perhaps you could give me a message."

A fresh-faced young woman's eyes were travelling up and down her. Pinching her accent hard, she said: "Oh! I'm afraid I couldn't do that."

The travelling gaze stopped at her face. "If you'll come with me, I'll see if he can see you."

Alone in a small waiting-room, Victorine sat without movement, till she saw a young man's face poked through the doorway, and heard the words:

"Will you come in?"

She took a deep breath, and went. Once in the presence, she looked from Michael to his secretary and back again, subtly daring his youth, his chivalry, his sportsmanship, to refuse her a private interview. Through Michael passed at once the thought: 'Money, I suppose. But what an interesting face!' The secretary drew down the corners of her mouth and left the room.

"Well, Miss—er—Manuelli?"

"Not Manuelli, please—Mrs. Bicket; my husband used to be here."

"What!" The chap that had snooped "Copper Coin"! Phew! Bicket's yarn—his wife—pneumonia! She looked as if she might have had it.

"He often spoke of you, sir. And, please, he hasn't any work. Couldn't you find room for him again, sir?"

Michael stood silent. Did this terribly interesting-looking girl know about the snooping?

"He just sells balloons in the street now; I can't bear to see him. Over by St. Paul's he stands, and there's no money in it; and we do so want to get out to Australia. I know he's very nervy, and gets wrong with people. But if you *could* take him back here. . . ."

No! she did not know!

"Very sorry, Mrs. Bicket. I remember your husband well, but we haven't a place for him. Are *you* all right again?"

"Oh! yes. Except that I can't get work again either."

What a face for wrappers! Sort of Mona Lisaish! Storbert's novel! Ha!

"Well, I'll have a talk with your husband. I suppose you wouldn't like to sit to an artist for a book-wrapper? It might lead to work in that line if you want it. You're just the type for a friend of mine. Do you know Aubrey Greene's work?"

"No, sir."

"It's pretty good—in fact, very good in a decadent way. You wouldn't mind sitting?"

"I wouldn't mind anything to save some money. But I'd rather you didn't tell my husband I'd been to see you. He might take it amiss."

"All right! I'll see him by accident. Near St. Paul's, you said? But there's no chance here, Mrs. Bicket. Besides, he couldn't make two ends meet on this job, he told me."

"When I was ill, sir."

"Of course, that makes a difference."

"Yes, sir."

"Well, let me write you a note to Mr. Greene. Will you sit down a minute?"

He stole a look at her while she sat waiting. Really, her sallow, large-eyed face, with its dead-black, bobbed, frizzy-ended hair, was extraordinarily interesting—a little too refined and anæmic for the public; but, dash it all! the public couldn't always have its Reckitt's blue eyes, corn-coloured hair, and poppy cheeks. "She's not a peach," he wrote, "on the main tree of taste; but so striking in her way that she really might become a type, like Beardsley's or Dana's."

When she had taken the note and gone, he rang for his secretary.

"No, Miss Perren, she didn't take anything off me. But some type, eh?"

"I thought you'd like to see her. She wasn't an authoress, was she?"

"Far from it."

"Well, I hope she got what she wanted."

Michael grinned. "Partly, Miss Perren—partly. You think I'm an awful fool, don't you?"

"I'm sure I don't; but I think you're too soft-hearted."

Michael ran his fingers through his hair.

"Would it surprise you to hear that I've done a stroke of business?"

"Yes, Mr. Mont."

"Then I won't tell you what it is. When you've done pouting, go on with that letter to my father about 'Duet': 'We are sorry to say that in the present state of the trade we should not be justified in reprinting the dialogue between those two old blighters; we have already lost money by it!' You must translate, of course. Now can we say something to cheer the old boy up? How about this? 'When the French have recovered their wits, and the birds begin to sing—in short, when spring comes—we hope to reconsider the matter in the light of—of—'er—what, Miss Perren?"

" 'The experience we shall have gained.' Shall I leave out about the French and the birds?"

"Excellent! 'Yours faithfully, Danby and Winter.' Don't you think it was a scandalous piece of nepotism bringing the book here at all, Miss Perren?"

"What is 'nepotism'?"

"Taking advantage of your son. He's never made a sixpence by any of his books."

"He's a very distinguished writer, Mr. Mont."

"And we pay for the distinction. Well, he's a good old

Bart. That's all before lunch, and mind you have a good one. That girl's figure wasn't usual either, was it? She's thin, but she stands up straight. There's a question I always want to ask. Miss Perren: Why do modern girls walk in a curve with their heads poked forward? They can't all be built like that."

The secretary's cheeks brightened.

"There *is* a reason, Mr. Mont."

"Good! What is it?"

The secretary's cheeks continued to brighten. "I don't really know whether I can——"

"Oh! sorry. I'll ask my wife. Only she's quite straight herself."

"Well, Mr. Mont, it's this, you see: They aren't supposed to have anything be—behind, and, of course, they have, and they can't get the proper effect unless they curve their chests in and poke their heads forward. It's the fashion-plates and mannequins that do it."

"I see," said Michael; "thank you, Miss Perren; awfully good of you. It's the limit, isn't it?"

"Yes, I don't hold with it, myself."

"No, quite!"

The secretary lowered her eyelids and withdrew.

Michael sat down and drew a face on his blotting-paper. It was not Victorine's. . . .

Armed with the note to Aubrey Greene, Victorine had her usual lunch, a cup of coffee and a bit of heavy cake, and took the tube towards Chelsea. She had not succeeded, but the gentleman had been friendly and she felt cheered.

At the studio door was a young man inserting a key—very elegant in smoke-grey Harris tweeds, a sliding young man with no hat, beautifully brushed-back bright hair, and a soft voice.

"Model?" he said.

"Yes, sir, please. I have a note for you from Mr. Mont."

"Michael! Come in."

Victorine followed him in. It was 'not half' sea-green in there; a high room with rafters and a top light, and lots of pictures and drawings on the walls, and as if they had slipped off on to the floor. A picture on an easel of two ladies with their clothes sliding down troubled Victorine. She became conscious of the gentleman's eyes, sea-green like the walls, sliding up her.

"Will you sit for anything?" he asked.

Victorine answered mechanically: "Yes, sir."

"Do you mind taking your hat off?"

Victorine took off the toque, and shook out her hair.

"Ah!" said the gentleman. "I wonder."

Victorine wondered what.

"Just sit down on the dais, will you?"

Victorine looked about her, uncertain. A smile seemed to fly up his forehead and over his slippery bright hair.

"This is your first shot, then?"

"Yes, sir."

"All the better." And he pointed to a small platform.

Victorine sat down on it in a black oak chair.

"You look cold."

"Yes, sir."

He went to a cupboard and returned with two small glasses of a brown fluid.

"Have a Grand Marnier?"

She noticed that he tossed his off in one gulp, and did the same. It was sweet, strong, very nice, and made her gasp.

"Take a cigarette."

Victorine took one from a case he handed, and put it between her lips. He lit it. And again a smile slid up away over the top of his head.

"You draw it in," he said. "Where were you born?"

"In Putney, sir."

"That's very interesting. Just sit still a minute. It's not as bad as having a tooth out, but it takes longer. The great thing is to keep awake."

"Yes, sir."

He took a large piece of paper and a bit of dark stuff, and began to draw.

"Tell me," he said, "Miss——"

"Collins, sir—Victorine Collins." Some instinct made

her give her maiden name. It seemed somehow more professional.

"Are you at large?" He paused, and again the smile slid up over his bright hair: "Or have you any other occupation?"

"Not at present, sir. I'm married, but nothing else."

For some time after that the gentleman was silent. It was interesting to see him, taking a look, making a stroke on the paper, taking another look. Hundreds of looks, hundreds of strokes. At last he said: "All right! Now we'll have a rest. Heaven sent you here, Miss Collins. Come and get warm."

Victorine approached the fire.

"Do you know anything about expressionism?"

"No, sir."

"Well, it means not troubling about the outside except in so far as it expresses the inside. Does that convey anything to you?"

"No, sir."

"Quite! I think you said you'd sit for the—er—altogether?"

Victorine regarded the bright and sliding gentleman. She did not know what he meant, but she felt that he meant something out of the ordinary.

"Altogether what, sir?"

"Nude."

"Oh!" She cast her eyes down, then raised them to the sliding clothes of the two ladies. "Like that?"

"No, I shouldn't be treating you cubistically."

A slow flush was burning out the sallow in her cheeks. She said slowly:

"Does it mean more money?"

"Yes, half as much again—more perhaps. I don't want you to if you'd rather not. You can think it over and let me know next time."

She raised her eyes again, and said: "Thank you, sir."

"Righto! Only please don't 'sir' me."

Victorine smiled. It was the first time she had achieved this functional disturbance, and it seemed to have a strange effect. He said hurriedly: "By George! When you smile, Miss Collins, I see you *im*pressionistically. If you've rested, sit up there again."

Victorine went back.

The gentleman took a fresh piece of paper.

"Can you think of anything that will keep you smiling?"

She shook her head. That was a fact.

"Nothing comic at all? I suppose you're not in love with your husband, for instance?"

"Oh! yes."

"Well, try that."

Victorine tried that, but she could only see Tony selling his balloons.

"That won't do," said the gentleman. "Don't think of him! Did you ever see *'L'après midi d'un Faune'?*"

"No, sir."

"Well, I've got an idea. *'L'après midi d'une Dryade.'* About the nude you really needn't mind. It's quite impersonal. Think of art, and fifteen bob a day. Shades of Nijinsky, I see the whole thing!"

All the time that he was talking his eyes were sliding off and on to her, and his pencil off and on to the paper. A sort of infection began to ferment within Victorine. Fifteen shillings a day! Blue butterflies!

There was profound silence. His eyes and hand slid off and on. A faint smile had come on Victorine's face—she was adding up the money she might earn.

At last his eyes and hand ceased moving, and he stood looking at the paper.

"That's all for to-day, Miss Collins. I've got to think it out. Will you give me your address?"

Victorine thought rapidly.

"Please, sir, will you write to me at the post-office. I don't want my husband to know that I'm—I'm——"

"Affiliated to art? Well! Name of post-office?"

Victorine gave it and resumed her hat.

"An hour and a half, five shillings, thank you. And to-morrow, at half-past two, Miss Collins—not 'sir.' "

"Yes, s——, thank you."

Waiting for her 'bus in the cold January air, the altogether appeared to Victorine improbable. To sit in front of a strange gentleman in her skin! If Tony knew! The slow flush again burned up the sallow in her cheeks. She climbed into the 'bus. But fifteen shillings! Six days a week—why, it would be four pound ten! In four months she could earn their passage out. Judging by the pictures in there, lots must be doing it. Tony must know nothing, not even that she was sitting for her face. He was all nerves, and that fond of her! He would imagine things; she had heard him say those artists were just like cats. But that gentleman had been very nice, though he did seem as if he were laughing at everything. She wished he had shown her the drawing. Perhaps she would see herself in an exhibition some day. But without—oh! And suddenly she thought: 'if I ate a bit more, I'd look nice like that, too!' And as if to escape from the daring of that thought, she stared up into the face opposite. It had two chins, was calm and smooth and pink, with light eyes staring back at her. People had thoughts, but you couldn't tell what they were! And the smile which Aubrey Greene desired crept out on his model's face.

Chapter Three

MICHAEL WALKS AND TALKS

———•—◆—•———

THE face Michael drew began by being Victorine's, and ended by being Fleur's. If physically Fleur stood up straight, was she morally as erect? This was the speculation for which he continually called himself a cad. He saw no change in her movements, and loyally refrained from enquiring into the movements he could not see. But his aroused attention made him more and more aware of a certain cynicism, as if she were continually registering the belief that all values were equal and none of much value.

Wilfrid, though still in London, was neither visible nor spoken of. "Out of sight and hearing, out of mind," seemed to be the motto. It did not work with Michael— Wilfrid was constantly in his mind. If Wilfrid were not seeing Fleur, how could he bear to stay within such tantalising reach of her? If Fleur did not want Wilfrid to stay, why had she not sent him away? He was finding it difficult, too, to conceal from others the fact that Desert and he were no longer pals. Often the impetus to go and have it out with him surged up and was beaten back. Either there was nothing beyond what he already knew, or there was something—and Wilfrid would say there wasn't. Michael accepted that without cavil; one did not

133

give a woman away! But he wanted to hear no lies from a
War comrade. Between Fleur and himself no word had
passed; for words, he felt, would add no knowledge,
merely imperil a hold weak enough already. Christmas at
the ancestral manor of the Monts had been passed in
covert-shooting. Fleur had come and stood with him at
the last drive on the second day, holding Ting-a-ling on a
lead. The Chinese dog had been extraordinarily excited,
climbing the air every time a bird fell, and quite unaf-
fected by the noise of guns. Michael, waiting to miss his
birds—he was a poor shot—had watched her eager face
emerging from grey fur, her form braced back
against Ting-a-ling. Shooting was new to her; and under
the stimulus of novelty she was always at her best. He
had loved even her "Oh, Michaels!" when he missed. She
had been the success of the gathering, which meant seeing
almost nothing of her except a sleepy head on a pillow;
but, at least, down there he had not suffered from lurking
uneasiness.

Putting a last touch to the bobbed hair on the blotting-
paper, he got up. St. Paul's, that girl had said. He might
stroll up and have a squint at Bicket. Something might
occur to him. Tightening the belt of his blue overcoat
round his waist, he sallied forth, thin and sprightly, with
a little ache in his heart.

Walking east, on that bright cheerful day, nothing
struck him so much as the fact that he was alive, well, and
in work. So very many were dead, ill, or out of a job. He
entered Covent Garden. Amazing place! A human nature
which, decade after decade, could put up with Covent
Garden was not in danger of extinction from its many
ills. A comforting place—one needn't take anything too
seriously after walking through it. On this square island
were the vegetables of the earth and the fruits of the
world, bounded on the west by publishing, on the east by
opera, on the north and south by rivers of mankind.
Among discharging carts and litter of paper, straw and
men out of drawing, Michael walked and sniffed. Smell
of its own, Covent Garden, earthly and just not rotten! He
had never seen—even in the War—any place that so

utterly lacked form. Extraordinarily English! Nobody
looked as if they had anything to do with the soil—
drivers, hangers-on, packers, and the salesmen inside the
covered markets, seemed equally devoid of acquaintance-
ship with sun, wind, water, earth or air—town types all!
And—Golly!—how their faces jutted, sloped, sagged and
swelled, in every kind of featural disharmony. What was
the English type amongst all this infinite variety of disproportion? There just wasn't one! He came on the
fruits, glowing piles, still and bright—foreigners from the
land of the sun—globes all the same size and colour.
They made Michael's mouth water. 'Something in the
sun,' he thought; 'there really is.' Look at Italy, at the
Arabs, at Australia—the Australians came from England,
and see the type now! Nevertheless—a Cockney for good
temper! The more regular a person's form and features,
the more selfish they were! Those grape-fruit looked horribly self-satisfied, compared with the potatoes!

He emerged still thinking about the English. Well!
They were now one of the plainest and most distorted
races of the world; and yet was there any race to compare
with them for good temper and for "guts"? And they
needed those in their smoky towns, and their climate—
remarkable instance of adaptation to environment, the
modern English character! 'I could pick out an Englishman anywhere,' he thought, 'and yet, physically, there's
no general type now!' Astounding people! So ugly in the
mass, yet growing such flowers of beauty, and such
strange sprigs—like that little Mrs. Bicket; so unimagina-
tive in bulk, yet with such a blooming lot of poets! How
would old Danby like it, by the way, when Wilfrid took
his next volume to some other firm; or rather what should
he—Wilfrid's particular friend!—say to old Danby? Aha!
He knew what he should say:

"Yes, sir, but you should have let that poor blighter off
who snooped the 'Copper Coins.' Desert hasn't forgotten
your refusal." One for old Danby and his eternal in-the-
rightness! "Copper Coin" had done uncommonly well. Its
successor would probably do uncommonly better. The
book was a proof of what he—Michael—was always say-

ing: The "cockyollybird period" was passing. People wanted life again. Sibley, Walter Nazing, Linda—all those who had nothing to say except that they were superior to such as had—were already measured for their coffins. Not that they would know when they were in them; not blooming likely! They would continue to wave their noses and look down them!

'*I'm* fed-up with them,' thought Michael. 'If only Fleur would see that looking down your nose is a sure sign of inferiority!' And, suddenly, it came to him that she probably did. Wilfrid was the only one of the whole lot she had ever been thick with; the others were there because—well, because she was Fleur, and had the latest things about her. When, very soon, they were no longer the latest things, she would drop them. But Wilfrid she would not drop. No, he felt sure that she had not dropped, and would not drop Wilfrid.

He looked up. Ludgate Hill! "Near St. Paul's—sells balloons?" And there—sure enough—the poor beggar was!

Bicket was deflating with a view to going off his stand for a cup of cocoa. Remembering that he had come on him by accident, Michael stood for a moment preparing the tones of surprise. Pity the poor chap couldn't blow himself into one of those coloured shapes and float over St. Paul's to Peter. Mournful little cuss he looked, squeezing out the air! Memory tapped sharply on his mind. Balloon—in the square—November the first—joyful night! Special! Fleur! Perhaps they brought luck. He moved and said in an astounded voice: "*You*, Bicket? Is this your stunt now?"

The large eyes of Bicket regarded him over a puce-coloured six-pennyworth.

"Mr. Mont! Often thought I'd like to see you again, sir."

"Same here, Bicket. If you're not doing anything, come and have some lunch."

Bicket completed the globe's collapse, and, closing his tray-lid, said: "Reelly, sir?"

"Rather! I was just going into a fish place."

Bicket detached his tray.

"I'll leave this with the crossing-sweeper." He did so, and followed at Michael's side.

"Any money in it, Bicket?"

"Bare livin', sir."

"How about this place? We'll have oysters."

A little saliva at the corner of Bicket's mouth was removed by a pale tongue.

At a small table decorated with white oilcloth and a cruet stand, Michael sat down.

"Two dozen oysters, and all that; then two good soles, and a bottle of Chablis. Hurry up, please."

When the white-aproned fellow had gone about it, Bicket said simply:

"My Gawd!"

"Yes, it's a funny world, Bicket."

"It *is,* and that's a fact. This lunch'll cost you a pound, I shouldn' wonder. If I take twenty-five bob a week, it's all I do."

"You touch it there, Bicket. I eat my conscience every day."

Bicket shook his head.

"No, sir, if you've got money, spend it. I would. Be 'appy if you can—there yn't too many that are."

The white-aproned fellow began blessing them with oysters. He brought them fresh-opened, three at a time. Michael bearded them; Bicket swallowed them whole. Presently above twelve empty shells, he said:

"That's where the Socialists myke their mistyke, sir. Nothing keeps me going but the sight of other people spendin' money. It's what we might all come to with a bit of luck. Reduce the world to a level of a pound a dy— and it won't ever run to that, they sy! It's not good enough, sir. I'd rather 'ave less with the 'ope of more. Take away the gamble, and life's a frost. Here's luck!"

"Almost thou persuadest me to be a capitalist, Bicket."

A glow had come up in the thin and large-eyed face behind the greenish Chablis glass.

"I wish to Gawd I had my wife here, sir. I told you about her and the pneumonia. She's all right agyne now, only thin. She's the prize I drew. I don't want a world where you can't draw prizes. If it were all bloomin' conscientious an' accordin' to merit, I'd never have got her. See?"

'Same here,' thought Michael, mentally drawing that face again.

"We've all got our dreams; mine's blue butterflies—Central Austrylia. The Socialists won't 'elp me to get there. Their ideas of 'eaven don't run beyond Europe."

"Cripes!" said Michael. "Melted butter, Bicket?"

"Thank you, sir."

Silence was not broken for some time, but the soles were.

"What made you think of balloons, Bicket?"

"You don't 'ave to advertise, they do it for you."

"Saw too much of advertising with us, eh?"

"Well, sir, I did use to read the wrappers. Astonished me, I will sy—the number of gryte books."

Michael ran his hands through his hair.

"Wrappers! The same young woman being kissed by the same young man with the same clean-cut jaw. But what can you do, Bicket? They *will* have it. I tried to make a break only this morning—I shall see what comes of it." 'And I hope *you* won't!' he thought: 'Fancy coming on Fleur outside a novel!'

"I did notice a tendency just before I left," said Bicket, "to 'ave cliffs or landskips and two sort of dolls sittin' on the sand or in the grass lookin' as if they didn't know what to do with each other."

"Yes," murmured Michael, "we tried that. It was supposed not to be vulgar. But we soon exhausted the public's capacity. What'll you have now—cheese?"

"Thank you, sir; I've had too much already, but I won't say 'No.' "

"Two Stiltons," said Michael.

"How's Mr. Desert, sir?"

Michael reddened.

"Oh! He's all right."

Bicket had reddened also.

"I wish—I wish you'd let him know that it was quite a

—an accident my pitchin' on his book. I've always regretted it."

"It's usually an accident, I think," said Michael slowly, "when we snoop other people's goods. We never *want* to."

Bicket looked up.

"No, sir, I don't agree. 'Alf mankind is predytory—only, I'm not that sort, meself."

In Michael loyalty tried to stammer "Nor is he." He handed his cigarette case to Bicket.

"Thank you, sir, I'm sure."

His eyes were swimming, and Michael thought: 'Dash it! This is sentimental. Kiss me good-bye and go!' He beckoned up the white-aproned fellow.

"Give us your address, Bicket. If integuments are any good to you, I might have some spare slops."

Bicket backed the bill with his address and said, hesitating: "I suppose, sir, Mrs. Mont wouldn't 'ave anything to spare. My wife's about my height."

"I expect she would. We'll send them along." He saw the 'little snipe's' lips quivering, and reached for his overcoat. "If anything blows in, I'll remember you. Good-bye, Bicket, and good luck."

Going east, because Bicket was going west, he repeated to himself the maxim: "Pity is tripe—pity is tripe!" Then getting on a 'bus, he was borne back past St. Paul's. Cautiously "taking a lunar"—as old Forsyte put it—he saw Bicket inflating a balloon; little was visible of his face or figure behind that rosy circumference. Nearing Blake Street, he developed an invincible repugnance to work, and was carried on to Trafalgar Square. Bicket had stirred him up. The world was sometimes almost unbearably jolly. Bicket, Wilfrid, and the Ruhr! "Feeling is tosh! Pity is tripe!" He descended from his 'bus, and passed the lions towards Pall Mall. Should he go into 'Snooks' and ask for Bart? No use—he would not find Fleur there. That was what he really wanted—to see Fleur in the daytime. But—where? She was everywhere to be found, and that was nowhere.

She was restless. Was that his fault? If he had been

Wilfrid—would she be restless? 'Yes,' he thought stoutly, 'Wilfrid's restless, too.' They were all restless—all the people he knew. At least all the young ones—in life and in letters. Look at their novels! Hardly one in twenty had any repose, any of that quality which made one turn back to a book as a corner of refuge. They dashed and sputtered and skidded and rushed by like motor cycles— violent, oh! and clever. How tired he was of cleverness! Sometimes he would take a manuscript home to Fleur for her opinion. He remembered her saying once: "This is exactly like life, Michael, it just rushes—it doesn't dwell on anything long enough to mean anything anywhere. Of course the author didn't mean it for satire, but if you publish it, I advise you to put: 'This awful satire on modern life' outside the cover." And they had. At least, they had put: "This wonderful satire on modern life." Fleur *was* like that! She could see the hurry, but, like the author of the wonderful satire, she didn't know that she herself veered and hurried, or—did she know? Was she conscious of licking at life, like a flame at air?

He had reached Piccadilly, and suddenly he remembered that he had not called on her aunt for ages. That was a possible draw. He bent his steps towards Green Street.

"Mrs. Dartie at home?"

"Yes, sir."

Michael moved his nostrils. Fleur used—but he could catch no scent, except incense. Winifred burnt joss-sticks when she remembered what a distinguished atmosphere they produced.

"What name?"

"Mr. Mont. My wife's not here, I suppose?"

"No, sir. Only Mrs. Val Dartie."

Mrs. Val Dartie! Yes, he remembered, nice woman— but not a substitute for Fleur! Committed, however, he followed the maid.

In the drawing-room Michael found three people, one of them his father-in-law, who had a grey and brooding aspect, and, from an Empire chair, was staring at blue Australian butterflies' wings under glass on a round scarlet table. Winifred had jazzed the Empire foundations of her room with a superstructure more suitable to the age. She greeted Michael with fashionable warmth. It was good of him to come when he was so busy with all these young poets. "I thought 'Copper Coin,' " she said—"what a *nice* title!—such an intriguing little book. I do think Mr. Desert is clever! What is he doing now?"

Michael said: "I don't know," and dropped on to a settee beside Mrs. Val. Ignorant of the Forsyte family feud, he was unable to appreciate the relief he had brought in with him. Soames said something about the French, got up, and went to the window; Winifred joined him—their voices sounded confidential.

"How is Fleur?" said Michael's neighbour.

"Thanks, awfully well."

"Do you like your house?"

"Oh, fearfully. Won't you come and see it?"

"I don't know whether Fleur would——?"

"Why not?"

"Oh! Well!"

"She's frightfully accessible."

She seemed to be looking at him with more interest than he deserved, to be trying to make something out from his face, and he added:

"You're a relation—by blood as well as marriage, aren't you?"

"Yes."

"Then what's the skeleton?"

"Oh! nothing. I'll certainly come. Only—she has so many friends."

Michael thought: 'I like this woman!' "As a matter of fact," he said, "I came here this afterooon thinking I might find Fleur. I should like her to know you. With all the jazz there is about, she'd appreciate somebody restful."

"Thank you."

"You've never lived in London?"

"Not since I was six."

"I wish she could get a rest—pity there isn't a d-desert handy." He had stuttered; the word was not pronounced the same—still! He glanced, disconcerted, at the butter-flies. "I've just been talking to a little Cockney whose S.O.S. is 'Central Austrylia.' But what do you say—Have we got souls to save?"

"I used to think so, but now I'm not so sure—something's struck me lately."

"What was that?"

"Well, I notice that any one at all out of proportion, or whose nose is on one side, or whose eyes jut out, or even have a special shining look, always believes in the soul; people who are in proportion, and have no prominent physical features, don't seem to be really interested."

Michael's ears moved.

"By Jove!" he said; "some thought! Fleur's beautifully proportioned—*she* doesn't seem to worry. I'm not—and I certainly do. The people in Covent Garden must have lots of soul. You think 'the soul's' the result of loose-gearing in the organism—sort of special consciousness from not working in one piece."

"Yes, rather like that—what's called psychic power is, I'm almost sure."

"I say, is your life safe? According to your theory, though, we're in a mighty soulful era. I must think over my family. How about yours?"

"The Forsytes! Oh, they're quite too well-propor-tioned."

"I agree, they haven't any special juts so far as I've seen. The French, too, are awfully close-knit. It really is an idea, only, of course, most people see it the other way. They'd say the soul produces the disproportion, makes the eyes shine, bends the nose, and all that; where the soul is small, it's not trying to get out of the body, whence the barber's block. I'll think about it. Thanks for the tip. Well, do come and see us. Good-bye! I don't think I'll disturb them in the window. Would you mind saying I had to scoot?" Squeezing a slim, gloved hand, receiving and returning a smiling look, he slid out, thinking: 'Dash the soul, where's her body?'

Chapter Four

FLEUR'S BODY

———————•❈•❈•❈•———————

FLEUR'S body, indeed, was at the moment in one of
those difficult positions which continually threaten
the spirit of compromise. It was in fact in Wilfrid's arms;
sufficiently, at least, to make her say:

"No, Wilfrid—you promised to be good."

It was a really remarkable tribute to her powers of
skating on thin ice that the word "good" should still have
significance. For eleven weeks exactly this young man
had danced on the edge of fulfilment, and was even now
divided from her by two clenched hands pressed firmly
against his chest, and the word "good"; and this after
not having seen her for a fortnight.

When she said it, he let her go, with a sort of violence,
and sat down on a piece of junk. Only the sense of
damnable iteration prevented him from saying: "It can't
go on, Fleur." She knew that! And yet it did! This was
what perpetually amazed him. How a poor brute could
hang on week after week saying to her and to himself:
"Now or never!" when it wasn't either? Subconsciousness,
that, until the word "now" had been reached, Fleur would
not know her own mind, alone had kept him dancing. His
own feelings were so intense that he almost hated her for
indecision. And he was unjust. It was not exactly indeci-

sion. Fleur wanted the added richness and excitement which Wilfrid's affection gave to life, but without danger and without loss. How natural! His frightful passionateness was making all the trouble. Neither by her wish, nor through her fault, was he passionate! And yet—it was both nice and proper to inspire passion; and, of course, she had the lurking sense that she was not "in the mode" to cavil at a lover, especially since life owed her one.

Released, she smoothed herself and said: "Talk of something sensible; what have you been writing?"

"This."

Fleur read. Flushing and biting her lips, she said:

"It's frightfully bitter."

"It's frightfully true. Does *he* ever ask you now whether you see me?"

"Never."

"Why?"

"I don't know."

"What would you answer if he did?"

Fleur shrugged her shoulders.

Desert said quietly: "Yes, that's your attitude. It can't last, Fleur." He was standing by the window. She put the sheets down on his desk and moved towards him. Poor Wilfrid! Now that he was quiet she was sorry.

He said suddenly: "Stop! Don't move! *He's* down there in the street."

Recoiling, she gasped: "Michael! Oh! But how—how could he have known?"

Desert said grimly: "Do you only know him as little as that? Do you suppose he'd be there if he knew you were here?"

Fleur winced.

"Why *is* he there, then?"

"He probably wants to see me. He looks as if he couldn't make up his mind. Don't get the wind up, he won't be let in."

Fleur sat down; she felt weak in the legs. The ice seemed suddenly of an appalling thinness—the water appallingly cold.

"Has he seen you?" she said.

"No."

The thought flashed through him: 'If I were a blackguard, I could force her hand, by moving one step and crooking my finger.' Pity one wasn't a blackguard—at all events, not to that point—things would be so much simpler!

"Where is he now?" asked Fleur.

"Going away."

In profound relief, she sighed out:

"But it's queer, isn't it, Wilfrid?"

"You don't suppose he's easy in his mind, do you?"

Fleur bit her lips. He was jeering, because she didn't or couldn't really love either of them. It was unjust. She *could* have loved—she *had* loved! Wilfrid and Michael—they might go to the deuce!

"I wish I had never come here," she said, suddenly: "and I'll never come again!"

He went to the door, and held it open.

"You are right."

Fleur stood quite still, her chin on the collar of her fur, her clear-glancing eyes fixed on his face, her lips set and mutinous.

"You think I'm a heartless beast," she said slowly. "So I am—now. Good-bye!"

He neither took her hand nor spoke, he only bowed. His eyes were very tragic. Trembling with mortification, Fleur went out. She heard the door closed, while she was going down the stairs. At the bottom she stood uncertain. Suppose Michael had come back! Almost opposite was that gallery where she had first met him and—Jon. Slip across in there! If he were still hovering round the entrance of the little street, she could tell him with a good conscience where she had been. She peeped. Not in sight! Swiftly she slid across into the doorway opposite. They would be closing in a minute—just on four o'clock! She put down a shilling and slipped in. She must see—in case! She stood, revolving—one-man show, the man—Claud Brains! She put down another shilling for a catalogue, and read as she went out. "No. 7. Woman getting the wind up." It told her everything; and with a lighter

heart she skimmed along, and took a taxi. Get home before Michael! She felt relieved, almost exhilarated. So
much for skating on thin ice! It wasn't good enough.
Wilfrid must go. Poor Wilfrid! Well, he shouldn't have
sneered—what did he know of her? Nobody knew anything of her! She was alone in the world. She slipped her
latch-key into the hall door. No Michael. She sàt down in
the drawing-room before the fire, and took up Walter
Nazing's last. She read a page three times. It meant no
more with every reading—it meant less; he was the kind
of author who must be read at a gallop, and given away
lest a first impression of wind in the hair be lost in a sensation of wind lower down; but Wilfrid's eyes came between her and the words. Pity! Nobody pitied her; why,
then, should she pity them? Besides, pity was "pop," as
Amabel would say. The situation demanded cast-iron
sense. But Wilfrid's eyes! Well—she wouldn't be seeing
them again! Beautiful eyes when they smiled or when—
so much more often—they looked at her with longing, as
now between her and the sentence: "Solemnly and with a
delicious egoism he more than awfully desired her who
snug and rosy in the pink shell of her involuted and so
petulant social periphrasis——" Poor Wilfrid! Pity was
"pop," but there was pride! Did she choose that he should
go away thinking that she had "played him up" just out
of vanity, as Walter Nazing said American women did?
Did she? Would it not be more in the mode, really dramatic—if one "went over the deep end," as they said,
just once? Would that not be something they could both
look back on—he in that East he was always talking of,
she in this West? The proposition had a momentary popu-
larity in that organism called Fleur too finely proportioned for a soul according to the theory which Michael
was thinking over. Like all popularities, it did not last.
First: Would she like it? She did not think she would;
one man, without love, was quite enough. Then there
was the danger of passing into Wilfrid's power. He was
a gentleman, but he was passionate; the cup once sipped,
would he consent to put it down? But more than all was
a physical doubt of the last two or three weeks which

awaited verification, and which made her feel solemn. She stood up and passed her hands all over her, with a definite recoil from the thought of Wilfrid's hands doing the same. No! To have his friendship, his admiration, but not at that price. She viewed him, suddenly, as a bomb set on her copper floor; and in fancy ran and seized and flung him out into the Square—poor Wilfrid! Pity was "pop"! But one might be sorry for *oneself,* losing him; losing too that ideal of modern womanhood expounded to her one evening by Marjorie Ferrar, pet of the "panjoys," whose red-gold hair excited so much admiration: "My ambition—old thing—is to be the perfect wife of one man, the perfect mistress of another, and the perfect mother of a third, all at once. It's perfectly possible—they do it in France."

But was it really so perfectly possible—even if pity *was* posh? How be perfect to Michael, when the slightest slip might reveal to him that she was being perfect to Wilfrid; how be perfect to Wilfrid, when every time she was perfect to Michael would be a dagger in Wilfrid's heart? And if—if her physical doubt should mature into certainty, how be perfect mother to the certainty, when she was either torturing two men, or lying to them like a trooperess? Not so perfectly possible as all that! 'If only I were all French!' thought Fleur. . . .

The clicking door startled her—the reason that she was not all French was coming in. He looked very grey, as if he had been thinking too much. He kissed her, and sat down moodily before the fire.

"Have you come for the night, Dad?"

"If I may," murmured Soames. "Business."

"Anything unpleasant, ducky?"

Soames looked up as if startled.

"Unpleasant? Why should it be unpleasant?"

"I only thought from your face."

Soames grunted. "This Ruhr!" he said. "I've brought you a picture. Chinese!"

"Oh, Dad! How jolly!"

"It isn't," said Soames; "it's a monkey eating fruit."

"But that's perfect! Where is it—in the hall?"

Soames nodded.

Stripping the coverings off the picture, Fleur brought it in, and setting it up on the jade-green settee, stood away and looked at it. The large white monkey with its brown haunting eyes, as if she had suddenly wrested its interest from the orange-like fruit in its crisped paw, the grey background, the empty rinds all round—bright splashes in a general ghostliness of colour, impressed her at once.

"But, Dad, it's a masterpiece—I'm sure it's of a frightfully good period."

"I don't know," said Soames. "I must look up the Chinese."

"But you oughtn't to give it to me, it must be worth any amount. You ought to have it in your collection."

"They didn't know its value," said Soames, and a faint smile illumined his features. "I gave three hundred for it. It'll be safer here."

"Of course it'll be safe. Only why safer?"

Soames turned towards the picture.

"I can't tell. Anything may come of this."

"Of what, dear?"

"Is 'Old Mont' coming in to-night?"

"No, he's at Lippinghall still."

"Well, it doesn't matter—he's no good."

Fleur took his hand and gave it a squeeze.

"Tell me!"

Soames' tickled heart quivered. Fancy her wanting to know what was troubling him! But his sense of the becoming, and his fear of giving away his own alarm, forbade response.

"Nothing you'd understand," he said. "Where are you going to hang it?"

"There, I think; but we must wait for Michael."

Soames grumbled out:

"I saw him just now at your aunt's. Is that the way he attends to business?"

'Perhaps,' thought Fleur, 'he was only on his way back to the office. Cork Street *is* more or less between! If he passed the end of it, he would think of Wilfrid, he might have been wanting to see him about books.'

"Oh, here's Ting! Well, darling!"

The Chinese dog, let in, as it were, by Providence, seeing Soames, sat down suddenly with snub upturned and eyes brilliant. "The expression of your face," he seemed to say, "pleases me. We belong to the past and could sing hymns together, old man."

"Funny little chap," said Soames; "he always knows me."

Fleur lifted him. "Come and see the new monkey, ducky."

"Don't let him lick it."

Held rather firmly by his jade-green collar and confronted by an inexplicable piece of silk smelling of the past, Ting-a-ling raised his head higher and higher to correspond with the action ot his nostrils, and his little tongue appeared, tentatively savouring the emanation of his country.

"It's a nice monkey, isn't it, darling?"

"No," said Ting-a-ling, rather clearly. "Put me down!"

Restored to the floor, he sought a patch where the copper came through between two rugs, and licked it quietly.

"Mr. Aubrey Greene, ma'am!"

"H'm!" said Soames.

The painter came gliding and glowing in; his bright hair slipping back, his green eyes sliding off.

"Ah!" he said, pointing to the floor. "That's what I've come about."

Fleur followed his finger in amazement.

"Ting!" she said severely, "stop it! He will lick the copper, Aubrey."

"But how perfectly Chinese! They do everything we don't."

"Dad—Aubrey Greene. My father's just brought me this picture, Aubrey—isn't it a gem?"

The painter stood quite still, his eyes ceased sliding off, his hair ceased slipping back.

"Phew!" he said.

Soames rose. He had waited for the flippant; but he

recognized in the tone something reverential, if not aghast.

"By George," said Aubrey Greene, "those eyes! Where did you pick it up, sir?"

"It belonged to a cousin of mine—a racing man. It was his only picture."

"Good for him! He must have had taste."

Soames stared. The idea that George should have had taste almost appalled him.

"No," he said, with a flash of inspiration: "What he liked about it was that it makes you feel uncomfortable."

"Same thing! I don't know where I've seen a more pungent satire on human life."

"I don't follow," said Soames dryly.

"Why, it's a perfect allegory, sir! Eat the fruits of life, scatter the rinds, and get copped doing it. When they're still, a monkey's eyes are the human tragedy incarnate. Look at them! He thinks there's something beyond, and he's sad or angry because he can't get at it. That picture ought to be in the British Museum, sir, with the label: 'Civilisation, caught out.' "

"Well, it won't be," said Fleur. "It'll be here, labelled 'The White Monkey.' "

"Same thing."

"Cynicism," said Soames abruptly, "gets you nowhere. If you'd said '*Modernity* caught out'——"

"I do, sir; but why be narrow? You don't seriously suppose this age is worse than any other?"

"Don't I?" said Soames. "In my belief the world reached its highest point in the 'eighties, and will never reach it again."

The painter stared.

"That's frightfully interesting. I wasn't born, and I suppose you were about my age then, sir. You believed in God and drove in *diligences*."

Diligences! The word awakened in Soames a memory which somehow seemed appropriate.

"Yes," he said, "and I can tell you a story of those days that you can't match in these. When I was a youngster in Switzerland with my people, two of my sisters had some black cherries. When they'd eaten about half a dozen they discovered that they all had little maggots in them. An English climber there saw how upset they were, and ate the whole of the rest of the cherries—about two pounds—maggots, stones and all, just to show them. That was the sort of men they were then."

"Oh! Father!"

"Gee! He must have been gone on them."

"No," said Soames, "not particularly. His name was Powley; he wore side-whiskers."

"Talking of God and diligences; I saw a hansom yesterday."

'More to the point if you'd seen God,' thought Soames, but he did not say so; indeed, the thought surprised him, it was not the sort of thing he had ever seen himself.

"You mayn't know it, sir, but there's more belief now than there was before the war—they've discovered that we're not all body."

"Oh!" said Fleur. "That reminds me, Aubrey. Do you know any mediums? Could I get one to come here? On our floor, with Michael outside the door, one would know there couldn't be any hanky. Do the dark *séance* people ever go out?—they're much more thrilling, they say."

"Spiritualism!" said Soames. "H'mph!" He could not in half an hour have expressed himself more clearly.

Aubrey Greene's eyes slid off to Ting-a-ling. "I'll see what I can do, if you'll lend me your Peke for an hour or so to-morrow afternoon. I'd bring him back on a lead, and give him every luxury."

"What do you want him for?"

"Michael sent me a most topping little model to-day. But, you see, she can't smile."

"Michael?"

"Yes. Something quite new; and I've got a scheme. Her smile's like sunlight going off an Italian valley; but when you tell her to, she can't. I thought your Peke could make her, perhaps."

"May I come and see?" said Fleur.

"Yes, bring him to-morrow; but, if I can persuade her, it'll be in the 'altogether.' "

"Oh! Will you get me a *séance,* if I lend you Ting?"

"I will."

"H'mph!" said Soames again. *Séance,* Italian sunlight, the "altogether!" It was time he got back to Elderson, and what was to be done now, and left this fiddling while Rome burned. "Good-bye, Mr. Greene," he said; "I've got no time."

"Quite, sir," said Aubrey Greene.

"Quite!" mimicked Soames to himself, going out.

Aubrey Greene took his departure a few minutes later, crossing a lady in the hall who was delivering her name to the manservant.

Alone with her body, Fleur again passed her hands all over it. The "altogether"—was a reminder of the dangers of dramatic conduct.

Chapter Five

FLEUR'S SOUL

———◆◆———

"MRS. VAL DARTIE, ma'am."

A name which could not be distorted even by Coaker affected her like a finger applied suddenly to the head of the sciatic nerve. Holly! Not seen since the day when she did not marry Jon. Holly! A flood of remembrance—Wansdon, the Downs, the gravel pit, the apple orchard, the river, the copse at Robin Hill! No! It was not a pleasant sensation—to see Holly, and she said: "How awfully nice of you to come!"

"I met your husband this afternoon at Green Street; he asked me. What a lovely room!"

"Ting! Come and be introduced! This is Ting-a-ling; isn't he perfect? He's a little upset because of the new monkey. How's Val, and dear Wansdon? It was too wonderfully peaceful."

"It's a nice backwater. I don't get tired of it."

"And——" said Fleur, with a little hard laugh, "Jon?"

"He's growing peaches in North Carolina. British Columbia didn't do."

"Oh! Is he married?"

"No."

"I suppose he'll marry an American."

"He isn't twenty-two, you know."

153

"Good Lord!" said Fleur: "Am I only twenty-one? I feel forty-eight."

"That's living in the middle of things and seeing so many people——"

"And getting to know none."

"But don't you?"

"No, it isn't done. I mean we all call each other by our Christian names; but *après*——"

"I like your husband very much."

"Oh! yes, Michael's a dear. How's June?"

"I saw her yesterday—she's got a new painter, of course—Claud Brains. I believe he's what they call a Vertiginist."

Fleur bit her lip.

"Yes, they're quite common. I suppose June thinks he's the only one."

"Well, she thinks he's a genius."

"She's wonderful."

"Yes," said Holly, "the most loyal creature in the world while it lasts. It's like poultry farming—once they're hatched. You never saw Boris Strumolowski?"

"No."

"Well, don't."

"I know his bust of Michael's uncle. It's rather sane."

"Yes. June thought it a pot-boiler, and he never forgave her. Of course it was. As soon as her duck becomes a swan she looks round for another duck, and the lamer the better. She's a darling."

"Yes," murmured Fleur; "I liked June."

Another flood of remembrance—from a teashop, from the river, from June's little dining-room, from where in Green Street she had changed her wedding-dress under the upward gaze of June's blue eyes. She seized the monkey and held it up.

"Isn't it a picture of 'life'?" Would she have said that, if Aubrey Greene hadn't? Still it seemed very true at the moment.

"Poor monkey!" said Holly. "I'm always frightfully sorry for monkeys. But it's marvellous, I think."

"Yes. I'm going to hang it here. If I can get one more,

I shall have done in this room; only people have so got on to Chinese things. This was luck—somebody died —George Forsyte, you know, the racing one."

"Oh!" said Holly softly. She saw again her old kinsman's japing eyes in the church when Fleur was being married, heard his throaty whisper, "Will she stay the course?" And was she staying it, this pretty filly? "Wish she could get a rest. If only there were a desert handy!" Well, one couldn't ask a question so personal, and Holly took refuge in a general remark.

"What do all you smart young people feel about life, nowadays, Fleur?—when one's not of it and has lived twenty years in South Africa, one still feels out of it."

"Life! Oh! well, we know it's supposed to be a riddle, but we've given it up. We just want to have a good time because we don't believe anything can last. But I don't think we know how to have it. We just fly on, and hope for it. Of course, there's art, but most of us aren't artists; besides, expressionism—Michael says it's got no inside. We gas about it, but I suppose it hasn't. I see a frightful lot of writers and painters, you know; they're supposed to be amusing."

Holly listened, amazed. Who would have thought that this girl *saw?* She might be seeing wrong, but anyway she saw!

"Surely," she said, "you enjoy yourselves?"

"Well, I like getting hold of nice things, and interesting people; I like seeing everything that's new and worth while, or seems so at the moment. But that's just how it is—nothing lasts. You see, I'm not of the 'Pan-joys,' nor of the 'new-faithfuls.' "

"The new-faithfuls?"

"Oh! don't you know—it's a sort of faith-healing done on oneself, not exactly the old 'God-good, good-God!' sort; but a kind of mixture of will-power, psycho-analysis, and belief that everything will be all right on the night if you say it will. You must have come across them. They're frightfully in earnest."

"I know," said Holly; "their eyes shine."

"I daresay. I don't believe in them—I don't believe in anyone; or anything—much. How can one?"

"How about simple people, and hard work?"

Fleur sighed. "I daresay. I will say for Michael—*he's* not spoiled. Let's have tea. Tea, Ting?" and turning up the lights, she rang the bell.

When her unexpected visitor had gone, she sat very still before the fire. To-day, when she had been so very near belonging to Wilfrid! So Jon was not married! Not that it made any odds! Things did not come round as they were expected to in books. And anyway sentiment was swosh! Cut it out! She tossed back her hair; and, getting hammer and nail, proceeded to hang the white monkey. Between the two tea-chests with their coloured pearl-shell figures, he would look his best. Since she couldn't have Jon, what did it matter—Wilfrid or Michael, or both, or neither? Eat the orange in her hand, and throw away the rind! And suddenly she became aware that Michael was in the room. He had come in very quietly and was standing before the fire behind her. She gave him a quick look and said:

"I've had Aubrey Greene here about a model you sent him, and Holly—Mrs. Val Dartie—she said she'd seen you. Oh! and father's brought us this. Isn't it perfect?"

Michael did not speak.

"Anything the matter, Michael?"

"No, nothing." He went up to the monkey. From behind him now Fleur searched his profile. Instinct told her of a change. Had he, after all, seen her going to Wilfrid's—coming away?

"Some monkey!" he said. "By the way, have you any spare clothes you could give the wife of a poor snipe—nothing too swell?"

She answered mechanically: "Yes, of course!" while her brain worked furiously.

"Would you put them out, then? I'm going to make up a bunch for him myself—they could go together."

Yes! He was quite unlike himself, as if the spring in him had run down. A sort of *malaise* overcame her. Michael not cheerful! It was like the fire going out on a cold day. And, perhaps for the first time, she was conscious that his cheerfulness was of real importance to her. She watched him pick up Ting-a-ling and sit down. And going up behind him, she bent over till her hair was against his cheek. Instead of rubbing his cheek on hers, he sat quite still, and her heart misgave her.

"What is it?" she said, coaxing.

"Nothing!"

She took hold of his ears.

"But there is. I suppose you know somehow that I went to see Wilfrid."

He said stonily: "Why not?"

She let go, and stood up straight.

"It was only to tell him that I couldn't see him again." The half-truth seemed to her the whole.

He suddenly looked up, a quiver went over his face; he took her hand.

"It's all right, Fleur. You must do what you like, you know. That's only fair. I had too much lunch."

Fleur withdrew to the middle of the room.

"You're rather an angel," she said slowly, and went out.

Up-stairs she looked out garments, confused in her soul.

Chapter Six

MICHAEL GETS "WHAT-FOR"

❧———◆———❧

AFTER his Green Street quest Michael had wavered back down Piccadilly, and, obeying one of those impulses which make people hang around the centres of disturbance, on to Cork Street. He stood for a minute at the mouth of Wilfrid's backwater.

'No,' he thought, at last, 'ten to one he isn't in; and if he is, twenty to one that I get any change except bad change!'

He was moving slowly on to Bond Street, when a little light lady, coming from the backwater, and reading as she went, ran into him from behind.

"Why don't you look where you're going! Oh! You? Aren't you the young man who married Fleur Forsyte? I'm her cousin, June. I thought I saw her just now." She waved a hand which held a catalogue with a gesture like the flirt of a bird's wing. "Opposite my gallery. She went into a house, or I should have spoken to her—I'd like to have seen her again."

Into a house! Michael dived for his cigarette-case. Hard-grasping it, he looked up. The little lady's blue eyes were sweeping from side to side of his face with a searching candour.

"Are you happy together?" she said.

A cold sweat broke out on his forehead. A sense of general derangement afflicted him—hers, and his own.

"I beg your pardon?" he gasped.

"I hope you are. She ought to have married my little brother—but I hope you are. She's a pretty child."

In the midst of a dull sense of stunning blows, it staggered him that she seemed quite unconscious of inflicting them. He heard his teeth gritting, and said dully: "Your little brother, who was he?"

"What! Jon—didn't you know Jon? He was too young, of course, and so was she. But they were head over—the family feud stopped that. Well! it's all past. I was at your wedding. I hope you're happy. Have you seen the Claud Brains show at my gallery? He's a genius. I was going to have a bun in here; will you join me? You ought to know his work."

She had paused at the door of a confectioner's. Michael put his hand on his chest.

"Thank you," he said, "I have just had a bun—two, in fact. Excuse me!"

The little lady grasped his other hand.

"Well, good-bye, young man! Glad to have met you. You're not a beauty, but I like your face. Remember me to that child. You should go and see Claud Brains. He's a real genius."

Stock-still before the door, he watched her turn and enter, with a scattered motion, as of flying, and a disturbance among those seated in the pastry-cook's. Then he moved on, the cigarette unlighted in his mouth, dazed, as a boxer from a blow which knocks him sideways, and another which knocks him straight again.

Fleur visiting Wilfrid—at this moment in his rooms up there—in his arms, perhaps! He groaned. A well-fed young man in a new hat skipped at the sound. Never! He could never stick that! He would have to clear out! He had believed Fleur honest! A double life! The night before last she had smiled on him. Oh! God! He dashed across into Green Park. Why hadn't he stood still and let something go over him? And that lunatic's little brother —John—family feud! Himself—a *pis aller,* then—taken

ness to give the consideration; Danby's to turn the affair down with the words: "Write him (or her) a civil letter, say we were greatly interested, regret we do not see our way—hope to have the privilege of considering next effort, and so forth. What!"

He turned up his reading-lamp and pulled out a manuscript he had already begun.

"No retreat, no retreat; they must conquer or die who have
    no retreat;
  No retreat, no retreat; they must conquer or die who have
    no retreat!"

The black footmen's refrain from "Polly" was all that happened in his mind. Dash it! He must read the thing! Somehow he finished the chapter. He remembered now. The manuscript was all about a man who, when he was a boy, had been so greatly impressed by the sight of a maid-servant changing her clothes in a room over the way, that his married life was a continual struggle not to be unfaithful with his wife's maids. They had just discovered his complex, and he was going to have it out. The rest of the manuscript no doubt would show how that was done. It went most conscientiously into all those precise bodily details which it was now so timorous and Victorian to leave out. Genuine piece of work, and waste of time to go on with it! Old Danby—Freud bored him stiff; and for once Michael did not mind old Danby being in the right. He put the thing back into the drawer. Seven o'clock! Tell Fleur what he had been told about that cousin? Why? Nothing could mend *that!* If only she were speaking the truth about Wilfrid! He went to the window —stars above, and stripes below, stripes of courtyard and back garden. "No retreat, no retreat; they must conquer or die who have no retreat!"

A voice said:

"When will your father be up?"

Old Forsyte! Lord! Lord!

"To-morrow, I believe, sir. Come in! You don't know my den, I think."

"No," said Soames. "Snug! Caricatures. You go in for them—poor stuff!"

"But not modern, sir—a revived art."

"Queering your neighbours—I never cared for them. They only flourish when the world's in a mess and people have given up looking straight before them."

"By Jove!" said Michael; "that's good. Won't you sit down, sir?"

Soames sat down, crossing his knees in his accustomed manner. Slim, grey, close—a sealed book, neatly bound! What was *his* complex? Whatever it was, he had never had it out. One could not even imagine the operation.

"I shan't take away my Goya," he said very unexpectedly; "consider it Fleur's. In fact, if I only knew you were interested in the future, I should make more provision. In my opinion death duties will be prohibitive in a few years' time."

Michael frowned. "I'd like you to know, sir, once for all, that what you do for Fleur, you do for Fleur. I can be Epicurus whenever I like—bread, and on feast days a little bit of cheese."

Soames looked up with shrewdness in his glance. "I know that," he said, "I always knew it."

Michael bowed.

"With this Land depression your father's hard hit, I should think."

"Well, he talks of being on the look out for soap or cars; but I shouldn't be surprised if he mortgages again and lingers on."

"A title without a place," said Soames, "is not natural. He'd better wait for me to go, if I leave anything, that is. But listen to me: I've been thinking. Aren't you happy together, you two, that you don't have children?"

Michael hesitated.

"I don't think," he said slowly, "that we have ever had a scrap, or anything like it. I have been—I am—terribly fond of her, but you have known better than I that I only picked up the pieces."

"Who told you that?"

"To-day—Miss June Forsyte."

"*That* woman!" said Soames. "She can't keep her foot out of anything. A boy and girl affair—over months before you married."

"But deep, sir," said Michael gently.

"Deep—who knows at that age? Deep?" Soames paused: "You're a good fellow—I always knew. Be patient—take a long view."

"Yes, sir," said Michael, very still in his chair, "if I can."

"She's everything to me," muttered Soames abruptly.

"And to me—which doesn't make it easier."

The line between Soames' brows deepened.

"Perhaps not. But hold on! As gently as you like, but hold on! She's young. She'll flutter about; there's nothing in it."

'Does he know about the other thing?' thought Michael.

"I have my own worries," went on Soames, "but they're nothing to what I should feel if anything went wrong with her."

Michael felt a twinge of sympathy, unusual towards that self-contained grey figure.

"I shall try my best," he said quietly; "but I'm not naturally Solomon at six stone seven."

"I'm not so sure," said Soames, "I'm not so sure. Anyway, a child—well, a child would be—a—sort of insur——" He baulked, the word was not precisely——!

Michael froze.

"As to that, I can't say anything."

Soames got up.

"No," he said, wistfully, "I suppose not. It's time to dress."

To dress—to dine, and if to dine, to sleep—to sleep, to dream! And then what dreams might come!

On the way to his dressing-room Michael encountered Coaker; the man's face was long.

"What's up, Coaker?"

"The little dog, sir, has been sick in the drawing-room."

"The deuce he has!"

"Yes, sir; it appears that some one left him there alone.

He makes himself felt, sir. I always say: He's an important little dog. . . ."

During dinner, as if visited by remorse for having given them advice and two pictures worth some thousands of pounds, Soames pitched a tale like those of James in his palmy days. He spoke of the French—the fall of the mark—the rise in Consols—the obstinacy of Dumetrius, the picture-dealer, over a Constable skyscrape which Soames wanted and Dumetrius did not, but to which the fellow held on just for the sake of a price which Soames did not mean to pay. He spoke of the trouble which he foresaw with the United States over their precious Prohibition. They were a headstrong lot. They took up a thing and ran their heads against a stone wall. He himself had never drunk anything to speak of, but he liked to feel that he could. The Americans liked to feel that he couldn't, that was tyranny. They were overbearing. He shouldn't be surprised if everybody took to drinking over there. As to the League of Nations, a man that morning had palavered it up. That cock wouldn't fight—spend money, and arrange things which would have arranged themselves, but as for anything important, such as abolishing Bolshevism, or poison gas, they never would, and to pretend it was all-me-eye-and-Betty-Martin. It was almost a record for one habitually taciturn, and deeply useful to two young people only anxious that he should continue to talk, so that they might think of other things. The conduct of Ting-a-ling was the sole other subject of consideration. Fleur thought it due to the copper floor. Soames that he must have picked up something in the Square—dogs were always picking things up. Michael suggested that it was just Chinese—a protest against there being nobody to watch his self-sufficiency. In China there were four hundred million people to watch each other being self-sufficient. What would one expect of a Chinaman suddenly placed in the Gobi Desert? He would certainly be sick.

"No retreat, no retreat; they must conquer or die who have no retreat!"

When Fleur left them, both felt that they could not so

soon again bear each other's company, and Soames said: "I've got some figures to attend to—I'll go to my room."

Michael stood up. "Wouldn't you like my den, sir?"

"No," said Soames, "I must concentrate. Say goodnight to Fleur for me."

Michael remained smoking above the porcelain effigies of Spanish fruits. That white monkey couldn't eat those and throw away the rinds! Would the fruits of his life be porcelain in future? Live in the same house with Fleur, estranged? Live with Fleur as now, feeling a stranger, even an unwelcome stranger? Clear out, and join the Air Force, or the "Save the Children" corps? Which of the three courses was least to be deplored? The ash of his cigar grew long, dropped incontinent, and grew again; the porcelain fruits mocked him with their sheen and glow; Coaker put his head in and took it away again. (The Governor had got the hump—good sort, the Governor!) Decision waited for him, somewhere, somewhen— Fleur's, not his own. His mind was too miserable and disconcerted to be known; but she would know hers. She had the information which alone made decision possible about Wilfrid, that cousin, her own actions and feelings. Yes, decision would come, and would it matter in a world where pity was punk and only a Chinese philosophy of any use?

But not be sick in the drawing-room, try and keep one's end up, even if there were no one to see one being important! . . .

He had been asleep and it was dark, or all but, in his bed-dressing-room. Something white by his bed. A fragrant faint warmth close to him; a voice saying low: "It's only me. Let me come in your bed, Michael." Like a child— like a child! Michael reached out his arms. The whiteness and the warmth came into them. Curls smothered his mouth, the voice said in his ear: "I wouldn't have come, would I, if there'd—if there'd been anything?" Michael's heart, wild, confused, beat against hers.

Chapter Seven

THE ALTOGETHER

———◆———

TONY BICKET, replete, was in vein that fine afternoon; his balloons left him freely, and he started
for home in the mood of a conqueror.

Victorine, too, had colour in her cheeks. She required
the story of his afternoon with the story of hers. A false
tale for a true—no word of Danby and Winter, the gentleman with the sliding smile, of the Grand Marnier, or "the
altogether." She had no compunction. It was her secret,
her surprise; if, by sitting in or out of "the altogether,"
not yet decided, she could make their passage money—
well, she should tell him she had won it on a horse. That
night she asked:

"Am I so very thin, Tony?" more than once. "I do so
want to get fat."

Bicket, still troubled that she had not shared that lunch,
patted her tenderly, and said he would soon have her as
fat as butter—he did not explain how.

They dreamed together of blue butterflies, and awoke
to chilly gaslight and a breakfast of cocoa and bread-and-
butter. Fog! Bicket was swallowed up before the eyes
of Victorine ten yards from the door. She returned to
the bedroom with anger in her heart. Who would buy
balloons in a fog? She would do anything rather than let

Tony go on standing out there all the choking days! Undressing again, she washed herself intensively, in case
——! She had not long finished when her landlady announced the presence of a messenger boy. He bore an enormous parcel entitled "Mr. Bicket."

There was a note inside. She read:

"DEAR BICKET,—Here are the togs. Hope they'll be useful.—
"Yours,
MICHAEL MONT."

In a voice that trembled she said to the boy:

"Thank you, it's O.K. Here's twopence."

When his rich whistle was heard writhing into the fog, she flung herself down before the "togs" in ecstasy. The sexes were divided by tissue paper. A blue suit, a velour hat, some brown shoes, three pairs of socks with two holes in them, four shirts only a little frayed at the cuffs, two black-and-white ties, six collars, not too new, some handkerchiefs, two vests beautifully thick, two pairs of pants, and a brown overcoat with a belt and just two or three nice little stains. She held the blue suit up against her arms and legs, the trousers and sleeves would only need taking-in about two inches. She piled them in a pyramid, and turned with awe to the spoil beneath the tissue paper. A brown knitted frock with little clear yellow buttons—unsoiled, uncreased. How could anybody spare a thing like that! A brown velvet toque with a little tuft of goldeny-brown feathers. She put it on. A pair of pink stays ever so little faded, with only three inches of bone above the waist, and five inches of bone below, pink silk ribbons, and suspenders—a perfect dream. She could not resist putting them on also. Two pairs of brown stockings; brown shoes; two combinations, a knitted camisole. A white silk jumper with a hole in one sleeve, a skirt of lilac linen that had gone a little in the wash; a pair of pallid pink silk pants; and underneath them all an almost black-brown coat, long and warm and cosy, with great jet buttons, and in the pocket six small handkerchiefs. She took a deep breath of sweetness—geranium!

Her mind leaped forward. Clothed, trousseaued, fitted out—blue butterflies—the sun! Only the money for the tickets wanting. And suddenly she saw herself with nothing on standing before the gentleman with sliding eyes. Who cared! The money!

For the rest of the morning she worked feverishly, shortening for Tony, mending the holes in his socks, turning the fray of his cuffs. She ate a biscuit, drank another cup of cocoa—it was fattening, and went for the hole in the white silk jumper. One o'clock. In panic she stripped once more, put on a new combination, pair of stockings, and the stays, then paused in superstition. No! Her own dress and hat—like yesterday! Keep the rest until——! She hastened to her 'bus, overcome alternately by heat and cold. Perhaps he would give her another glass of that lovely stuff. If only she could go swimmy and not care for anything!

She reached the studio as two o'clock was striking, and knocked. It was lovely and warm in there, much warmer than yesterday, and the significance of this struck her suddenly. In front of the fire was a lady with a little dog.

"Miss Collins—Mrs. Michael Mont; she's lending us her Peke, Miss Collins."

The lady—only her own age, and ever so pretty—held out her hand. Geranium! This, then was she whose clothes——!

She took the hand, but could not speak. If this lady were going to stay, it would be utterly impossible. Before her—so pretty, so beautifully covered—oh! no!

"Now, Ting, be good, and as amusing as you can. Good-bye, Aubrey! Good luck to the picture! Good-bye, Miss Collins; it ought to be wonderful."

Gone! The scent of geranium fading; the little dog snuffling at the door. The sliding gentleman had two glasses in his hands.

'Ah!' thought Victorine, and drank hers at a gulp.

"Now, Miss Collins, you don't mind, do you? You'll find everything in there. It's really nothing. I shall want you lying on your face just here with your elbows on the ground and your head up and a little turned this way;

your hair as loose as it can be, and your eyes looking at this bone. You must imagine that it's a faun or some other bit of all right. The dog'll help you when he settles down to it. F-a-u-n, you know, not f-a-w-n."

"Yes," said Victorine faintly.

"Have another little tot?"

"Oh, please."

He brought it.

"I quite understand; but you know, really, it's absurd. You wouldn't mind with a doctor. That's right. Look here, I'll put this little cow-bell on the ground. When you're in position, give it a tinkle, and I'll come out. That'll help you."

Victorine murmured:

"You *are* kind."

"Not at all—it's natural. Now will you start in? The light won't last for ever. Fifteen bob a day, we said."

Victorine saw him slide away behind a screen, and looked at the little cow-bell. Fifteen bob! And fifteen bob! And fifteen bob! Many, many fifteen bobs before——! But not more times of sitting than of Tony's standing, from foot to foot, offering balloons. And as if wound up by that thought, she moved like clockwork off the dais, into the model's room. Cosy in there, too; warm, a green silk garment thrown on a chair. She took off her dress. The beauty of the pink stays struck her afresh. Perhaps the gentleman would like—no, that would be even worse——! A noise reached her—from Ting-a-ling complaining of solitude. If she delayed, she never would——! Stripping hastily, she stood looking at herself in a glass. If only that slim ivory-white image could move out on to the dais and she could stay here! Oh! It was awful—awful! She couldn't—no! she couldn't. She caught up her final garment again. Fifteen bob! But fifteen bob! Before her eyes, wild and mournful, came a vision: Of a huge dome, and a tiny Tony, with little, little balloons in a hand held out! Something cold and steely formed over her heart as icicles form on a window. If that was all they would do for him, she would do better! She dropped the garment; and, confused, numb, stepped forth in the "altogether." Ting-a-ling growled at her above his bone. She reached the cow-bell and lay down on her face as she had been told, with feet in the air, crossed. Resting her chin on one hand, she wagged the bell. It made a sound like no bell she had ever heard; and the little dog barked —he did look funny!

"Perfect, Miss Collins! Hold that!"

Fifteen bob! and fifteen bob!

"Just point those left toes a bit more. That's right! the flesh tone's perfect! My God, why must one walk before one runs! Drawing's a bore, Miss Collins; one ought to draw with a brush only; a sculptor draws with a chisel, at least when he's a Michelangelo. How old are you?"

"Twenty-one," came from lips that seemed to Victorine quite far away.

"I'm thirty-two. They say our generation was born so old that it can never get any older. Without illusions. Well! I never had any beliefs that I can remember. Had you?"

Victorine's wits and senses were astray, but it did not matter, for he was rattling on:

"We don't even believe in our ancestors. All the same, we're beginning to copy them again. D'you know a book called 'The Sobbing Turtle' that's made such a fuss?— sheer Sterne, very well done; but sheer Sterne, and the author's tongue in his cheek. That's it in a nut-shell, Miss Collins—our tongues are in our cheeks—bad sign. Never mind; I'm going to out-Piero Cosimo with this. Your head an inch higher, and that curl out of your eye, please. Thanks! Hold that! By the way, have you Italian blood? What was your mother's name, for instance?"

"Brown."

"Ah! You can never tell with Browns. It may have been Brune—or Bruno—but very likely she was Iberian. Probably all the inhabitants of Britain left alive by the Saxons were called Brown. As a fact, that's all tosh, though. Going back to Edward the Confessor, Miss Collins—a mere thirty generations—we each of us have close on a thousand million ancestors, and the population of this island was then well under a million. We're as inbred as racehorses, but not so nice to look at, are we? I assure you, Miss Collins, you're something to be grateful for. So is Mrs. Mont. Isn't she pretty? Look at that dog?"

Ting-a-ling, indeed, with forelegs braced, and wrinkled nose, was glaring, as if under the impression that Victorine was another bone.

"He's funny," she said, and again her voice sounded far away. Would Mrs. Mont lie here if he'd asked her? *She* would look pretty! But *she* didn't need the fifteen bob!

"Comfortable in that position?"

In alarm, she murmured:

"Oh! yes, thank you!"

"Warm enough?"

"Oh! yes, thank you!"

"That's good. Just a little higher with the head."

Slowly in Victorine the sense of the dreadfully unusual faded. Tony should never know. If he never knew, he couldn't care. She could lie like this all day—fifteen bob, and fifteen bob! It was easy. She watched the quick, slim fingers moving, the blue smoke rising from the cigarette. She watched the little dog.

"Like a rest? You left your gown; I'll get it for you."

In that green silk gown, beautifully padded, she sat up, with her feet on the floor over the dais edge.

"Cigarette? I'm going to make some Turkish coffee. You'd better walk about."

Victorine obeyed.

"You're out of a dream, Miss Collins. I shall have to do a Mathew Maris of you in that gown."

The coffee, like none she had ever tasted, gave her a sense of well-being. She said:

"It's not like coffee."

Aubrey Greene threw up his hands.

"You have said it. The British are a great race—nothing will ever do them in. If they could be destroyed, they must long ago have perished of their coffee. Have some more?"

"Please," said Victorine. There was such a little in the cup.

"Ready, again?"

She lay down, and let the gown drop off.

"That's right! Leave it there—you're lying in long grass, and the green helps me. Pity it's winter; I'd have hired a glade."

Lying in long grass—flowers, too, perhaps. She did love flowers. As a little girl she used to lie in the grass, and make daisy-chains, in the field at the back of her grandmother's lodge at Norbiton. Her grandmother kept the lodge. Every year, for a fortnight, she had gone down there—she had liked the country ever so. Only she had always had something on. It would be nicer with nothing. Were there flowers in Central Australia? With butterflies there must be! In the sun—she and Tony—like the Garden of Eden! ...

"Thank you, that's all for to-day. Half a day—ten bob. To-morrow at eleven. You're a first-rate sitter, Miss Collins."

Putting on the pink stays, Victorine had a feeling of elation. She had done it! Tony should never know! The thought that he never would gave her pleasure. And once more divested of the "altogether," she came forth.

Aubrey Greene was standing before his handiwork.

"Not yet, Miss Collins," he said; "I don't want to depress you. That hip-bone's too high. We'll put it right to-morrow. Forgive my hand, it's all chalk. *Au revoir!* Eleven o'clock. And we shan't need this chap. No, you don't!"

For Ting-a-ling was showing signs of accompanying the larger bone. Victorine passed out smiling.

Chapter Eight

SOAMES TAKES THE MATTER UP

SOAMES had concentrated, sitting before the fire in his bedroom till Big Ben struck twelve. His reflections sum-totalled in a decision to talk it over with "Old Mont" after all. Though light-brained, the fellow was a gentleman, and the matter delicate. He got into bed and slept, but awoke at half-past two. There it was! '*I won't* think of it,' he thought; and instantly began to. In a long life of dealings with money, he had never had such an experience. Perfectly straightforward conformity with the law—itself so often far from perfectly straightforward—had been the *sine qua non* of his career. Honesty, they said, was the best policy. But was it anything else? A perfectly honest man couldn't keep out of a perfect penitentiary for a week. But then a perfect penitentiary had no relation to prison, or the Bankruptcy Court. The business of working honesty was to keep out of those two institutions. And so far he had never had any difficulty. What, besides the drawing of fees and the drinking of tea, were the duties of a director? That was the point. And how far, if he failed in them, was he liable? It was a director's duty to be perfectly straightforward. But if a director were perfectly straightforward, he couldn't be a director. That was clear. In the first place, he would have to tell his shareholders that he didn't anything like earn his fees. For what did he do on his Boards? Well, he sat and signed his name and talked a little, and passed that which the general trend of business decided must be passed. Did he initiate? Once in a blue moon. Did he calculate? No, he read calculations. Did he check payments out and in? No, the auditors did that. There was policy! A comforting word, but—to be perfectly straightforward—a director's chief business was to let the existing policy alone. Take his own case! If he had done his duty, he would have stopped this foreign insurance business which he had instinctively distrusted the moment he heard of it—within a month of sitting on the Board, or, having failed in doing so, resigned his seat. But he had not. Things had been looking better! It was not the moment, and so forth! If he had done his duty as a perfectly straightforward director, indeed, he would never have become a director of the P.P.R.S., because he would have looked into the policy of the Society much more closely than he had before accepting a position on the Board. But what with the names, and the prestige, and not looking a gift horse too closely in the mouth—there it had been! To be perfectly straightforward, he ought now to be circularising the shareholders, saying: "My *laissez-faire* has cost you two hundred odd thousand pounds. I have lodged this amount in the hands of trustees for your benefit, and am suing the rest of the directors for their quotas of the amount." But he was not proposing to do so, because—well—because it wasn't done, and the other directors wouldn't like it. In sum: You waited till the shareholders found out the mess, and you hoped they wouldn't. In fact, just like a Government, you confused the issues, and made the best case you could for yourselves. With a sense of comfort Soames thought of Ireland: The late Government had let the country in for all that mess in Ireland, and at the end taken credit for putting an end to what need never have been! The Peace, too, and the Air Force, and Agriculture, and Egypt—the five most important issues they'd had to deal with—they had put the chestnuts into the fire in every case! But had they confessed to it? Not they. One didn't confess. One said: "The question of policy made it imperative at the time." Or, better still, one said nothing; and trusted to the British character. With his chin resting on the sheet, Soames felt a momentary relief. The late Government weren't sweating into *their* sheets—not they —he was convinced of it! Fixing his eyes on the dying embers in the grate, he reflected on the inequalities and injustices of existence. Look at the chaps in politics and business, whose whole lives were passed in skating on thin ice, and getting knighted for it. They never turned a hair. And look at himself, for the first time in forty years on thin ice, and suffering confoundedly. There was a perfect cult of hoodwinking the public, a perfect cult of avoiding the consequences of administrative acts; and here was he, a man of the world, a man of the law, ignorant of those cults, and—and glad of it. From engrained caution and a certain pride, which had in it a touch of the fine, Soames shrank from that coarse-grained standard of honesty which conducted the affairs of the British public. In anything that touched money he was, he always had been, stiff-necked, stiff-kneed. Money was money, a pound a pound, and there was no way of pretending it wasn't and keeping your self-respect. He got up, drank some water, took a number of deep breaths, and stamped his feet. Who was it said the other day that nothing had ever lost him five minutes' sleep? The fellow must have the circulation of an ox, or the gift of Baron Munchausen. He took up a book. But his mind would only turn over and over the realisable value of his resources. Apart from his pictures, he decided that he could not be worth less than two hundred and fifty thousand pounds, and there was only Fleur—and she already provided for more or less. His wife had her settlement, and could live on it perfectly well in France. As for himself—what did he care? A room at his club near Fleur—he would be just as happy, perhaps happier! And suddenly he found that he had reached a way out of his disturbance and anxiety. By imagining the farfetched, by facing the loss of his wealth, he had exorcised the demon. The book, "The

Sobbing Turtle," of which he had not read one word, dropped from his hand; he slept. . . .

His meeting with "Old Mont" took place at 'Snooks'' directly after lunch. The tape in the hall, at which he glanced on going in, recorded a further heavy drop in the mark. Just as he thought: The thing was getting valueless!

Sitting there, sipping coffee, the baronet looked to Soames almost offensively spry. Two to one he had realised nothing! 'Well!' thought Soames, 'as old Uncle Jolyon used to say, I shall astonish his weak nerves!'

And without preamble he began.

"How are you, Mont? This mark's valueless. You realise we've lost the P.P.R.S. about a quarter of a million by that precious foreign policy of Elderson's. I'm not sure an action won't lie against us for taking unjustifiable risk. But what I've come to see you about is this." He retailed the interview with the clerk, Butterfield, watching the eyebrows of his listener, and finished with the words: "What do you say?"

Sir Lawrence, whose foot was jerking his whole body, fixed his monocle.

"Hallucination, my dear Forsyte! I've known Elderson all my life. We were at Winchester together."

Again! Again! Oh! Lord! Soames said slowly:

"You can't tell from that. A man who was at Marlborough with me ran away with his mess fund and his colonel's wife, and made a fortune in Chile out of canned tomatoes. The point is this: If the young man's story's true, we're in the hands of a bad hat. It won't do, Mont. Will you tackle him, and see what he says to it? You wouldn't like a story of that sort about yourself. Shall we both go?"

"Yes," said Sir Lawrence, suddenly. "You're right. We'll both go, Forsyte. I don't like it, but we'll both go. He ought to hear it."

"Now?"

"Now."

With solemnity they assumed top hats, and issued.

"I think, Forsyte, we'll take a taxi."

"Yes," said Soames.

The cab ground its way slowly past the lions, then dashed on down to the Embankment. Side by side its occupants held their noses steadily before them.

"He was shooting with me a month ago," said Sir Lawrence. "Do you know the hymn 'O God, our help in ages past'? It's very fine, Forsyte."

Soames did not answer. The fellow was beginning to tittup!

"We had it that Sunday," went on Sir Lawrence. "Elderson used to have a fine voice—sang solos. It's a fog-horn now, but a good delivery still." He gave his little whinnying laugh.

'Is it possible,' thought Soames, 'for this chap to be serious?' and he said:

"If we find this is true of Elderson, and conceal it, we could all be put in the dock."

Sir Lawrence refixed his monocle. "The deuce!" he said.

"Will you do the talking," said Soames, "or shall I?"

"I think you had better, Forsyte; ought we to have the young man in?"

"Wait and see," said Soames.

They ascended to the offices of the P.P.R.S. and entered the Board Room. There was no fire, the long table was ungarnished; an old clerk, creeping about like a fly on a pane, was filling inkstands out of a magnum.

Soames addressed him:

"Ask the manager to be so kind as to come and see Sir Lawrence Mont and Mr. Forsyte."

The old clerk blinked, put down the magnum, and went out.

"Now," said Soames in a low voice, "we must keep our heads. He'll deny it, of course."

"I should hope so, Forsyte; I should hope so. Elderson's a gentleman."

"No liar like a gentleman," muttered Soames, below his breath.

After that they stood in their overcoats before the empty grate, staring at their top hats placed side by side on the table.

"One minute!" said Soames, suddenly, and crossing the room, he opened a door opposite. There, as the young clerk had said, was a sort of lobby between Board Room and Manager's Room, with a door at the end into the main corridor. He stepped back, closed the door, and, rejoining Sir Lawrence, resumed his contemplation of the hats.

"Geography correct," he said with gloom.

The entrance of the manager was marked by Sir Lawrence's monocle dropping on to his coat-button with a tinkle. In cutaway black coat, clean-shaven, with grey eyes rather baggy underneath, a pink colour, every hair in place on a rather bald egg-shaped head, and lips alternately pouting, compressed, or smiling, the manager reminded Soames ridiculously of old Uncle Nicholas in his middle period. Uncle Nick was a clever fellow—"cleverest man in London," some one had called him—but none had ever impugned his honesty. A pang of doubt and disinclination went through Soames. This seemed a monstrous thing to have to put to a man of his own age and breeding. But young Butterfield's eyes—so honest and doglike! Invent a thing like that—was it possible? He said abruptly:

"Is that door shut?"

"Yes; do you feel a draught?" said the manager. "Would you like a fire?"

"No, thank you," said Soames. "The fact is, Mr. Elderson, a young man in this office came to me yesterday with a very queer story. Mont and I think you should hear it."

Accustomed to watching people's eyes, Soames had the impression of a film (such as passes over the eyes of parrots) passing over the eyes of the manager. It was gone at once, if, indeed, it had ever been.

"By all means."

Steadily, with that power he had over his nerves when it came to a point, and almost word for word, Soames repeated a story which he had committed to heart in the watches of the night. He concluded with:

"You'd like him in, no doubt. His name is Butterfield."

During the recital Sir Lawrence had done nothing but scrutinise his finger-nails; he now said:

"You had to be told, Elderson."

"Naturally."

The manager was crossing to the bell. The pink in his cheeks looked harder; his teeth showed, they had a pointed look.

"Ask Mr. Butterfield to come here."

There followed a minute of elaborate inattention to each other. Then the young man came in, neat, commonplace, with his eyes on the manager's face. Soames had a moment of compunction. This young fellow held his life in his hands, as it were—one of the great army who made their living out of self-suppression and respectability, with a hundred ready to step into his shoes at his first slip. What was that old tag of the provincial actor's declamation—at which old Uncle Jolyon used to cackle so? "Like a pale martyr with his shirt on fire."

"So, Mr. Butterfield, you have been good enough to exercise your imagination in my regard."

"No, sir."

"You stick to this fantastic story of eavesdropping?"

"Yes, sir."

"We have no further use for your services then. Good morning!"

The young man's eyes, doglike, sought the face of Soames; a string twitched in his throat, his lips moved without a sound. He turned and went out.

"So much for that," said the manager's voice; *"he'll* never get another job."

The venom in those words affected Soames like the smell of Russian fat. At the same moment he had the feeling: This wants thinking out. Only if innocent, or guilty and utterly resolved, would Elderson have been so drastic. Which was he?

The manager went on:

"I thank you for drawing my attention to the matter, gentlemen. I have had my eye on that young man for some time. A bad hat all round."

Soames said glumly:

"What do you make out he had to gain?"

"Foresaw dismissal, and thought he would get in first."

"I see," said Soames. But he did not. His mind was back in his own office with Gradman rubbing his nose, shaking his grey head, and Butterfield's: "No, sir, I've nothing against Mr. Elderson, and he's nothing against me."

'I shall require to know more about that young man,' he thought.

The manager's voice again cut through.

"I've been thinking over what you said yesterday, Mr. Forsyte, about an action lying against the Board for negligence. There's nothing in that; our policy has been fully disclosed to the shareholders at two general meetings, and has passed without comment. The shareholders are just as responsible as the Board."

"H'm!" said Soames, and took up his hat. "Are you coming, Mont?"

As if summoned from a long distance, Sir Lawrence galvanitically refixed his monocle.

"It's been very distasteful," he said; "you must forgive us, Elderson. You had to be told. I don't think that young man can be quite all there—he had a peculiar look; but we can't have this sort of thing, of course. Good-bye, Elderson."

Placing their hats on their heads simultaneously the two walked out. They walked some way without speaking. Then Sir Lawrence said:

"Butterfield? My brother-in-law has a head gardener called Butterfield—quite a good fellow. Ought we to look into that young man, Forsyte?"

"Yes," said Soames, "leave him to me."

"I shall be very glad to. The fact is, when one has been at school with a man, one has a feeling, don't you know."

Soames gave vent to a sudden outburst.

"You can't trust any one nowadays, it seems to me," he said. "It comes of—well, I don't know what it comes of. But I've not done with this matter yet."

is young man into my own firm for obvious
I can trust you."

ouched his forelock.

ly bucked, sir. Protection of the poor—some
I'll see him to-night, and let you know what
."

odded. 'Good Gad!' he thought; 'what jar-

view served Michael the good turn of taking
s off himself. Temperamentally he sided al-
the young man Butterfield; and, lighting a
went into the card-room. Sitting on the high
was impressed—the room was square, and
ere three square card tables, set askew to the
hree triangles of card players.

thought Michael, 'the fourth player sat under
he pattern would be complete. It's having the
loose that spoils the cubes.' And with some-
hrill he saw that Elderson was a fourth player!
impassive, he was engaged in applying a knife
of a cigar. Gosh! what sealed books faces were!
pages and pages of private thoughts, inter-
es, fancies, passions, hopes and fears; and
death—splosh!—and a creature wiped out,
n a wall, and nobody any more could see its
mechanism working away for its own ends in
vacy and its own importance; nobody any more
late on whether it was a clean or a dirty little
. Hard to tell! They ran in all shapes! Elder-
stance—was he a nasty mess, or just a lamb
o didn't look it? 'Somehow,' thought Michael,
a womaniser. Now why?' He spread his hands
him to the fire, rubbing them together like a
s been in treacle. If one couldn't tell what
g in the mind of one's own wife in one's own
on earth could one tell anything from the face
er, and he one of the closest bits of mechanism
ld—an English gentleman of business! If only
ke "The Idiot" or "The Brothers Karamazov,"
ody went about turning out their inmost hearts

Chapter Nine

SLEUTH

THE 'Hotch-potch' Club went back to the eighteen-
sixties. Founded and nicknamed by a posse of
young sparks, social and political, as a convenient place
in which to smoulder, while qualifying for the hearths of
'Snooks,' The Remove, The Wayfarers, Burton's, Ostrich
Feather, and other more permanent resorts, the Club had,
chiefly owing to a remarkable *chef* in its early days, acquired a stability and distinction of its own. It still, however, retained a certain resemblance to its nickname, and
this was its attraction to Michael—all sorts of people belonged. From Walter Nazing, and young semi-writers
and patrons of the stage, who went to Venice, and talked
of being amorous in gondolas, or of how so-and-so ought
to be made love to; from such to bottle-brushed demi-
generals, who had sat on courts-martial and shot men out
of hand for the momentary weaknesses of human nature;
from Wilfrid Desert (who never came there now) to
Maurice Elderson, in the card-room, he could meet them
all, and take the temperature of modernity. He was doing
this in the 'Hotch-potch' smoking-room, the late afternoon but one after Fleur had come into his bed, when he
was informed:

"A Mr. Forsyte, sir, in the hall for you. Not the member we had here many years before he died; his cousin, I think."

Conscious that his associates at the moment would not be his father-in-law's "dream", nor he theirs, Michael went out, and found Soames on the weighing machine.

"I don't vary," he said, looking up. "How's Fleur?"

"Very well, thank you, sir."

"I'm at Green Street. I stayed up about a young man. Have you any vacancy in your office for a clerk—used to figures. I want a job for him."

"Come in here, sir," said Michael, entering a small room.

Soames followed and looked round him.

"What do you call this?" he said.

"Well, we call it 'the grave'; it's nice and quiet. Will you have a sherry?"

"Sherry!" repeated Soames. "You young people think you've invented sherry; when I was a boy no one dreamed of dining without a glass of fine old sherry with his sweet. Sherry!"

"I quite believe you, sir. There really is nothing new. Venice, for instance—wasn't that the fashion, too; and knitting, and Royalties? It's all cyclic. Has your young man had the boot?"

Soames stared. "I know nothing about a boot. His name is Butterfield; he wants a job."

"That's frightfully rife; we get applications every day. I don't want to be swanky, but ours is a rather specialised business. It has to do with books."

"He strikes me as capable, orderly, and civil; I don't see what more you want in a clerk. He writes a good hand, and, so far as I can see, he tells the truth."

"That's important, of course," said Michael; "but is he a good liar as well? I mean, there's more likely to be something in the travelling line; selling special editions, and that kind of thing. Could you open up about him a bit? Anything human is to the good—I don't say old Danby would appreciate that, but he needn't know."

"H'm! Well—he—er—did his duty—quite against his

interest—in fact, it's ruination married and to have two childr

"Ho, ho! Jolly! If I got him he be doing his duty again, do

"I am serious," said Soames mind."

"Yes," said Michael, rumi such a case is to get him on Could I see him?"

"I told him to step round dinner. I thought you'd prefer before considering him for you

"Very thoughtful of you, s Don't you think I ought to confidence? I don't see how I into my mouth without, do you

Soames stared at his sor mouth was wide; for the *nth* certain liking and confidence; i

"Well," he said, going to that it was opaque, "this is m action, so for your own sake a it strictly to yourself"; and in facts.

"As I expected," he ended me again this morning. He is keep my hand on him. With make up my mind whether sides——" Soames hesitated; repulsive to him: "I—it seen getting three hundred and fifty.

"Dashed hard!" said Mic member here."

Soames looked with renew it still seemed opaque, and he you know him?"

"I've played bridge with taken some of the best off me—

"Ah!" said Soames—he ne

at the tops of their voices! If only club card-rooms had a dash of epilepsy in their composition! But—nothing! Nothing! The world was full of wonderful secrets which everybody kept to themselves without captions or close-ups to give them away!

A footman came in, looked at the fire, stood a moment expressionless as a stork, waiting for an order to ping out, staccato, through the hum, turned and went away.

Mechanism! Everywhere—mechanism! Devices for getting away from life so complete that there seemed no life to get away from.

'It's all,' he thought, 'awfully like a man sending a registered letter to himself. And perhaps it's just as well. Is "life" a good thing—is it? Do I want to see "life" raw again?'

Elderson was seated now, and Michael had a perfect view of the back of his head. It disclosed nothing.

'I'm no sleuth,' he thought; 'there ought to be something in the way he doesn't part his hair behind.' And, getting off the fender, he went home.

At dinner he caught one of his own looks at Fleur and didn't like it. Sleuth! And yet how not try to know what were the real thoughts and feelings of one who held his heart, like an accordion, and made it squeak and groan at pleasure!

"I saw the model you sent Aubrey yesterday," she said. "She didn't say anything about the clothes, but she looked ever so! What a face, Michael! Where did you come across her?"

Through Michael sped the thought: 'Could I make her jealous?' And he was shocked at it. A low-down thought —mean and ornery! "She blew in," he said. "Wife of a little packer we had who took to snooping—er—books. He sells balloons now; they want money badly."

"I see. Did you know that Aubrey's going to paint her in the nude?"

"Phew! No! I thought she'd look good on a wrapper. I say! Ought I to stop that?"

Fleur smiled. "It's more money and her look-out. It doesn't matter to you, does it?"

Again that thought; again the recoil from it!

"Only," he said, "that her husband is a decent little snipe for a snooper, and I don't want to be more sorry for him."

"She won't tell him, of course."

She said it so naturally, so simply, that the words disclosed a whole attitude of mind. One didn't tell one's mate what would tease the poor brute! He saw by the flutter of her white eyelids that she also realised the giveaway. Should he follow it up, tell her what June Forsyte had told him—have it all out—all out? But with what purpose—to what end? Would it change things, make her love him? Would it do anything but harass her a little more; and give him the sense that he had lost his wicket trying to drive her to the pavilion? No! Better adopt the principle of secrecy she had unwittingly declared her own, bite on it, and grin. He muttered:

"I'm afraid he'll find her rather thin."

Her eyes were bright and steady; and again he was worried by that low-down thought: 'Could he make her——?'

"I've only seen her once," he added, "and then she was dressed."

"I'm not jealous, Michael."

'No,' he thought, 'I wish to heaven you were!'

The words: "A young man called Butterfill to see you, sir," were like the turning of a key in a cell door.

In the hall the young man "called Butterfill" was engaged in staring at Ting-a-ling.

'Judging by his eyes,' thought Michael, 'he's more of a dog than that little Djinn!'

"Come up to my study," he said, "it's cold down here. My father-in-law tells me you want a job."

"Yes, sir," said the young man, following up the stairs.

"Take a pew," said Michael; "and a cigarette. Now then! I know all about the turmoil. From your moustache, you were in the war, I suppose, like me? As between fellow-sufferers: Is your story O.K.?"

"God's truth, sir; I only wish it wasn't. I'd nothing to gain and everything to lose. I'd have done better to hold my tongue. It's his word against mine, and here I am in the street. That was my first job since the war, so I can whistle for a reference."

"Wife and two children, I think?"

"Yes, and I've put them in the cart for the sake of my conscience! It's the last time I'll do that, I know. What did it matter to me, whether the Society was cheated? My wife's quite right, I was a fool, sir."

"Probably," said Michael. "Do you know anything about books?"

"Yes, sir; I'm a good book-keeper."

"Holy Moses! *Our* job is getting rid of them. My firm are publishers. We were thinking of putting on an extra traveller. Is your tongue persuasive?"

The young man smiled wanly.

"I don't know, sir."

"Well, look here," said Michael, carried away by the look in his eyes, "it's all a question of a certain patter. But, of course, that's got to be learned. I gather that you're not a reader."

"Well, sir, not a great reader."

"That, perhaps, is fortunate. What you would have to do is to impress on the poor brutes who sell books that every one of the books on your list—say about thirty-five—is necessary in large numbers to his business. It's lucky you've just chucked your conscience, because, as a matter of fact most of them won't be. I'm afraid there's nowhere you could go to get lessons in persuasion, but you can imagine the sort of thing, and if you like to come here for an hour or two this week, I'll put you wise about our authors, and ready you up to go before Peter."

"Before Peter, sir?"

"The Johnny with the keys; luckily it's Mr. Winter, not Mr. Danby; I believe I could get him to let you in for a month's trial."

"Sir, I'll try my very best. My wife knows about books, she could help me a lot. I can't tell you what I think of your kindness. The fact is, being out of a job has put the wind up me properly. I've not been able to save with two children; it's like the end of the world."

"Right-o, then! Come here to-morrow evening at nine, and I'll stuff you. I believe you've got the face for the job, if you can get the patter. Only one book in twenty is a necessity really, the rest are luxuries. Your stunt will be to make them believe the nineteen are necessaries, and the twentieth a luxury that they need. It's like food or clothes, or anything else in civilisation."

"Yes, sir, I quite understand."

"All right, then. Good-night, and good luck!"

Michael stood up and held out his hand. The young man took it with a queer reverential little bow. A minute later he was out in the street; and Michael in the hall was thinking: 'Pity is tripe! Clean forgot I was a sleuth!'

Chapter Ten

FACE

———◆———

WHEN Michael rose from the refectory table, Fleur had risen, too. Two days and more since she left Wilfrid's rooms, and she had not recovered zest. The rifling of the oyster Life, the garlanding of London's rarer flowers, which kept colour in her cheeks, seemed stale, unprofitable. Those three hours, when from shock off Cork Street she came straight to shocks in her own drawing-room, had dislocated her so that she had settled to nothing since. The wound re-opened by Holly had nearly healed again. Dead lion beside live donkey cuts but dim figure. But she could not get hold again of what? That was the trouble: What? For two whole days she had been trying. Michael was still strange, Wilfrid still lost, Jon still buried alive, and nothing seemed novel under the sun. The only object that gave her satisfaction during those two dreary, disillusioned days was the new white monkey. The more she looked at it, the more Chinese it seemed. It summed up the satirical truth of which she was perhaps subconscious, that all her little modern veerings and flutterings and rushings after the future showed that she believed in nothing but the past. The age had overdone it and must go back to ancestry for faith. Like a little bright fish out of a warm bay, making a splash in chill, strange waters, Fleur felt a subtle nostalgia.

In her Spanish room, alone with her own feelings, she stared at the porcelain fruits. They glowed, cold, un-eatable! She took one up. Meant for a passion fruit? Alas! Poor passion! She dropped it with a dull clink on to the pyramid, and shuddered a little. Had she blinded Michael with her kisses? Blinded him to—what? To her incapacity for passion?

'But I'm not incapable,' she thought; 'I'm not. Some day I'll show him; I'll show them all.' She looked up at "the Goya" hanging opposite. What gripping determina-tion in the painting—what intensity of life in the black eyes of a rather raddled dame! *She* would know what she wanted, and get it, too! No compromise and uncertainty there—no capering round life, wondering what it meant, and whether it was worth while, nothing but hard living for the sake of living!

Fleur put her hands where her flesh ended, and her dress began. Wasn't she as warm and firm—yes, and ten times as pretty, as that fine and evil-looking Spanish dame, with the black eyes and the wonderful lace? And, turning her back on the picture, she went into the hall. Michael's voice and another's! They were coming down! She slipped across into the drawing-room and took up the manuscript of a book of poems, on which she was to give Michael her opinion. She sat, not reading, wondering if he were coming in. She heard the front door close. No! He had gone out! A relief, yet chilling! Michael not warm and cheerful in the house—if that were to go on, it would be wearing. She curled herself up and tried to read. Dreary poems—free verse, blank, introspective, all about the author's inside! No lift, no lilt! Duds! She seemed to have read them a dozen times before. She lay quite still —listening to the click and flutter of the burning logs! If the light were out she might go to sleep. She turned it off, and came back to the settee. She could see herself sitting there, a picture in the firelight; see how lonely she looked, pretty, pathetic, with everything she wished for, and— nothing! Her lip curled. She could even see her own spoiled-child ingratitude. And what was worse, she could see herself seeing it—a triple-distilled modern, so subtly arranged in life-tight compartments that she could not be submerged. If only something would blow in out of the unkempt cold, out of the waste and wilderness of a London whose flowers she plucked. The firelight—soft, uncertain—searched out spots and corners of her Chinese room, as on a stage in one of those scenes, seductive and mysterious, where one waited, to the sound of tambourines, for the next moment of the plot. She reached out and took a cigarette. She could see herself lighting it, blowing out the smoke—her own half-curled fingers, her parted lips, her white rounded arm. She was decorative! Well, and wasn't that all that mattered? To be decorative, and make little decorations; to be pretty in a world that wasn't pretty! In "Copper Coin" there was a poem of a flicker-lit room, and a spoiled Columbine before the fire, and a Harlequin hovering without, like "the spectre of the rose." And sudddenly, without warning, Fleur's heart ached. It ached definitely, rather horribly, and, slipping down on to the floor before the fire, she snuggled her face against Ting-a-ling. The Chinese dog raised his head —his black eyes lurid in the glow.

He licked her cheek, and turned his nose away. Huf! Powder! But Fleur lay like the dead. And she saw herself lying—the curve of her hip, the chestnut glow in her short hair; she heard the steady beat of her heart. Get up! Go out! Do something! But what—what was worth doing? What had any meaning in it? She saw herself doing—extravagant things; nursing sick women; tending pale babies; making a speech in Parliament; riding a steeplechase; hoeing turnips in knickerbockers—decorative. And she lay perfectly still, bound by the filaments of her self-vision. So long as she saw herself she would do nothing—she knew it—for nothing would be worth doing! And it seemed to her, lying there so still, that not to see herself would be worse than anything. And she felt that to feel this was to acknowledge herself caged for ever.

Ting-a-ling growled, turning his nose towards the

windows. "In here," he seemed to say, "we are cosy; we think of the past. We have no use for anything outside. Kindly go away—whoever it is out there!" And again he growled—a low, continuous sound.

"What is it, Ting?"

Ting-a-ling rose on his fore-legs, with muzzle pointed at the window.

"Do you want your walk?"

"No," said the growl.

Fleur picked him up. "Don't be so silly!" And she went to the window. The curtains were closely drawn; rich, Chinese, lined, they excluded the night. Fleur made a chink with one hand, and started back. Against the pane was a face, the forehead pressed against the glass, the eyes closed, as if it had been there a long time. In the dark it seemed featureless, vaguely pale. She felt the dog's body stiffen under her arm—she felt his silence. Her heart pumped. It was ghastly—face without body.

Suddenly the forehead was withdrawn, the eyes opened. She saw—the face of Wilfrid. Could he see in—see her peering out from the darkened room? Quivering all over, she let the curtains fall to. Beckon? Let him in? Go out to him? Wave him away? Her heart beat furiously. How long had he been out there—like a ghost? What did he want of her? She dropped Ting-a-ling with a flump, and pressed her hands to her forehead, trying to clear confusion from her brain. And suddenly she stepped forward and flung the curtains apart. No face! Nothing! He was gone! The dark, draughty square—not a soul in it! Had he ever been—or was the face her fancy? But Ting-a-ling! Dogs had no fancies. He had gone back to the fire and settled down again.

'It's not my fault,' she thought passionately. 'It's not! I didn't want him to love me. I only wanted his—his ——!' Again she sank down before the fire. "Oh! Ting, have a feeling heart!" But the Chinese dog, mindful of the flump, made no response. . . .

Chapter Eleven

COCKED HAT

———◆◆◆———

AFTER missing his vocation with the young man Butterfield, Michael had hesitated in the hall. At last he had gone not upstairs again but quietly out. He walked past the Houses of Parliament and up Whitehall. In Trafalgar Square, it occurred to him that he had a father. Bart might be at 'Snooks',' The Coffee House, the Aeroplane; and, with the thought, 'He'd be restful,' he sought the most modern of the three.

"Yes, Sir Lawrence Mont is in the lounge, sir."

He was sitting with knees crossed, and a cigar between his fingertips, waiting for some one to talk to.

"Ah! Michael! Can you tell me why I come here?"

"To wait for the end of the world, sir?"

Sir Lawrence sniggered. "An idea," he said. "When the skies are wrecking civilisation, this will be the best-informed tape in London. The wish to be in at the death is perhaps the strongest of our passions, Michael. I should very much dislike being blown up, especially after dinner; but I should still more dislike missing the next show, if it's to be a really good one. The air raids were great fun, after all."

Michael sighed.

"Yes," he said, "The war got us used to thinking of the

millennium, and then it went and stopped, and left the millennium hanging over us. Now we shall never be happy till we get it. Can I take one of your cigars, sir?"

"My dear fellow! I've been reading Frazer again. Extraordinary how remote all superstition seems, now that we've reached the ultimate truth: That enlightenment never can prevail."

Michael stopped the lighting of his cigar.

"Do you really think that, sir?"

"What else can one think? Who can have any reasonable doubt now that with the aid of mechanics the headstrong part of man must do him in? It's an unavoidable conclusion from all recent facts. *'Per ardua ad astra,'* 'Through hard knocks we shall see stars.' "

"But it's always been like that, sir, and here we are alive?"

"They say so, but I doubt it. I fancy we're really dead, Michael. I fancy we're only living in the past. I don't think—no, I don't think we can be said to expect a future. We talk of it, but I hardly think we hope for one. Underneath our protestations we subconsciously deduce. From the mess we've made of it these last ten years, we can feel the far greater mess we shall make of it in the next thirty. Human nature can argue the hind leg off a donkey, but the donkey will be four-legged at the end of the discussion."

Michael sat down suddenly and said:

"You're a bad, bold Bart."

Sir Lawrence smiled.

"I should be glad to think that men really believed in humanity, and all that, but you know they don't—they believe in novelty and getting their own way. With rare exceptions they're still monkeys, especially the scientific variety; and when you put gunpowder and a lighted match into the paws of monkeys, they blow themselves up to see the fun. Monkeys are only safe when deprived of means to be otherwise."

"Lively, that!" said Michael.

"Not livelier than the occasion warrants, my dear boy. I've been thinking. We've got a member here who knows a trick worth twenty of any played in the way—an extraordinarily valuable fellow. The Government have got their eye on him. He'll help the other valuable fellows in France and Germany and America and Russia to make history. Between them, they'll do something really proud—something that'll knock all the other achievements of man into a cocked hat. By the way, Michael, new device of '*Homo sapiens*'—the cocked hat."

"Well," said Michael, "what are you going to do about it?"

Sir Lawrence's eyebrow sought his hair.

"Do, my dear fellow? What should I do? Can I go out and grab him and the Government by the slack of their breeches; yes, and all the valuable fellows and Governments of the other countries? No! All I can do is to smoke my cigar and say: 'God rest you, merry gentlemen, let nothing you dismay!' By hook or crook, they will come into their own, Michael; but in the normal course of things I shall be dead before they do."

"I shan't," said Michael.

"No, my dear; but think of the explosions, the sights, the smells. By Jove, you've got something to live for, yet. Sometimes I wish I were your age. And sometimes," Sir Lawrence relighted his cigar, "I don't. Sometimes I think I've had enough of our pretences, and that there's nothing left but to die like gentlemen."

"Some Jeremiad, Dad!"

"Well," said Sir Lawrence, with a twirl of his little grizzled moustache, "I hope I'm wrong. But we're driving fast to a condition of things when millions can be killed by the pressing of a few buttons. What reason is there to suppose that our bumps of benevolence will increase in time to stop our using these great new toys of destruction, Michael!"

" 'Where you know little, place terrors.' "

"Very nice; where did you get that?"

"Out of a life of Christopher Columbus."

"Old C. C.! I could bring myself to wish sometimes that he hadn't been so deucedly inquisitive. We were snugger in the dark ages. There was something to be said for not discovering the Yanks."

"Well," said Michael, "*I* think we shall pedal through, yet. By the way, about this Elderson stunt: I've just seen the clerk—he doesn't look to me the sort that would have made that up."

"Ah! That! But if Elderson could do such a thing, well —really, anything might happen. It's a complete stumper. He was such a pretty bat, always went in first wicket down. He and I put on fifty-four against Eton. I suppose old Forsyte told you?"

"Yes, he wanted me to find the chap a job."

"Butterfield. Ask him if he's related to old Butterfield the gardener? It would be something to go on. D'you find old Forsyte rather trying?"

Loyal to Fleur, Michael concealed his lips. "No, I get on very well with him."

"He's straight, I admit that."

"Yes," said Michael, "very straight."

"But somewhat reticent."

"Yes," said Michael.

On this conclusion they were silent, as though terrors had been placed beyond it. And soon Michael rose.

"Past ten, I'd better go home."

Returning the way he came, he could think of nothing but Wilfrid. What wouldn't he give to hear him say: "It's all right, old man; I've got over it!"—to wring him by the hand again. Why should one catch this fatal disease called love? Why should one be driven half crazy by it? They said love was Nature's provision against Bart's terrors, against the valuable fellows. An insistent urge— lest the race die out. Prosaic, if true! Not that he cared whether Fleur had children. Queer how Nature camou- flaged her schemes—leery old bird! But overreaching her- self a bit, wasn't she? Children might yet go clean out of fashion if Bart was right. A very little more would do it; who would have children for the mere pleasure of seeing them blown up, poisoned, starved to death? A few fanatics would hold on, the rest of the world go barren. The cocked hat! Instinctively Michael straightened his

own, ready for crossing under Big Ben. He had reached
the centre of Parliament Square, when a figure coming
towards him swerved suddenly to its left and made in
the direction of Victoria. Tall, with a swing in its walk.
Wilfrid! Michael stood still. Coming from—South
Square! And suddenly he gave chase. He did not run,
but he walked his hardest. The blood beat in his tem-
ples, and he felt confused to a pitch past bearing. Wilfrid
must have seen him, or he wouldn't have swerved,
wouldn't be legging it away like a demon. Black!—black!
He was not gaining, Wilfrid had the legs on him—to
overtake him, he must run! But there rose in Michael a
sort of exaltation. His best friend—his wife! There was a
limit. One might be too proud to fight that. Let him go
his ways! He stood still, watched the swift figure disap-
pear, and slowly, head down under the now cocked hat,
turned towards home. He walked quite quietly, and with
a sense of finality. No use making a song about it! No
fuss, but no retreat! In the few hundred yards before he
reached his Square he was chiefly conscious of the tallness
of houses, the shortness of men. Such midgets to have
made this monstrous pile, lighted it so that it shone in an
enormous glittering heap whose glow blurred the colour of
the sky! What a vast business this midget activity! Absurd to think that his love for another midget mattered!
He turned his key in the lock, took off his cocked hat
and went into the drawing-room. Unlighted—empty? No.
She and Ting-a-ling were on the floor before the fire! He
sat down on the settee, and was abruptly conscious that
he was trembling and sweating as if he had smoked a too
strong cigar. Fleur had raised herself, crosslegged, and
was staring up at him. He waited to get the better of his
trembling. Why didn't she speak? Why was she sitting
there, in the dark? 'She knows'; he thought: 'we both
know this is the end. O God, let me behave like a sport!'
He took a cushion, put it behind him, crossed his legs,
and leaned back. His voice surprised him suddenly:

"May I ask you something, Fleur? And will you please
answer me quite truly?"

"Yes."

"It's this: I know you didn't love me when you married me. I don't think you love me now. Do you want me to clear out?"

A long time seemed to pass.

"No."

"Do you mean that?"

"Yes."

"Why?"

"Because I don't."

Michael got up.

"Will you answer one thing more?"

"Yes."

"Was Wilfrid here to-night?"

"Yes—no. That is——"

His hands clutched each other; he saw her eyes fix on them, and kept them still.

"Fleur, don't!"

"I'm not. He came to the window there. I saw his face —that's all. His face—it—Oh! Michael, don't be unkind to-night!"

Unkind! Unkind! Michael's heart swelled at that strange word.

"It's all right," he stammered: "So long as you tell me what it is you want."

Fleur said, without moving:

"I want to be comforted."

Ah! She knew exactly what to say, how to say it! And going on his knees, he began to comfort her.

Chapter Twelve

GOING EAST

———⊷◦◅═╼◦╾═▻◦⊶———

HE had not been on his knees many minutes before
they suffered from reaction. To kneel there comforting Fleur brought him a growing discomfort. He believed her to-night, as he had not believed her for
months past. But what was Wilfrid doing? Where wandering? The face at the window—face without voice,
without attempt to reach her! Michael ached in that il-
legitimate organ the heart. Withdrawing his arms, he
stood up.

"Would you like me to have a look for him? If it's all
over—he might—I might——"

Fleur, too, stood up. She was calm enough now.

"Yes, I'll go to bed." With Ting-a-ling in her arms, she
went to the door; her face, between the dog's chestnut fur
and her own, was very pale, very still.

"By the way," she said, "this is my second no go,
Michael; I suppose it means——"

Michael gasped. Currents of emotion, welling, ebbing,
swirling, rendered him incapable of speech.

"The night of the balloon," she said: "Do you mind?"

"Mind? Good God! Mind!"

"That's all right, then. I don't. Good-night!"

She was gone. Without reason, Michael thought: 'In

the beginning was the Word, and the Word was with God, and the Word was God.' And he stood, as if congealed, overcome by an uncontrollable sense of solidity. A child coming! It was as though the barque of his being, tossed and drifted, suddenly rode tethered—anchor down. He turned and tore at the curtains. Night of stars! Wonderful world! Jolly—jolly! And—Wilfrid! He flattened his face against the glass. Outside there Wilfrid's had been flattened. He could see it if he shut his eyes. Not fair! Dog lost—man lost! S.O.S. He went into the hall, and from the mothless marble coffer rived his thickest coat. He took the first taxi that came by.

"Cork Street! Get along!" Needle in bundle of hay! Quarter past eleven by Big Ben! The intense relief of his whole being in that jolting cab seemed to him brutal. Salvation! It *was*—he had a strange certainty of that as though he saw Fleur suddenly "close-up" in a very strong light, concrete beneath her graceful veerings. Family! Continuation! He had been unable to anchor her, for he was not of her! But her child could and would! And, perhaps, he would yet come in with the milk. Why did he love her so—it was not done! Wilfrid and he were donkeys—out of touch, out of tune with the times!

"Here you are, sir—what number?"

"All right! Cool your heels and wait for me! Have a cigarette!"

With one between his own lips which felt so dry, he went down the backwater.

A light in Wilfrid's rooms! He rang the bell. The door was opened, the face of Wilfrid's man looked forth.

"Yes, sir?"

"Mr. Desert in?"

"No, sir. Mr. Desert has just started for the East. His ship sails tomorrow."

"Oh!" said Michael, blankly: "Where from?"

"Plymouth, sir. His train leaves Paddington at midnight. You might catch him yet."

"It's very sudden," said Michael, "he never——"

"No, sir. Mr. Desert is a sudden gentleman."

"Well, thanks; I'll try and catch him."

Back in the cab with the words: "Paddington—flick her along!" he thought: 'A sudden gentleman!' Perfect! He remembered the utter suddenness of that little interview beside the bust of Lionel Charwell. Sudden their friendship, sudden its end—sudden even Wilfrid's poems —offspring of a sudden soul! Staring from window to window in that jolting, rattling cab, Michael suffered from St. Vitus's dance. Was he a fool? Could he not let well alone? Pity was posh! And yet! With Wilfrid would go a bit of his heart, and in spite of all he would like him to know that. Upper Brook Street, Park Lane! Emptying streets, cold night, stark plane trees painted-up by the lamps against a bluish dark. And Michael thought: 'We wander! What's the end—the goal? To do one's bit, and not worry! But what is my bit? What's Wilfrid's? Where will he end up, now?'

The cab rattled down the station slope and drew up under cover. Ten minutes to twelve, and a long heavy train on platform one!

'What shall I do?' thought Michael: 'It's so darned crude! Must I go down—carriage by carriage? "Couldn't let you go, old man, without"—blurb!'

Bluejackets! If not drunk—as near as made no matter. Eight minutes still! He began slowly walking along the train. He had not passed four windows before he saw his quarry. Desert was sitting back to the engine in the near corner of an empty first. An unlighted cigarette was in his mouth, his fur collar turned up to his eyes, and his eyes fixed on an unopened paper on his lap. He sat without movement; Michael stood looking at him. His heart beat fast. He struck a match, took two steps, and said:

"Light, old boy?"

Desert stared up at him.

"Thanks," he said, and took the match. By its flare his face was dark, thin, drawn; his eyes dark, deep, tired. Michael leaned in the window. Neither spoke.

"Take your seat, if you're going, sir."

"I'm not," said Michael. His whole inside seemed turning over.

"Where are you going, old man?" he said suddenly.

"Jericho."

"God, Wilfrid, I'm sorry!"

Desert smiled.

"Cut it out!"

"Yes, I know! Shake hands?"

Desert held out his hand.

Michael squeezed it hard.

A whistle sounded.

Desert rose suddenly and turned to the rack above him. He took a parcel from a bag. "Here," he said, "these wretched things! Publish them if you like."

Something clicked in Michael's throat.

"Thanks, old man! That's great! Good-bye!"

A sort of beauty came into Desert's face.

"So long!"

The train moved. Michael withdrew his elbows; quite still, he stared at the motionless figure slowly borne along, away. Carriage after carriage went by him, full of bluejackets leaning out, clamoring, singing, waving handkerchiefs and bottles. Guard's van now—the tail light—all spread—a crimson blur—setting East—going—going—gone!

And that was all—was it? He thrust the parcel into his coat pocket. Back to Fleur, now! Way of the world—one man's meat, another's poison! He passed his hand over his eyes. The dashed things were full of—blurb!

PART THREE

Chapter One

BANK HOLIDAY

———◆❖◆———

WHITSUNTIDE Bank Holiday was producing its seasonal invasion of Hampstead Heath, and among the ascending swarm were two who meant to make money in the morning and spend it in the afternoon.

Tony Bicket, with balloons and wife, embarked early on the Hampstead Tube.

"You'll see," he said, "I'll sell the bloomin' lot by twelve o'clock, and we'll go on the bust."

Squeezing his arm, Victorine fingered, through her dress, a slight swelling just above her right knee. It was caused by fifty-four pounds fastened in the top of her stocking. She had little feeling, now, against balloons. They afforded temporary nourishment, till she had the few more pounds needful for their passage-money. Tony still believed he was going to screw salvation out of his blessed balloons: he was 'that hopeful—Tony,' though their heads were only just above water on his takings. And she smiled. With her secret she could afford to be indifferent now to the stigma of gutter hawking. She had her story pat. From the evening paper, and from communion on 'buses with those interested in the national pastime, she had acquired the necessary information about racing. She even talked of it with Tony, who had street-corner knowledge. Already she had prepared chapter and verse of two imaginary coups; a sovereign made out of stitching imaginary blouses, invested on the winner of the Two Thousand Guineas, and the result on the deadheater for the Jubilee at nice odds; this with a third winner, still to be selected, would bring her imaginary winnings up to the needed sixty pounds odd she would so soon have saved now out of 'the altogether.' This tale she would pitch to Tony in a week or two, reeling off by heart the wonderful luck she had kept from him until she had the whole of the money. She would slip her forehead against his eyes if he looked at her too hard, and kiss his lips till his head was no longer clear. And in the morning they would wake up and take their passages. Such was the plan of Victorine, with five ten-pound and four one-pound notes in her stocking, attached to the pink silk stays.

"Afternoon of a Dryad" had long been finished, and was on exhibition at the Dumetrius Gallery, with other works of Aubrey Greene. Victorine had paid a shilling to see it; had stood some furtive minutes gazing at that white body glimmering from among grass and spikey flowers, at the face, turned as if saying: "I know a secret!"

"Bit of a genius, Aubrey Greene—that face is jolly good!" Scared, and hiding the face, Victorine had slipped away.

From the very day when she had stood shivering outside the studio of Aubrey Greene she had been in full work. He had painted her three times—always nice, always polite, quite the gentleman! And he had given her introductions. Some had painted her in clothes, some half-draped, some in that "altogether," which no longer troubled her, with the money swelling her stocking and Tony without suspicion. Not every one had been "nice"; advances had been made to her, but she had nipped them in the bud. It would have meant the money quicker, but —Tony! In a fortnight now she could snap her fingers at it all. And often on the way home she stood by that plate-glass window, before the fruits, and the corn, and the blue butterflies. ...

In the packed railway carriage they sat side by side, Bicket, with tray on knee, debating where he had best stand.

"I fyvour the mokes," he said at last, "up by the pond. People'll have more money than when they get down among the swings and cocoanuts; and you can go and sit in a chair by the pond, like the seaside—I don't want you with me not till I've sold out."

Victorine pressed his arm.

Along the top and over on to the heath to north and south the holiday swarms surged, in perfect humour, carrying paper bags. Round the pond children, with thin, grey-white, spindly legs, were paddling and shrilly chattering, too content to smile. Elderly couples crawled slowly by, with jutting stomachs, and faces discoloured by the unaccustomed climb. Girls and young men were few, for they were dispersed already on the heath, in search of a madder merriment. On benches, in chairs of green canvas or painted wood, hundreds were sitting, contemplating their feet, as if imagining the waves of the sea. Now and again three donkeys would start, urged from behind, and slowly tittup their burdens along the pond's margin. Hawkers cried goods. Fat dark women told fortunes. Policemen stood cynically near them. A man talked and talked and took his hat round.

Tony Bicket unslung his tray. His cockney voice, wheedling and a little husky, offered his coloured airs without intermission. This was something like! It was brisk! And now and again he gazed through the throng away across the pond, to where Victorine would be seated in a canvas chair, looking different from every one—he knew.

"Fine balloons—fine balloons! Six for a bob! Big one, Madam? Only sixpence. See the size! Buy, buy! Tyke one for the little boy!"

No "aldermen" up here, but plenty in the mood to spend their money on a bit of brightness!

At five minutes before noon he snapped his tray—not a bally balloon left! With six Bank Holidays a week he would make his fortune! Tray under arm, he began to tour the pond. The kiddies were all right, but—good Lord—how thin and pale! If he and Vic had a kid—but not they—not till they got out there! A fat brown kid, chysin' blue butterflies, and the sun oozin' out of him. Rounding the end of the pond, he walked slowly along the chairs. Lying back, elegant, with legs crossed, in brown stockings showing to the knees, and neat brown shoes with the flaps over—— My! she looked a treat—in a world of her own, like that! Something caught Bicket by the throat. Gosh! He wanted things for her!

"Well, Vic! Penny!"

"I was thinkin' of Australia."

"Ah! It's a gaudy long wait. Never mind—I've sold the bally lot. Which shall we do, go down among the trees, or get to the swings, at once?"

"The swings."

The Vale of Health was in rhapsodic mood. The crowd flowed here in a slow, speechless stream, to the cries of the booth-keepers, and the owners of swings and cocoanuts. "Roll—bowl—or pitch! Now for the milky ones! Penny a shy! . . . Who's for the swings? . . . Ices . . . Ices . . . Fine bananas!"

On the giant merry-go-round under its vast umbrella the thirty chain-hung seats were filled with girls and men. Round to the music—slowly—faster—whirling out to the full extent of the chain, bodies bent back, legs stuck forward, laughter and speech dying, faces solemn, a little lost, hands gripping the chains hard. Faster, faster; slowing, slowing to a standstill, and the music silent.

"My word!" murmured Victorine. "Come on, Tony!"

They entered the enclosure and took their seats. Victorine, on the outside, locked her feet, instinctively, one over the other, and tightening her clasp on the chains, curved her body to the motion. Her lips parted:

"Lor, Tony!"

Faster, faster—every nerve and sense given to that motion! O-o-h! It *was* a feeling—flying round like that above the world! Faster—faster! Slower—slow, and the descent to earth.

"Tony—it's 'eaven!"

"Queer feelin' in yer inside, when you're swung right out!"

"I'd like it level with the top. Let's go once more!"

"Right-o!"

Twice more they went—half his profit on balloons! But who cared? He liked to see her face. After that, six shies at the milky ones without a hit, an ice apiece; then arm-in-arm to find a place to eat their lunch. That was the time Bicket enjoyed most, after the ginger-beer and sandwiches; smoking his fag, with his head on her lap, and the sky blue. A long time like that; till at last she stirred.

"Let's go and see the dancin'!"

In the grass enclosure ringed by the running path, some two dozen couples were jigging to a band.

Victorine pulled at his arm. "I *would* love a turn!"

"Well, let's 'ave a go," said Bicket. "This one-legged bloke'll 'old my tray."

They entered the ring.

"Hold me tighter, Tony!"

Bicket obeyed. Nothing he liked better; and slowly their feet moved—to this side and that. They made little way, revolving, keeping time, oblivious of appearances.

"You dance all right, Tony."

"*You* dance a treat!" gasped Bicket.

In the intervals, panting, they watched over the one-legged man; then to it again, till the band ceased for good.

"My word!" said Victorine. "They dance on board ship, Tony!"

Bicket squeezed her waist.

"I'll do the trick yet, if I 'ave to rob the Bank. There's nothin' I wouldn't do for you, Vic."

But Victorine smiled. She had done the trick already.

The crowd with parti-coloured faces, tired, good-humoured, frowsily scented, strolled over a battlefield thick-strewn with paper bags, banana peel, and newspapers.

"Let's 'ave our tea, and one more swing," said Bicket; "then we'll get over on the other side among the trees."

Away over on the far side were many couples. The sun went very slowly down. Those two sat under a bush and watched it go. A faint breeze swung and rustled the birch leaves. There was little human sound out here. All seemed to have come for silence, to be waiting for darkness in the hush. Now and then some stealthy spy would pass and scrutinise.

"Foxes!" said Bicket. "Gawd! I'd like to rub their noses in it!"

Victorine sighed, pressing closer to him.

Some one was playing on a banjo now; a voice singing. It grew dusk, but a moon was somewhere rising, for little shadows stole out along the ground.

They spoke in whispers. It seemed wrong to raise the voice, as though the grove were under a spell. Even their whisperings were scarce. Dew fell, but they paid no heed to it. With hands locked, and cheeks together, they sat very still. Bicket had a thought. This was poetry—this was! Darkness now, with a sort of faint and silvery glow, a sound of drunken singing on the Spaniard's Road, the whirr of belated cars returning from the north—and suddenly an owl hooted.

"My!" murmured Victorine, shivering: "An owl! Fancy! I used to hear one at Norbiton. I 'ope it's not bad luck!"

Bicket rose and stretched himself.

"Come on!" he said: "we've 'ad a dy. Don't you go catchin' cold!"

Arm-in-arm, slowly, through the darkness of the birch-grove, they made their way upwards—glad of the lamps, and the street, and the crowded station, as though they had taken an overdose of solitude.

Huddled in their carriage on the Tube, Bicket idly turned the pages of a derelict paper. But Victorine sat thinking of so much, that it was as if she thought of nothing. The swings, and the grove in the darkness, and the money in her stocking. She wondered Tony hadn't noticed when it crackled—there wasn't a safe place to keep it in! What was he looking at, with his eyes so fixed? She peered, and read: " 'Afternoon of a Dryad.' The striking picture by Aubrey Greene, on exhibition at the Dumetrius Gallery."

Her heart stopped beating.

"Cripes!" said Bicket. "Ain't that like you?"

"Like me? No!"

Bicket held the paper closer. "It *is*. It's like you all over. I'll cut that out. I'd like to see that picture."

The colour came up in her cheeks, released from a heart beating too fast now.

" 'Tisn't decent," she said.

"Dunno about that; but it's awful like you. It's even got your smile."

Folding the paper, he began to tear the sheet. Victorine's little finger pressed the notes beneath her stocking.

"Funny," she said, slowly, "to think there's people in the world so like each other."

"I never thought there could be one like you. Charin' Cross; we gotta change."

Hurrying along the rat-runs of the Tube, she slipped her hand into his pocket, and soon some scraps of torn paper fluttered down behind her following him in the crush. If only he didn't remember where the picture was!

Awake in the night, she thought:

'I don't care; I'm going to get the rest of the money—that's all about it.'

But her heart moved queerly within her, like that of one whose feet have trodden suddenly the quaking edge of a bog.

Chapter Two

OFFICE WORK

━━━━◆━◆━◆━━━━

MICHAEL sat correcting the proofs of "Counterfeits"—the book left by Wilfrid behind him.

"Can you see Butterfield, sir?"

"I can."

In Michael the word Butterfield excited an uneasy pride. The young man fulfilled with increasing success the function for which he had been engaged, on trial, four months ago. The head traveller had called him "a find." Next to "Copper Coin" he was the finest feather in Michael's cap. The Trade were not buying, yet Butterfield was selling books, or so it was reported; he appeared to have a natural gift of inspiring confidence where it was not justified. Danby and Winter had even entrusted to him the private marketing of that vellum-bound "Limited" of "Duet," by which they were hoping to recoup their losses on the ordinary edition. He was now engaged in working through a list of names considered likely to patronise the little masterpiece. This method of private approach had been suggested by himself.

"You see, sir," he had said to Michael: "I know a bit about Coué. Well, you can't work that on the Trade— they've got no capacity for faith. What can you expect? Every day they buy all sorts of stuff, always basing them-

selves on past sales. You can't find one in twenty that'll
back the future. But with private gentlemen, and especially private ladies, you can leave a thought with them
like Coué does—put it into them again and again that
day by day in every way the author's getting better and
better; and ten to one when you go round next, it's got
into their subconscious, especially if you take 'em just after
lunch or dinner, when they're a bit drowsy. Let me take my
own time, sir, and I'll put that edition over for you."

"Well," Michael had answered, "if you can inspire confidence in the future of my governor, Butterfield, you'll
deserve more than your ten per cent."

"I can do it, sir; it's just a question of faith."

"But you haven't any, have you?"

"Well, not, so to speak, in the author—but I've got faith
that I can give *them* faith in him; that's the real point."

"I see—the three-card stunt; inspire the faith you
haven't got, that the card is there, and they'll take it.
Well, the disillusion is not immediate—you'll probably
always get out of the room in time. Go ahead, then!"

The young man Butterfield had smiled.

The uneasy part of the pride inspired in Michael by
the name was due to old Forsyte's continually saying to
him that he didn't know—he couldn't tell—there was
that young man and his story about Elderson, and they
got no further. . . .

"Good morning, sir. Can you spare me five minutes?"

"Come in, Butterfield. Bunkered with 'Duets'?"

"No, sir. I've placed forty already. It's another matter."
Glancing at the shut door, the young man came closer.

"I'm working my list alphabetically. Yesterday I was
in the E's." His voice dropped. "Mr. Elderson."

"Phew!" said Michael. "You can give *him* the go-by."

"As a fact, sir, I haven't."

"What! Been over the top?"

"Yes, sir. Last night."

"Good for you, Butterfield! What happened?"

"I didn't send my name in, sir—just the firm's card."

Michael was conscious of a very human malice in the
young man's voice and face.

"Well?"

"Mr. Elderson, sir, was at his wine. I'd thought it out, and I began as if I'd never seen him before. What struck me was—he took my cue!"

"Didn't kick you out?"

"Far from it, sir. He said at once: 'Put my name down for two copies.'"

Michael grinned. "You both had a nerve."

"No, sir; that's just it. Mr. Elderson got it between wind and water. He didn't like it a little bit."

"I don't twig," said Michael.

"My being in this firm's employ, sir. He knows you're a partner here, and Mr. Forsyte's son-in-law, doesn't he?"

"He does."

"Well, sir, you see the connection—two directors believing me—not *him*. That's why I didn't miss him out. I fancied it'd shake him up. I happened to see his face in the sideboard glass as I went out. *He's* got the wind up all right."

Michael bit his forefinger, conscious of a twinge of sympathy with Elderson, as for a fly with the first strand of cob-web round his hind leg.

"Thank you, Butterfield," he said.

When the young man was gone, he sat stabbing his blotting-paper with a paper-knife. What curious "class" sensation was this? Or was it merely fellow-feeling with the hunted, a tremor at the way things found one out? For, surely, this was real evidence, and he would have to pass it on to his father, and "Old Forsyte." Elderson's nerve must have gone phut, or he'd have said: "You impudent young scoundrel—get out of here!" That, clearly, was the only right greeting from an innocent, and the only advisable greeting from a guilty man. Well! Nerve did fail sometimes—even the best. Witness the very proof-sheet he had just corrected:

THE COURT MARTIAL

"See 'ere! I'm myde o' nerves and blood
    The syme as you, not meant to be
Froze stiff, up to me ribs in mud,
    You try it, like I 'ave, an' see!

"Aye, you snug beauty brass hats, when
 You stick what I stuck out that d'y,
An' keep yer ruddy 'earts up—then
 You'll learn, maybe, the right to s'y:

" 'Take aht an' shoot 'im in the snow,
 Shoot 'im for cowardice! 'E who serves
His King and Country's got to know
 There's no such bloody thing as nerves.' "

Good old Wilfrid!

"Yes, Miss Perren?"

The letter to Sir James Foggart, Mr. Mont; you told me to remind you. And will you see Miss Manuelli?"

"Miss Manu—— Oh! Ah! Yes."

Bicket's girl wife, whose face they had used on Storbert's novel, the model for Aubrey Greene's——! Michael rose, for the girl was in the room already.

'I remember that dress!' he thought: 'Fleur never liked it.'

'What can I do for you, Mrs. Bicket? How's Bicket, by the way?"

"Fairly, sir, thank you."

"Still in balloons?"

"Yes."

"Well, we all are, Mrs. Bicket."

"Beg pardon?"

"In the air—don't you think? But you didn't come to tell me that?"

"No, sir."

A slight flush in those sallow cheeks, fingers concerned with the tips of the worn gloves, lips uncertain; but the eyes steady—really an uncommon girl!

"You remember givin' me a note to Mr. Greene, sir?"

"I do; and I've seen the result; it's topping, Mrs. Bicket."

"Yes. But it's got into the papers—my husband saw it there last night; and, of course, he doesn't know about me."

Phew! For what had he let this girl in?

"I've made a lot of money at it, sir—almost enough for our passage to Australia; but now I'm frightened. 'Isn't it like you?' he said to me. I tore the paper up, but suppose he remembers the name of the Gallery and goes to see the picture! That's even much more like me! He might go on to Mr. Greene. So would you mind, sir, speaking to Mr. Greene, and beggin' him to say it was some one else, in case Tony did go?"

"Not a bit," said Michael. "But do you think Bicket would mind so very much, considering what it's done for you? It can be quite a respectable profession."

Victorine's hands moved up to her breast.

"Yes," she said, simply. "I have been quite respectable. And I only did it because we do so want to get away, and I couldn't bear seein' him standin' in the gutter there sellin' those balloons in the fogs. But I'm ever so scared, sir, now."

Michael stared.

"My God!" he said; "money's an evil thing!"

Victorine smiled faintly. "The want of it is, I know."

"How much more do you need, Mrs. Bicket?"

"Only another ten pound, about, sir."

"I can let you have that."

"Oh! thank you; but it's not that—I can easy earn it—I've got used to it; a few more days don't matter."

"But how are you going to account for having the money?"

"Say I won it bettin'."

"*Thin!*" said Michael. "Look here! Say you came to me and I advanced it. If Bicket repays it from Australia, I can always put it to your credit again at a bank out there. I've got you into a hole, in a way, and I'd like to get you out of it."

"Oh! no, sir; you did me a service. I don't want to put you about, telling falsehoods for me."

"It won't worry me a bit, Mrs. Bicket. I can lie to the umteenth when there's no harm in it. The great thing for you is to get away sharp. Are there many other pictures of you?"

"Oh! yes, a lot—not that you'd recognise them, I think, they're so square and funny."

"Ah! well—Aubrey Greene has got you to the life!"

"Yes; it's like me all over, Tony says."

"Quite. Well, I'll speak to Aubrey, I shall be seeing him at lunch. Here's the ten pounds! That's agreed, then?

You came to me today—see? Say you had a brain wave. I quite understand the whole thing. You'd do a lot for him; and he'd do a lot for you. It's all right—don't cry!"

Victorine swallowed violently. Her hand in the worn glove returned his squeeze.

"I'd tell him to-night, if I were you," said Michael, "and I'll get ready."

When she had gone he thought: 'Hope Bicket won't think I received value for that sixty pounds!' And, pressing his bell, he resumed the stabbing of his blotting-paper.

"Yes, Mr. Mont?"

"Now let's get on with it, Miss Perren."

" 'DEAR SIR JAMES FOGGART,—We have given the utmost consideration to your very interesting—er—production. While we are of opinion that the views so well expressed on the present condition of Britain in relation to the rest of the world are of great value to all—er—thinking persons, we do not feel that there are enough—er—thinking persons to make it possible to publish the book, except at a loss. The—er—thesis that Britain should now look for salvation through adjustment of markets, population, supply and demand, within the Empire, put with such exceedingly plain speech, will, we are afraid, get the goat of all the political parties; nor do we feel that your plan of emigrating boys and girls in large quantities before they are spoiled by British town life, can do otherwise than irritate a working-class which knows nothing of conditions outside its own country, and is notably averse to giving its children a chance in any other.' "

"Am I to put that, Mr. Mont?"

"Yes; but tone it in a bit. Er——

" 'Finally, your view that the land should be used to grow food is so very unusual in these days, that we feel your book would have a hostile Press except from the Old Guard and the Die-hard, and a few folk with vision.' "

"Yes, Mr. Mont?"

" 'In a period of veering—er—transitions'—keep that, Miss Perren—'and the airy unreality of hopes that have long gone up the spout'—almost keep that—'any scheme that looks forward and defers harvest for twenty years, must be extraordinarily unpopular. For all these reasons you will see how necessary it is for you to—er—seek another publisher. In short, we are not taking any.

"'With—er—' what you like—'dear Sir James Foggart,

"'We are your obedient servants,

"'DANBY AND WINTER.'"

"When you've translated that, Miss Perren, bring it in, and I'll sign it for the firm."

"Yes. Only, Mr. Mont—I thought you were a Socialist. This almost seems—forgive my asking?"

"Miss Perren, it's struck me lately that labels are 'off.' How can a man be anything at a time when everything's in the air? Look at the Liberals. They can't see the situation whole because of Free Trade; nor can the Labour Party because of their Capital levy; nor can the Tories because of Protection; they're all hag-ridden by catch-words! Old Sir James Foggart's jolly well right, but nobody's going to listen to him. His book will be wastepaper if anybody ever publishes it. The world's unreal just now, Miss Perren; and of all countries we're the most unreal."

"Why, Mr. Mont?"

"Why? Because with the most stickfast of all the national temperaments, we're holding on to what's gone more bust for us than for any other country. Anyway, Mr. Danby shouldn't have left the letter to me, if he didn't mean me to enjoy myself. Oh! and while we're about it—I've got to refuse Harold Master's new book. It's a mistake, but they won't have it."

"Why not, Mr. Mont? 'The Sobbing Turtle' was such a success!"

"Well, in this new thing Master's got hold of an idea which absolutely forces him to say something. Winter says those who hailed 'The Sobbing Turtle' as such a work of art, are certain to be down on this for that; and Mr. Danby calls the book an outrage on human nature. So there's nothing for it. Let's have a shot:

"'MY DEAR MASTER,—In the exhilaration of your subject it has obviously not occurred to you that you've bust up the show. In 'The Sobbing Turtle' you were absolutely in tune with half the orchestra, and that—er—the noisiest half. You were charmingly archaic, and securely cold-blooded. But now, what have you gone and done? Taken the last Marquesan islander for your hero and put him down in London town! The thing's a searching satire, a real criticism of life. I'm sure you didn't mean to be contemporary, or want to burrow into reality; but your subject has run off with you. Cold acid and cold blood are very different things, you know, to say nothing of your having had to drop the archaic. Personally, of course, I think this new thing miles better than 'The Sobbing Turtle,' which was a nice little affair, but nothing to make a song about. But I'm not the public, and I'm not the critics. The young and thin will be aggrieved by your lack of modernity, they'll say you're moralising; the old and fat will call you bitter and destructive; and the ordinary public will take your Marquesan seriously, and resent your making him superior to themselves. The prospects, you see, are not gaudy. How d'you think we're going to 'get away' with such a book? Well, we're not! Such is the fiat of the firm. I don't agree with it. I'd publish it tomorrow; but needs must when Danby and Winter drive. So, with every personal regret, I return what is really a masterpiece.

> " 'Always yours,
>
> " 'MICHAEL MONT.' "

"D'you know, Miss Perren, I don't think you need translate that?"

"I'm afraid it would be difficult."

"Right-o, then; but do the other, please. I'm going to take my wife out to see a picture; back by four. Oh! and if a little chap called Bicket, that we used to have here, calls any time and asks to see me, he's to come up; but I want warning first. Will you let them know downstairs?"

"Yes, Mr. Mont! Oh! didn't—wasn't that Miss Manuelli the model for the wrapper on Mr. Storbert's novel?"

"She was, Miss Perren; alone I found her."

"She's very interesting-looking, isn't she?"

"She's unique, I'm afraid."

"She needn't mind that, I should think."

"That depends," said Michael; and stabbed his blotting-paper.

Chapter Three

"AFTERNOON OF A DRYAD"

***

FLEUR was still gracefully concealing most of what Michael called "the eleventh baronet," now due in about two months' time. She seemed to be adapting herself, in mind and body, to the quiet and persistent collection of the heir. Michael knew that, from the first, following the instructions of her mother, she had been influencing his sex, repeating to herself, every evening before falling asleep, and every morning on waking, the words: "Day by day, in every way, he is getting more and more male," to infect the subconscious which, everybody now said, controlled the course of events; and that she was abstaining from the words: "I *will* have a boy," for this, setting up a reaction, everybody said, was liable to produce a girl. Michael noted that she turned more and more to her mother, as if the French, or more naturalistic, side of her, had taken charge of a process which had to do with the body. She was frequently at Mapledurham, going down in Soames' car, and her mother was frequently in South Square. Annette's handsome presence, with its tendency to black lace, was always pleasing to Michael, who had never forgotten her espousal of his suit in days when it was a forlorn hope. Though he still felt only on the threshold of Fleur's heart, and was preparing to play second fiddle to "the eleventh baronet," he was infinitely easier in mind since Wilfrid had been gone. And he watched, with a sort of amused adoration, the way in which she focussed her collecting powers on an object that had no epoch, a process that did not date.

Personally conducted by Aubrey Greene, the expedition to view his show at the Dumetrius Gallery left South Square after an early lunch.

"Your Dryad came to me this morning, Aubrey," said Michael in the cab. "She wanted me to ask you to put up a barrage if by any chance her husband blows round to accuse you of painting his wife. It seems he's seen a reproduction of the picture."

"Umm!" murmured the painter: "Shall I, Fleur?"

"Of course you must, Aubrey!"

Aubrey Greene's smile slid from her to Michael.

"Well, what's his name?"

"Bicket."

Aubrey Greene fixed his eyes on space, and murmured slowly:

> "An angry young husband called Bicket
> Said: 'Turn your self round, and I'll kick it;
> You have painted my wife
> In the nude to the life,
> Do you think, Mr. Greene, it was cricket?' "

"Oh! Aubrey!"

"Chuck it!" said Michael, "I'm serious. She's a most plucky little creature. She's made the money they wanted, and remained respectable."

"So far as I'm concerned, certainly."

"Well, I should think so."

"Why, Fleur?"

"You're not a vamp, Aubrey!"

"As a matter of fact, she excited my aesthetic sense."

"Much that'd save her from some aesthetes!" muttered Michael.

"Also, she comes from Putney."

"There you have a real reason. Then, you *will* put up a barrage if Bicket blows in?"

Aubrey Greene laid his hand on his heart. "And here we are!"

For the convenience of the eleventh baronet Michael had chosen the hour when the proper patrons of Aubrey Greene would still be lunching. A shock-headed young man and three pale-green girls alone wandered among the pictures. The painter led the way at once to his masterpiece; and for some minutes they stood before it in a suitable paralysis. To speak too soon in praise would never do; to speak too late would be equally tactless; to speak too fulsomely would jar; to mutter coldly: "Very nice—very nice indeed!" would blight. To say bluntly: "Well, old man, to tell you the truth, I don't like it a little bit!" would get his goat.

At last Michael pinched Fleur gently, and she said:

"It really is charming, Aubrey; and awfully like—at least——"

"So far as one can tell. But really, old man, you've done it in once. I'm afraid Bicket will think so, anyway."

"Dash that!" muttered the painter. "How do you find the colour values?"

"Jolly fine; especially the flesh; don't you think so, Fleur?"

"Yes; only I should have liked that shadow down the side a little deeper."

"Yes?" murmured the painter: "Perhaps!"

"You've caught the spirit," said Michael. "But I tell you what, old man, you're for it—the thing's got meaning. I don't know what the critics will do to you."

Aubrey Greene smiled. "That was the worst of her. She led me on. To get an idea's fatal."

"Personally, I don't agree with that; do you, Fleur?"

"Of course not; only one doesn't say so."

"Time we did, instead of kow-towing to the Café C'rillon. I say, the hair's all right, and so are the toes— they curl as you look at 'em."

"And it *is* a relief not to get legs painted in streaky cubes. The asphodels rather remind one of the flowers in Leonardo's 'Virgin of the Rocks,' Aubrey."

"The whole thing's just a bit Leonardoish, old man. You'll have to live that down."

"Oh! Aubrey, my father's seen it. I believe he's biting. Something you said impressed him—about our white monkey, d'you remember?"

Aubrey Greene threw up his hands. "Ah! That white monkey—to have painted that! Eat the fruit and chuck the rinds around, and ask with your eyes what it's all about."

"A moral!" said Michael: "Take care, old man! Well! Our taxi's running up. Come along, Fleur; we'll leave Aubrey to his conscience."

Once more in the cab, he took her arm.

"That poor little snipe, Bicket! Suppose I'd come on *you* as he'll come on his wife!"

"I shouldn't have looked so nice."

"Oh! yes; much nicer; though she looks nice enough, I must say."

"Then why should Bicket mind, in these days of emancipation?"

"Why? Good Lord, ducky! You don't suppose Bicket——! I mean, we emancipated people have got into the habit of thinking we're the world—well! we aren't; we're an excrescence, small, and noisy. We talk as if all the old values and prejudices had gone; but they've no more gone, really, you know, than the rows of villas and little grey houses."

"Why this outburst, Michael?"

"Well, darling, I'm a bit fed-up with the attitude of our crowd. If emancipation were true, one could stick it; but it's not. There isn't ten per cent difference between now and thirty years ago."

"How do you know? You weren't alive."

"No; but I read the papers, and talk to the man in the street, and look at people's faces. Our lot think they're the tablecloth, but they're only the fringe. D'you know, only one hundred and fifty thousand people in this country have ever heard a Beethoven Symphony? How many, do you suppose, think old B. a back number? Five thousand, perhaps, out of forty-two millions. How's that for emancipation?"

He stopped, observing that her eyelids had drooped.

"I was thinking, Michael, that I should like to change my bedroom curtains to blue. I saw the exact colour yesterday at Harton's. They say blue has an effect on the mind—the present curtains really are too jazzy."

The eleventh baronet!

"Anything you like, darling. Have a blue ceiling if it helps."

"Oh, no! But I think I'll change the carpet, too; there's a lovely powder blue at Harton's."

"Then get it. Would you like to go there now? I can take the Tube back to the office."

"Yes, I think I'd better. I might miss it."

Michael put his head out of the window. "Harton's, please!" And, replacing his hat, he looked at her. Emancipated forsooth!

Chapter Four

AFTERNOON OF A BICKET

—◆◆◆◆◆—

JUST about that moment Bicket re-entered his sitting-room and deposited his tray. All the morning under the shadow of St. Paul's he had re-lived Bank Holiday. Exceptionally tired in feet and legs, he was also itching mentally. He had promised himself a refreshing look from time to time at what was almost like a photo of Vic herself. And he had lost the picture! Yet he had taken nothing out of his pockets—just hung his coat up. Had it joggled out in the crush at the station, or had he missed his pocket opening and dropped it in the carriage? And he had wanted to see the original, too. He remembered that the Gallery began with a "D," and at lunch-time squandered a penny-halfpenny to look up the names. Foreign, he was sure—the picture being naked. "Dumetrius"? Ah!

Back at his post, he had a bit of luck. 'That alderman,' whom he had not seen for months, came by. Intuition made him say at once: "Hope I see you well, sir. Never forgotten your kindness."

The "alderman," who had been staring up as if he saw a magpie on the dome of St. Paul's, stopped as though attacked by cramp.

"Kindness?" he said; "what kindness? Oh, balloons! They were no good to me!"

"No, sir, I'm sure," said Bicket humbly.

"Well, here you are!" muttered the "alderman"; "don't expect it again."

Half-a-crown! A whole half-crown! Bicket's eyes pursued the hastening form. "Good luck!" he said softly to himself, and began putting up his tray. "I'll go home and rest my feet, and tyke Vic to see that picture. It'll be funny lookin' at it together."

But she was not in. He sat down and smoked a fag. He felt aggrieved that she was out, this the first afternoon he had taken off. Of course she couldn't stay in all day! Still——! He waited twenty minutes, then put on Michael's suit and shoes.

'I'll go and see it alone,' he thought. 'It'll cost half as much. They charge you sixpence, I expect.'

They charged him a shilling—a shilling! One fourth of his day's earnings, to see a picture! He entered bashfully. There were ladies who smelled of scent and had drawling voices, but not a patch on Vic for looks. One of them, behind him, said:

"See! There's Aubrey Greene himself! And that's the picture they're talking of—'Afternoon of a Dryad.' "

They passed him and moved on. Bicket followed. At the end of the room, between their draperies and catalogues, he glimpsed the picture. A slight sweat broke out on his forehead. Almost life-size, among the flowers and spiky grasses, the face smiled round at him—very image of Vic! Could some one in the world be as like her as all that? The thought offended him, as a collector is offended finding the duplicate of an unique possession.

"It's a wonderful picture, Mr. Greene! What a type!"

A young man without hat, and fair hair sliding back, answered:

"A find, wasn't she?"

"Oh! perfect!—the very spirit of a wood nymph; so mysterious!"

The word that belonged to Vic! It was unholy. There

she lay for all to look at, just because some beastly
woman was made like her! A kind of rage invaded
Bicket's throat, caused his cheeks to burn; and with it
came a queer physical jealousy. That painter! What
business had he to paint a woman so like Vic as that
—a woman that didn't mind lyin' like that! They and
their talk about cahryscuro, and paganism, and a bloke
called Leneardo! Blast their drawling and their tricks! He
tried to move away, and could not, fascinated by that
effigy, so uncannily resembling what he had thought
belonged to himself alone. Silly to feel so bad over a
"coincidence," but he felt like smashing the glass and
cutting the body up into little bits. The ladies and the
painter passed on, leaving him alone before the picture.
Alone, he did not mind so much. The face was mourn-
ful-like, and lonely, and—and teasing, with its smile. It
sort of haunted you—it did! 'Well!' thought Bicket, 'I'll
get home to Vic. Glad I didn't bring her, after all, to
see herself-like. If I was an alderman, I'd buy the blinkin'
thing, and burn it!'

And there, in the entrance-lobby, talking to a "dago,"
stood—his very own "alderman"! Bicket paused in sheer
amazement.

"It's a rithing name, Mr. Forthyte," he heard the
Dago say: "hith prithes are going up."

"That's all very well, Dumetrius, but it's not everybody's money in these days—too highly-finished, altogether!"

"Well, Mr. Forthyte, to *you* I take off ten per thent."

"Take off twenty and I'll buy it."

That Dago's shoulders mounted above his hairy ears—
they did; and what a smile!

"Mithter Forthyte! Fifteen, thir!"

"Well, you're doing me; but send it round to my
daughter's in South Square—you know the number. When
do you close?"

"Day after to-morrow, thir."

So! The counterfeit of Vic had gone to that "alderman,"

had it? Bicket uttered a savage little sound, and slunk out.

He walked with a queer feeling. Had he got unnecessary wind up? After all, it wasn't her. But to know that another woman could smile that way, have frizzy-ended short black hair, and be all curved the same! And at every woman's passing face he looked—so different, so utterly unlike Vic's!

When he reached home she was standing in the middle of the room, with her lips to a balloon. All around her, on the floor, chairs, table, mantelpiece, were the blown-out shapes of his stock; one by one they had floated from her lips and selected their own resting-places: puce, green, orange, purple, blue, enlivening with their colour the dingy little space. All his balloons blown up! And there, in her best clothes, she stood, smiling, queer, excited.

"What in thunder!" said Bicket.

Raising her dress, she took some crackling notes from the top of her stocking, and held them out to him.

"See! Sixty-four pounds, Tony! I've got it all. We can go."

"*What!*"

"I had a brain wave—went to that Mr. Mont who gave us the clothes, and he's advanced it. We can pay it back, some day. Isn't it a marvel?"

Bicket's eyes, startled like a rabbit's, took in her smile, her excited flush, and a strange feeling shot through all his body, as if *they* were taking *him* in! She wasn't like Vic! No! Suddenly he felt her arms round him, felt her moist lips on his. She clung so tight, he could not move. His head went round.

"At last! At last! Isn't it fine? Kiss me, Tony!"

Bicket kissed; his vertigo was real, but behind it, for the moment stifled, what sense of unreality! . . .

Was it before night, or in the night, that the doubt first came—ghostly, tapping, fluttering, haunting—then, in the dawn, jabbing through his soul, turning him rigid. The money—the picture—the lost paper—that sense of unreality! This story she had told him! Were such things possible? Why should Mr. Mont advance that money? She had seen him—that was certain; the room, the secretary—you couldn't mistake her description of that Miss Perren. Why, then, feel this jabbing doubt? The money —such a lot of money! Not with Mr. Mont—never—he was a gent! Oh! Swine that he was, to have a thought like that—of Vic! He turned his back to her and tried to sleep. But once you got a thought like that—sleep? No! Her face among the balloons, the way she had smothered his eyes and turned his head—so that he couldn't think, couldn't go into it and ask her questions! A prey to dim doubts, achings, uncertainty, thrills of hope, and visions of "Austrylia," Bicket arose haggard.

"Well," he said, over their cocoa and margarined bread: "I must see Mr. Mont, that's certain." And suddenly he added: "Vic?" looking straight into her face.

She answered his look—straight, yes, straight. Oh! he was a proper swine! . . .

When he had left the house Victorine stood quite still, with hands pressed against her chest. She had slept less than he. Still as a mouse, she had turned and turned the thought: 'Did I take him in? Did I?' And if not— what? She took out the notes which had bought—or sold?—their happiness, and counted them once more. And the sense of injustice burned within her. Had she wanted to stand like that before men? Hadn't she been properly through it about that? Why, she could have had the sixty pounds three months ago from that sculptor, who was wild about her; or—so he said! But she had stuck it; yes, she had. Tony had nothing against her really— even if he knew it all. She had done it for him—Well! mostly—for him selling those balloons day after day in all weathers! But for her, they would still be stuck, and another winter coming, and unemployment—so they said in the paper—to be worse and worse! Stuck in the fogs and the cold, again! Ugh! Her chest was still funny sometimes; and he always hoarse. And this poky little room, and the bed so small that she couldn't stir without waking him. Why should Tony doubt her? For he did—

she had felt it, heard it in his "Vic?" Would Mr. Mont convince him? Tony was sharp! Her head drooped. The unfairness of it all! Some had everything to their hand, like that pretty wife of Mr. Mont's! And if one tried to find a way and get out to a new chance—then—then this! She flung her hair back. Tony *must* believe—he should! If he wouldn't, let him look out. She had done nothing to be ashamed of! No, indeed! And with the longing to go in front and lead her happiness along, she got out her old tin trunk, and began with careful method to put things into it.

Chapter Five

MICHAEL GIVES ADVICE

———————

ICHAEL still sat, correcting the proofs of "Counterfeits." Save "Jericho," there had been no address
to send them to. The East was wide, and Wilfrid had
made no sign. Did Fleur ever think of Wilfrid now? He
had the impression that she did not. And Wilfrid—well,
probably he was forgetting her already. Even passion required a little sustenance.

"A Mr. Forsyte to see you, sir."

Apparition in bookland!

"Ah! Show him in."

Soames entered with an air of suspicion.

"This your place?" he said. "I've looked in to tell you
that I've bought that picture of young Greene's. Have
you anywhere to hang it?"

"I should think we had," said Michael. "Jolly good,
sir, isn't it?"

"Well," muttered Soames, "for these days, yes. He'll
make a name."

"He's an intense admirer of that White Monkey you
gave us."

"Ah! I've been looking into the Chinese. If I go on
buying——" Soames paused.

235

"They *are* a bit of an antidote, aren't they, sir? That 'Earthly Paradise'! And those geese—they don't seem to mind your counting their feathers, do they?"

Soames made no reply; he was evidently thinking: 'How on earth I missed those things when they first came on the market!' Then, raising his umbrella, and pointing it as if at the book trade, he asked:

"Young Butterfield—how's he doing?"

"Ah! I was going to let you know, sir. He came in yesterday and told me that he saw Elderson two days ago. He went to sell him a copy of my father's 'Limited'; Elderson said nothing and bought two."

"The deuce he did!"

"Butterfield got the impression that his visit put the wind up him. Elderson knows, of course, that I'm in this firm, and your son-in-law."

Soames frowned. "I'm not sure," he said, "that sleeping dogs——! Well, I'm on my way there now."

"Mention the book, sir, and see how Elderson takes it. Would you like one yourself? You're on the list. E, F—Butterfield should be reaching you to-day. It'll save you a refusal. Here it is—nice get-up. One guinea."

" 'Duet,' " read Soames. "What's it about? Musical?"

"Not precisely. A sort of cat-calling between the ghosts of the G.O.M. and Dizzy."

"I'm not a reader," said Soames. He pulled out a note. "Why didn't you make it a pound? Here's the shilling."

"Thanks awfully, sir; I'm sure my father'll be frightfully bucked to think you've got one."

"Will he?" said Soames, with a faint smile. "D'you ever do any *work* here?"

"Well, we try to turn a doubtful penny."

"What d'you make at it?"

"Personally, about five hundred a year."

"That all?"

"Yes, but I doubt if I'm worth more than three."

"H'm! I thought you'd got over your Socialism."

"I fancy I have, sir. It didn't seem to go with my position."

"No," said Soames. "Fleur seems well."

"Yes, she's splendid. She does the Coué stunt, you know."

Soames stared. "That's her mother," he said. "I can't tell. Goodbye! Oh! I want to know; what's the meaning of that expression 'got his goat'?"

"'Got his goat'? Oh, raised his dander, if you know what that means, it was before my time."

"I see," said Soames; "I had it right, then. Well!" He turned. His back was very neat and real. It vanished through the doorway, and with it seemed to go the sense of definition.

Michael took up the proofs, and read two poems. Bitter as quinine! The unrest in them—the yearning behind the words! Nothing Chinese there! After all, the ancients—like Old Forsyte, and his father in a very different way—had an anchor down. 'What is it?' thought Michael. 'What's wrong with us? We're quick, and clever, cock-sure, and dissatisfied. If only something would enthuse us, or get *our* goats! We've chucked religion, tradition, property, pity; and in their place we put—what? Beauty? Gosh! See Walter Nazing, and the Café C'rillon! And yet—we must be after something! Better world? Doesn't look like it. Future life? Suppose I ought to "look into spiritualism," as Old Forsyte would say. But —half in this world, half in that—deuced odd if spirits are less restive than we are!'

To what—to what, then, was it all moving?

'Dash it!' thought Michael, getting up, 'I'll try dictating an advertisement!'

"Will you come in, please, Miss Perren? For the new Desert volume—Trade Journals: 'Danby and Winter will shortly issue "Counterfeits," by the author of "Copper Coin," the outstanding success of the last publishing season.' I wonder how many publishers have claimed that, Miss Perren, for how many books this year? 'These poems show all the brilliancy of mood, and more than the technical accomplishment of the young author's first volume.' How's that?"

"Brilliancy of mood, Mr. Mont? Do you think?"

"No. But what am I to say? 'All the pangs and pessimism'?"

"Oh, no! But possibly: 'All the brilliancy of diction, the strangeness and variety of mood.' "

"Good. But it'll cost more. Say: 'All the brilliant strangeness'; that'll ring their bells in once. We're nuts on 'the strange,' but we're not getting it—the *outré*, yes, but not the strange."

"Surely Mr. Desert gets——"

"Yes, sometimes; but hardly any one else. To be strange, you've got to have guts, if you'll excuse the phrase, Miss Perren."

"Certainly, Mr. Mont. That young man Bicket is waiting to see you."

"He is, is he?" said Michael, taking out a cigarette. "Give me time to tighten my belt, Miss Perren, and ask him up."

'The lie benevolent,' he thought; 'now for it!'

The entrance of Bicket into a room where his last appearance had been so painful, was accomplished with a certain stolidity. Michael stood, back to the hearth, smoking; Bicket, back to a pile of modern novel, with the words "This great new novel" on it. Michael nodded.

"Hallo, Bicket!"

Bicket nodded.

"Hope you're keeping well, sir?"

"Frightfully well, thank you." And there was silence.

"Well," said Michael, at last, "I suppose you've come about that little advance to your wife. It's quite all right; no hurry whatever."

While saying this he had become conscious that the "little snipe" was dreadfully disturbed. His eyes had a most peculiar look, those large, shrimp-like eyes which seemed, as it were, in advance of the rest of him. He hastened on:

"I believe in Australia myself. I think you're perfectly right, Bicket, and the sooner you go, the better. She doesn't look too strong."

Bicket swallowed.

"Sir," he said, "you've been a gent to me, and it's hard to say things."

"Then don't."

Bicket's cheeks became suffused with blood: queer effect in that pale, haggard face.

"It isn't what you think," he said: "I've come to ask you to tell me the truth." Suddenly he whipped from his pocket what Michael perceived to be a crumpled novel-wrapper.

"I took this from a book on the counter as I came by, downstairs. There! Is that my wife?" He stretched it out.

Michael beheld with consternation the wrapper of Storbert's novel. One thing to tell the lie benevolent already determined on—quite another to deny this!

Bicket gave him little time.

"I see it is, from your fyce," he said. "What's it all mean? I want the truth—I must 'ave it! I'm gettin' wild over all this. If that's 'er fyce there, then that's 'er body in the Gallery—Aubrey Greene; it's the syme nyme. What's it all mean?" His face had become almost formidable; his cockney accent very broad. "What gyme 'as she been plyin'? You gotta tell me before I go aht of 'ere."

Michael's heels came together. He said quietly:

"Steady, Bicket."

"Steady! You'd be steady if *your* wife——! All that money! *You* never advanced it—you never give it 'er—never! Don't tell me you did!"

Michael had taken his line. No lies!

"I lent her ten pounds to make a round sum of it—that's all; the rest she earned—honourably; and you ought to be proud of her."

Bicket's mouth fell open.

"Proud? And how's she earned it? Proud! My Gawd!"

Michael said coldly:

"As a model. I myself gave her the introduction to

my friend, Mr. Greene, the day you had lunch with me. You've heard of models, I suppose?"

Bicket's hands tore the wrapper, and the pieces fell to the floor. "Models!" he said: "Pynters—yes, I've 'eard of 'em—Swines!"

"No more swine than you are, Bicket. Be kind enough not to insult my friend. Pull yourself together, man, and take a cigarette."

Bicket dashed the proffered case aside.

"I—I—was stuck on her," he said passionately, "and she's put this up on me!" A sort of sob came out of his lungs.

"You were stuck on her," said Michael; his voice had sting in it. "And when she does her best for you, you turn her down—is that it? Do you suppose she liked it?"

Bicket covered his face suddenly.

"What should I know?" he muttered from behind his hands.

A wave of pity flooded up in Michael. Pity! Blurb!

He said drily: "When you've quite done, Bicket. D'you happen to remember what *you* did for *her?*"

Bicket uncovered his face and stared wildly. "You've never told her that?"

"No; but I jolly well will if you don't pull yourself together."

"What do I care if you do, now—lyin' like that, for all the men in the world! Sixty pound! Honourably! D'you think I believe that?" His voice had desolation in it.

"Ah!" said Michael. "You don't believe simply because you're ignorant, as ignorant as the swine you talk of. A girl can do what she did and be perfectly honest, as I haven't the faintest doubt she is. You've only to look at her, and hear the way she speaks of it. She did it because she couldn't bear to see you selling those balloons. She did it to get you out of the gutter, and give you both a chance. And now you've got the chance, you kick up like this. Dash it all, Bicket, be a sport! Suppose I tell her what you did for her—d'you think she's going to squirm and squeal? Not she! It was damned human of you, and it was damned human of her; and don't you forget it!"

Bicket swallowed violently again.

"It's all very well," he said, sullenly; "it 'asn't 'appened to you."

Michael was afflicted at once. No! It hadn't happened to him! And all his doubts of Fleur in the days of Wilfrid came hitting him.

"Look here, Bicket," he said, "do you doubt your wife's affection? The whole thing is there. I've only seen her twice, but I don't see how you can. If she weren't fond of you, why should she want to go to Australia, when she knows she can make good money here, and enjoy herself if she wants? I can vouch for my friend Greene. He's dashed decent, and I *know* he's played cricket."

But, searching Bicket's face, he wondered: Were all the others she had sat to as dashed decent?

"Look here, Bicket! We all get up against it sometimes; and that's the test of us. You've just *got* to believe in her; there's nothing else to it."

"To myke a show of herself for all the world to see!" The words seemed to struggle from the skinny throat. "I saw that picture bought yesterday by a ruddy alderman."

Michael could not conceal a grin at this description of "Old Forsyte."

"As a matter of fact," he said, "it was bought by my own father-in-law as a present to us, to hang in our house. And, mind you, Bicket, it's a fine thing."

"Ah!" cried Bicket, "it *is* a fine thing! Money! It's money bought her. Money'll buy anything. It'll buy the 'eart out of your chest."

And Michael thought: 'I can't get away with it a bit! What price emancipation? He's never heard of the Greeks! And if he had, they'd seem to him a lot of loose-living foreigners. I must quit.' And, suddenly, he saw tears come out of those shrimp's eyes, and trickle down the hollowed cheeks.

Very disturbed, he said hastily:

"When you get out there, you'll never think of it again. Hang it all, Bicket, be a man! She did it for the best. If I were you, I'd never let on to her that I knew. That's what she'd do if I told her how you snooped those 'Copper Coins.' "

Bicket clenched his fists—the action went curiously with the tears; then, without a word, he turned and shuffled out.

'Well,' thought Michael, 'giving advice is clearly not my stunt. Poor little snipe!"

Chapter Six

QUITTANCE

━━◆━━

BICKET stumbled, half-blind, along the Strand. Naturally good-tempered, such a nerve-storm made him feel ill, and bruised in the brain. Sunlight and motion slowly restored some power of thought. He had got the truth. But was it the whole and nothing but the truth? Could she have made all that money without——? If he could believe that, then, perhaps—out of this country where people could see her naked for a shilling—he might forget. But—all that money! And even if all earned "honourable," as Mr. Mont had put it, in how many days, exposed to the eyes of how many men? He groaned aloud in the street. The thought of going home to her—of a scene, of what he might learn if there *were* a scene, was just about unbearable. And yet—must do it, he supposed. He could have borne it better under St. Paul's, standing in the gutter, offering his balloons. A man of leisure for the first time in his life, a blooming "alderman" with nothing to do but step in and take a ticket to the ruddy butterflies! And he owed that leisure to what a man with nothing to take his thoughts off simply could not bear! He would rather have snaffled the money out of a shop till. Better that on his soul, than the jab of this dark fiendish sexual jealousy. 'Be a man!' Easy said! 'Pull yourself together! She did it for you!' He would a hundred times rather she had not. Blackfriars Bridge! A dive, and an end in the mud down there? But you had to rise three times; they would fish you out alive, and run you in for it—and nothing gained—not even the pleasure of thinking that Vic would see what she had done, when she came to identify the body. Dead was dead, anyway, and he would never know what she felt post-mortem! He trudged across the bridge, keeping his eyes before him. Little Ditch Street—*how* he used to scuttle down it, back to her, when she had pneumonia! Would he never feel like that again? He strode past the window, and went in.

Victorine was still bending over the brown tin trunk. She straightened herself, and on her face came a cold, tired look.

"Well," she said, "I see you know."

Bicket had but two steps to take in that small room. He took them, and put his hands on her shoulders. His face was close, his eyes, so large and strained, searched hers.

"I know you've myde a show of yerself for all London to see; what I want to know is—the rest!"

Victorine stared back at him.

"The rest!" she said—it was not a question, just a repetition, in a voice that seemed to mean nothing.

"Ah!" said Bicket hoarsely; "the rest— Well?"

"If you think there's a 'rest,' that's enough."

Bicket jerked his hands away.

"Aoh! for the land's sake, daon't be mysterious. I'm 'alf orf me nut!"

"I see that," said Victorine; "and I see this: You aren't what I thought you. D'you think I liked doing it?" She raised her dress and took out the notes. "There you are! You can go to Australia without me."

Bicket cried hoarsely: "And leave you to the blasted pynters?"

"And leave me to meself. Take them!"

But Bicket recoiled against the door, staring at the notes with horror. "Not me!"

"Well, *I* can't keep 'em. I earned them to get you out of this."

There was a long silence, while the notes lay between them on the table, still crisp if a little greasy—the long-desired, the dreamed-of means of release, of happiness together in the sunshine. There they lay; neither would take them! What then?

"Vic," said Bicket at last, in a hoarse whisper, "swear you never let 'em touch you!"

"Yes, I can swear that."

And she could smile, too, saying it—that smile of hers! How believe her—living all these months, keeping it from him, telling him a lie about it in the end! He sank into a chair by the table and laid his head on his arms.

Victorine turned and began pulling an old cord round the trunk. He raised his head at the tinny sound. Then she really meant to go away! He saw his life devastated, empty as a cocoanut on Hampstead Heath; and all defence ran melted out of his cockney spirit. Tears rolled from his eyes.

"When you were ill," he said, "I stole for you. I got the sack for it."

She spun round. "Tony—you never told me! What did you steal?"

"Books. All your extra feedin' was books."

For a long minute she stood looking at him, then stretched out her hands without a word. Bicket seized them.

"I don't care about anything," he gasped, "so 'elp me, so long as you're fond of me, Vic!"

"And I don't neither. Oh! let's get out of this, Tony!— this awful little room, this awful country. Let's get out of it all!"

"Yes," said Bicket; and put her hands to his eyes.

Chapter Seven

LOOKING INTO ELDERSON

———— ❖——❖——❖ ————

$\mathfrak{S}$OAMES had left Danby and Winter divided in thought between Elderson and the White Monkey. As Fleur surmised, he had never forgotten Aubrey Greene's words concerning that bit of salvage from the wreck of George Forsyte. "Eat the fruits of life, scatter the rinds, and get copped doing it." His application of them tended towards the field of business.

The country was still living on its capital. With the collapse of the carrying trade and European markets, they were importing food they couldn't afford to pay for. In his opinion they would get copped doing it, and that before long. British credit was all very well, the wonder of the world and that, but you couldn't live indefinitely on wonder. With shipping idle, concerns making a loss all over the place, and the unemployed in swarms, it was a pretty pair of shoes! Even insurance must suffer before long. Perhaps that chap Elderson had foreseen this already, and was simply feathering his nest in time. If one was to be copped in any case, why bother to be honest? This was cynicism so patent, that all the Forsyte in Soames rejected it; and yet it would keep coming back. In a general bankruptcy, why trouble with thrift, farsightedness, integrity? Even the Conservatives were refusing to call themselves Conservatives again, as if there were something ridiculous about the word, and they knew there was really nothing left to conserve. "Eat the fruit, scatter the rinds, and get copped doing it." That young painter had said a clever thing—yes, and his picture was clever, though Dumetrius had done one over the price—as usual! Where would Fleur hang it? In the hall, he shouldn't be surprised—good light there; and the sort of people they knew wouldn't jib at the nude. Curious—where all the nudes went to! You never saw a nude—no more than you saw the proverbial dead donkey! Soames had a momentary vision of dying donkeys laden with pictures of the nude, stepping off the edge of the world. Refusing its extravagance, he raised his eyes, just in time to see St. Paul's as large as life. That little beggar with his balloons wasn't there to-day! Well—he'd nothing for him! At a tangent his thoughts turned towards the object of his pilgrimage—the P.P.R.S. and its half-year's accounts. At his suggestion, they were writing off that German business wholesale—a dead loss of two hundred and thirty thousand pounds. There would be no interim dividend, and even then they would be carrying forward a debit towards the next half-year. Well! better have a rotten tooth out at once and done with; the shareholders would have six months to get used to the gap before the general meeting. He himself had got used to it already, and so would they in time. Shareholders were seldom nasty unless startled—a long-suffering lot!

In the board room the old clerk was still filling his inkpots from the magnum.

"Manager in?"

"Yes, sir."

"Say I'm here, will you?"

The old clerk withdrew. Soames looked at the clock. Twelve! A little shaft of sunlight slanted down the wainscoting and floor. There was nothing else alive in the room save a bluebottle and the tick of the clock; not even a daily paper. Soames watched the bluebottle. He remembered how, as a boy, he had preferred bluebottles and greenbottles to the ordinary fly, because of their bright colour. It was a lesson. The showy things, the brilliant people, were the dangerous. Witness the Kaiser, and that precious Italian poet—what was his name! And this Jack-o'-lantern of their own! He shouldn't be surprised if Elderson were brilliant in private life. Why didn't the chap come? Was that encounter with young Butterfield giving him pause? The bluebottle crawled up the pane, buzzed down, crawled up again; the sunlight stole inward along the floor. All was vacuous in the board room, as though embodying the principle of insurance: "Keep things as they are."

'Can't kick my heels here for ever,' thought Soames, and moved to the window. In that wide street leading to the river, sunshine illumined a few pedestrains and a brewer's dray, but along the main artery at the end the traffic streamed and rattled. London! A monstrous place! And all insured! 'What'll it be like thirty years hence?' he thought. To think that there would be London, without himself to see it! He felt sorry for the place, sorry for himself. Even old Gradman would be gone. He supposed the insurance societies would look after it, but he didn't know. And suddenly he became aware of Elderson. The fellow looked quite jaunty, in a suit of dittoes and a carnation.

"Contemplating the future, Mr. Forsyte?"

"No," said Soames. How had the fellow guessed his thoughts?

"I'm glad you've come in. It gives me a chance to say how grateful I am for the interest you take in the concern. It's rare. A manager has a lonely job."

Was he mocking? He seemed altogether very spry and uppish. Light-heartedness always made Soames suspicious —there was generally some reason for it.

"If every director were as conscientious as you, one would sleep in one's bed. I don't mind telling you that the amount of help I got from the Board before you came on it was—well—negligible."

Flattery! The fellow must be leading up to something! Elderson went on:

"I can say to you what I couldn't say to any of the others: I'm not at all happy about business, Mr. Forsyte. England is just about to discover the state she's really in."

Faced with this startling confirmation of his own thoughts, Soames reacted.

"No good crying out before we're hurt," he said; "the pound's still high. We're good stayers."

"In the soup, I'm afraid. If something drastic isn't done—we *shall* stay there. And anything drastic, as you know, means disorganisation and lean years before you reap reward."

How could the fellow talk like this, and look as bright and pink as a new penny? It confirmed the theory that he didn't care what happened. And, suddenly, Soames resolved to try a shot.

"Talking of lean years—I came in to say that I think we must call a meeting of the shareholders over this dead loss of the German business." He said it to the floor, and looked quickly up. The result was disappointing. The manager's light-grey eyes met his without a blink.

"I've been expecting that from you," he said.

'The deuce you have!' thought Soames, for it had but that moment come into his mind.

"By all means call one," went on the manager; "but I'm afraid the Board won't like it."

Soames refrained from saying: "Nor do I."

"Nor the shareholders, Mr. Forsyte. In a long experience I've found that the less you rub their noses in anything unpleasant, the better for every one."

"That may be," said Soames, stiffening in contrariety; "but it's all a part of the vice of not facing things."

"I don't think, Mr. Forsyte, that you will accuse *me* of not facing things, in the time to come."

Time to come! Now, what on earth did the fellow mean by that?

"Well, I shall moot it at the next Board," he said.

"Quite!" said the manager. "Nothing like bringing things to a head, is there?"

Again that indefinable mockery, as if he had something up his sleeve. Soames looked mechanically at the fellow's cuffs—beautifully laundered, with a blue stripe; at his holland waistcoat, and his bird's-eye tie—a regular dandy. He would give him a second barrel!

"By the way," he said, "Mont's written a book. I've taken a copy."

Not a blink! A little more show of teeth, perhaps—false, no doubt!

"I've taken two—poor, dear Mont!"

Soames had a sense of defeat. This chap was armoured like a crab, varnished like a Spanish table.

"Well," he said, "I must go."

The manager held out his hand.

"Good-bye, Mr. Forsyte. I'm so grateful to you."

The fellow was actually squeezing his hand. Soames went out confused. To have his hand squeezed was so rare! It undermined him. And yet, it might be the crown of a consummate bit of acting. He couldn't tell. He had, however, less intention even than before of moving for a meeting of the shareholders. No, no! That had just been a shot to get a rise; and it had failed. But the Butterfield shot had gone home, surely! If innocent, Elderson must certainly have alluded to the impudence of the young man's call. And yet such a cool card was capable of failing to rise, just to tease you! No! Nothing doing—as they said nowadays. He was as far as ever from a proof of guilt; and to speak truth, glad of it. Such a scandal could serve no purpose save that of blackening the whole concern, directors and all. People were so careless, they never stopped to think, or apportion blame where it was due. Keep a sharp eye open, and go on as they were! No good stirring hornets' nests! He had got so far in thought and progress, when a voice said:

"Well met, Forsyte! are you going my way?"

"Old Mont," coming down the steps of 'Snooks'!

"I don't know," said Soames.

"I'm off to the Aeroplane for lunch."

"That new-fangled place?"

"Rising, you know, Forsyte—rising."

"I've just been seeing Elderson. He's bought two copies of your book."

"Dear me! Poor fellow!"

Soames smiled faintly. "That's what he said of you! And who d'you think sold them to him? Young Butterfield."

"Is he still alive?"

"He was, this morning."

Sir Lawrence's face took on a twist:

"I've been thinking, Forsyte. They tell me Elderson keeps two women."

Soames stared. The idea was attractive; would account for everything.

"My wife says it's one too many, Forsyte. What do you say?"

"I?" said Soames. "I only know the chap's as cool as a cucumber. I'm going in here. Good-bye!"

One could get no help from that baronet fellow; he couldn't take anything seriously. Two women! At Elderson's age! What a life! There were always men like that, not content with one thing at a time—living dangerously. It was mysterious to him. You might look and look into chaps like that, and see nothing. And yet, there they were! He crossed the hall, and went into the room where Connoisseurs were lunching. Taking down the menu at the service table, he ordered himself a dozen oysters; but, suddenly remembering that the month contained no "r," changed them to a fried sole.

Chapter Eight

LEVANTED

❧❧❧

"NO, dear heart, Nature's 'off'!"

"How d'you mean, Michael?"

"Well, look at the Nature novels we get. Sedulous stuff pitched on Cornish cliffs or Yorkshire moors—ever been on a Yorkshire moor?—it comes off on you; and the Dartmoor brand. Gosh! Dartmoor, where the passions come from—ever been on Dartmoor? Well, they don't, you know. And the South Sea bunch! Oh, la, la! And the poets, the splash-and-splutter school don't get within miles of Nature. The village idiot school is a bit better, certainly. After all, old Wordsworth made Nature, and she's a bromide. Of course, there's raw nature with the small 'n'; but if you come up against that, it takes you all your time to keep alive—the Nature we gas about is licensed, nicely blended and bottled. She's not modern enough for contemporary style."

"Oh! well, let's go on the river, anyway, Michael. We can have tea at 'The Shelter.' "

They were just reaching what Michael always called 'this desirable residence,' when Fleur leaned forward, and, touching his knee, said:

"I'm not half as nice to you as you deserve, Michael."

253

"Good Lord, darling! I thought you were."

"I know I'm selfish; especially just now."

"It's only the eleventh baronet."

"Yes; it's a great responsibility. I only hope he'll be like you."

Michael slid in to the landing-stage, shipped his sculls, and sat down beside her.

"If he's like me, I shall disown him. But sons take after their mothers."

"I meant in character. I want him frightfully to be cheerful and not restless, and have the feeling that life's worth while."

Michael stared at her lips—they were quivering; at her cheek, slightly browned by the afternoon's sunning; and, bending sideways, he put his own against it.

"He'll be a sunny little cuss, I'm certain."

Fleur shook her head.

"I don't want him greedy and self-centred; it's in my blood, you know. I can see it's ugly, but I can't help it. How do you manage not to be?"

Michael ruffled his hair with his free hand.

"The sun isn't too hot for you, is it, ducky?"

"No. Seriously, Michael—how?"

"But I *am* greedy. Look at the way I want you. Nothing will cure me of that."

A slight pressure of her cheek on his own was heartening, and he said:

"Do you remember coming down the garden one night, and finding me in a boat just here? When you'd gone, I stood on my head, to cool it. I was on my uppers; I didn't think I'd got an earthly——" He stopped. No! He would not remind her, but that was the night when she said: "Come again when I know I can't get my wish!" The unknown cousin!

Fleur said quietly:

"I was a pig to you, Michael, but I was awfully unhappy. That's gone. It's gone at last; there's nothing wrong now, except my own nature."

Conscious that his feelings betrayed the period, Michael said:

"Oh! if that's all! What price tea?"

They went up the lawn arm-in-arm. Nobody was at home—Soames in London, Annette at a garden-party.

"We'll have tea on the verandah, please," said Fleur.

Sitting there, happier than he ever remembered being, Michael conceded a certain value to Nature, to the sunshine stealing down, the scent of pinks and roses, the sighing in the aspens. Annette's pet doves were cooing; and, beyond the quietly-flowing river, the spires of poplar trees rose along the further bank. But, after all, he was only enjoying them because of the girl beside him, whom he loved to touch and look at, and because, for the first time, he felt as if she did not want to get up and flutter off to some one or something else. Curious that there could be, outside oneself, a being who completely robbed the world of its importance, "snooped," as it were, the whole "bag of tricks"—and she one's own wife! Very curious, considering what one was! He heard her say:

"Of course, mother's a Catholic; only, living with father down here, she left off practising. She didn't even bother me much. I've been thinking, Michael—what shall we do about *him?*"

"Let him rip."

"I don't know. He must be taught something, because of going to school. The Catholics, you know, really do get things out of their religion."

"Yes; they go it blind; it's the only logical way now."

"I think having no religion makes one feel that nothing matters."

Michael suppressed the words: "We could bring him up as a sunworshipper," and said, instead:

"It seems to me that whatever he's taught will only last till he can think for himself; then he'll settle down to what suits him."

"But what do *you* think about things, Michael? You're as good as any one I know."

"Gosh!" murmured Michael, strangely flattered: "Is that so?"

"What *do* you think? Be serious!"

"Well, darling, doctrinally nothing—which means, of course, that I haven't got religion. I believe one has to play the game—but that's ethics."

"But surely it's a handicap not to be able to rely on anything but oneself? If there's something to be had out of any form of belief, one might as well have it."

Michael smiled, but not on the surface.

"You're going to do just as you like about the eleventh baronet, and I'm going to abet you. But considering his breeding—I fancy he'll be a bit of a sceptic."

"But I don't *want* him to be. I'd rather he were snug, and convinced and all that. Scepticism only makes one restless."

"No white monkey in him? Ah! I wonder! It's in the air, I guess. The only thing will be to teach him a sense of other people, as young as possible, with a slipper, if necessary."

Fleur gave him a clear look, and laughed.

"Yes," she said: "Mother used to try, but father wouldn't let her generally."

They did not reach home till past eight o'clock.

"Either your father's here, or mine," said Michael, in the hall; "there's a prehistoric hat."

"It's Dad's. His is grey inside. Bart's is buff."

In the Chinese room Soames indeed was discovered, with an opened letter, and Ting-a-ling at his feet. He held the letter out to Michael, without a word.

There was no date, and no address; Michael read:

"Dear Mr. Forsyte,—Perhaps you will be good enough to tell the Board at the meeting on Tuesday that I am on my way to immunity from the consequences of any peccadillo I may have been guilty. By the time you receive this, I shall be there. I have always held that the secret of life, no less than that of business, is to know when not to stop. It will be no use to proceed against me, for my person will not be attachable, as I believe you call it in the law, and I have left no property behind. If your object was to corner me, I cannot congratulate you on your tactics. If, on the other hand, you inspired that young man's visit as a warning that you were still pursuing the matter, I should like to add new thanks to those which I expressed when I saw you a few days ago.

"Believe me, dear Mr. Forsyte,

"Faithfully yours,

"ROBERT ELDERSON."

Michael said cheerfully:

"Happy release! Now you'll feel safer, sir."

Soames passed his hand over his face, evidently wiping off its expression. "We'll discuss it later," he said. "This dog's been keeping me company."

Michael admired him at that moment. He was obviously swallowing his 'grief,' to save Fleur.

"Fleur's a bit tired," he said. "We've been on the river, and had tea at 'The Shelter'; Madame wasn't in. Lets have dinner at once, Fleur."

Fleur had picked up Ting-a-ling, and was holding her face out of reach of his avid tongue.

"Sorry you've had to wait, Dad," she murmured, behind the yellow fur; "I'm just going to wash; shan't change."

When she had gone, Soames reached for the letter.

"A pretty kettle of fish!" he muttered. "Where it'll end, I can't tell!"

"But isn't this the end, sir?"

Soames stared. These young people! Here he was, faced with a public scandal, which might lead to he didn't know what—the loss of his name in the city, the loss of his fortune, perhaps; and they took it as if——! They had no sense of responsibility—none! All his father's power of seeing the worst, all James's nervous pessimism, had come to the fore in him during the hour since, at the Connoisseurs' Club, he had been handed that letter. Only the extra 'form' of the generation that succeeded James saved him, now that Fleur was out of the room, from making an exhibition of his fears.

"Your father in town?"

"I believe so, sir."

"Good!" Not that he felt relief. That baronet chap was just as irresponsible—getting him to go on that Board! It all came of mixing with people brought up in a sort of incurable levity, with no real feeling for money.

"Now that Elderson's levanted," he said, "the whole thing must come out. Here's his confession in my hand—"

"Why not tear it up, sir, and say Elderson has developed consumption?"

The impossibility of getting anything serious from this young man afflicted Soames like the eating of heavy pudding.

"You think that would be honourable?" he said grimly.

"Sorry, sir!" said Michael, sobered. "Can I help at all?"

"Yes; by dropping your levity, and taking care to keep wind of this matter away from Fleur."

"I will," said Michael, earnestly: "I promise you. I'll Dutch-oyster the whole thing. What's your line going to be?"

"We shall have to call the shareholders together and explain this dicky-dealing. They'll very like take it in bad part."

"I can't see why they should. How could you have helped it?"

Soames sniffed.

"There's no connection in life between reward and your deserts. If the war hasn't taught you that, nothing will."

"Well," said Michael, "Fleur will be down directly. If you'll excuse me a minute; we'll continue it in our next."

Their next did not occur till Fleur had gone to bed.

"Now, sir," said Michael, "I expect my governor's at the Aeroplane. He goes there and meditates on the end of the world. Would you like me to ring him up, if your Board meeting's to-morrow?"

Soames nodded. He himself would not sleep a wink— why should "Old Mont"?

Michael went to the Chinese tea chest.

"Bart? This is Michael. Old For——my father-in-law is here; he's had a pill. . . . No; Elderson. Could you blow in by any chance and hear? . . . He's coming, sir. Shall we stay down, or go up to my study?"

"Down," muttered Soames, whose eyes were fixed on the white monkey. "I don't know what we're all coming to," he added, suddenly.

"If we did, sir, we should die of boredom."

"Speak for yourself. All this unreliability! I can't tell where it's leading."

"Perhaps there's somewhere, sir, that's neither heaven nor hell."

"A man of *his* age!"

"Same age as my dad; it was a bad vintage, I expect. If you'd been in the war, sir, it would have cheered you up no end."

"Indeed!" said Soames.

"It took the linch-pins out of the cart—admitted; but, my Lord! it did give you an idea of the grit there is about, when it comes to being up against it."

Soames stared. Was this young fellow reading him a lesson against pessimism?

"Look at young Butterfield, the other day," Michael went on, "going over the top, to Elderson! Look at the girl who sat for 'the altogether' in that picture you bought us! She's the wife of a packer we had, who got hoofed for snooping books. She made quite a lot of money by standing for the nude, and never lost her wicket. They're going to Australia on it. Yes, and look at that little snooper himself; he snooped to keep her alive after pneumonia, and came down to selling balloons."

"I don't know what you're talking about," said Soames.

"Only grit, sir. You said you didn't know what we were coming to. Well, look at the unemployed! Is there a country in the world where they stick it as they do here? I get awfully bucked at being English every now and then. Don't you?"

The words stirred something deep in Soames; but, far from giving it away, he continued to gaze at the white monkey. The restless, inhuman, and yet so human, angry sadness of the creature's eyes! 'No whites to them!' thought Soames: 'that's what does it, I expect!' And George had liked that picture to hang opposite his bed! Well, George had grit—joked with his last breath: very English, George! Very English, all the Forsytes! Old Uncle Jolyon, and his way with shareholders; Swithin, upright, puffy, huge in a too-little arm-chair at Timothy's: 'All these small fry!' he seemed to hear the words again; and Uncle Nicholas, whom that chap Elderson reproduced as it were unworthily, spry, and all-there, and pretty sensual, but quite above suspicion of dishonesty. And old Roger, with his crankiness, and German mutton! And his own father, James—how he had hung on, long and frail as a reed, hung on and on! And Timothy, preserved in Consols, dying at a hundred! Grit and body in those old English boys, in spite of their funny ways. And there stirred in Soames a sort of atavistic will-power. He would see, and they would see—and that was all about it!

The grinding of a taxi's wheels brought him back from reverie. Here came "Old Mont," tittuppy, and light in the head as ever, no doubt. And, instead of his hand, Soames held out Elderson's letter.

"Your precious schoolfellow's levanted," he said.

Sir Lawrence read it through, and whistled.

"What do you think, Forsyte—Constantinople?"

"More likely Monte Carlo," said Soames gloomily. "Secret commission—it's not an extraditable offence."

The odd contortions of that baronet's face were giving him some pleasure—the fellow seemed to be feeling it, after all.

"I should think he's really gone to escape his women, Forsyte."

The chap was incorrigible! Soames shrugged his shoulders almost violently.

"You'd better realise," he said, "that the fat is in the fire."

"But surely, my dear Forsyte, it's been there ever since the French occupied the Ruhr. Elderson has cut his lucky; we appoint some one else. What more is there to it?"

Soames had the peculiar feeling of having overdone his own honesty. If an honourable man, a ninth baronet, couldn't see the implications of Elderson's confession, were they really there? Was any fuss and scandal necessary? Goodness knew, *he* didn't want it! He said heavily:

"We now have conclusive evidence of a fraud; we *know* Elderson was illegally paid for putting through business by which the shareholders have suffered a dead loss. How can we keep this knowledge from them?"

"But the mischief's done, Forsyte. How will the knowledge help them?"

Soames frowned.

"We're in a fiduciary position. I'm not prepared to run the risks of concealment. If we conceal, we're accessory after the fact. The thing might come out at any time." If that was caution, not honesty, he couldn't help it.

"I should be glad to spare Elderson's name. We were at——"

"I'm aware of that," said Soames, drily.

"But what risk is there of its coming out, Forsyte? Elderson won't mention it; nor young Butterfield, if you tell him not to. Those who paid the commission certainly won't. And beyond us three here, no one else knows. It's not as if we profited in any way."

Soames was silent. The argument was specious. Entirely unjust, of course, that he should be penalised for what Elderson had done!

"No," he said, suddenly, "it won't do. Depart from the law, and you can't tell where it'll end. The shareholders have suffered this loss, and they have the right to all the facts within the directors' knowledge. There might be some means of restitution they could avail themselves of. We can't judge. It may be they've a remedy against ourselves."

"If that's so, Forsyte, I'm with you."

Soames felt disgust. Mont had no business to put it

with a sort of gallantry that didn't count the cost; when
the cost, if cost there were, would fall, not on Mont,
whose land was heavily mortgaged, but on himself, whose
property was singularly realisable.

"Well," he said, coldly, "remember that to-morrow.
I'm going to bed."

At his open window upstairs he felt no sense of
virtue, but he enjoyed a sort of peace. He had taken
his line, and there it was!

Chapter Nine

SOAMES DOESN'T GIVE A DAMN

DURING the month following the receipt of Elder-son's letter, Soames aged more than thirty days. He had forced his policy of disclosure on a doubting Board, the special meeting had been called, and, just as, twenty-three years ago, pursuing divorce from Irene, he had to face the public eye, so now he suffered day and night in dread of that undiscriminating optic. The French had a proverb: *"Les absents ont toujours tort!"* but Soames had grave doubts about it. Elderson would be absent from that meeting of the shareholders, but—unless he was much mistaken—he himself, who would be present, would come in for the blame. The French were not to be relied on. What with his anxiety about Fleur, and his misgiving about the public eye, he was sleeping badly, eating little, and feeling below par. Annette had recommended him to see a doctor. That was probably why he did not. Soames had faith in doctors for other people; but they had never—he would say—done anything for *him,* possibly because, so far, there had not been anything to do.

Failing in her suggestion, and finding him every day less sociable, Annette had given him her book on Coué.

After running it through, he had meant to leave it in the train, but the theory, however extravagant, had somehow clung to him. After all, Fleur was doing it; and the thing cost you nothing: there might be something in it! There was. After telling himself that night twenty-five times that he was getting better and better, he slept so soundly that Annette, in the next room, hardly slept at all.

"Do you know, my friend," she said at breakfast, "you were snoring last night so that I could not hear the cock crow."

"Why should you want to?" said Soames.

"Well, never mind—if you had a good night. Was it my little Coué who gave you that nice dream?"

Partly from fear of encouraging Coué, and partly from fear of encouraging her, Soames avoided a reply; but he had a curious sense of power, as if he did not care what people said of him.

'I'll do it again to-night,' he thought.

"You know," Annette went on, "you are just the temperament for Coué, Soames. When you cure yourself of worrying you will get quite fat."

"Fat!" said Soames, looking at her curves. "I'd as soon grow a beard."

Fatness and beards were associated with the French. He would have to keep an eye on himself if he went on with this—er—what was one to call it?—Tomfoolery was hardly the word to conciliate the process, even if it did require you to tie twenty-five knots in a bit of string: very French, that, like telling your beads! He himself had merely counted on his fingers. The sense of power lasted all the way up to London; he had the conviction that he could sit in a draught if he wanted to, that Fleur would have her boy all right; and as to the P.P.R.S.— ten to one he wouldn't be mentioned by name in any report of the proceedings.

After an early lunch and twenty-five more assurances over his coffee, he set out for the City.

This Board, held just a week before the special meeting

of the shareholders, was in the nature of a dress rehearsal. The details of confrontation had to be arranged, and Soames was chiefly concerned with seeing that a certain impersonality should be preserved. He was entirely against disclosure of the fact that young Butterfield's story and Elderson's letter had been confided to himself. The phrase to be used should be a "member of the Board." He saw no need for anything further. As for explanations, they would fall, of course, to the chairman and the senior director, Lord Fontenoy. He found, however, that the Board thought he himself was the right person to bring the matter forward. No one else—they said—could supply the personal touch, the necessary conviction; the chairman should introduce the matter briefly, then call on Soames to give the evidence within his knowledge. Lord Fontenoy was emphatic.

"It's up to you, Mr. Forsyte. If it hadn't been for you, Elderson would be sitting there to-day. From beginning to end you put the wind up him; and I wish the deuce you hadn't. The whole thing's a confounded nuisance. He was a very clever fellow, and we shall miss him. Our new man isn't a patch on him. If he did take a few thou. under the rose, he took 'em off the Huns."

Old guinea-pig! Soames replied, acidly:

"And the quarter of a million he's lost the shareholders, for the sake of those few thou.? Bagatelle, I suppose?"

"Well, it might have turned out a winner; for the first year it did. We all back losers sometimes."

Soames looked from face to face. They did not support this blatant attitude, but in them all, except perhaps "Old Mont's," he felt a grudge against himself. Their expressions seemed to say: "Nothing of this sort ever happened till you came on the Board." He had disturbed their comfort, and they disliked him for it. They were an unjust lot! He said doggedly:

"You leave it to me, do you? Very well!"

What he meant to convey, or whether he meant to convey anything, he did not know; but even that "old guinea-pig" was more civil afterwards. He came away from the Board, however, without any sense of power at all. There he would be on Tuesday next, bang in the public eye.

After calling to enquire after Fleur, who was lying down rather poorly, he returned home with a feeling of having been betrayed. It seemed that he could not rely, after all, on this fellow with his twenty-five knots. However much better he might become, his daughter, his reputation, and possibly his fortune, were not apparently at the disposition of his subconscious self. He was silent at dinner, and went up afterwards to his picture gallery, to think things over. For half an hour he stood at the open window, alone with the summer evening; and the longer he stood there, the more clearly he perceived that the three were really one. Except for his daughter's sake, what did he care for his reputation or his fortune? His reputation! Lots of fools—if they couldn't see that he was careful and honest so far as had lain within his reach; so much the worse for them! His fortune—well, he had better make another settlement on Fleur and her child at once, in case of accidents; another fifty thousand. Ah! if she were only through her trouble! It was time Annette went up to her for good; and there was a thing they called twilight sleep. To have her suffering was not to be thought of!

The evening lingered out; the sun went down behind familiar trees; Soames' hands, grasping the window-ledge, felt damp with dew; sweetness of grass and river stole up into his nostrils. The sky had paled, and now began to darken; a scatter of stars came out. He had lived here a long time, through all Fleur's childhood—best years of his life; still, it wouldn't break his heart to sell. His heart was up in London. Sell? That was to run before the hounds with a vengeance. No—no!—it wouldn't come to *that!* He left the window and, turning up the lights, began the thousand and first tour of his pictures. He had made some good purchases since Fleur's marriage, and without wasting his money on fashionable favourites. He had made some good sales, too. The pictures in this gallery, if he didn't mistake, were worth from seventy to a hundred thousand pounds; and, with the profits on his sales from time to time, they stood him in at not half the money—not a bad result from a life's hobby, to say nothing of the pleasure! Of course, he might have taken up something else—butterflies, photography, archaeology, or first editions; some other sport in which you backed your judgment against the field, and collected the results; but he had never regretted choosing pictures. Not he! More to show for your money, more kudos, more profit, and more risk! The thought startled him a little; had he really taken to pictures because of the risk? A risk had never appealed to him; at least, he hadn't realised it, so far. Had his "subconscious" some part in the matter? He suddenly sat down and closed his eyes. Try the thing once more; very pleasant feeling, that morning, of not "giving a damn"; he never remembered having it before! He had always felt it necessary to worry—kind of insurance against the worst; but worry was wearing, no doubt about it, wearing. Turn out the light! They said in that book, you had to relax. In the now dim and shadowy room, with the starlight, through many windows, dusted over its reality, Soames, in his easy chair, sat very still. A faint drone rose on the words: "fatter and fatter" through his moving lips. 'No, no,' he thought: 'that's wrong!' And he began the drone again. The tips of his fingers ticked it off; on and on—he would give it a good chance. If only one needn't worry! On and on—"better and better!" If only——! His lips stopped moving; his grey head fell forward into the subconscious. And the stealing starlight dusted over him, too, a little unreality.

Chapter Ten

BUT TAKES NO CHANCES

———❖———◆———

ICHAEL knew nothing of the City; and, in the spirit of the old cartographers: "Where you know nothing, place terrors," made his way through the purlieus of the Poultry, towards that holy of holies, the offices of Cuthcott, Kingson and Forsyte. His mood was attuned to meditation, for he had been lunching with Sibley Swan at the Café C'rillon. He had known all the guests—seven chaps even more modern than old Sib—save only a Russian so modern that he knew no French and nobody could talk to him. Michael had watched them demolish everything, and the Russian closing his eyes, like a sick baby, at mention of any living name. . . . 'Carry on!' he thought, several of his favourites having gone down in the *mêlée*. 'Stab and bludge! Importance awaits you at the end of the alley.' But he had restrained his irreverence till the moment of departure.

"Sib," he said, rising, "all these chaps here are dead—ought they to be about in this hot weather?"

"What's that?" ejaculated Sibley Swan, amidst the almost painful silence of the chaps.

"I mean—they're alive—so they *must* be damned!" And avoiding a thrown chocolate which hit the Russian, he sought the door.

Outside, he mused: 'Good chaps, really! Not half so darned superior as they think they are. Quite a human touch—getting that Russian on the boko. Phew! It's hot!'

On that first day of the Eton and Harrow match all the forfeited heat of a chilly summer had gathered and shimmered over Michael on the top of his Bank 'bus; shimmered over straw hats, and pale, perspiring faces, over endless other 'buses, business men, policemen, shopmen at their doors, sellers of newspapers, laces, jumping toys, endless carts and cabs, letterings and wires, all the confusion of the greatest conglomeration in the world—adjusted almost to a hair's breadth, by an unseen instinct. Michael stared and doubted. Was it possible that, with every one pursuing his own business, absorbed in his own job, the thing could work out? An ant-heap was not busier, or more seemingly confused. Live wires crossed and crossed and crossed—inextricable entanglement, you'd say; and yet, life, the order needful to life, somehow surviving! 'No slouch of a miracle!' he thought, 'modern town life!' And suddenly it seemed to cease, as if demolished by the ruthless dispensation of some super Sibley Swan; for he was staring down a *cul-de-sac*. On both sides, flat houses, recently re-buffed, extraordinarily alike; at the end, a flat buff house, even more alike, and down to it, grey virgin pavement, unstained by horse or petrol; no cars, cats, carts, policemen, hawkers, flies, or bees. No sign of human life, except the names of legal firms to right and left of each open doorway.

" 'Cuthcott, Kingson and Forsyte, Commissioners for Oaths: First Floor.' "

'Rule Britannia!' thought Michael, ascending wide stone steps.

Entering the room to which he had been ushered, he saw an old and pug-faced fellow with a round grizzled beard, a black alpaca coat, and a roomy holland waistcoat round his roomy middle, who rose from a swivel chair.

"Aoh!" he said, "Mr. Michael Mont, I think. I've been expecting you. We shan't be long about it, after Mr.

Forsyte comes. He's just stepped around the corner. Mrs. Michael well, I hope?"

"Thanks; as well as——"

"Ye-es; it makes you anxious. Take a seat. Perhaps you'd like to read the draft?"

Thus prescribed for, Michael took some foolscap from a pudgy hand, and sat down opposite. With one eye on the old fellow, and the other on the foolscap, he read steadily.

"It seems to mean something," he said at last.

He saw a gape, as of a frog at a fly, settle in the beard; and hastened to repair his error.

"Calculating what's going to happen if something else doesn't, must be rather like being a bookmaker."

He felt at once that he had not succeeded. There was a grumpy mutter:

"We don't waste our time, 'ere. Excuse me, I'm busy."

Michael sat, compunctious, watching him tick down a long page of entries. He was like one of those old dogs which lie outside front doors, keeping people off the premises, and notifying their fleas. After less than five minutes of that perfect silence Soames came in.

"You're here, then?" he said.

"Yes, sir; I thought it best to come at the time you mentioned. What a nice cool room!"

"Have you read this?" asked Soames, pointing to the draft.

Michael nodded.

"Did you understand it?"

"Up to a point, I think."

"The interest on *this* fifty thousand," said Soames, "is Fleur's until her eldest child, if it's a boy, attains the age of twenty-one, when the capital becomes his absolutely. If it's a girl, Fleur retains half the income for life, the rest of the income becomes payable to the girl when she attains the age of twenty-one or marries, and the capital of that half goes to her child or children lawfully begotten, at majority or marriage, in equal shares.

The other half of the capital falls into Fleur's estate, and is possible by her will, or follows the laws of intestacy."

"You make it wonderfully clear," said Michael.

"Wait!" said Soames. "If Fleur has no children——"

Michael started.

"Anything is possible," said Soames gravely, "and my experience is that the contingencies not provided for are those which happen. In such a case the income of the whole is hers for life, and the capital hers at death to do as she likes with. Failing that, it goes to the next of kin. There are provisions against anticipation and so forth."

"Ought she to make a fresh will?" asked Michael, conscious of sweat on his forehead.

"Not unless she likes. Her present will covers it."

"Have I to do anything?"

"No. I wanted you to understand the purport before I sign; that's all. Give me the deed, Gradman, and get Wickson in, will you?"

Michael saw the old chap produce from a drawer a fine piece of parchment covered with copper-plate writing and seals, look at it lovingly, and place it before Soames. When he had left the room Soames said in a low voice:

"This meeting on Tuesday—I can't tell! But, whatever happens, so far as I can see, this ought to stand."

"It's awfully good of you, sir."

Soames nodded, testing a pen.

"I'm afraid I've got wrong with your old clerk," said Michael; "I like the look of him frightfully, but I accidentally compared him to a bookmaker."

Soames smiled. "Gradman," he said, "is a 'character.' There aren't many, nowadays."

Michael was wondering: Could one be a 'character' under the age of sixty?—when the 'character' returned, with a pale man in dark clothes.

Lifting his nose sideways, Soames said at once:

"This is a post-nuptial settlement on my daughter. I deliver this as my act and deed."

He wrote his name, and got up.

The pale person and Gradman wrote theirs, and the former left the room. There was a silence as of repletion.

"Do you want me any more?" asked Michael.

"Yes. I want you to see me deposit it at the bank with the marriage settlement. Shan't come back, Gradman!"

"Good-bye, Mr. Gradman."

Michael heard the old fellow mutter through his beard half buried in a drawer to which he was returning the draft, and followed Soames out.

"Here's where I used to be," said Soames as they went along the Poultry; "and my father before me."

"More genial, perhaps," said Michael.

"The trustees are meeting us at the bank; you remember them?"

"Cousins of Fleur's, weren't they, sir?"

"Second cousins; young Roger's eldest, and young Nicholas's. I chose them youngish. Very young Roger was wounded in the war—he does nothing. Very young Nicholas is at the Bar."

Michael's ears stood up. "What about the next lot, sir? Very very young Roger would be almost insulting, wouldn't it?"

"There won't be one," said Soames, "with taxation where it is. He can't afford it; he's a steady chap. What are you going to call your boy, if it *is* one?"

"We think Christopher, because of St. Paul's and Columbus. Fleur wants him solid, and I want him enquiring."

"H'm! And if it's a girl?"

"Oh!—if it's a girl—Anne."

"Yes," said Soames: "Very neat. Here they are!"

They had reached the bank, and in the entrance Michael saw two Forsytes between thirty and forty, whose chinny faces he dimly remembered. Escorted by a man with bright buttons down his front, they all went to a room, where a man without buttons produced a japanned box. One of the Forsytes opened it with a key; Soames muttered an incantation, and deposited the deed. When he and the chinnier Forsyte had exchanged a few remarks with the manager on the question of the bank rate, they all went back to the lobby and parted with the words: "Well, good-bye!"

"Now," said Soames, in the din and hustle of the street, "he's provided for, so far as I can see. When exactly do you expect it?"

"It should be just a fortnight."

"Do you believe in this—this twilight sleep?"

"I should like to," said Michael, conscious again of sweat on his forehead. "Fleur's wonderfully calm; she does Coué night and morning."

"That!" said Soames. He did not mention that he himself was doing it, thus giving away the state of his nerves. "If you're going home, I'll come, too."

"Good!" said Michael.

He found Fleur lying down with Ting-a-ling on the foot of the sofa.

"Your father's here, darling. He's been anointing the future with another fifty thou. I expect he'd like to tell you all about it."

Fleur moved restlessly.

"Presently. If it's going on as hot as this, it'll be rather a bore, Michael."

"Oh! but it won't, ducky. Three days and a thunderstorm."

Taking Ting-a-ling by the chin, he turned his face up.

"And how on earth is your nose going to be put out of joint, old man? There's no joint to put."

"He knows there's something up."

"He's a wise little brute, aren't you, old son?"

Ting-a-ling sniffed.

"Michael!"

"Yes, darling?"

"I don't seem to care about anything now—it's a funny feeling."

"That's the heat."

"No. I think it's because the whole business is **too** long. Everything's ready, and now it all seems rather stupid. One more person in the world or one more out of it—what does it matter?"

"Don't! It matters frightfully!"

"One more gnat to dance, one more ant to run about!"

Anguished, Michael said again:

"Don't, Fleur! That's just a mood."

"Is Wilfrid's book out?"

"It comes out to-morrow."

"I'm sorry I gave you such a bad time, there. I only didn't want to lose him."

Michael took her hand.

"Nor did I—goodness knows!" he said.

"He's never written. I suppose?"

"No."

"Well, I expect he's all right by now. Nothing lasts."

Michael put her hand to his cheek.

"*I* do, I'm afraid," he said.

The hand slipped round over his lips.

"Give Dad my love, and tell him I'll be down to tea. Oh! I'm so hot!"

Michael hovered a moment, and went out. Damn the heat, upsetting her like this!

He found Soames standing in front of the white monkey.

"I should take this down, if I were you," he muttered, "until it's over."

"Why, sir?" asked Michael, in surprise.

Soames frowned.

"Those eyes!"

Michael went up to the picture. Yes! He was a haunting kind of brute!

"But it's such top-hole work, sir."

Soames nodded.

"Artistically, yes. But at such times you can't be too careful what she sees."

"I believe you are right. Let's have him down."

"I'll hold him," said Soames, taking hold of the bottom of the picture.

"Got him tight? Right-o. Now!"

"You can say I wanted an opinion on his period,"

said Soames, when the picture had been lowered to the floor.

"There can hardly be a doubt of that, sir—the present!"

Soames stared. "What? Oh! You mean——? Ah! H'm! Don't let her know he's in the house."

"No. I'll lock him up." Michael lifted the picture. "D'you mind opening the door, sir?"

"I'll come back at tea-time," said Soames. "That'll look as if I'd taken him off. You can hang him again, later."

"Yes. Poor brute!" said Michael, bearing the monkey off to limbo.

Chapter Eleven

WITH A SMALL "N"

———▶◀———

ON the night of the Monday following, after Fleur
had gone to bed, Michael and Soames sat listening to the mutter of London coming through the windows
of the Chinese room opened to the brooding heat.

"They say the war killed sentiment," said Soames suddenly: "Is that true?"

"In a way, yes, sir. We had so much reality that we
don't want any more."

"I don't follow you."

"I meant that only reality really makes you feel. So
if you pretend there *is* no reality, you don't have to
feel. It answers awfully well, up to a point."

"Ah!" said Soames. "Her mother comes up to-morrow
morning, to stay. This P.P.R.S. meeting of mine is at
half-past two. Good-night!"

Michael, at the window, watched the heat gathered
black over the Square. A few tepid drops fell on his
outstretched hand. A cat stole by under a lamp-post, and
vanished into shadow so thick that it seemed uncivilised.

Queer question of "Old Forsyte's" about sentiment;
odd that he should ask it! 'Up to a point! But don't
we all get past that point?' he thought. Look at Wilfrid,

and himself—after the war they had deemed it blasphemous to admit that anything mattered except eating and drinking, for to-morrow they died; even fellows like Nazing, and Master, who were never in the war, had felt like that ever since. Well, Wilfrid had got it in the neck; and he himself had got it in the wind; and he would bet that—barring one here and there whose blood was made of ink—they would all get in the neck or wind soon or late. Why, he would cheerfully bear Fleur's pain and risk, instead of her! But if nothing mattered, why should he feel like that?

Turning from the window, he leaned against the lacquered back of the jade-green settee, and stared at the wall space between the Chinese tea-chests. Jolly thoughtful of the "old man" to have that white monkey down! The brute was potent—symbolic of the world's mood: beliefs cancelled, faiths withdrawn! And, dash it! not only the young—but the old—were in that temper! "Old Forsyte," or he would never have been scared by that Monkey's eyes; yes, and his own governor, and Elderson, and all the rest. Young and old—no real belief in anything! And yet—revolt sprang up in Michael, with a whirr, like a covey of partridges. It *did* matter that some person or some principle outside oneself should be more precious than oneself—it dashed well did! Sentiment, then, wasn't dead—nor faith, nor belief, which were the same things. They were only shedding shell, working through chrysalis, into—butterflies, perhaps. Faith, sentiment, belief, had gone underground, possibly. but they were there, even in "Old Forsyte" and himself. He had a good mind to put the monkey up again. No use exaggerating his importance! . . . By George! Some flare! A jagged streak of vivid light had stripped darkness off the night. Michael crossed, to close the windows. A shattering peal of thunder blundered overhead; and down came the rain, slashing and sluicing. He saw a man running, black, like a shadow across a dark blue screen; saw him by the light of another flash, suddenly made lurid and full of small meaning, with face of cheerful anxiety, as if he were saying: "Hang it, I'm getting wet!" Another frantic crash!

'Fleur!" thought Michael; and clanging the last window down, he ran upstairs.

She was sitting up in bed, with a face all round, and young, and startled.

'Brutes!' he thought—guns and the heavens confounded in his mind: 'They've waked her up!'

"It's all right, darling! Just another little summer kick-up! Were you asleep?"

"I was dreaming!" He felt her hand clutching within his own, saw a sudden pinched look on her face, with a sort of rage. What infernal luck!

"Where's Ting?"

No dog was in the corner.

"Under the bed—you bet! Would you like him up?"

"No. Let him stay; he hates it."

She put her head against his arm, and Michael curled his hand round her other ear.

"I never liked thunder much!" said Fleur, "and now it—it hurts!"

High above her hair Michael's face underwent the contortions of an overwhelming tenderness. One of those crashes which seem just overhead sent her face burrowing against his chest, and, sitting on the bed, he gathered her in, close.

"I wish it were over," came, smothered, from her lips.

"It will be directly, darling; it came on so suddenly!" But he knew she didn't mean the storm.

"If I come through, I'm going to be quiet different to you, Michael."

Anxiety was the natural accompaniment of such events, but the words "If I come through" turned Michael's heart right over. Incredible that one so young and pretty should be in even the remotest danger of extinction; incredibly painful that she should be in fear of it! He hadn't realised. She had been so calm, so matter-of-fact about it all.

"Don't!" he mumbled; "of course you'll come through."

"I'm afraid."

The sound was small and smothered, but the words hurt horribly. Nature, with the small "n," forcing fear into this girl he loved so awfully! Nature kicking up this godless din above her poor little head!

"Ducky, you'll have twilight sleep and know nothing about it; and be as right as rain in no time."

Fleur freed her hand.

"Not if it's not good for him. Is it?"

"I expect so, sweetheart; I'll find out. What makes you think——?"

"Only that it's not natural. I want to do it properly. Hold my hand hard, Michael. I—I'm not going to be a fool. Oh! Some one's knocking—go and see."

Michael opened the door a crack. Soames was there—unnatural—in a blue dressing gown and scarlet slippers!

"Is she all right?" he whispered.

"Yes, yes."

"In this bobbery she oughtn't to be left."

"No, sir, of course not. I shall sleep on the sofa."

"Call me, if anything's wanted."

"I will."

Soames' eyes slid past, peering into the room. A string worked in his throat, as if he had things to say which did not emerge. He shook his head, and turned. His slim figure, longer than usual, in its gown, receded down the corridor, past the Japanese prints which he had given them. Closing the door again, Michael stood looking at the bed. Fleur had settled down; her eyes were closed, her lips moving. He stole back on tiptoe. The thunder, travelling away south, blundered and growled as if regretfully. Michael saw her eyelids quiver, her lips stop, then move again. 'Coué!' he thought.

He lay down on the sofa at the foot of the bed, whence, without sound, he could raise himself and see her. Many times he raised himself. She had dropped off, was breathing quietly. The thunder was faint now, the flashes imperceptible. Michael closed his eyes.

A faint last mutter roused him to look at her once more, high on her pillows by the carefully shaded light. Young—young! Colourless, like a flower in wax! No scheme in her brain, no dread—peaceful! If only she could stay like that and wake up with it all over! He looked away. And there she was at the far end, dim, reflected in a glass; and there to the right, again. She lay, as it were, all round him in the pretty room, the inhabiting spirit—of his heart.

It was quite still now. Through a chink in those powder blue curtains he could see some stars. Big Ben chimed one.

He had slept, perhaps, dozed at least, dreamed a little. A small sound woke him. A very little dog, tail down, yellow, low and unimportant, was passing down the room, trailing across it to the far corner. 'Ah!" thought Michael, closing his eyes again: 'You!'

Chapter Twelve

ORDEAL BY SHAREHOLDER

———◆━◆━◆———

REPAIRING, next day, to the Aeroplane Club, where, notably spruce, Sir Lawrence was waiting in the lounge, Michael thought: 'Good old Bart! he's got himself up for the guillotine all right!'

"That white piping will show the blood!" he said. "Old Forsyte's neat this morning, but not so gaudy."

"Ah! How is 'Old Forsyte'? In good heart?"

"One doesn't ask him, sir. How do you feel yourself?"

"Exactly as I used to before the Eton and Winchester match. I think I shall have shandy-gaff at lunch."

When they had taken their seats, Sir Lawrence went on:

"I remember seeing a man tried for murder in Colombo; the poor fellow was positively blue. I think my favourite moment in the past, Michael, is Walter Raleigh asking for a second shirt. By the way, it's never been properly settled yet whether the courtiers of that day were lousy. What are you going to have, my dear fellow?"

"Cold beef, pickled walnuts, and gooseberry tart."

"Excellent for the character. I shall have curry; they give you a very good Bombay duck here. I rather fancy we shall be fired, Michael. *'Nous sommes trahis!'* used to be the prerogative of the French, but I'm afraid we're getting the attitude, too. The Yellow Press has made a difference."

Michael shook his head.

"We say it, but we don't act on it; the climate's too uncertain."

"That sounds deep. This looks very good curry—will you change your mind? Old Fontenoy sometimes comes in here; he has no inside. It'll be serious for him if we're shown the door."

"Deuced rum," said Michael suddenly, "how titles still go down. There can't be any belief in their business capacity."

"Character, my dear fellow—the good old English gentleman. After all, there's something in it."

"I fancy, sir, it's more a case of complex in the shareholders. Their parents show them a lord when they're young."

"Shareholders," said Sir Lawrence; "the word is comprehensive. Who are they, what are they, when are they?"

"This afternoon," said Michael, "and I shall have a good look at them."

"They won't let you in, my dear."

"No?"

"Certainly not."

Michael frowned.

"What paper," he said, "is sure not to be represented?"

Sir Lawrence gave his whinnying laugh.

"*The Field,*" he said; "*The Horse and Hound; The Gardener's Weekly.*"

"I'll slide in on them."

"You'll see us die game, I hope," said Sir Lawrence, with sudden gravity.

They took a cab together to the meeting, but separated before reaching the door of the hotel.

Michael had thought better of the Press, and took up a position in the passage, whence he could watch for a chance. Stout men, in dark suits, with a palpable look of having lunched off turbot, joints, and cheese, kept passing him. He noticed that each handed the janitor a paper.

'I'll hand him a paper, too,' he thought, 'and scoot in.' Watching for some even stouter men, he took cover between two of them, and approached the door, with an announcement of "Counterfeits" in his left hand. Handing it across a neighbouring importance, he was quickly into a seat. He saw the janitor's face poked round the door. 'No, my friend,' thought Michael, 'if you could tell duds from shareholders, you wouldn't be in that job!"

He found a report before him, and holding it up, looked at other things. The room seemed to him to have been got by a concert-hall out of a station waiting-room. It had a platform with a long table behind which were seven empty chairs, and seven inkpots, with seven quill pens upright in them. 'Quills!' thought Michael; 'symbolic, I suppose—they'll all use fountain-pens!

Back-centre of the platform was a door, and in front, below it, a table, where four men were sitting, fiddling with notebooks. 'Orchestra,' thought Michael. He turned his attention to the eight or ten rows of shareholders. They looked what they were, but he could not tell why. Their faces were cast in an infinity of moulds, but all had the air of waiting for something they knew they would not get. What sort of lives did they lead, or did their lives lead them? Nearly all wore moustaches. His neighbours to right and left were the same stout shareholders between whom he had slipped in; they both had thick lobes to their ears, and necks even broader than the straight broad backs of their heads. He was a good deal impressed. Dotted here and there he noticed a woman, or a parson. There was practically no conversation, from which he surmised that no one knew his neighbour. He had a feeling that a dog somewhere would have humanised the occasion. He was musing on the colour-scheme of green picked out with chocolate and chased with gold, when the door behind the platform was thrown open, and seven men in black coats filed in, and with little bows took their seats behind the quills. They reminded him of people getting up on horses, or about to play the piano—full of small adjustments. That—on the

Chairman's right—would be old Fontenoy, with a face entirely composed of features. Michael had an odd conceit: a little thing in a white top-hat sat inside the brain, driving the features eight-in-hand. Then came a face straight from a picture of Her Majesty's Government in 1850, round and pink, with a high nose, a small mouth, and little white whiskers; while at the end on the right was a countenance whose jaw and eyes seemed boring into a conundrum beyond the wall at Michael's back. 'Legal!' he thought. His scrutiny passed back to the Chairman. Chosen? Was he—or was he not? A bearded man, a little behind on the Chairman's left, was already reading from a book, in a rapid monotonous voice. That must be the secretary letting off his minute-guns. And in front of him was clearly the new manager, on whose left Michael observed his own father. The dark pothooks over Sir Lawrence's right eye were slightly raised, and his mouth was puckered under the cut line of his small moustache. He looked almost Oriental, quick but still. His left hand held his tortoiseshell-rimmed monocle between thumb and finger. 'Not quite in the scene!' thought Michael; 'poor old Bart!' He had come now to the last of the row. "Old Forsyte" was sitting precisely as if alone in the world; with one corner of his mouth just drawn down, and one nostril just drawn up, he seemed to Michael quite fascinatingly detached; and yet not out of the picture. Within that still, neat figure, whereof only one patent-leather boot seemed with a slight movement to be living, was intense concentration, entire respect for the proceedings, and yet, a queer contempt for them; he was like a statue of reality, by one who had seen that there was precious little reality in it. 'He chills my soup,' thought Michael, 'but—dash it!—I can't help half admiring him!'

The Chairman had now risen. 'He *is*'—thought Michael; 'no, he isn't—yes—no—I can't tell!' He could hardly attend to what the Chairman said, for wondering whether he was chosen or not, though well aware that it did not matter at all. The Chairman kept steadily on. Distracted, Michael caught words and words: "European situation—misguided policy—French—totally unexpected—position disclosed—manager—unfortunate circumstances shortly to be explained to you—future of this great concern—no reason to doubt——"

'Oil,' thought Michael, 'he is—and yet——'

"I will now ask Mr. Forsyte, one of your directors, to give you at first hand an account of this painful matter."

Michael saw Soames, pale and deliberate, take a piece of paper from his breast-pocket, and rise. Was it to the occasion?

"I will give you the facts shortly," he said in a voice which reminded Michael of a dry, made-up wine. "On the eleventh of January last I was visited by a clerk in the employ of the Society——"

Familiar with these details, Michael paid them little attention, watching the shareholders for signs of reaction. He saw none, and it was suddenly borne in on him why they wore moustaches: They could not trust their mouths! Character was in the mouth. Moustaches had come in when people no longer went about, like the old Duke, saying: "Think what you damned well like of my character!" Mouths had tried to come in again, of course, before the war; but what with majors, shareholders, and the working classes, they now had little or no chance! He heard Soames say: "In these circumstances we came to the conclusion that there was nothing for it but to wait and see." Michael saw a sudden quiver pass over the moustaches, as might wind over grass.

'Wrong phrase,' he thought; 'we all do it, but we can't bear being reminded of it.'

"Six weeks ago, however," he heard Soames intone, "an accidental incident seems to have warned your late manager that Sir Lawrence and I still entertained suspicions, for I received a letter from him practically admitting that he had taken this secret commission on the German business, and asking me to inform the Board that he had gone abroad and left no property behind him. This statement we have been at pains to verify.

In these circumstances we had no alternative but to call you together, and lay the facts before you."

The voice, which had not varied an iota, ceased its recital; and Michael saw his father-in-law return to his detachment—stork on one leg, about to apply beak to parasite, could have inspired no greater sense of loneliness. 'Too like the first account of the battle of Jutland!' he thought: 'He mentioned all the losses, and never once struck the human note.'

A pause ensued, such as occurs before an awkward fence, till somebody has found a gate. Michael rapidly reviewed the faces of the Board. Only one showed any animation. It was concealed in a handkerchief. The sound of the blown nose broke the spell. Two share-holders rose to their feet at once—one of them Michael's neighbour on the right.

"Mr. Sawdry," said the Chairman, and the other share-holder sat down.

With a sonorous clearing of the throat, Michael's neighbour turned his blunt red face towards Soames.

"I wish to ask you, sir, why you didn't inform the Board when you first 'eard of this?"

Soames rose slightly.

"You are aware, I presume, that such an accusation, unless it can be fully substantiated, is a matter for criminal proceedings?"

"No; it would ha' been privileged."

"As between members of the Board, perhaps; but any leakage would have rendered us liable. It was a mere case of word against word."

"Perhaps Sir Lawrence Mont will give us 'is view of that?"

Michael's heart began to beat. There was an air of sprightliness about his father's standing figure.

"You must remember, sir," he said, "that Mr. Elderson had enjoyed our complete confidence for many years; he was a gentleman, and, speaking for myself, an old schoolfellow of his, I preferred, in common loyalty, to give his word preference, while—er—keeping the matter in mind."

"Oh!" said Michael's neighbour: "What's the Chairman got to say about bein' kept in the dark?"

"We are all perfectly satisfied, sir, with the attitude of our co-directors, in a very delicate situation. You will kindly note that the mischief was already done over this unfortunate assurance, so that there was no need for undue haste."

Michael saw his neighbour's neck grow redder.

"I don't agree," he said. 'Wait and see'—We might 'ave 'ad that commission out of him, if he'd been tackled promptly." And he sat down.

He had not reached mahogany before the thwarted share-holder had started up.

"Mr. Bottterill," said the Chairman.

Michael saw a lean and narrow head, with two hollows in a hairy neck, above a back slightly forward, as of a doctor, listening to a chest.

"I take it from you then, sir," he said, "that these two directors represent the general attitude of the Board, and that the Board were content to allow a suspected person to remain manager. The gentleman on your extreme left—Mr. Forsyte, I think—spoke of an accidental incident. But for that, apparently, we should still be in the hands of an unscrupulous individual. The symptoms in this case are very disquieting. There appears to have been gross overconfidence; a recent instance of the sort must be in all our minds. The policy of assuring foreign business was evidently initiated by the manager for his own ends. We have made a severe loss by it. And the question for us shareholders would seem to be whether a Board who placed confidence in such a person, and continued it after their suspicions were aroused, are the right people to direct this important concern."

Throughout this speech Michael had grown very hot. ' "Old Forsyte" was right,' he thought; 'they're on their uppers after all.'

There was a sudden creak from his neighbour on the left.

"Mr. Tolby," said the Chairman.

"It's a serious matter, this, gentlemen. I propose that the Board withdraw, an' leave us to discuss it."

"I second that," said Michael's neighbour on the right.

Searching the vista of the Board, Michael saw recognition gleam for a second in the lonely face at the end, and grinned a greeting.

The Chairman was speaking.

"If that is your wish, gentlemen, we shall be happy to comply with it. Will those who favour the motion hold up their hands?"

All hands were held up, with the exception of Michael's, of two women whose eager colloquy had not permitted them to hear the request, and of one shareholder, just in front of Michael, so motionless that he seemed to be dead.

"Carried," said the Chairman, and rose from his seat.

Michael saw his father smiling, and speaking to "Old Forsyte" as they both stood up. They all filed out, and the door was closed.

'Whatever happens,' Michael thought, 'I've got to keep my head shut, or I shall be dropping a brick.'

"Perhaps the Press will kindly withdraw, too," he heard some one say.

With a general chinny movement, as if enquiring their rights of no one in particular, the four Pressmen could be seen to clasp their notebooks. When their pale reluctance had vanished, there was a stir among the shareholders, like that of ducks when a dog comes up behind. Michael saw why, at once. They had their backs to each other. A shareholder said:

"Perhaps Mr. Tolby, who proposed the withdrawal, will act as Chairman."

Michael's left-hand neighbour began breathing heavily.

"Right-o!" he said. "Any one who wants to speak, kindly ketch my eye."

Every one now began talking to his neighbour, as though to get at once a quiet sense of proportion, before speaking. Mr. Tolby was breathing so heavily that Michael felt a positive draught.

" 'Ere, gentlemen," he said suddenly, "this won't do! We don't want to be too formal, but we must preserve some order. I'll open the discussion myself. Now, I didn't want to 'urt the feelin's of the Board by plain speakin' in their presence. But, as Mr. What's-'is-name there, said: The public 'as got to protect itself against sharpers, and against slackness. We all know what 'appened the other day, and what'll 'appen again in other concerns, unless we shareholders look after ourselves. In the first place, then, what I say is: They ought never to 'ave touched anything to do with the 'Uns. In the second place, I say they showed bad judgment. And in the third place I say they were too thick together. In my opinion, we should propose a vote of no confidence."

Cries of: "Hear, hear!" mixed with indeterminate sounds, were broken sharply by a loud: "No!" from the shareholder who had seemed dead. Michael's heart went out to him, the more so as he still seemed dead. The negative was followed by the rising of a thin, polished-looking shareholder, with a small grey moustache.

"If you'll forgive my saying so, sir," he began, "your proposal seems to me very rough-and-ready justice. I should be interested to know how you would have handled such a situation if you had been on the Board. It is extremely easy to condemn other people!"

"Hear, hear!" said Michael, astonished at his own voice.

"It is all very well," the polished shareholder went on, "when anything of this sort happens, to blame a directorate, but, speaking as a director myself, I should be glad to know whom one is to trust, if not one's manager. As to the policy of foreign insurance, it has been before us at two general meetings; and we have pocketed the profit from it for nearly two years. Have we raised a voice against it?"

The dead shareholder uttered a "No!" so loud that Michael almost patted his head.

The shareholder, whose neck and back were like a doctor's, rose to answer.

"I differ from the last speaker in his diagnosis of the case. Let us admit all he says, and look at the thing more widely. The proof of pudding is in the eating. When a Government makes a bad mistake of judgment, the electorate turns against it as soon as it feels the effects. This is a very sound check on administration; it may be rough and ready, but it is the less of two evils. A Board backs its judgment; when it loses, it should pay. I think, perhaps, Mr. Tolby, being our informal Chairman, was out of order in proposing a vote of no confidence; if that be so, I should be happy to do so, myself."

The dead shareholder's "No!" was so resounding this time that there was a pause for him to speak; he remained, however, without motion. Both of Michael's neighbours were on their feet. They bobbed at each other over Michael's head, and Mr. Tolby sat down.

"Mr. Sawdry," he said.

"Look 'ere, gentlemen," said Mr. Sawdry, "and ladies, this seems to me a case for compromise. The directors that knew about the manager ought to go; but we might stop at that. The gentleman in front of me keeps on saying 'No.' Let 'im give us 'is views."

"No," said the dead shareholder, but less loudly.

"If a man can't give 'is views," went on Mr. Sawdry, nearly sitting down on Michael, " 'e shouldn't interrupt, in my opinion."

A shareholder in the front row now turned completely round so that he faced the meeting.

"I think," he said, "that to prolong this discussion is to waste time; we are evidently in two, if not three, minds. The whole of the business of this country is now conducted on a system of delegated trust; it may be good, it may be bad—but there it is. You've got to trust somebody. Now, as to this particular case, we've had no reason to distrust the Board, so far; and, as I take it, the Board had no previous reason to distrust the late manager. I think it's going too far at present, to propose anything definite like a vote of no confidence; it seems to me that we should call the Board in and hear what assurances they have to give us against a repetition of anything of the sort in the future."

The sounds which greeted this moderate speech were so inextricable that Michael could not get the sense of them. Not so with the speech which followed. It came from a shareholder on the right, with reddish hair, light eyelashes, a clipped moustache, and a scraped colour.

"I have no objection whatever to having the Board in," he said in a rather jeering voice, "and passing a vote of no confidence in their presence. There is a question, which no one has touched on, of how far, if we turn them out, we could make them liable for this loss. The matter is not clear, but there is a good sporting chance, if we like to take it. Whereas, if we don't turn them out, it's obvious we can't take it, even if we wish."

The impression made by this speech was of quite a different order from any of the others. It was followed by a hush, as though something important had been said at last. Michael stared at Mr. Tolby. The stout man's round, light, rather prominent eye was extraordinarily reflective. 'Trout must look like that,' thought Michael, 'when they see a mayfly.' Mr. Tolby suddenly stood up.

"All right," he said, " 'ave 'em in!"

"Yes," said the dead shareholder. There was no dissent.

Michael saw some one rise and ascend the platform.

"Let the Press know!" said Mr. Tolby.

Chapter Thirteen

SOAMES AT BAY

————— ◆◆ —————

WHEN the door had closed behind the departing
directors, Soames sought a window as far as possible from the lunch eaten before the meeting.

"Funeral baked meats, eh, Forsyte?" said a voice in his
ear. "Our number's up, I think. Poor old Mothergill's
looking very blue. I think he ought to ask for a second
shirt!"

Soames' tenacity began wriggling within him.

"The thing wants tackling," he grumbled; "the
Chairman's not the man for the job!" Shades of old Uncle
Jolyon! He would have made short work of this! It
wanted a masterful hand.

"Warning to us all, Forsyte, against loyalty! It's not in
the period. Ah! Fontenoy!"

Soames became conscious of features rather above the
level of his own.

"Well, Mr. Forsyte, hope you're satisfied? A pretty
damned mess! If I'd been the Chairman, I'd never have
withdrawn. Always keep hounds under your eye, Mont.
Take it off, and they'll go for you! Wish I could get
among 'em with a whip; I'd give it those two heavy pug-

faced chaps—they mean business! Unless you've got something up your sleeve, Mr. Forsyte, we're dished."

"What should I have up my sleeve?" said Soames coldly.

"Damn it, sir, you put the chestnuts in the fire; it's up to you to pull 'em out. I can't afford to lose these fees!"

Soames heard Sir Lawrence murmur: "Crude, my dear Fontenoy!" and said with malice:

"You may lose more than your fees!"

"Can't! They may have Eaglescourt to-morrow, and take a loss off my hands." A gleam of feeling burned up suddenly in the old eyes: "The country drives you to the wall, skins you to the bone, and expects you to give 'em public service gratis. Can't be done, Mont—can't be done!"

Soames turned away; he had an utter disinclination for talk, like one standing before an open grave, watching a coffin slowly lowered. Here was his infallibility going—going! He had no illusions. It would all be in the papers, and his reputation for sound judgment gone for ever! Bitter! No more would the Forsytes say: "Soames says ——" No more would old Gradman follow him with eyes like an old dog's, grudging sometimes, but ever submitting to infallibility. It would be a nasty jar for the old fellow. His business acquaintances—after all, they were not many, now!—would no longer stare with envious respect. He wondered if the reverberations would reach Dumetrius, and the picture market! The sole comfort was: Fleur needn't know. Fleur! Ah! If only her business were safely over! For a moment his mind became empty of all else. Then with a rush the present filled it up again. Why were they all talking as if there were a corpse in the room? Well! There was—the corpse of his infallibility! As for monetary loss—that seemed secondary, remote, incredible—like a future life. Mont had said something about loyalty. He didn't know what loyalty had to do with it! But if they thought he was going to show any white feather, they were extremely mistaken. Acid courage welled up into his brain. Shareholders, directors—

they might howl and shake their fists; he was not going to be dictated to. He heard a voice say:

"Will you come in, please, gentlemen?"

Taking his seat again before his unused quill, he noticed the silence—shareholders waiting for directors, directors for shareholders. "Wish I could get among 'em with a whip!" Extravagant words of that "old guinea-pig's," but expressive, somehow!

At last the Chairman, whose voice always reminded Soames of a raw salad with oil poured over it, said ironically:

"Well, gentlemen, we await your pleasure."

That stout, red-faced fellow, next to Michael, stood up, opening his pug's mouth.

"To put it shortly, Mr. Chairman, we're not at all satisfied; but before we take any resolution, we want to 'ear what you've got to say."

Just below Soames, some one jumped up and added:

"We'd like to know, sir, what assurances you can offer us against anything of this sort in the future."

Soames saw the Chairman smile—no real backbone in that fellow!

"In the nature of things, sir," he said, "none whatever! You can hardly suppose that if we had known our manager was not worthy of our confidence, we should have continued him in the post for a moment!"

Soames thought: 'That won't do—he's gone back on himself!' Yes, and that other pug-faced chap has seen it!

"That's just the point, sir," he was saying: "Two of you *did* know, and yet, there the fellow was for months afterwards, playin' 'is own 'and, cheatin' the Society for all he was worth, I shouldn't wonder."

One after another, they were yelping now:

"What about your own words?"

"You admitted collective responsibility."

"You said you were perfectly satisfied with the attitude of your co-directors in the matter." Regular pack!

Soames saw the Chairman incline his head as if he wanted to shake it; old Fontenoy muttering, old Mothergill blowing his nose, Meyricke shrugging his sharp shoulders. Suddenly he was cut off from view of them—Sir Lawrence was standing up between.

"Allow me a word! Speaking for myself, I find it impossible to accept the generous attempt of the Chairman to shoulder a responsibility which clearly rests on me. If I made a mistake of judgement in not disclosing our suspicions, I must pay the penalty; and I think it will clear the—er—situation if I tender my resignation to the meeting."

Soames saw him give a little bow, place his monocle in his eye, and sit down.

A murmur greeted the words—approval, surprise, deprecation, admiration? It had been gallantly done. Soames distrusted gallantry—there was always a dash of the peacock about it. He felt curiously savage.

"I, apparently," he said, rising, "am the other incriminated director. Very good! I am not conscious of having done anything but my duty from beginning to end of this affair, I am confident that I made no mistake of judgment. And I consider it entirely unjust that I should be penalised. I have had worry and anxiety enough, without being made a scapegoat by shareholders who accepted this policy without a murmur, before ever I came on the Board, and are now angry because they have lost by it. You owe it to me that the policy has been dropped: You owe it to me that you have no longer a fraudulent person for a manager. And you owe it to me that you were called together to-day to pass judgment on the matter. I have no intention whatever of singing small. But there is another aspect to this affair. I am not prepared to go on giving my services to people who don't value them. I have no patience with the attitude displayed this afternoon. If any one here thinks he has a grievance against me, let him bring an action. I shall be happy to carry it to the House of Lords, if necessary. I have been familiar with the City all my life, and I have not been in the habit of meeting with suspicions and ingratitude. If this is an instance of present manners, I have been familiar with the

City long enough. I do not tender my resignation to the meeting; I resign."

Bowing to the Chairman, and pushing back his chair, he walked doggedly to the door, opened it and passed through.

He sought his hat. He had not the slightest doubt but that he had astonished their weak nerves! Those pug-faced fellows had their mouths open! He would have liked to see what he had left behind, but it was hardly consistent with dignity to open the door again. He took a sandwich instead, and began to eat it with his back to the door and his hat on. He felt better than he had for months. A voice said:

" 'And the subsequent proceedings interested him no more!' I'd no idea, Forsyte, you were such an orator! You gave it 'em between the eyes! Never saw a meeting so knocked out! Well, you've saved the Board by focussing their resentment entirely on yourself. It was very gallant, Forsyte!"

Soames growled through his sandwich:

"Nothing of the sort! Are you out, too?"

"Yes. I pressed my resignation. That red-faced fellow was proposing a vote of confidence in the Board when I left—and they'll pass it, Forsyte—they'll pass it! Something was said about financial liability, by the way!"

"Was there?" said Soames, with a grim smile: "That cock won't fight. Their only chance was to claim against the Board for initiating foreign assurance *ultra vires;* if they're re-affirming the Board, after the question's been raised in open meeting, they're dished. Nothing'll lie against you and me, for not disclosing our suspicions—that's certain."

"A relief, I confess," said Sir Lawrence, with a sigh. "It was the speech of your life, Forsyte!"

Perfectly well aware of that, Soames shook his head. Apart from the horror of seeing himself in print, he was beginning to feel that he had been extravagant. It was always a mistake to lose your temper! A bitter little smile came on his lips. Nobody, not even Mont, would see how unjustly he had been treated.

"Well," he said, "I shall go."

"I think I shall wait, Forsyte, and hear the upshot."

"Upshot? They'll appoint two other fools and slaver over each other. Shareholders! Good-bye!" He moved to the door.

Passing the Bank of England, he had a feeling of walking away from his own life. His acumen, his judgment, his manner of dealing with affairs—aspersed! They didn't like it; well—he would leave it! Catch him meddling, in future! It was all of a piece with the modern state of things. Hand to mouth, and the steady men pushed to the wall! The men to whom a pound was a pound, and not a mess of chance and paper. The men who knew that the good of the country was the strict, straight conduct of their own affairs. They were not wanted. One by one, they would get the go-by—as he had got it—in favour of Jack-o'-lanterns, revolutionaries, restless chaps, or clever, unscrupulous fellows, like Elderson. It was in the air. No amount of eating your cake and wanting to have it could take the place of common honesty.

He turned into the Poultry before he knew why he had come there. Well, he might as well tell Gradman at once that he must exercise his own judgment in the future. At the mouth of the backwater he paused for a second, as if to print its buffness on his brain. He would resign his trusts, private and all! He had no notion of being sneered at in the family. But a sudden wave of remembrance almost washed his heart into his boots. What a tale of trust deeds executed, leases renewed, houses sold, investments decided on—in that back room up there; what a mint of quiet satisfaction in estates well managed! Ah! well! He would continue to manage his own. As for the others, they must look out for themselves, now. And a precious time they'd have of it, in face of the spirit there was about!

He mounted the stone steps slowly.

In the repository of Forsyte affairs, he was faced by the

unusual—not Gradman, but, on the large ripe table, a large ripe melon alongside a straw bag. Soames sniffed. The thing smelled delicious. He held it to the light. Its greeny yellow tinge, its network of threads—quite Chinese! Was old Gradman going to throw its rind about, like that white monkey?

He was still holding it when a voice said:

"Aoh! I wasn't expecting you to-day, Mr. Soames. I was going early; my wife's got a little party."

"So I see!" said Soames, restoring the melon to the table. "There's nothing for you to do at the moment, but I came in to tell you to draw my resignations from the Forsyte trusts."

The old chap's face was such a study that he could not help a smile.

"You can keep me in Timothy's; but the rest must go. Young Roger can attend to them. He's got nothing to do."

A gruff and deprecating: "Dear me! They won't like it!" irritated Soames.

"Then they must lump it! I want a rest."

He did not mean to enter into the reason—Gradman could read it for himself in the *Financial News,* or whatever he took in.

"Then I shan't be seeing you so often, Mr. Soames; there's never anything in Mr. Timothy's. Dear me! I'm quite upset. Won't you keep your sister's?"

Soames looked at the old fellow, and compunction stirred within him—as ever, at any sign that he was appreciated.

"Well," he said, "keep me in hers; I shall be in about my own affairs, of course. Good afternoon, Gradman. That's a fine melon."

He waited for no more words. The old chap! *He* couldn't last much longer anyway, sturdy as he looked! Well, they would find it hard to match him!

On reaching the Poultry, he decided to go to Green Street and see Winifred—queerly and suddenly homesick for the proximity of Park Lane, for the old secure days, the efflorescent privacy of his youth under the wings of James and Emily. Winifred alone represented for him now, the past; her solid nature never varied, however much she kept up with the fashions.

He found her, a little youthful in costume, drinking Chinese tea, which she did not like—but what could one do, other teas were "common!" She had taken to a parrot. Parrots were coming in again. The bird made a dreadful noise. Whether under its influence or that of the Chinese tea—which, made in the English way, of a brand the Chinese grew for foreign stomachs, always upset him— he was soon telling her the whole story.

When he had finished, Winifred said comfortably:

"Well, Soames, I think you did splendidly; it serves them right!"

Conscious that his narrative must have presented the truth as it would not appear to the public, Soames muttered:

"That's all very well; you'll find a very different version in the financial papers."

"Oh! but nobody reads them. I shouldn't worry. Do you do Coué? Such a comfortable little man, Soames; I went to hear him. It's rather a bore sometimes, but it's quite the latest thing."

Soames became inaudible—he never confessed a weakness.

"And how," asked Winifred, "is Fleur's little affair?"

" 'Little affair!' " echoed a voice above his head. That bird! It was clinging to the brocade curtains, moving its neck up and down.

"Polly!" said Winifred: "don't be naughty!"

"Soames!" said the bird.

"I've taught him that. Isn't he rather sweet?"

"No," said Soames. "I should shut him up; he'll spoil your curtains."

The vexation of the afternoon had revived within him suddenly. What was life, but parrotry? What did people see of the real truth? They just repeated each other, like a lot of shareholders, or got their precious sentiments out of

The Daily Liar. For one person who took a line, a hundred followed on, like sheep!

"You'll stay and dine, dear boy!" said Winifred.

Yes! he would dine. Had she a melon, by any chance? He'd no inclination to go and sit opposite his wife at South Square. Ten to one Fleur would not be down. And as to young Michael—the fellow had been there that afternoon and witnessed the whole thing; he'd no wish to go over it again.

He was washing his hands for dinner, when a maid, outside, said:

"You are wanted on the 'phone, sir."

Michael's voice came over the wire, strained and husky.

"That you, sir?"

"Yes. What is it?"

"Fleur. It began this afternoon at three. I've been trying to reach you."

"What?" cried Soames. "How? Quick!"

"They say it's all normal. But it's so awful. They say quite soon, now." The voice broke off.

"My God!" said Soames. "My hat!"

By the front door the maid was asking: "Shall you be back to dinner, sir?"

"Dinner!" muttered Soames, and was gone.

He hurried along, almost running, his eyes searching for a cab. None to be had, of course! None to be had! Opposite the 'Iseeum' Club he got one, open in the fine weather after last night's storm. That storm! He might have known. Ten days before her time. Why on earth hadn't he gone straight back, or at least telephoned where he would be? All that he had been through that afternoon was gone like smoke. Poor child! Poor little thing! And what about twilight sleep? Why hadn't he been there? He might have—nature! Damn it! Nature—as if it couldn't leave even her alone!

"Get on!" he said, leaning out: "Double fare!"

Past the Connoisseurs, and the Palace, and Whitehall; past all preserves whence nature was excluded, deep in the waters of primitive emotion Soames sat, grey, breathless. Past Big Ben—eight o'clock! Five hours! Five hours of it!

"Let it be over!" he muttered aloud: "Let it be over, God!"

Chapter Fourteen

ON THE RACK

━━━━◦◦━━◦◦◦━━◦◦━━

WHEN his father-in-law bowed to the Chairman and withdrew, Michael had restrained a strong desire to shout: "Bravo!" Who'd have thought the "old man" could let fly like that? He had "got their goats" with a vengeance. Quite an interval of fine mixed vociferation followed, before his neighbour, Mr. Sawdry, made himself heard at last.

"Now that the director implicated has resigned, I shall 'ave pleasure in proposing a vote of confidence in the rest of the Board."

Michael saw his father rise, a little finicky and smiling, and bow to the Chairman. "I take my resignation as accepted also; if you permit me, I will join Mr. Forsyte in retirement."

Some one was saying:

"I shall be glad to second that vote of confidence."

And brushing past the knees of Mr. Sawdry, Michael sought the door. From there he could see that nearly every hand was raised in favour of the vote of confidence; and with the thought: 'Thrown to the shareholders!' he made his way out of the hotel. Delicacy prevented him from seeking out those two. They had saved their dignity; but the dogs had had the rest.

Hurrying west, he reflected on the rough ways of justice. The shareholders had a grievance, of course; and some one had to get it in the neck to satisfy their sense of equity. They had pitched on "Old Forsyte," who, of all, was least to blame; for if Bart had only held his tongue, they would certainly have lumped him into the vote of confidence. All very natural and illogical;—and four o'clock already!

"Counterfeits"! The old feeling for Wilfrid was strong in him this day of publication. One must do everything one could for his book—poor old son! There simply must not be a frost.

After calling in at two big booksellers, he made for his club, and closeted himself in the telephone booth. In old days they "took cabs and went about." Ringing-up was quicker—was it? With endless vexations, he tracked down Sibley, Nazing, Upshire, Master, and half-a-dozen others of the elect. He struck a considered note likely to move them. The book—he said—was bound to "get the goat of the old guard" and the duds generally; it would want a bit of drum-beating from the cognoscenti. To each of them he appealed as the only one whose praise really mattered. "If you haven't reviewed the book, old chap, will you? It's you who counts, of course." And to each he added: "I don't care two straws whether it sells, but I do want old Wilfrid to get his due." And he meant it. The publisher in Michael was dead during that hour in the telephone booth, the friend alive and kicking hard. He came out with sweat running down his forehead, quite exhausted; and it was half-past five.

'Cup of tea—and home!' he thought. He reached his door at six. Ting-a-ling, absolutely unimportant, was cowering in the far corner of the hall.

"What's the matter, old man?"

A sound from above, which made his blood run cold, answered—a long, low moaning.

Oh, God!" he gasped, and ran upstairs.

Annette met him at the door. He was conscious of her speaking in French of being called *"Mon cher,"* of the words *"vers trois heures. . . ."* The doctor says one must not worry—all goes for the best." Again that moan, and the door shut in his face; she was gone. Michael remained standing on the rug with perfectly cold sweat oozing from him, and nails dug deep into his palms.

'This is how one becomes a father!' he thought: 'This is how I became a son!' That moaning! He could not bear to stay there, and he could not bear to go away. It might be hours, yet! He kept repeating to himself: "One must not worry—must not worry!" How easily said! How meaningless! His brain, his heart, ranging for relief, lighted on the strangest relief which could possibly have come to him. Suppose this child being born, had not been his—had been—been Wilfrid's; how would he have been feeling, here, outside this door? It might—it might so easily have been—since nothing was sacred, now! Nothing except—yes, just that which was dearer than one-self—just that which was in there, moaning. He could not bear it on the rug, and went downstairs. Across and across the copper floor, a cigar in his mouth, he strode in vague, rebellious agony. Why should birth be like this? And the answer was: It isn't—not in China! To have the creed that nothing mattered—and then run into it like this! Something born at such a cost, must matter, should matter. One must see to that! Speculation ceased in Michael's brain; he stood, listening terribly. Nothing! He could not bear it down there, and went up again. No sound at first, and then another moan! This time he fled into his study, and ranged round the room, looking at the cartoons of Aubrey Greene. He did not see a single one, and suddenly bethought him of "Old Forsyte." He ought to be told!

He rang up the "Connoisseurs," the "Remove," and his own father's clubs, in case they might have gone there together after the meeting. He drew blank everywhere. It was half-past seven. How much longer was this going on? He went back to the bedroom door; could hear nothing. Then down again to the hall. Ting-a-ling was lying by the front door, now. "Fed-up!' thought Michael, stroking his back, and mechanically clearing the letter-box. Just one letter—Wilfrid's writing! He took it to the foot of the stairs, and read it with half his brain, the other half wondering—wandering up there.

"DEAR MONT,—I start to-morrow to try and cross Arabia. I thought you might like a line in case Arabia crosses me. I have recovered my senses. The air here is too clear for sentiment of any kind; and passion in exile soon becomes sickly. I am sorry I made you so much disturbance. It was a mistake for me to go back to England after the war, and hang about writing drival for smart young women and inky folk to read. Poor old England—she's in for a bad time. Give her my love; the same to yourselves.

"Yours ever,

"WILFRID DESERT.

"P.S.—If you've published the things I left behind, send any royalties to me care of my governor.—W.D."

Half Michael's brain thought: 'Well, that's that! And the book coming out to-day!' Queer! Was Wilfrid right —was it all a blooming gaff—the inky stream? Was one just helping on England's sickness? Ought they all to get on camels and ride the sun down? And yet, in books were comfort and diversion; and they were wanted! England had to go on—go on! 'No retreat, no retreat, they must conquer or die who have no retreat!' . . . God! There it was again! Back he flew upstairs, with his ears covered, and his eyes wild. The sounds ceased; Annette came out to him.

"Her father, *mon cher;* try to find her father!"

"I have—I can't!" gasped Michael.

"Try Green Street—Mrs. Dartie. *Courage!* All is normal—it will be quite soon, now."

When he had rung up Green Street and been answered at last, he sat with the door of his study open, waiting for "Old Forsyte" to come. Half his sight remarked a round hole burnt in his trouser leg—he hadn't even noticed the smell; hadn't even realised that he had been smoking. He must pull himself together for the "old man." He heard the bell ring, and ran down to open.

"Well?" said Soames.

"Not yet, sir. Come up to my study. It's nearer."

They went up side by side. That trim grey head, with the deep furrow between the eyes, and those eyes staring as if at pain behind them, steadied Michael. Poor old chap! He was "for it," too! They were both on "their uppers"!

"Have a peg, sir? I've got brandy here."

"Yes," said Soames. "Anything."

With the brandies in their hands, half-raised, they listened—jerked their hands up, drank. They were automatic, like two doll figures worked by the same string.

"Cigarette, sir?" said Michael.

Soames nodded.

With the lighted cigarettes just not in their mouths, they listened, put them in, took them out, puffed smoke. Michael had his right arm tight across his chest, Soames his left. They formed a pattern, thus, side by side.

"Bad to stick, sir. Sorry!"

Soames nodded. His teeth were clenched. Suddenly his hand relaxed.

"Listen!" he said. Sounds—different—confused!

Michael's hand seized something, gripped it hard; it was cold, thin—the hand of Soames. They sat thus, hand in hand, staring at the doorway, for how long neither knew.

Suddenly that doorway darkened; a figure in grey stood there—Annette!

"It is all r-right! A son!"

Chapter Fifteen

CALM

><><><><

ON waking from deep sleep next morning, Michael's first thought was: 'Fleur is back!' He then remembered.

To his: "O.K.?" whispered at her door, he received an emphatic nod from the nurse.

In the midst of excited expectation he retained enough modernity to think: 'No more blurb! Go and eat your breakfast quietly!'

In the dining-room Soames was despising the broken egg before him. He looked up as Michael entered, and buried his face in his cup. Michael understood perfectly; they had sat hand in hand! He saw, too, that the journal opened by his plate was of a financial nature.

"Anything about the meeting, sir? Your speech must read like one o'clock!"

With a queer little sound Soames held out the paper. The headlines ran: "Stormy meeting—resignation of two directors—a vote of confidence." Michael skimmed down till he came to:

"Mr. Forsyte, the director involved, in a speech of some length, said he had no intention of singing small. He deprecated the behaviour of the shareholders; he had not been accustomed to meet with suspicions. He tendered his resignation."

Michael dropped the sheet.

"By Jove!" he said—" 'Involved—suspicions!' They've given it a turn, as though——!"

"The papers!" said Soames and resumed his egg.

Michael sat down, and stripped the skin off a banana. " 'Nothing became him like his death,' " he thought; 'Poor old boy!'

"Well, sir," he said, "I was there, and all I can say is: You and my father were the only two people who excited my respect."

"That!" said Soames, putting down his spoon.

Michael perceived that he wished to be alone, and swallowing the banana, went to his study. Waiting for his summons, he rang up his father.

"None the worse for yesterday, sir?"

Sir Lawrence's voice came clear and thin, rather high.

"Poorer and wiser. What's the bulletin?"

"Top-hole."

"Our love to both. Your mother wants to know if he has any hair?"

"Haven't seen him yet. I'm just going."

Annette, indeed, was beckoning him from the doorway.

"She wants you to bring the little dog, *mon cher*."

With Ting-a-ling under his arm, and treading on tiptoe, Michael entered. The eleventh baronet! He did not seem to amount to much, beneath her head bent over him. And surely her hair was darker! He walked up to the bed, and touched it reverently.

Fleur raised her head, and revealed the baby sucking vigorously at her little finger. "Isn't he a monkey?" said her faint voice.

Michael nodded. A monkey clearly—but whether white—that was the question!

"And you, sweetheart?"

"All right now, but it was——" She drew her breath in, and her eyes darkened: "Ting, look!"

The Chinese dog, with nostrils delicately moving, drew backward under Michael's arm. His whole demeanour displayed a knowing criticism. "Puppies," he seemed to say, "we do it in China. Judgment reserved!"

"What eyes!" said Michael: "We needn't tell *him* that this was brought from Chelsea by the doctor."

Fleur gave the tiniest laugh.

"Put him down, Michael."

Michael put him down, and he went to his corner.

"I mustn't talk," said Fleur, "but I want to, frightfully; as if I'd been dumb for months."

'Just as I felt,' thought Michael, 'she's been away, away somewhere, utterly away.'

"It was like being held down, Michael. Months of not being yourself."

Michael said softly: "Yes! the process *is* behind the times! Has he got any hair? My mother wants to know."

Fleur revealed the head of the eleventh baronet, covered with dark down.

"Like my grandmother's; but it'll get lighter. His eyes are going to be grey. Oh! and, Michael, about god-parents? Alison, of course—but men?"

Michael dwelled a little before answering:

"I had a letter from Wilfrid yesterday. Would you like him? He's still out there, but I could hold the sponge for him in church."

"Is he all right again?"

"He says so."

He could not read the expression of her eyes, but her lips were pouted slightly.

"Yes," she said: "and I think one's enough, don't you? Mine never gave me anything."

"One of mine gave me a bible, and the other gave me a wigging. Wilfrid, then." And he bent over her.

Her eyes seemed to make him a little ironic apology. He kissed her hair, and moved hurriedly away.

By the door Soames was standing, awaiting his turn.

"Just a minute only, sir," the nurse was saying.

Soames walked up to the bedside, and stood looking at his daughter.

"Dad, dear!" Michael heard her say.

Soames just touched her hand, nodded, as if implying approval of the baby, and came walking back, but, in a mirror, Michael saw his lips quivering.

On the ground floor once more, he had the most intense desire to sing. It would not do; and, entering the Chinese room, he stood staring out into the sunlit square. Gosh! It was good to be alive! Say what you liked, you couldn't beat it! They might turn their noses up at life, and look down them at it; they might bolster up the future and the past, but—give him the present!

'I'll have that white monkey up again!' he thought. 'I'll see the brute further before he shall depress me!'

He went out to a closet under the stairs, and, from beneath four pairs of curtains done up in moth-preserver and brown paper, took out the picture. He held it away from him in the dim light. The creature's eyes! It was all in those eyes!

"Never mind, old son!" he said: "Up you go!" And he carried it into the Chinese room.

Soames was there.

"I'm going to put him up again, sir."

Soames nodded.

"Would you hold him, while I hook the wire?"

Soames held the picture.

Returning to the copper floor, Michael said:

"All right, sir!" and stood back.

Soames joined him. Side by side they contemplated the white monkey.

"He won't be happy till he gets it," said Michael, at last: "The only thing is, you see, he doesn't know what *it* is."

INTERLUDE

A SILENT WOOING

ON the first of February, 1926, Jon Forsyte, con-
valescing from the 'flu, was sitting in the lounge
of an hotel at Camden, South Carolina, with his bright
hair slowly rising on his scalp. He was reading about a
lynching.

A voice behind him said:

"Will you join our picnic over at those old-time mounds
to-day?"

Looking up, he saw a young acquaintance called Francis Wilmot, who came from further south.

"Very glad to. Who's going?"

"Why, just Mr. and Mrs. Pulmore Hurrison, and that
English novelist, Gurdon Minho, and the Blair girls and
their friends, and my sister Anne and I. You could ride
over horseback, if you want exercise."

"All right; they've got some new horses in this morning from Columbia."

"Why, that's fine! My sister and I'll ride horseback too,
and some of the Blair girls. The Hurrisons can take the
others."

"I say," said Jon, "this is a pretty bad case of lynching."

317

The young man to whom he spoke leaned in the window. Jon admired his face, **as** of ivory, with dark hair and eyes, and narrow nose and lips, and his lissom attitude.

"All you Britishers go off the deep-end when you read of a lynching. You haven't got the negro problem up where you are at Southern Pines. They don't have it any to speak of in North Carolina."

"No, and I don't profess to understand it. But I can't see why negroes shouldn't be tried the same as white men. There may be cases where you've got to shoot at sight; but how can you defend mob law? Once you catch a man, he ought to be tried properly."

"We're not taking any chances with that particular kind of trouble."

"But without trial, how can you tell he's guilty?"

"Well, we'd sooner do without an innocent darkie now and again than risk our women."

"But killing a man for a thing he hasn't done is the limit."

"Maybe, in Europe. But, here, things are in the large, still."

"What do they think about lynching in the North?"

"They squeal a bit, but they've no call to. If we've got negroes, they've got the Reds, and they surely have a wholesale way with them.'"

Jon Forsyte tilted back his rocking-chair, with a puzzled frown.

"I reckon there's too much space left in this country," said Francis Wilmot; "a man has all the chances to get off. So where we feel strong about a thing, we take the law into our own hands."

"Well, every country to its own fashions. What are these mounds we're going to?"

"Old Indian remains that go way back thousands of years, they say. You haven't met my sister? She only came last night."

"No. What time do we start?"

"Noon; it's about an hour's ride by the woods."

At noon then, in riding kit, Jon came out to the five horses, for more than one of the Blair girls had elected to ride. He started between them, Francis Wilmot going ahead with his sister.

The Blair girls were young and pretty with a medium-coloured, short-faced, well-complexioned, American prettiness, of a type to which he had become accustomed during the two and a half years he had spent in the United States. They were at first extremely silent, and then extremely vocal. They rode astride, and very well. Jon learned that they, as well as the givers of the picnic, Mr. and Mrs. Pulmore Hurrison, inhabited Long Island. They asked him many questions about England, to which Jon, who had left it at the age of nineteen, invented many answers. He began to look longingly between his horse's ears at Francis Wilmot and his sister, cantering ahead in a silence that, from a distance, seemed extremely restful. Their way led through pine woods—of trees spindly and sparse, and over a rather sandy soil; the sunlight was clear and warm, the air still crisp. Jon rode a single-footing bay horse, and felt as one feels on the first day of recovered health.

The Blair girls wished to know what he thought of the English novelist—they were dying to see a real highbrow. Jon had only read one of his books, and of the characters therein could only remember a cat. The Blair girls had read none; but they had heard that his cats were "just too cunning."

Francis Wilmot, reining up in front, pointed at a large mound which certainly seemed to be unnaturally formed. They all reined up, looked at it for two minutes in silence, remarked that it was "very interesting," and rode on. In a hollow the occupants of two cars were disembarking food. Jon led the horses away to tether them alongside the horses of Wilmot and his sister.

"My sister," said Francis Wilmot.

"Mr. Forsyte," said the sister.

She looked at Jon, and Jon looked at her. She was slim but distinctly firm, in a long dark-brown coat and breeches and boots; her hair was bobbed and dark under a soft brown felt hat. Her face was pale, rather browned, and had a sort of restrained eagerness—the brow broad and clear, the nose straight and slightly sudden, the mouth unreddened, rather wide and pretty. But what struck Jon were her eyes, which were exactly his idea of a water nymph's. They slanted a little, and were steady and brown and enticing; whether there was ever such a slight squint in them he could not tell, but if there were it was an improvement. He felt shy. Neither of them spoke.

Francis Wilmot reckoned that he was hungry, and they walked side by side towards the eatables.

Jon said suddenly to the sister:

"You've just come then, Miss Wilmot?"

"Yes, Mr. Forsyte."

"Where from?"

"From Naseby. It's way down between Charleston and Savannah."

"Oh, Charleston! I like Charleston."

"Anne likes Savannah best," said Francis Wilmot.

Anne nodded. She was not talkative, it seemed, though her voice had sounded pleasant in small quantities.

"It's kind of lonely where we live," said Francis. "Mostly darkies. Anne's never seen an Englishman to speak to."

Anne smiled. Jon also smiled. Neither pursued the subject. They arrived at the eatables, spread in a manner calculated to give the maximum of muscular and digestive exertion. Mrs. Pulmore Hurrison, a lady of forty or so, and of defined features, was seated with her feet turned up; next to her, Gurdon Minho, the English novelist, had his legs in a more reserved position; and then came quantities of seated girls, all with pretty, unreserved legs; Mr. Pulmore Hurrison, somewhat apart, was pursuing a small mouth over the cork of a large bottle. Jon and the Wilmots also sat down. The picnic had begun.

Jon soon realised that everybody was expecting Gurdon Minho to say something beyond "Yes" "Really!" "Ah!" "Quite!" This did not occur. The celebrated novelist was at first almost painfully attentive to what everybody else said, and then seemed to go into a coma. Jon felt a patriotic disappointment, for he himself was, if anything, even more silent. He could see that, among the three Blair girls and their two girl friends, a sort of conspiracy was brewing, to quiz the silent English in the privacy of the future. Francis Wilmot's speechless sister was a comfort to him, therefore, for he felt that she would neither be entitled nor inclined to join that conspiracy. He took refuge in handing victuals and was glad when the period of eating on constricted stomachs was over. Picnics were like Christmas Day, better in the future and the past than in the present. After the normal period of separation into genders, the baskets were repacked, and all resorted to their vehicles. The two cars departed for another mound said to be two miles off. Francis Wilmot and the two Blair girls believed that they would get back and watch the polo. Jon asked Anne Wilmot which she wished to do. She elected to see the other mound.

They mounted and pursued a track through the woods in silence, till Jon said:

"Do you like picnics?"

"I certainly do not."

"Nor do I. But riding?"

"I just adore it more than anything in the world."

"More than dancing?"

"Surely. Riding and swimming."

"Ah! I *thought*——" And he was silent.

"What did you think?"

"Well, I thought somehow you were a good swimmer."

"Why?"

Jon said with embarrassment:

"By your eyes——"

"What! Are they fishy?"

Jon laughed.

"Not exactly. They're like a water nymph's."

"I don't just know if that's a compliment."

"Of course it is."

"I thought nymphs weren't respectable."

"Oh! *Water* nymphs—very! Shy, of course."

"Do you have many in England?"

"No. As a matter of fact I've never seen one before."

"Then how do you know?"

"Just a general sense of what's fitting."

"I suppose you had a classical education. Don't you all have that in England?"

"Far from it."

"And how do you like America, Mr. Forsyte?"

"Very much. I get homesick sometimes."

"I'd love to travel."

"You never have?"

She shook her head. "I just stay at home and look after things. But I reckon we'll have to sell the old home—cotton doesn't pay any more."

"I grow peaches near Southern Pines, you know, up in North Carolina; that's paying at present."

"D'you live there alone?"

"No; with my mother."

"Is she English?"

"Yes."

"Have you a father?"

"He died four years ago."

"Francis and I have been orphans ten years."

"I wish you'd both come and stay with us some day; my mother would be awfully glad."

"Is she like you?"

Jon laughed.

"No. She's beautiful."

The eyes regarded him gravely, the lips smiled faintly.

"I'd just love to come, but Francis and I can't ever be away together."

"But," said Jon, "you're both here."

"We go back to-morrow; I wanted to see Camden." The eyes resumed their steady consideration of Jon's face. "Won't you come back with us and see our home—it's old? Francis would like to have you come."

"Do you always know what your brother would like?"

"Surely."

"That must be jolly. But do you really mean you want me?"

"I certainly do."

"I'd enjoy it awfully; I hate hotels. I mean—well, you know——" But as *he* didn't, he was not so sure that she did.

She touched her horse, and the single-footing animal broke into a canter.

Along the alleys of the eternal pinewood the sun was in their eyes; a warmed scent rose from pine needles, and herbs; the going was sandy and soft; the horses in good mood. Jon felt happy. This girl had strange eyes, enticing; and she rode better even than the Blair girls.

"I suppose all the English ride well?" she said.

"Most do, when they ride at all; but we don't ride much nowadays."

"I'd love to see England; our folk came from England in 1700—Worcestershire. Where is that?"

"It's our middle west," said Jon. "But as unlike as ever you can imagine. It's a fruit-growing county—very pretty; white timbered houses, pastures, orchards, woods, green hills. I went there walking one holiday with a school friend."

"It sounds just lovely. Our ancestors were Roman Catholics. They had a place called Naseby; that's why we call ours Naseby. But my grandmother was French Creole, from Louisiana. Is it true that in England they think Creoles have negro blood in them?"

"We're very ignorant," said Jon. "*I* know the Creoles are the old French and Spanish families. You both look as if you had French blood."

"Francis does. Do you think we've passed that mound? We've come all of four miles, and I thought it was only two."

"Does it matter? The other mound was rather over-rated."

The lips smiled; she didn't ever quite laugh, it seemed.

"What Indians hereabouts?" asked Jon.

"I'm not too sure; Seminoles, if any, I think. But Francis says these mounds would be from way back before the present tribes. What made you come to America, Mr. Forsyte?"

Jon bit his lip. To give the reason—family feud—broken love affair—was not exactly possible.

"I went first to British Columbia; but I didn't get on too well. Then I heard of peaches in North Carolina."

"But why did you leave England?"

"I suppose I just wanted to see the world."

"Yes," she said. It was a quiet but comprehending sound; Jon was the more gratified, because she had not comprehended. The image of his first love did not often haunt him now—had not for a year or more. He had been so busy with his peaches. Besides, Holly had written that Fleur had a boy. He said suddenly: "I think we ought to turn. Look at the sun!" The sun, indeed, was well down behind the trees.

"My—yes!"

Jon turned his steed. "Let's gallop, it'll be down in half an hour; and there's no moon till late."

They galloped back along the track. The sun went down even faster than he had thought, the air grew cold, the light grey. Jon reined up suddenly.

"I'm awfully sorry; I don't believe we're on the track we came by from the picnic. I feel we've gone off to the right. The tracks are all alike and these horses only came in from Columbia yesterday; they don't know the country any more than we do."

The girl laughed.

"We'll be lost."

"M'm! That'll be no joke in these woods. Don't they ever end?"

"I reckon not, in these parts. It's an adventure."

"Yes; but you'll catch cold. It's jolly cold at night."

"And you've had 'flu!"

"Oh! That's all right. Here's a track to the left. Shall we go on, or shall we take it?"

"Take it."

They cantered on. It was too dark now for galloping, and soon too dark for cantering. And the track wound on and on.

"This is a pretty business," said Jon. "I *am* sorry." He peered towards her riding beside him, and could just see her smile.

"Why! It's lots of fun."

He was glad she thought so, but he could not see it.

"I *have* been an ass. Your brother'll be pretty sick with me."

"He'll know I'm with you."

"If we only had a compass. We may be out all night at this rate. Here's another fork! Gosh, it *is* going to be dark."

And, almost as he spoke, the last of the light failed; he could barely see her five yards away. He came up close alongside, and she touched his sleeve.

"Don't worry," she said; "that spoils it."

Shifting his reins, he gave her hand a squeeze.

"You're splendid, Miss Wilmot."

"Oh! do call me Anne. Surnames seem kind of chilly when you're lost."

"Thank you very much. My name's Jon. Without an h, you know—short for Jolyon."

"Jolyon—Jon; I like it."

"Well, Anne's always been my favourite name. Shall we stop till the moon rises, or ride on?"

"When will the moon rise?"

"Not for hours, judging from last night."

"Let's ride on and leave it to the horses."

"Right! Only if they make for anywhere I'm pretty sure it'll be towards Columbia, which must be miles and miles."

They pursued the narrow track at a foot's pace. It was really dark now. Jon said: "Are you cold? You'd be warmer walking. I'll go ahead; stick close enough to see me."

He went ahead, and soon dismounted, feeling cold himself; there was utter silence among unending trees.

"I'm cold now," said the voice of Anne. "I'll get off too."

They had trailed on perhaps half an hour like this, leading their horses, and almost feeling their way, when Jon said: "Look! There's some sort of a clearing here! And what's that blackness on the left?"

"It's a mound."

"Which mound, I wonder? The one we saw, or the other, or neither?"

"I reckon we'd better stop here till the moon rises, then maybe we'll see which it is, and know our way."

"You're right. There'll be swamps, I expect. I'll tether the horses to leeward, and we'll try to find a nook. It *is* cold."

He tethered the horses out of the wind, and, turning back, found her beside him.

"It's creepy here," she said.

"We'll find a snug place, and sit down."

He put his hand through her arm, and they moved round the foot of the mound.

"Here," said Jon suddenly; "they've been digging. This'll be sheltered." He felt the ground—dry enough. "Let's squat here and talk."

Side by side, with their backs to the wall of the ex- cavated hollow, they lighted cigarettes, and sat listening to the silence. But for a snuffle or soft stamp now and then from the horses, there was not a sound. Trees and wind, both, were too sparse for melody, and nothing but their two selves and their horses seemed alive. A sprinkle of stars in a very dark sky and the deeper blackness of the pine stems was all they could see. Ah! and the glowing tips of their cigarettes, and each other's faces thereby illumined, now and then.

"I don't expect you'll ever forgive me for this," said Jon, with gloom.

"Why! I'm just loving it."

"Very sweet of you to say so; but you must be awfully cold. Look here—have my coat!"

He had begun to take it off when she said: "If you do that I'll run out into the woods and get really lost."

Jon resumed his coat.

"It might have been one of those Blair girls," he said.

"Would you rather?"

"For your sake, of course. Not for my own—no, indeed!"

They were looking round at each other so that the tips of their cigarettes were almost touching. Just able to see her eyes, he had a very distinct impulse to put his arm round her. It seemed the natural and proper thing to do, but of course it was not "done"!

"Have some chocolate," she said.

Jon ate a very little. The chocolate should be reserved for her!

"This is a real adventure. It *is* black. I'd have been scared alone—seems kind of spooky here."

"Spirits of the old Indians," muttered Jon. "Only I don't believe in spirits."

"You would if you'd had a coloured mammy."

"Did you have one?"

"Surely, with a voice as soft as mush melon. We have one old darkie still, who was a slave as a boy. He's the best of all the negroes round—nearly eighty, with quite white hair."

"Your father couldn't have been in the Civil War, could he?"

"No; my two grandfathers and my great-grandfather."

"And how old are you, Anne?"

"Nineteen."

"I'm twenty-three."

"Tell me about your home in England."

"I haven't one now." He began an expurgated edition of his youth, and it seemed to him that she listened beautifully. He asked for her story in return; and, while she was telling it, wondered whether he liked her voice or not. It dwelled and slurred, but was soft and had great flavour. When she had finished her simple tale, for she

had hardly been away from home, there was silence, till
Jon said:

"I'll go and see that the horses are all right; then perhaps you could get a snooze."

He moved round the foot of the mound till he came
to the horses, and stayed a little talking to them and
stroking their noses. A feeling, warm and protective,
stirred within him. This was a nice child, and a brave
one. A face to remember, with lots behind it. Suddenly
he heard her voice, low and as if pretending not to call:
"Jon, oh, Jon!" He felt his way back through the darkness. Her hands were stretched out.

"It *is* so spooky! That funny rustling! I've got creeps
down my back!"

"The wind's got up a bit. Let's sit back to back—it'll
keep you warm. Or, look here, I'll sit against the bank; if
you lean up against me you could go to sleep. It's only an
hour or two now before we can ride on by moonlight."

They took up the suggested postures, her back against
his side, and her head in the hollow of his arm and
shoulder.

"Comfy?"

"Surely. It stops the creeps."

They smoked and talked a little more. The stars were
brighter now, and their eyes more accustomed to the
darkness. And they were grateful for each other's warmth.
Jon enjoyed the scent, as of hay, that rose from her hair
not far below his nose. Then came a long silence, while
the warm protective feeling grew and grew within him.
He would have liked to slip his arms round and hold her
closer. But of course he did not. It was, however, as
much as he could do to remain a piece of warmth impersonal enough for her to recline against. This was the
very first time since he left England that he had felt an
inclination to put his arms round anyone, so badly burnt
had he been in that old affair. The wind rose, talked in
the trees, died away again; the stillness was greater than
ever. He was very wide awake, and it seemed curious to
him that she could sleep, for, surely, she was asleep—so

still. The stars twinkled, and he gazed up at them. His limbs began to ache and twitch, and suddenly he realised that she was no more asleep than he. She slowly turned her head till he could see her eyes, grave, enticing.

"I'm cramping you," she said, and raised herself; but his arm restored her.

"Not a bit; so long as you're warm and comfy."

Her head settled in again; and the vigil was resumed. They talked a little now, of nothing important, and he thought: 'It's queer—one could live months knowing people and not know them half so well as we shall know each other now.'

Again a long silence fell; but this time his arm was round her, it was more comfortable so, for both of them. And Jon began to have the feeling that it would be inadvisable for the moon to rise. Had she that feeling too? He wondered. But if she had, the moon in its courses paid no attention. For suddenly he became conscious that it was there, behind the trees somewhere lurking, a curious kind of stilly glimmer creeping about the air, along the ground, in and out of the tree-stems.

"The moon!" he said. She did not stir, and his heart beat rather fast. So! She did not want the moon to rise any more than he! And slowly the creeping glimmer became light, and, between the tree-stems, stole, invading their bodies till they were visible. And still they sat, unstirring, as if afraid to break a spell. The moon gained power and a cold glory, and rose above the trees; the world was alive once more. Jon thought, 'Could I kiss her?' and at once recoiled. As if she would want! But, as though she divined his thought, she turned her head, and her eyes looked into his.

"I'm in charge of you!" he did not exactly say.

Her answer was a little sigh, and she got up. They stood, gazing into the whitened mysterious wood.

"Look!" said Jon; "it *is* the mound. There's the path down to the hollow where we had the picnic. Now we can find the way all right."

She made a sound that he could not interpret, and they

went towards the horses, untethered them, and mounted. They set forth, riding side by side.

"This'll be something to remember," said Jon.

"Yes, I shall always remember it."

They said no more, except to consult about the way, but this was soon so clear, that they cantered till they came out on the polo ground close to the hotel.

"Go in and relieve your brother's mind. I'll take the horses round, and then come on."

When he entered the hotel lounge Francis Wilmot, still in riding clothes, was alone. His expression was peculiar, not exactly hostile, but certainly not friendly.

"Anne's gone up," he said, "I reckon you haven't much bump of locality. You surely had me scared."

"I'm awfully sorry," said Jon humbly, "I forgot the horses were new to the country."

"Well!" said Francis Wilmot, and shrugged his shoulders. Jon looked at the young man steadily.

"You don't think that I got bushed on purpose? Because you look as if you did."

Again Francis Wilmot shrugged his shoulders.

"Forgive me," said Jon, "but aren't you forgetting that your sister's a lady, and that one doesn't behave like a cad with a lady?"

Francis Wilmot did not answer; he went to a window and stood looking out. Jon felt very angry. He sat down on the arm of a long chair, suddenly extremely tired. He sat there looking at the ground, and frowning heavily. Damn the fellow! Had he been bullying Anne? If he had —! A voice behind him said: "I reckon I didn't mean it. I certainly am sorry. It was just the scare. Shake hands!"

Jon stretched out his own impulsively, and they shook hands, looking straight into each other's eyes.

"You must be about through," said Francis Wilmot. "Come on to my room; I've gotten a flask. I've given Anne a dram already."

They went up. Jon sat in the only chair, Francis Wilmot on the bed.

"Anne tells me she's asked you to come home with us to-morrow. I surely hope you will."

"I should simply love to."

"That's fine!"

They drank, talked a little, smoked.

"Good night," said Jon, suddenly, "or I shall go to sleep here."

They shook hands again, and Jon staggered to his room. He fell asleep at once.

They travelled next day, all three, through Columbia and Charleston, to the Wilmot's place. It stood in the bend of a red river, with cotton fields around, and swampy ground where live oaks grew, melancholy, festooned with Florida moss. The old slave quarters, disused except as kennels, were still standing; the two-storied house had flights of wooden steps running up on each side, on to the wide wisteria-covered porch, and needed a coat of paint; and, within, rooms ran one into the other, hung with old portraits of dead Wilmots and de Frevilles; and darkies wandered around and talked their soft drawled speech.

Jon was happier than he had been since he landed in the New World three and a half years ago. In the mornings he sauntered with the dogs in the sunlight or tried to write poetry—for the two young Wilmots were busy. After the midday meal he rode with them or with Anne alone. In the evening he learned from her to play the ukulele before a wood fire lighted at sundown, or heard about cotton culture from Francis, with whom, since that moment of animosity, he was on the best of terms.

Between Anne and himself there was little talk; they had, as it were, resumed the silence which had fallen when they sat in the dark under the old Indian mound. But he watched her; indeed, he was always trying to catch the grave enticing look in her dark eyes. More and more she seemed to him unlike any girl he had ever known; quicker, more silent, and with more "sand." The days went on, in warm sun, and the nightly scent of wood smoke; and his holiday drew to an end. He could play the ukulele now, and they sang to it—negro spirituals, songs from comic operas, and other immortal works. The last day came, and dismay descended on Jon. To-morrow, early, he was going back to his peaches at Southern Pines! That afternoon, riding with her for the last time, the silence was almost unnatural, and she did not even look at him. Jon went up to change, with panic in his heart. He knew now that he wanted to take her back with him, and he thought he knew that she did not want to come. How he would miss watching for those eyes to be fixed on him. He was thirsty with the wish to kiss her. He went down moodily, and sat in a long chair before the wood fire, pulling a spaniel's ears and watching the room darken. Perhaps she wouldn't even come for a last sing-song. Perhaps there would be nothing more but dinner and an evening *à trois;* not even a chance to say he loved her and be told that she didn't love him. And he thought, miserably: 'It's my fault—I'm a silent fool; I've missed my chance.' The room darkened till there was nothing but firelight, and the spaniel went to sleep. Jon, too, closed his eyes. It was as if he could wait better, thus —for the worst. When he opened them she was standing in front of him with the ukuleles in her hands.

"Do you want to play Jon?"

"Yes," said Jon, "let's play. It's the last time"; and he took his ukulele.

She sat down on the rug before the fire, and began to tune hers. Jon slipped down beside the spaniel and began to tune his. The spaniel got up and went away.

"What shall we sing?"

"I don't want to sing, Anne. You sing; I'll just accompany."

She didn't look at him! She would not look at him! It was all up! What a fool he'd been!

Anne sang. She sang a crooning phrase—some Spanish air. Jon plucked his strings, and the tune plucked his heart. She sang it through. She sang it again, and her eyes slid round. God! She *was* looking at him. She mustn't see that he knew she was! It was too good—that long dark look over the ukulele. Between him and her were her ukulele and his own. He dropped the beastly thing. And, suddenly shifting along the floor, he put his arm round her. Without a word she drooped her head against his shoulder, as when they sat under the Indian mound. He bent his cheek down to her hair. It smelled, as it had then, of hay. And, just as she had screwed her face round in the moonlight, she turned it to him now. But this time Jon kissed her lips.

About the Author

JOHN GALSWORTHY, the son of a well-to-do solicitor, was born in 1867 and educated at Harrow and Oxford. Although called to the bar in 1890, he rarely practiced, devoting his time to reading and to travel—particularly in the Far East, where he met Joseph Conrad who became a lifelong friend. On his return to England, Galsworthy settled down to writing, and produced some stories and two novels. It was not, however, until *The Man of Property* (1906), the first book in *The Forsyte Saga*, together with his first play, *The Silver Box*, that his name was established in the public mind. Many other novels and plays followed, but it was only after World War I that he completed the first Forsyte trilogy with *In Chancery* (1920) and *To Let* (1921). The complete edition of *The Forsyte Saga*, first published in 1922, has since been through hundreds of impressions in many languages around the world. The second Forsyte trilogy, *A Modern Comedy*, appeared in 1929, and the third, *End of the Chapter*, posthumously in 1934. In 1932 Galsworthy was awarded the Nobel Prize for *The Forsyte Saga*. He died in 1933, one of the most popular writers in the world.

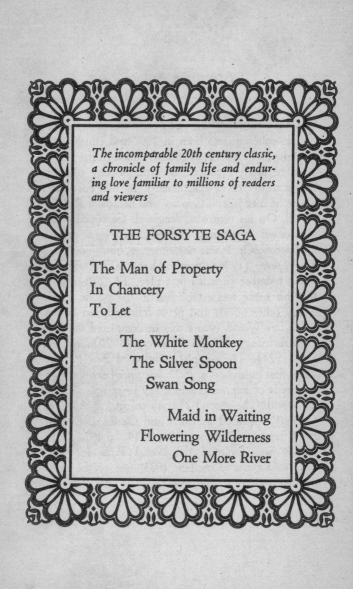

*The incomparable 20th century classic,
a chronicle of family life and enduring love familiar to millions of readers
and viewers*

THE FORSYTE SAGA

The Man of Property
In Chancery
To Let

The White Monkey
The Silver Spoon
Swan Song

Maid in Waiting
Flowering Wilderness
One More River

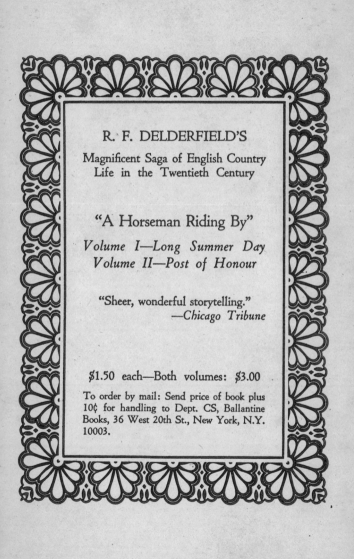